P9-DEE-828

MEDITATIONS
ON THE
SOUL

MEDITATIONS
ON THE
SOUL

SELECTED
LETTERS OF
MARSILIO
FICINO

Translated from the Latin by members of the
Language Department of the School of Economic Science, London

Inner Traditions International
Rochester, Vermont

Inner Traditions International
One Park Street
Rochester, Vermont 05767

First published in the United States of America 1996

These letters have been selected from *The Letters of Marsilio Ficino* originally
published by Shepheard Watwyn (Publishers) Ltd, London

Copyright © The School of Economic Science, London 1975, 1978, 1981,
1988, 1994, 1996

All rights reserved. No part of this book may be reproduced or utilized in
any form or by any means, electronic or mechanical, including photo-
copying, recording, or by any information storage and retrieval
system, without permission in writing from the publisher.

LIBRARY OF CONGRESS CATALOGING-IN-PUBLICATION DATA
Ficino, Marsilio, 1433-1499.
[Correspondence. English. Selections]
Meditations on the soul : selected letters of Marsilio Ficino /
Marsilio Ficino.
p.   cm.
"Selected from The letters of Marsilio Ficino, originally published by
Shepheard Walwyn (Publishers) Ltd., London"—T.p. verso.
Includes bibliographical references (p.   ) and index.
ISBN 0-89281-567-1
1. Philosophers—Italy—Correspondence.   2. Philosophy.   I. Title.
B785.F434A4   1996
186.4—dc20   96-4623
CIP

Printed and bound in the United States
10 9 8 7 6 5 4 3 2 1
Text design and layout by Kristin Camp
This book was typeset in Italian,
with MBembo for the correspondence numbers

Distributed to the book trade in Canada by Publishers Group West (PGW),
Toronto, Ontario

Contents

INTRODUCTION

There are few who would pick up a book of fifteenth-century philosophy from anything other than a sense of duty. But the letters of Marsilio Ficino (1433–1499) of Florence are an exception. They are philosophical, inspired by Plato; but they also have an instant appeal because they connect with what we all know, but mostly ignore: the knowledge of our own soul. In so many of these letters Ficino urges us either directly or indirectly to cultivate our soul, a message that in our own times has been taken up with great eloquence and power by Thomas Moore.[1] In the Moore sense these letters are "soulful." They invite us to look again at those areas of our lives that we have neglected or on which we have fixed views. Above all, they advise us not to pursue sensory objects for their own sake. Ficino writes (letter 19), "I can only judge it the most foolish act of all, that many people most diligently feed a beast, that is, their body, a wild, cruel and dangerous animal; but allow themselves, that is, the soul, insofar as they have one, to starve to death."

Yet Ficino is no hair-shirt ascetic. He is no medieval mystic turning away from the world in disgust. He is drawing our attention to what is truly good and truly beautiful in the world and in ourselves and inviting us to turn to that. Only in this way can everything really be enjoyed, only in this way can the soul really be fed. He writes in letter 2.34:[2] "Shame on mortals, again and again shame on them, I say, for no other reason save this: they delight in mortal goods, and in so doing they ignore the eternal good itself."

Ficino is not telling us that the good things of the world are not to be enjoyed, but that they cannot truly be enjoyed without being related to a greater good of which they are a part.

---

1. See especially Thomas Moore, *Care of the Soul* (New York: HarperCollins, 1992).
2. Some references in this introduction are to letters that do not appear in this selection. These are cited by volume and number (for example, 2.34) as they appear in *The Letters of Marsilio Ficino.*

What makes Ficino's letters relevant today is that he gives so many examples of the ways in which our souls may be fed—in situations that are as ordinary, common, and difficult as they were five hundred years ago. Only a few may be cited here, but there are many examples. In letter 1.11 he speaks of finding time to be alone for contemplation. He says: "Whoever desires to attain God avoids large numbers and movement as much as he can. Let us therefore, my Gregorio, retire into that one unmoving watchtower of the mind, where, as Plato says, the unseen light will shine unceasingly upon us."

Even the blow of bereavement can become an occasion for the cultivation of the soul. In August 1473 he writes to Gismondo della Stufa (letter 1.15):

> If each of us, essentially, is that which is greatest within us, which always remains the same and by which we understand ourselves, then certainly the soul is the man himself and the body but his shadow. Whatever wretch is so deluded as to think that the shadow of man is man, like Narcissus is dissolved in tears. You will only cease to weep, Gismondo, when you cease looking for your Albiera degli Albizzi in her dark shadow and begin to follow her by her own clear light.

The conscious possession of outstanding talents can be used for feeding the soul—or for starving it. This depends upon whether the enjoyer of these talents attributes them to his ego and his own achievement, or whether he recognizes that they come from above and are for the service of God. After praising the extraordinary gifts of Lorenzo de' Medici in a letter to him dated 21 January 1474 (letter 1.26), Ficino continues as follows: "Dear friend, I say these qualities are in you, but do not originate from you. For such wonders are the work of omnipotent God alone. Excellent man, you are the instrument of God, fitted to perform great deeds. . . . You will therefore continue to perform successfully these wonderful works, so long as you obey the divine creator."

The pain of being wronged and insulted can also be turned to the good of the soul. Ficino explains in a letter to his friend Giovanni Cavalcanti (letter 10) written in March 1474:

> You say that one of your relatives felt injured the other day by the insults of some impudent people. The man who acts unjustly, Giovanni, does injustice to himself; for he upsets the mind and stamps it with the

mark of an evil disposition. Because of his dishonorable conduct he suffers hatred, danger, and misfortune. He who accepts injury receives it from himself and not from the offender. For the rational soul—which is man himself—cannot be offended unless he considers the injustice as bad for him; and this depends on our judgment. Let therefore no man blame another, but himself; for no man can be offended but by himself, and let he who complains think how he may punish himself, that is, by discipline and correction, instead of hatching punishment for the offender.

Have you not seen puppies snapping at a stone that has been thrown at them, even though it has not hit them? Although they have not been hurt by the stone, they hurt their teeth when they bite it. In the same way the imprudent, when kicked by a donkey, flay the animal with their fists, or rather flay themselves. Indeed, from their opinions they receive many injuries which, like balls, rebound against the thrower. You will perhaps say that it is difficult not to desire vengeance. But be in no doubt that if men forgive, the most just God will settle the balance a little later.

Ficino's care for the souls of mankind came from profound love. The basis of this love was that he saw others in himself. He says that the lover forms in his heart an image of the beloved. Seeing this image the beloved recognizes himself in the lover, but is himself purified and transformed by that very love. With this radiant self he himself falls in love. Thus the pair become both lovers and beloved. But this radiant Self is divine. It is ever present, ever full, ever blissful. According to Ficino, wherever there are two friends, God always is the third. Hence, real friendship is always divine. For friendship is nothing but love made firm and fast. It is not easy to see any limits to Ficino's love or friendship. In so many of his letters he makes a point of saying that the friend addressed and himself are one. This great force of love is universal. Ficino says in the second speech of his *Commentary* on Plato's *Symposium* (often referred to by him as *De amore*) that the "Divine Beauty (which is God) creates in everything Love, that is, desire for Itself, because if God draws the world to Himself, and the world is drawn from Him, there is one continuous attraction, beginning with God, going to the world, and ending at last in God, an attraction that returns to the same place whence it began as though in a kind of circle."

In other words, the whole event of creation, both its beginning and its end, is set in motion by love. Of course, it is through this love that the soul is really fed. As this love becomes full, it sees itself reflected everywhere. The soul, recognizing its true nature, begins to grow wings; as Ficino says in letter 35, it starts to fly back to its true home. At last it realizes its infinite nature; a sublime transformation that Ficino describes in letter 29 and letter 59. This transformation of Man into God is Man's true destiny. In letter 12 Ficino writes: "It was not for small things but for great that God created men, who, knowing the great, are not satisfied with small things. Indeed, it was for the limitless alone that He created men, who are the only beings on earth to have rediscovered their infinite nature and who are not fully satisfied by anything limited, however great that thing may be." Here Ficino seems to express the essential spirit of the Renaissance.

We do not find Marsilio's letters filled with the personal anecdotes that characterize the correspondence of many authors: the details that seem to say so much but usually convey so little about their subject. The real nature of the man comes through the sense of being at one with his correspondents: the distinctive combination of total detachment and intense sympathy with their predicaments. Such personal details as seem important come mainly from the near-contemporary biography of Giovanni Corsi, written in the early years of the sixteenth century.[3]

Corsi tells us that Marsilio was the son of Diotifeci Ficino, physician to Cosimo de' Medici.[4] He goes on to say that at his father's insistence his education was directed toward medicine. Accordingly, so Corsi says, he went for a time to Bologna University, one of the leading medical universities of the age. Marsilio's interest and skill in medicine never left him. Corsi tells us that in later years the Medici always came to him first for medical advice, as did his friends, whom he always treated free of charge. His *Three Books on Life* (completed in 1489) are devoted to the preservation of health, particularly of those practicing philosophy. With characteristic dry humor he suggests that there is not much use in a scholar deciding to devote his life to philosophy if he loses the life he is intending

---

3. A translation from the Latin of the short biography is given in volume 3 of *The Letters of Marsilio Ficino*.

4. Three generations of Medici ruled Florence from 1434 to 1492: Cosimo to 1464, his son Piero to 1469, and his grandson Lorenzo to 1492.

to devote. In letter 34 Ficino refers to a certain Francesco Musano being cured by "our medicines," and Musano paying his respects to Ficino's "Academy," as if to his own doctor.

Of Ficino's father Diotifeci, who died in 1478, not much is known except that he was a successful surgeon as well as physician and that the nobility of Florence came to him for treatment. Marsilio in his "Consilio contro la Pestilentia" tells us that his treatment of the plague, endemic then in Florence as in the rest of Europe, was particularly successful. However, like his son later, Diotifeci was reluctant to charge his patients and therefore lived in somewhat straitened circumstances.

We know even less of Marsilio's mother, Alessandra, than of his father. She lived to an advanced age, dying only a year or two before Marsilio himself. Marsilio was convinced that she had psychic powers. He describes in letter 24 how her own mother, Angela, appeared to Alessandra and her husband simultaneously, although they were in different places, to announce her death at the moment it occurred, many miles from them both. Marsilio saw this as evidence that "the souls of the dead, freed from the chains of the body, can influence us, and care about human affairs." He looked after both his parents in their old age and took them to live with him. He appears also to have taken care of his brothers. When Lorenzo de' Medici, Cosimo's grandson, gave Ficino two ecclesiastical livings, Corsi tells us that "he left the whole of his patrimony to his brothers." One of his nephews he employed as his scribe.

The most decisive influence in Marsilio's education was his connection with Cosimo de' Medici. Cosimo was not only the undisputed ruler of Florence, one of the five main states into which Italy was divided in the fifteenth century, from 1434 till his death in 1464, but he was also one of the richest men in Europe since he controlled the enormously successful Medici bank. But he was far more than a successful statesman and businessman: he was a man of vision. He evidently aimed to restore in Florence the cultural glories of the classical past. Not only did he establish the conditions of peace and prosperity in which the new Renaissance could flourish, but he assembled around him the most gifted circle of men related to the arts. These included the sculptors Donatello and Luca della Robbia, the architect Michelozzi, the musician Squarcialuppi, the painters Filippo Lippi and Fra Angelico, and many others. He also worked indefatigably to recover and have copied the ancient texts upon which he clearly thought the ancient culture really rested. Many of these were obtained from Constantinople, which was doomed long before its final fall to the Turks in 1453. Many other manuscripts were brought from monasteries in Western Europe where they had long lain unregarded and, indeed, unremembered.

A decisive moment in the life of Cosimo was the calling of the Church Council that met in Florence in 1439. The council was called at the behest of the Greek emperor, John Palaeologus, who was hoping to achieve a union between the Eastern and Western churches that might in turn lead to the western states of Europe sending military help to the dwindling "empire" of Byzantium. A magnificent retinue of churchmen and scholars followed the emperor to Ferrara whither the council was first called. They were met by theologians and statesmen from the West; one of these was Cosimo who, feeling that the resources of Ferrara were not adequate to maintain such a gathering in sufficient state, invited the council to meet in Florence instead. The council failed in its objective; but among the scholars from the East was a certain Gemisthos Plethon who had established a Platonic Academy in Mistra, whence the members might have surveyed, with some sense of irony, the barren slopes that had once supported the wooden structures of the invincible state of Sparta. Corsi says of Gemisthos that he was "called by Marsilio a second Plato, and acclaimed equally for his eloquence and scholarship. When Cosimo heard him frequently discoursing before the scholars and winning their highest applause and admiration, it is said that he was set ablaze with an extraordinary desire to recall to Italy as soon as possible, the philosophy of Plato, as of ancient right." Corsi then adds, "Not many years later, as if by divine fate, he was able to accomplish this through Marsilio, who in his youth had been widely instructed in the humanities and was so kindled with a love of Plato, having been won over to him through Cicero, that, laying all else aside, he pondered this one thing: how, in entering within the portals of the Academy, he might be able to see Plato at close quarters and speak face to face with him and all his family."

The dates are elusive but it seems clear that Cosimo had selected Marsilio, when he was still a youth, to revive the study of Plato, not as a scholastic exercise but as a living philosophy. Corsi tells us that on one occasion when Marsilio "visited" Florence (perhaps on holiday from his studies in Bologna) his father took him to visit Cosimo: "He exhorted him to take special care over Marsilio's studies so that he should not go against his natural disposition. He said there was no reason to take account of domestic hardship, for he would never neglect him in any matter but would supply everything most generously. 'You, Ficino,' he said, 'have been sent to us to heal bodies, but your Marsilio here has been sent down from heaven to heal souls.'"

While we do not know the date that Cosimo's close association with Marsilio started, it must have been before 1452 (when Ficino was nineteen) because Ficino tells us in letter 1.86 that he had discussed philosophy fruitfully with Cosimo for more than twelve years; and Cosimo died in 1464.

But there were influences other than those of his father that delayed Marsilio's learning of Greek and therefore his study of Plato in the original. Antoninus, the great Dominican archbishop of Florence and chancellor of the university, whom Ficino greatly respected, advised him in the mid 1450s to study less Plato and more Thomas Aquinas.

It is clear therefore that it was not until his late twenties that Ficino had really mastered Greek. His first work, *The Platonic Institutions* (probably destroyed) was written in 1456, but Cosimo advised him not to publish anything until he could read Greek. His first translations into Latin did not appear until 1463, when he was twenty-nine.

The fact that Ficino learned Greek so comparatively late illustrates the genius of the man. In the first place, some of his finest letters (for instance, 29 and 35) were written before he had really studied Plato and his great family of like-minded philosophers. Second, he was able to master the language so quickly and comprehensively that even his early translations remained the standard ones until vernacular translations entirely superseded the Latin versions during the nineteenth century.

True to his word, Cosimo gave Ficino a small estate very close to his own villa at Careggi in 1462. The woods of Monte Vecchio where Ficino undertook spiritual practices in solitude rise up behind the site of his house. It must have been at this house that Ficino began the first translations of Plato that were commissioned by Cosimo. According to Corsi he completed the translations in the astonishingly short period of five years.

Even before he could embark on translating Plato, however, Ficino was asked by Cosimo to translate a newly discovered manuscript of *The Poimandres* attributed to the Egyptian sage Hermes Trismegistus. This work had been lost to the West since antiquity. It was of seminal importance both to Ficino and Cosimo because it was conclusive evidence to them that the two main strands in European culture, Judeo-Christian religion and Greek philosophy, both had Hermes (or Thoth as he was known in Egypt) as their ultimate source. Ficino thought that Hermes had instructed not only Moses but also Orpheus, who in turn had inspired a line of philosophers including Pythagoras and culminating with Plato. Until the writing of Isaac Causabon in the late sixteenth century, European scholars and theologians accepted the evidence presented by the translation and commentary of Ficino. The most dramatic instance of this acceptance is the large pavement illustration of Hermes, executed about 1488, at the entrance to Siena cathedral in Italy; beneath it is the inscription "Hermes Mercurius Trismegistus contemporaneus Moysi" (the contemporary of Moses). He hands a book of his wisdom to two figures on his right, one clearly from the East and one from the West. The division between philosophy and religion that characterized so much of the Middle Ages and gave rise to so much absurdity (such as the doctrine that there were two truths) seemed at an end, and Ficino was able to write, without fear of contradiction, that "lawful Philosophy is no different from true religion, and lawful religion exactly the same as true Philosophy" (letter 48).

It is clear that Ficino soon gathered around him a group of like-minded men, which he referred to as the Academy. How this group met and what happened at such meetings is far from clear. But it is certain that the Academy was of great importance to Ficino and he refers to it acting as a single entity quite often, for instance in the letter to Francesco Musano already mentioned. In a letter to Martin Preninger he lists the members of the Academy, dividing them into three classes: the Medici, his helpers, and his listeners. What is impressive about the membership is that it includes so many of the notable men of Florence besides the Medici. Ficino attributes his well-known work, the *Commentary* on Plato's *Symposium,* to a meeting of certain friends on the occasion of Plato's birthday (November 7th) in 1468 when different people had to speak on the orations by the characters in Plato's dialogue. These speeches, according to Ficino, form the text of the book. This kind of meeting may not have been untypical of the way the Academy worked.

Outwardly Ficino's life was not very eventful. Much of his time was spent at Careggi. Not content with translating and writing commentaries on the dialogues of Plato, he proceeded to translate and comment on the main Neoplatonic philosophers as well, including Plotinus, Iamblichus, Porphyry, Proclus, and Psellus. In addition to those already mentioned he wrote two other major works, *The Platonic Theology* and *The Chris-*

tian Religion. Never far from his thoughts in the composition of these
works was the reconciliation of Plato's philosophy to the Christian religion. But his vision of unity was much wider than this. Ultimately he
saw everything in the universe as a manifestation of the One, of the
Good, of God. To him this was the only reality. He writes in letter 65 "all
the time that we are pursuing merely one thing after another, we are
running away from the One itself, which is everything. But he who simply pursues the One itself, in that One soon attains everything."

In 1473 Ficino was ordained a priest. In September of the following
year he writes (letter 68) that he had just suffered a severe illness, and that
there were times when he "almost despaired of recovery." He says:

> I offered prayers to the divine Mary and begged for some sign of re-
> covery. I felt some relief immediately, and in dreams received a clear
> indication of recovery. So I do not owe a cock to Aesculapius, but my
> heart and body to Christ and His mother. One must always accept
> everything as leading to the good, Marescalchi. Could it be that God
> wished to warn me by a sign during this illness that I must in future
> declare the Christian teaching with greater zeal and depth?

It has sometimes been suggested that Ficino was suffering from some
sort of psychological crisis at this point in his life and that he felt he had
been devoting too much of his attention to Plato at the expense of the
Christian Scriptures. Corsi says it was at this point that he wrote his
book *The Christian Religion* and that "now, while he was still in his
forty-second year, from being a pagan he became a soldier of Christ."
But in fact letter 68 makes it clear that he had already started *The Christian Religion* before his illness and that he was not turning to Christ and
Mary at the expense of Plato, for he writes that during his illness, "Except for the Platonic authors, the writings of men did not help at all, but
the works of Christ brought much more comfort than the words of philosophers." The fact that he was also engaged at this time in writing *The
Platonic Theology* shows that he was turning his mind with added intensity to showing the unity in the teachings of Christ and Plato.

Like his patrons the Medici, in pursuance of the One he worked for
harmony and peace at every level. A single instance will suffice here. In
1478 a faction of discontented notables, egged on by Pope Sixtus IV
and his nephew, Girolamo Riario, hatched a plot, known as the Pazzi

conspiracy, against Lorenzo de' Medici and his brother Giuliano. The plot involved the assassination of the two brothers in Florence cathedral during the service on the Sunday before Ascension. Giuliano was in fact murdered, but Lorenzo escaped thanks to the inexperience of one of the assassins, Lorenzo's quick-wittedness, and the solid support for the Medici shown by the Florentine citizens. The vengeance on the plotters was terrible. The leader of the conspiracy, Jacopo de' Pazzi, head of a banking business that rivaled the Medici bank, was captured while trying to escape from Florence, tortured, and hanged, as was Jacopo Bracciolini; Francesco Salviati, the archbishop of Pisa, was hung upside down from the windows of the Signoria without even the show of a trial; and Bernardo Bandini, who had slain Giuliano and actually escaped to Constantinople, was returned by the sultan, tried, and hanged in Florence. Cardinal Raffaele Riario, the seventeen-year-old nephew of Girolamo Riario who had been conducting the service at which the assassination of Giuliano de' Medici took place, though imprisoned by Lorenzo immediately after the trial for his own safety, got off. He was young; there was no proof against him; and, after all, he was the great-nephew of the pope.

Before the assassination Ficino had been on good terms with Salviati, Bracciolini, and Riario. He clearly knew the nature of these men and probably of their wish to remove the Medici from power, although he would not have known of the actual plot to kill them. He wrote a number of letters that were clearly composed to turn them from violence to wisdom. Letter 5 is titled "Truth addresses Cardinal Riario on the education of a ruler." The main burden of the advice that "Truth" gives to Riario is to beware of flatterers and evil counselors. Letter 16 clearly refers to the recent preferments of Salviati to the archbishopric of Pisa and to Riario's appointment as cardinal. Ficino writes: "By some foolish, or rather, unhappy fate . . . most mortals make more perverse use of prosperity than adversity. . . . Let us remember that the nature of evil is to offer itself to us daily under the guise of good." It is then "very easily taken in . . . and given lodging as if it were good; but soon after, it secretly strikes down its unwary host with a sword, as he deserves." In letter 2.36 Ficino speaks to Jacopo Bracciolini in still more pointed terms. Quoting a letter purporting to be from the philosopher Plutarch to the Roman emperor Trajan, he writes "the further you are from the charge of ambition, the more worthy are you deemed . . . public opinion usually flings the transgres-

sion of disciples back at their teachers [Bracciolini was Riario's tutor] . . .
I have represented to you the essence of political order and practice. If
you are conforming to this, you have Plutarch as your authority. . . .
Otherwise I call upon the letter before us to witness that you are not
pursuing the ruin of government on Plutarch's authority." (For Plutarch,
read Ficino).

When Pope Sixtus IV found that his plan for getting rid of the Medici
by assassination had failed, he resorted to open warfare, since he was still
intent on increasing his hold over the Florentine clergy and expanding
the Papal State to the north, in both of which aims he found himself
balked by Lorenzo. The pope procured a ready ally in the ambitious
Ferdinand (or Ferrante), king of Naples. Florence, besieged by the two
armies, found itself in desperate straits from which it was only saved by
the heroic action of Lorenzo in going incognito and alone to negotiate
with Ferdinand; these negotiations were successful in bringing the war to
a close.

Ficino's part in this was to write magnificent letters to both the pope
and Ferdinand urging them to end their attacks. In letter 95 Ficino reminds Sixtus of his own true nature and assumes that he will act from it.
The letter needs to be read in its entirety, but the following passage could
perhaps be particularly noted as epitomizing Ficino's way of giving counsel: "If you have any hatred toward your flock, put it aside, so that you
may regain, if you have ever lost it, your accustomed charity, which,
being wholly innate, you cannot lose without losing yourself." Typically,
Ficino perceives by the end of the letter the change in the pope already
taking place: "Our Pontiff, the most far-sighted of all men, has not forgotten himself. He did not lose his own wisdom when he began to be
wise for all. He did not cast off his natural generosity when he put on the
mantle of the most generous Peter."

Ficino's relations with Lorenzo de' Medici were not as uniformly harmonious as they appear to have been with his grandfather Cosimo. An astute
diplomat, a superb patron of the arts, and an eloquent poet, Lorenzo did not
have the serious philosophic intent of Cosimo nor the steadiness of character of his own father, Piero. Certainly, before the Pazzi conspiracy he seems
to have spent much of his time in frivolous pastimes and under his direction
the great Medici bank began to drift toward insolvency. His generosity to
Ficino seems to have been spasmodic; occasional letters of thinly veiled
complaint and long periods of silence replace the earlier loving letters that

passed between the two. In later years, however, their good relationship was much restored.

Ficino saw clearly into the double nature of Lorenzo and wrote a letter of great penetration to him (letter 97). Ficino presents him with "a picture of the evil mind and the good." The first is "a wood dense with tangled thorns, bristling with savage beasts, infested with poisonous snakes," and regarding the second, "a mind endued with fine principles . . . is like a well tended and fertile field." Ficino was presenting the two sides of Lorenzo's nature to him with dramatic clarity; probably shortly before he set out on his fateful visit to King Ferdinand.

But Ficino was not just a man who gave good advice. He practiced the principles that he taught. According to Corsi, like Socrates, he was sparing in food and cared little for personal possessions. His life also appears to have been completely chaste, as befitted a philosopher and priest. But Corsi emphasizes that he was no grim killjoy. He tells us that "he did select the most excellent wines, for he was rather disposed toward wine, yet he never went away from parties drunk or fuddled, though often more cheerful." He had a flashing wit and lively sense of humor and Corsi mentions that many of his sayings in Italian were recorded. He also tells us that Ficino did not bear grudges or take offense, but always remembered kindnesses done to him. Ficino mentions that he suffered from black bile or melancholy, but we get hardly a hint of introspection or self-involvement from his letters.

Corsi tells us that in stature he was very short, and Ficino himself makes jokes about this in his letters. He was apparently a little hesitant in his speech but his face "presented a mild and pleasing aspect. His complexion was ruddy; his hair was golden and curly and stood up on his forehead." That his appearance was attractive is supported by the portrait that Ghirlandaio painted of him on the walls of the Church of Santa Maria Novella in Florence.

Above all, Corsi emphasizes the great love he felt for his fellow Florentines and the love they in turn felt for him. Like Socrates, from whom he drew so much of his inspiration, he used to walk around Florence, as Socrates did Athens, engaging in conversation particularly with the young people, who would become enraptured with his speech. When he died on 1 October 1499, Corsi tells us that the people of Florence attended the funeral with grief and tears.

But his inspiration lived on. Shortly before his death, he published in

1497 his *Commentaries on Dionysius,* whose teaching perhaps came closer to Platonism than any other Christian author of the ancient world. In 1498 a commentary on the Epistles of Paul appeared. He was in correspondence with Germain de Ganay, president of the Parlement of Paris, and Matthias Corvinus, the great warrior-king of Hungary. In 1496 he received a letter from Robert Gaguin, rector of the University of Paris who wrote "Your virtue and wisdom, Ficino, are widely known and appreciated, especially in our Academy of Paris, so that your name is loved and praised." After his death particularly, "academies" based on the model of Ficino's sprang up in various places in Europe, the most famous of which was that in Navarre (initiated by Margaret, sister of the French king, Francis I).

The importance of Ficino in influencing European thought right up to the present time has been very great. His teaching that the human soul was immortal and unlimited links directly with the unshakeable confidence and creative genius that so many of the giants of the Renaissance expressed in so many fields. His view that the whole creation was moved by love and inspired to return to God through His beauty was reflected in the intense beauty of physical form that the masters of the Renaissance manifested with such skill. His emphasis on the importance of human nature and the virtues that lie within it gave support to a new direction in education. Ultimately it is the practice of these virtues that leads to the discovery of the divine in man. "The reward of virtues," says Ficino in letter 91, "is the realization of God." There was an obvious connection between these views and the reintroduction of the great epics of antiquity into the educational system. John Colet of St. Paul's School, London, who was one of the first teachers to encourage this development of the curriculum, was one of Ficino's correspondents.

The fullness of Ficino's wisdom on so many topics is most clearly presented by the method adopted in this volume, that is, by collecting his letters together by topic. By studying the letters in this way, we may gain a fuller insight into the many aspects of this great man's wisdom.

CLEMENT SALAMAN

Translators' Note

Ficino's twelve books of letters were first printed in Venice in 1495. The letters contained in this volume cover the period from 1457 to 1481. Ficino probably began to gather his philosophical letters for publication toward the end of 1473. He may have been prompted to start this collection by the fact that letters falsely purporting to be his were being circulated (see letter 1).

The printed version of the first book of letters was translated into Italian during Ficino's lifetime; all twelve books were translated into Italian by Figliucci in the sixteenth century. The Venice edition was followed by a further one that appeared in Ficino's *Opera omnia*, which contained all his published works, printed in Basel in 1561 and 1576. The latter was reprinted by the Bottega d'Erasmo in Turin in 1959. The English translations are based on a comparison of the most reliable sources.

This selection is drawn from the first five volumes of letters published by Shepheard-Walwyn as *The Letters of Marsilio Ficino* (London, 1975–). For full bibliographic information on the various manuscript and printed sources used in the translations, the reader should consult the notes and supporting material in that edition. Letters have been renumbered for this selection; following each letter the original volume and letter number appear in brackets.

THE
LETTERS

TRUTH AND VIRTUE

1

Praise of truth

Marsilio Ficino to Angelo Poliziano, the Homeric poet: greetings.

As you say, some letters are being passed around under my name that are written in the style of Aristippus,[1] and to some extent in that of Lucretius,[2] rather than of Plato. If they are mine, Angelo, they are not like that: and if they are like that, they are definitely not mine, but fabricated by my detractors; for, as everyone knows, I have followed the divine Plato from my youth.

But you will easily distinguish my own writings from others in this way: in my letters, as far as in me lies, there is always a purpose relating to morals, natural subjects, or theology. But if occasionally there is anything in them in some way relating to love, it is certainly Platonic and honorable, not Aristippian and wanton.

Moreover, the praises they contain are genuine and such as to encourage and advise, not to flatter; and there are almost no unnecessary words, for I decided at the beginning of my studies always to write as briefly as possible; since in time's brief span to use words in excess is the mark of a lover of words rather than a lover of wisdom. And since there are very few people with much knowledge, often the loquacious speak falsely or unnecessarily, or both.

All this is alien to the dignity of a man, and very far from the profession of a philosopher.

Farewell. [1.16]

2

A picture of a beautiful body and a beautiful mind[1]

Marsilio Ficino of Florence to his friends.[2]

Philosophers debate, orators declaim, and poets sing at great length to exhort men to the true love of virtue. I admire their works and praise them. Indeed, if I did not praise good things, I would not be a good man. But I consider that if virtue herself were ever to be brought into the open she would encourage everyone to take hold of her far more easily and effectively than would the words of men.

It is pointless for you to praise a maiden to the ears of a young man and describe her in words in order to inflict upon him pangs of love, when you can bring her beautiful form before his eyes. Point, if you can, to her beautiful form; then you have no further need of words.[3] For it is impossible to say how much more easily and powerfully Beauty herself calls forth love than do words.

Therefore, if we bring into the view of men the marvelous sight of Virtue herself, there will be no further need for our persuading words: the vision itself will persuade more quickly than can be conceived.

Picture a man endowed with the most vigorous and acute faculties, a strong body, good health, a handsome form, well-proportioned limbs, and a noble stature.[4] Picture this man moving with alacrity and skill, speaking elegantly, singing sweetly, laughing graciously: you will love no one anywhere, you will admire no one, if you do not love and admire such a man as soon as you see him.

Now, in order to reflect more easily upon the divine aspect of the mind from the corresponding likeness of the beautiful body, refer each aspect of the body to an aspect of the mind. For the body is the shadow of the soul; the form of the body, as best it can, represents the form of the soul; thus liveliness and acuteness of perception in the body represent, in a measure, the wisdom and far-sightedness of the mind; strength of body represents strength of mind; health of body, which consists in the tempering of the humors, signifies a temperate mind. Beauty, which is determined by the proportions of the body and a becoming complexion, shows us the harmony and splendor of justice; also, size shows us liberality and nobility; and stature, magnanimity; in the same way dexterity indicates to us civility and courteousness; fine speaking, oratory; sweet singing, the power of poetry. Finally, gracious laughter represents serene happiness in life and perfect joy, which Virtue herself showers upon us.

Now bring into one whole each single part and attribute of Virtue, which we have mentioned; you will at once see clearly a spectacle to be admired and venerated. How worthy of love, how worthy of admiration, is this form of the soul, whose shadow is the form of the body so loved and admired by everyone. But just as Virtue, when she is seen, instantly draws each man to herself by her lovely form so, without doubt, will Vice, if clearly seen, immediately terrify by his deformity and drive everyone away.

Come, friends. Let us always hold before our eyes the divine idea and form of Virtue. She will at once draw us to herself by the grace of her splendor, unceasingly delight us with the sweetness of her proportion and harmony, and completely fill us with an abundance of all that is good. [4.51]

3

The definition, function and end of the virtues

Marsilio Ficino to Antonio Calderini: greetings.

You often ask me, Antonio, to define the virtues for you, expecting from me perhaps those very detailed analyses of the Aristotelians and Stoics. Calderini, this is not the way of our school of Plato. Surely the power of virtue lies in unity rather than in division. Hence the Pythagoreans held that unity belonged to the good, diversity to evil. So I shall be very brief in my definition, especially as it is better to practice the virtues than to know about them.

Virtue is a quality of the soul which leads a man by discrimination to bliss. Of the virtues there are two kinds.[1] There are those in the intellect and there are those in the heart, which may or may not be governed by reason. The first are called reflective virtues and the second moral.[2] The first are so called because they are developed in reflection and once developed are used for this purpose. The moral virtues are so called because they are acquired by practice and custom and, once acquired, are based on moral conduct and useful works.

Among the reflective virtues are wisdom, contemplation of the divine; science, which is knowledge of natural laws; prudence, that is, an awareness of the proper ordering of private and public affairs; and lastly art, which is the true measure in accomplishing any work. Among the moral virtues are justice, which freely gives each man his own; courage which, ever ready for true work, casts from us the burden of fear; and lastly, temperance, which dispels the wanton desire for pleasure, the other obstacle to true work. Justice is accompanied by generosity and magnanimity, and the other virtues likewise have their companions.

To sum up, reflective virtue is simply an acquired clarity of the intellect, and moral virtue is a constant warmth of heart kindled by that clarity. We should remember that of the human virtues none is more precious than discrimination.[3] As Plato observes in the *Republic*, to buy this one should sell everything else. For everything is an obstacle and nothing of use to a man who cannot distinguish the good from the bad and separate the bad from the good.

Do we not wish to attain this faculty of discrimination? Then in all matters we should consult elder and more proven men. First of all we should consult time. For among temporal things what is more ancient or better proven than time? But we consult time if we consider well and often the events of the past. For the past is master of the present and future. And consideration of the future instructs the present. For it is very difficult to deal properly with events of the present if you do not consider the end and issue of each action. Consider what is appropriate and leave the rest to God. Whatever follows, welcome as an action of God. For whoever rejects divine governance is rejected by God. Since God is indeed the beginning and end of all things, we are born not for ourselves but for God. Those virtues that have been described above are virtues to the extent that they are practiced by us for the sake of worshiping, imitating, and realizing God. The worship of God is therefore the virtue of virtues. But the reward of the virtues is the realization of God. [1.106]

4

No one is happy unless he rejoices truly;
no one rejoices truly unless he rejoices in the truth

Marsilio Ficino to Giovanni Cavalcanti, his unique friend: true joy.

Since my brother has only just told me that he will be passing your way, I have been unable to find anything that I could give him for you. But I have suddenly thought of giving you that one thing beyond which there is nothing to be found, or even sought. Though all mortals seek this, no one who seeks shall find it by mortal means. I have just been reading the following definition of happiness in the *Confessions* of our Augustine, whose divine footsteps I frequently follow, as far as I am able. To live happily is simply to rejoice in the truth; this very joy in the truth is happiness itself.[1] Be happy, my good Giovanni; but to be happy, rejoice truly; and that you may rejoice truly, rejoice in the truth. Absolute truth is in itself the light of God. The truth of things is the splendor of God in those things.

So, if you wish to rejoice in the truth, love, seek, and consider God for His own sake, and everything else for the sake of God. [2.20]

5

Truth addresses Cardinal Riario¹ on the education of a ruler²

I beg you, fortunate Cardinal, not to be surprised because you do not read any man's name inscribed as the author of this letter. How miraculous that at this moment no human mind is addressing you, but Truth herself! Truth comes to you now, not merely defenseless but naked,³ as you may see, not protected by the barbs and subtleties of disputation, not decked in the ornaments of fine words, for she knows that of all things she is the most powerful and beautiful. She knows that just as anything from outside that approaches a light does not illumine that light but obscures it, so Truth herself is weakened, so to speak, and deformed by additions from anywhere else.

Let her now earnestly entreat you to hear her awhile with a generous mind, as she speaks out for your benefit, for she may not know that you always hear her willingly; to hear anything in any other way is erroneous and unprofitable.

To Cardinal Riario, her most beloved son, Truth gives many greetings and promises true salvation.

The Skeptic philosophers and many others falsely slander me as being most obscure and nowhere to be found. This is far from being so; for what shines more clearly than my light, whereby the very Sun and the world are lit? Again, what can be more widely and clearly visible than Truth, through whom alone lies revealed all that is revealed anywhere, and outside whom whatever is said to be visible is nothing but darkness, in which all things are hidden? I am not in any way mean or of ill will; of my own accord I run to meet everything everywhere, and very willingly.

But many people grasp for me with clouded minds, whereas I am apprehended only by a mind that is clear. Most people think that I abide in the high palaces of princes. On the contrary, I am more often compelled to seek out cottages and to dwell in humble homes.⁴ Leaking roofs and cracked walls are no obstacle whatever to me; here the doors are open and a bare house receives me. But I am driven back from the thick roofs and walls of rich houses; and if these doors are ever opened, a tumult of countless falsehoods immediately streams out to meet me. Not thinking to stay among enemies, I instantly take flight. I leave that house that is full of gold and lies but impoverished and empty of truth. Today, however, I come to you willingly, fortunate cardinal, to dwell with you always, if you but wish it. I have come in haste at the very outset of your appointment before your hearth is beset by my enemies, the pernicious lies of flatterers and slanderers.

You should attribute your high rank of office to your ancestry and not to your own merits which, to speak truly, could not have achieved so much in your few tender years. You should not attribute it to fate and fortune either, for sacred mysteries and holy orders do not arise from the caprice of fortune but from the eternal wisdom of God. For divine providence has ordained that in our times she should nurture at her breast the perfect shepherd of the Christian flock, feeding him from his very birth on spiritual food alone. And before he is caught up in childish games and applies his mind to harmful or trivial things, she should lead him to conduct becoming a man and instruct him in the greatest and finest duties. Thus, as you have heard, it is God Himself who has recently brought you forth as a new man.[5] For your part, therefore, when you have put the world aside, by your godly conduct embrace your Heavenly Father, who embraces everything. Believe me, you will stand fast so long as you hold fast to Him who is not moved. Do not in any way trust in the high position and power of men. The highest positions are very often shaken by wind and lightning, and mighty edifices fall most heavily and are only with much difficulty reconstructed.[6] Arise, act in Him who cannot fall and you yourself will never fall. For men abandon themselves with unfortunate consequences whenever they foolishly and ungratefully abandon Him, without whom they can in no way exist. Alas, whoever attempts to desert such a protector hardly leaves Him at all, for he instantly encounters him again as an avenger. Anyone who wickedly disregards the merciful Father's light discovers in this same Father a fiery judge.

Hence you know that lawful cardinals are really vicars of the Apostles and pivots[7] of the Christian Church. For that reason, they ought not to consider any particular advantage, either for themselves or for another, but only the common good of the Church. Furthermore, they should do, think, and speak nothing that is unworthy of apostolic sanctity. Those who do the contrary are not cardinals, but robbers of the Church. They are not vicars of the Apostles, but their enemies. May I say this? May I with your permission say this one thing above all else? Of course, I may say it even without your permission, for who will ever be allowed to speak the truth, if not Truth herself? Understand that nothing should be more foreign to apostolic men than pride, pomp, and luxury.

Just as it pleases you to control your servants outside, take as much care to serve divine laws and to control your servants inside: the senses. Remember that your servants are men, equal to you in origin, and that the human species, which is by nature free, ought not to be, indeed cannot be, united by any fear, but only by love. Just as almost all men of power delight in their several possessions, neatly disposed and displayed in their homes, so will you delight in a mind that is ordered by fine language and conduct. It will be your art to temper both the desires of the mind and all your actions lest, when all external things are in harmony for you, the mind alone be in discord. It will also be your schooling to make frequent study of the most select writers lest the mind alone be impoverished in the midst of such great riches.

Let the hunters and fowlers around you be completely trustworthy and wise, men who by prudence and exceptional love of mankind[8] obtain for you the favor and goodwill of all. Love of mankind alone is the food by which men are won, and only by the favor of men do human affairs prosper.[9] Nothing is more dangerous for a prince than that a great many men should feel contempt for him or hate him or envy him too much. Contempt is avoided by knowledge, worth, and integrity. Hatred is softened by innocence and humanity, and envy is allayed by generosity, liberality, and greatness of action. Since all men are of the same kind and possessed of free will, no wonder they bear servitude with a most unwilling spirit, unless those who rule are equal to them in humility, even as they surpass them in rank, and clearly excel them far more through wisdom than through good fortune.

Nature has given to those parts of the body below the head only the power of touch, but she has furnished the head alone with the powers of all the senses. By doing this she seems to have warned men that those who, like the head, strive to rule others, should surpass the rest in wisdom, just as the head surpasses all members of the body in its range of sense.[10]

No great man ought to believe that his conduct can in any way be hidden. For the greatest things, whatever they be, are most fully exposed to view and are the envy of all who forgive little and disparage much. Since it is very difficult for a prince to conceal himself from others, let him see that nothing at all lies hidden either in private or in public life. Let him first be Argus; then let him raise a lynx in his house; Oedipus, too should be there were that possible.[11] It is dangerous to despise little things in great matters, for often a contemptible little spark kindles a great conflagration.[12] It is neither proper nor safe that one who should be watching over many men, and who is being watched by still more men, should ever go completely to sleep, or that the leader of many, by serving greed and lust, should become slave to a beast.

The best and safest thing is never to be roused to anger. For does not a ferment of anger end in intoxication and madness? However, if anger shakes off restraint and rage is boiling up, the tongue must be curbed. And as is customary with madmen, hands and feet should be bound so that nothing may be said or done in a frenzy. The disciples of Pythagoras were never able to detect in him any sign of anger.[13] Nor had the close friends of Socrates any indication of his anger, except silence.[14] Once Plato, father of philosophers, angered by a boy who had done wrong, said to Xenocrates: "Beat this boy, for I cannot while I am angry."[15]

Let your mind be at once humble and exalted, a blend of dignity and courtesy; may you live temperately and speak truthfully, but sparingly. May you be generous in giving but not rash in promising. May you be firm in faith, your vision wide. May your judgments stand the test of time, following carefully the words of the wise. Lest many men should find it easy to deceive you every day, do not trust many and do not trust easily. Let not smooth persuasion or vain speculation move you, but nothing less than sure reason. Do not make a start on anything unless you have first seen that the end is both good and well assured. Avoid servants who are evil or of ill repute, lest you yourself be reputed an evil master.

But why have we just passed with our eye closed what is most important of all? The poets depict love as blind because the lover is very often deceived when he makes a judgment either about himself or about the beloved.[16] Since men love themselves more than anyone else, they are deceived by no one more than themselves. Therefore, do not trust your own convictions in anything. Again, do not entrust yourself entirely to a single counsellor but have many; and these should be elders whom long experience has taught and whose fine characters have been commended to you by the most reliable report, which is clearly proved in practice. Whenever you are discussing a serious matter with your counsellors, take care that they understand your will, lest in their counsel they follow your pleasure rather than what is useful and honorable.

Furthermore, daily declare to your counsellors that the gift of truth, from wherever it may be offered, will be as pleasing to you as the most costly gifts are to the greedy tyrants who often receive them. I pray you to listen to those who would warn you, lest you be compelled to lay bare your very heart to the darts of fortune. Stop your ears totally to those who praise you, as you would to the evil songs of the Sirens. Remember that you are human and consequently you always have within you some things that can be shown to be false. For this reason those in your household who praise you indiscriminately are either blind themselves or wish you to be. If the laws punish with the greatest severity as sorcerers those who hypnotize with the eye or captivate the ear with incantations, or poison the body, what do we think should be done to those who, by always agreeing and pleasing, deprive the mind's eye of light or rob its ear of hearing? So if you wish to see, if you wish to hear, if you wish to live, banish far away all flatterers and ministers of pleasure as you would your enemies.

But what shall we say of those men who sometimes make accusations against members of your household? Perhaps it may sometimes seem that they should be heard for a while, yet you should never heed them. If you ever do listen to them, let them lead you to caution rather than to punishment. But if you do show the power of punishment, be content with this one sort: that you drive far from your doors slanderers, evil speakers and envious men as if they were rabid dogs.

Finally, let your house be a temple of God. Let it be the eye of prudence, the scales of justice, the seat of fortitude. Let it be an example of moderation, a standard of integrity, the splendor of love, the source of the Graces, and the chorus of the Muses. Let it be a school for orators and poets, a shrine for philosophers and theologians, and a council chamber for the wise. Let it be a nursery of genius, a reward for the learned, a table for the poor, the hope of the good, a refuge for the innocent, and a stronghold for the oppressed. If with all your strength you heed these things and others like them, you will at last hear those blessed words: "Upon this rock I will build my church."[17]

I commend to you Marsilio Ficino of Florence, through whose mouth I have spoken these things.

> 27 January 1478.
> Florence. [4.27]

6

Praise of generosity, praise of almsgiving

Marsilio Ficino to the magnanimous Lorenzo de' Medici: greetings.

I shall say what I feel, my dear Lorenzo, even if it may seem blasphemous; but in reality what is true is not blasphemous, for there is nothing more sacred than truth. So I shall say what I feel, freely.

God, Lorenzo, God Himself is for sale. But with what coin can He be bought? At the price that He Himself pays for others: that is, generous charity to the poor. God in His great love freely gives all things to all men, yet He gives to the poor alone, for every man, however rich he may seem, is quite destitute in relation to God.

Deservedly, we can buy God only by the practice of this virtue, for in this way alone do we act most truly like Him. No one wise, strong, or temperate would boast that he emulates God. These virtues are shadows, not copies of divine virtues: only he who gives generously to the poor acts like God exactly, for the principle in giving is the same both for the generous man and for God. Fortunate indeed is the merchant who for such a paltry sum redeems himself from his enemies, that is, his imperfections, and at the same time buys men and God. He who is rich of both men and God will never be poor. He, who in the midst of great riches often reflects on what it is to be poor, will never become poor, for from the summit he looks upon poverty with compassion. A man of small stature can do nothing better than ascend the heights with humility. A great man can do nothing better than descend to the lowest places with magnanimity. The other virtues for the most part benefit only the man using them; generosity benefits both him and others, and as its application is wider than the other virtues, so it is considered more excellent. The more far-reaching a good act is, the more is it God-like. If evil-doing is the worst of acts, being contrary to the nature of good and against human society, then we must consider doing good to be the best. The other virtues can sometimes arouse jealousy; this one alone always kindles love and completely extinguishes hatred and jealousy. This virtue works most fully when it succors man; both the needy because of his misfortune and the deserving because of his merit.

Therefore sow, my dear Lorenzo, sow I say, fortunate farmer, as you have long ago begun, this arid field of humankind with good will, and it will at length not only abound with fruit and vines, but also flow with milk and honey. But although it is said that the word "human" is derived from *humus*,[1] the principle of sowing among humankind is different from sowing in the earth. The man who sows on poor soil wastes the seed, but he who sows among poor men assuredly works to good purpose, for he shall harvest a hundredfold as was promised by Him who does not lie, and—more priceless yet—from a hundred seeds, he shall harvest the one God.

But why all this? When I heard that during this Holy Week you had compassionately distributed to the poor as much, and, indeed, more than you generally do, I did not wish to be miserly in praising your charity, which you have exercized generously and, if I may say so, lavishly.

12 April 1474.

Florence. [1.70]

7

Difficulty in life follows the easy path
of vice, ease in life follows the difficult path of virtue

Marsilio Ficino to Piero del Nero, a man of the greatest radiance.

How much more difficult it is to go forward in the certainty of reason than to stray by chance; to climb than to descend; to attempt the new rather than practice the habitual; to attain to the one center of the circle, rather than rush at any of its countless other points. How much more difficult it is to pierce with an arrow the target itself, that is the mark, rather than its surround; to keep to the footpath or furrow than to wander hither and thither; to hold perfectly straight than to slip to the side. It is just as difficult to act rightly rather than do wrong, to be good rather than bad. Indeed, it is evident that we all go astray every day, and only rarely do a few of us act honorably and justly.

Quote for 73rd!

Nevertheless, divine law compensates for the extreme difficulty of the path of virtue with two benefits. Firstly, the virtues are so closely linked together that whoever follows one attains them all. On the other hand, the vices are so mutually incompatible that they cannot all be in one person at the same time. For how can anyone be at once both miserly and extravagant? Or both reckless and timid? Secondly, that first difficulty of nascent virtue is followed by the easiest and most enjoyable life. Brief struggle is followed by everlasting reward. But the easiness of vice is soon followed by appalling difficulty and perpetual sorrow. Hence that saying of Pythagoras: "Do not touch the creature with the black tail!"[1] That is, flee from vice, for in its wake lie darkness of mind and torment of will.

Farewell, most radiant Nero! Having attained virtue through difficulty, you have attained ease of life through virtue. In order that from this place you may reach the summit of felicity, remember that it is hard and laborious to retrace steps out of the deep abyss of the vices and emerge into the upper air; so hard that no one has strength to make this ascent unless evenhanded Jupiter has loved him and ardent virtue has raised him from that place to the upper, pure, bright air.[2] [2.55]

8

There is no remedy for evils more fitting than patience

Marsilio Ficino to Sebastiano Salvini, his nephew: greetings.

The common saying has it, Sebastiano, that nothing is more difficult than patience. But we think the opposite: it is not at all difficult, because it involves no trouble; no trouble, because there is no toil; how can there be toil where there is no need for activity? What need is there of activity when it is a matter of not acting rather than acting? Patience, indeed, leads you not to act but to suffer things to be. Just as it is more difficult to act than to suffer things to be, so is it more difficult to act well than to suffer well. All the other virtues hinge on acting well, while patience alone consists in suffering well. What is suffering well, other than not adding to the suffering occasioned by evils? But what do we mean by this? Nothing but a willingness to suffer what you have to suffer, even if you do not wish to. Unless you suffer willingly, you will certainly suffer

J'attends la morte!

unwillingly; and unless you allow yourself to be led, you will be seized and violently dragged away.

O, the marvelous power of patience! The other virtues certainly battle against fate in one way or another, but it is patience alone, or patience more than all the others, that conquers fate; for patience, being in accord with the will of divine providence, changes what fate has decreed to be immutable and unavoidable, so that it makes the unavoidable voluntary. Just as he who acts badly turns what is good for him into evil, so he who suffers well turns what is bad for him into good. Certainly, in suffering ills, such a man ultimately becomes good. He is tested and made bright by adversity, as gold is tried by fire; and as a veteran soldier is made wily and dauntless by frequent experience of danger, so he who has first tasted bitterness appreciates sweet experiences all the more keenly, puts them to wiser use, and enjoys them with greater pleasure. The man who has not experienced evil cannot rightly appraise the magnitude of goodness, while he who has never learned to make use of evil will never know how to enjoy the good.

There is no prosperity more frail than that of the man whom everything seems to have touched with prosperity. The prudent man looks out for rain in a clear sky and for a clear sky[1] in rain, or rather, he regards nothing as clear in this dark life unless it is beneath a clear mind. The unabating storm batters us from without, and it is only within that peace is to be sought.

Clarity comes from the same source as heat, and heat from the same source as light. Light, however, does not proceed from the shadow of matter, but from the light of the mind.

They speak falsely, my friend, who say that the numerous sufferings in the life of mankind arise from its numerous evils. It would be much more accurate to say that life itself is a form of suffering that presses on the wretched without respite. The cures to be applied to chronic diseases are not those that have temporary effect but those that bring permanent benefit.

We are not always strong enough to deliberate, fight, and put up resistance, but we are always able to suffer well. We always suffer and, by suffering, are taught how to suffer. Certainly we can always do something when the power to do it lies within the will itself. As soon as we have the will to suffer well, we do suffer well, since suffering well is nothing other than having the will to suffer. If we do ill, we shall undoubtedly suffer ills and suffer them ill. If we suffer well, we act well. If, perversely, we fight, my friend, we shall grow weary and be utterly defeated, if not by the weariness then by our own selves. If we yield, as we should, we shall undoubtedly conquer.

Air, being totally fluid, yields to the blows of hard bodies and immediately returns to itself just as it was before. But hard bodies in direct collision are broken. All that is softest and most pliant endures unbroken and can bind the hardest things; because the hardest do not know how to yield, they are forced to be hewn, shattered, and bound.

Therefore, my Salvini, overcome fortune by bearing it, and that you may overcome all else, overcome yourself, as you have already begun to do. Remember that in this malign region of the universe nothing escapes the touch of evil, but that under a just judge, or rather under justice as judge, nothing good can be without just reward, nothing evil without due punishment. Remember, too, that patience is so perfectly good that without it none of the other good works of men can be perfected; for whatever arises from other virtues is perfected by patience.

Farewell, most beloved brother, and, so that others may bear with you, bear with others. Indeed, whenever I see in a man those things that offend me, I remember that I too am a man and therefore possess some attribute that may offend others. For this reason I bear with many every day, that many may bear with me. Even bear patiently the severity and length of this letter of mine, since otherwise I shall have spoken of patience fruitlessly or else you will seem to have heard these things in vain, although through your own sound judgment you began to affirm and practise them long ago. [4.12]

9

One cannot have patience without religion[1]

Marsilio Ficino to Antonio Cocci, the distinguished lawyer: greetings.

Three things in particular patience teaches us, it seems to me: first, that you should be willing to bear cheerfully the ills that nature herself bids you bear unwillingly; second, that you should make those things that fate has decreed to be inevitable, agreeable to your own will; third, that you should turn any evil whatsoever into good, which is the office of

God alone. In the first of these, patience requires you to oppose nature, in the second to confound fate, and in the third to raise yourself to the level of God.

It was far easier for Hercules long ago to obey the commands of Eurystheus[2] and to conquer those unconquerable monsters than it is for us to comply with the precepts of patience. And indeed the very great difficulty with which we strive to do this makes this point very clear to us; because in other matters, whatever we frequently put our hand to, in the end we usually accomplish in the best and easiest way. But I cannot see what progress most people are making in the practice of patience. This is not surprising, since the whole of man's life in this region of the universe, which is malign and opposed to celestial minds, seems to be nothing other than sickness and perpetual sorrow. But, as I was saying, although we continually suffer evils, almost continuously we suffer them badly. Added to the other evils, which are countless, impatience comes to us as the culmination of them all. Impatience is so bad that without it nothing is bad for us, and with it nothing good.

For impatience alone causes adversities, which could relate merely to external things and to the body, to pass right through to the soul as well. In addition, it allows us but scant enjoyment of the good things provided by nature or by fortune. Patience, on the other hand, both transforms evils into good by bearing them well and also finds the greatest delight in good things by using them well.

Assuredly, just as we bear evils badly, that is with difficulty and unhappiness, when we are separated from the supreme good, so in equal measure do we bear them well, that is easily and happily, when we are united with the supreme good. For where there is all good there alone is found the remedy for all evils. Moreover, we are united with the supreme good whenever we join wholeheartedly with the will of God, the governor of all. Finally, we join with that will if we love, especially if we acknowledge that in loving individual good things we are really loving nothing other than the supreme divine good itself. From this good, individual things have that whereby they are good and have to be loved and we have that whereby we have to be loved and are able to love.

Let us therefore acknowledge, O friend, I beseech you, let us finally acknowledge this: since nothing anywhere pleases except by its reflection of God, then it is God Himself who pleases us in things that please. From Him those individual things have precisely that which makes them please. Thus, in loving all things, we shall realize beyond doubt that it is God Himself who is being loved; in this way we shall join wholeheartedly with His will. Thus united with God, we shall successfully surmount fortune, nature, and fate. We shall readily understand that, just as individual particles of heat or light must return to absolute heat or light, so whatever has any part of the good, that is all things, so well and wisely ordered in the one system of the universe, must clearly come home to that one absolute goodness and wisdom. Since no good is lacking from absolute goodness, fully present are eternal life, full knowledge of all things, unlimited bounty, total service, and perfect happiness. And since everything is thence disposed in the best possible way, we shall always accept whatever happens as the best.

The whole virtue of patience consists in this alone, that we fully accept as good whatever takes place under the governance of infinite goodness. [4.40]

10

On bearing injury

Marsilio Ficino to Giovanni Cavalcanti, his unique friend: greetings.

You say that one of your relatives felt injured the other day by the insults of some impudent people. The man who acts unjustly, Giovanni, does injustice to himself; for he upsets the mind and stamps it with the mark of an evil disposition. Because of his dishonorable conduct he suffers hatred, danger, and misfortune. He who accepts injury receives it from himself and not from the offender. For the rational soul—which is man himself—cannot be offended unless he considers the injustice as bad for him; and this depends on our judgment. Let therefore no man blame another, but himself; for no man can be offended but by himself, and let him who complains think how he may punish himself, that is, by discipline and correction, instead of hatching punishment for the offender.

Have you not seen puppies snapping at a stone that has been thrown at them, even though it has not hit them? Although they have not been hurt by the stone they hurt their teeth when they bite it. In the same way the imprudent, when kicked by a donkey, flay the animal with their fists, or rather flay themselves. Indeed, from their opinions they receive many injuries, which like balls, rebound against the thrower. You will perhaps say that it is difficult not to desire vengeance. But be in no doubt that if men forgive, the most just God will settle the balance a little later. What could be easier, what more glorious than reliance on God as one's Lord and avenger, and to earn as much goodness from Him by patience, as the wicked meant to inflict injury, and thus to transform evil into good? O what a precious gift forbearance is! Socrates, the wisest among the Greeks, practiced this virtue alone, and Christ, the master of Life, practiced it above all others. Indeed, it is said that He descended among men virtually just for this.

Impatience should be condemned as much as patience should be praised. Apart from other things impatience disturbs the soul, erases past good, taints the present, and constricts the future. One should not listen to the voice of the worthless crowd if it urges one to vengeance. What is the crowd? A kind of polypus;[1] that is, some multilegged beast without a head.

The magnanimous man in his greatness sets small value on small things. Trivial and fleeting are all temporal things, for the past is no more, the future does not yet exist, and the present is indivisible; it starts and ends at the same time.

He is not strong who succumbs to injustice, but he who overcomes injustice is. For injustice to be conquered a man has to stand firm so that he is not moved from his place by its onslaught.

Read this letter to your relative and tell him to find his remedy in reason and not expect it from time. For time is a pernicious doctor and daily misleads the sick by their hope of the future, and before he heals old sores he adds new sorrows. Thus day by day time accumulates evil and leads man to death in a fallacious hope for life. We must live today, since he who lives for tomorrow never lives. If you desire to live now, live for God, in whom yesterday and tomorrow are nothing else but today.

Farewell.

30 March 1474. [1.49]

11

*Since the truth itself is unmoving and is eternal
happiness, only they live truly, beyond movement
and in bliss who devote their lives to the study of truth*

Marsilio Ficino of Florence to his nephew, Sebastiano Salvini: greetings.

I have received your letter[1] speaking unvaryingly about the changeability of things; by unvaryingly I mean truly, since I consider that which does not vary to be nothing other than truth. Indeed, truth itself is so totally unmoving that the truth even of movement is unmoving. For what is the truth of movement except its own unchanging law that is comprehended in the true definition of truth? Truth is such that it can never be other than itself. Consequently, truth is eternally present and neither passes from the past into the present nor flows from the present into the future. Truth is so present that the truth even of the future and of the past is present. For by that same truth by which it was true from the beginning of time that this or that would at some time be, and by which it will be true for all time to come that this or that once was, it is true in the present that this or that is, or was or will be.

Truth is so eternal that even if it is said to have had a beginning at some time, it would certainly have been true before the beginning of time, and it would not have been true except through the same truth, that truth itself would at some time be.[2] And even if truth should be thought ever to cease, then it would be true for all time, yet only through truth itself would it be true, that truth once was. If truth is unmoving in movement, if it is present in past and future, if it is in the beginning without a beginning, if likewise in the end without an end, it is certainly nothing other than the eternal unmoving itself.

The mind therefore, with its natural capacity for truth, partakes of this eternal unmoving. The will,[3] also by its nature longing for truth, can be granted its desire beyond movement and beyond time. Only a life dedicated by choice to the study and cultivation of truth is lived in the fullness of bliss beyond movement and beyond time. Be sure that those who unlawfully and willfully depart from truth, the fount of true happiness, thereupon fall in misery from the bliss of eternity. But those who with all their might draw near to truth, the source of true happiness, at once rise again in bliss to that blessed eternity.

Therefore live happily, as you have begun, in the study and cultivation of truth. For only those live truly and happily who live in truth itself, the fount of true happiness. But only those can ever live in truth itself who always, as far as possible, live for truth.

13 September 1480.
Careggi. [5.23]

Human Nature

12

It was not for small things but for great that God created men

Marsilio Ficino to Giovanni Cavalcanti, his unique friend: greetings.

Logicians say it is the nature of a contradiction that someone who is disposed to one point of view cannot at the same time be disposed to its opposite.[1] Yet this autumn my thoughts have been so divided that I wish neither to speak nor yet to remain silent; I can neither act nor yet refrain from acting. Perhaps this is because I am in some sense two, though I seem to be one. But let me be two, as in *Phaedrus*[2] Plato would have us, or even three, as he argues in the *Timaeus*,[3] as long as that within me which draws me to honorable labor always overcomes that which draws me back to indolence and torpor. See, that which stirs me to action and speech is now dominant, and so I am speaking and acting as best I can. But somehow we are now faced with another problem. For I would like to joke for a while in my usual way and to write something humorous at least to my Cavalcanti. I took up my pen chiefly with this intention, yet I am writing rather seriously; while attempting the lyrical or comic, I am producing elegy or tragedy.

Would you have me say, my friend, that in these times Saturn has chosen me alone on whom to test all his stern powers? No. I see you would not want that,[4] my Giovanni, and neither would I. Then what shall we say, my friend? We shall say that God wishes his priests to be the most serious of men and that he requires a serious rather than humorous attitude to sacred matters. This was perhaps what Pythagoras meant when he gave his disciples the symbolic instruction not to cut their fingernails at a sacrifice.[5]

It was not for small things but for great that God created men, who, knowing the great, are not satisfied with small things. Indeed, it was for the limitless alone that He created men, who are the only beings on earth to have rediscovered their infinite nature and who are not fully satisfied by anything limited, however great that thing may be. [4.6]

13

On humanity

Marsilio Ficino to Tommaso Minerbetti, a humane man: greetings.

Why are boys more cruel than old men, madmen more cruel than the sane, stupid men more than the clever? Because the former are, so to speak, less human than the others. Hence those who are more cruel are called inhuman and brutish. For those who fall far short of the full nature of Man, through lack of years, mental defect, physical disease, or an unfavorable position of the stars, mostly hate or ignore the human race, as if it were something alien and unconnected to them. Nero was not a man, I would say, but a monster in a man's skin. For if he had really been a man, he would have loved all other men as members of the same body.

Individual men, formed by one idea in the same image, are one man. It is for this reason, I think, that of all the virtues, wise men named only one after man himself: that is humanity, which loves and cares for all men as though they were brothers, born in a long succession of one father.

Therefore, most humane man, persevere in the service of humanity. Nothing is dearer to God than love. There is no surer sign of madness or of future misery than cruelty.

Remain a friend to Carlo Valguli of Brescia; for he is a man of outstanding humanity, as well as excelling in the humanities through his studies of Greek and Latin. [1.55]

14

He who pursues everything achieves nothing

Marsilio Ficino to Carlo Valguli of Brescia: greetings.

You ask, my Valguli, what am I doing today? That which I did yesterday. Again you ask, what am I planning to do tomorrow? That which I am doing today. Our Plato has persuaded me that I would in the end accomplish most if I always did the same thing.[1] And this is perfectly right. Assuredly a man who pursues everything achieves nothing; for many obstruct one, whereas one serves and unites many.

He is one of a crowd, who pursues many things; singular indeed is he who pursues one. It is the mark of an immature and weak mind to under-take different things at any one moment. It is also rash ambition daily to promise many things. Pythagoras teaches us that unity looks toward the good, but diversity toward the evil.[2] Just as when the natural force in the liver or the vital force in the heart is drawn apart into two, and as a conse-quence is weakened, so the conscious force in the brain does not equip us for diverse actions.[3] Besides, each man carries out most efficiently what each is best suited for by nature. One accords with one, therefore one is necessary, plurality brings confusion; one, I say, because it is in itself pure, and more appropriate than anything else for the man who acts.

Finally, if God is always the same and sets the same things in motion, a man is further away from God the more inclined he is to different things.

10 December 1476. [2.30]

15

Happy is the man who has all he desires;
only he has all he desires who desires all he has[1]

Marsilio Ficino speaks of happiness to Francesco Sassetti.

The wise, Sassetti, judge that man alone to be happy for whom all things come to pass according to his intent. All things come to pass according to his intent for him alone who has all he desires. Only he has all he desires who desires all he has.[2] That man alone desires everything he has (that is, whatever happens to him, either because of his nature or by chance) who first of all understands that there is nothing good that he should not desire. Secondly, he considers that He who from the beginning made all things good daily disposes everything everywhere for the good. Finally, since nothing anywhere is at variance with him, he is at one with the creator of all. So we judge him alone to be happy who has committed himself wholeheartedly to God, the helmsman. Whatever happens he either approves as something coming from God, or at least praises as something to be brought to its place in the good by God.

Perhaps you will ask by what reasoning I may best demonstrate this? By just this for the moment, because a letter delights in brevity: if the light of the sun were infinite or the heat of fire without limit, no place would admit of darkness, nor the least cold be felt anywhere. We know that the one ruler of the whole universe, who directs and moves such a great body so well over so great a span of time without ever wearying, is good and without limit. If He is indisputably without limit and reproduces Himself infinitely throughout space and surpasses everything infinitely in degree of virtue, where then does evil dwell, if it cannot exist with the good, and the good itself fills the universe? Evil therefore has no true place anywhere, only an imaginary one. It is certainly not in nature herself, but rather in that mind that deceives itself to such an extent about divine goodness that it thinks things could be disposed other than well under the infinite good. By contrast, nothing other than good happens to the man who realizes that there is nothing other than good. To be able to consider all things thus, and therefore live happily, only devotion to God can be of use to us. Moreover, it will always be twice as useful to you as to anyone else, my Francesco, if you surpass others in devotion to the same degree that that spacious mansion of yours surpasses the rest. Your home, Sassetti, is twice as fit for devotion as other homes. It is rare for other homes to have even one chapel. But yours contains two;[3] and very beautiful ones at that. Be twice as devoted as the rest, my Francesco. Be twice as happy. [4.33]

16

Our use of prosperity is even more perverse than our use of adversity

Marsilio Ficino to Cardinal Raffaele Riario and Francesco Salviati, Archbishop of Pisa

Aristotle writes in his book on Ethics[1] that it is more difficult to endure pain than to abstain from pleasure. Indeed, this seems probable by reason, since pain is more potent in destroying nature than pleasure is in preserving or restoring it. For this reason, a man of sound mind will choose, if the choice be given, to abstain from pleasure rather than to accept or suffer pain.

In spite of this, by some foolish, or rather unhappy, fate it happens that most mortals make more perverse use of prosperity than of adversity, and that those who have not yielded to the threat of pain may yet succumb to the allurements of pleasure. I could mention Achilles, Hannibal,[2] Mark Antony, and many others who had indeed stood firm while the north wind raged, yet collapsed when caressed by a gentle breeze; and although they freed themselves from a sea of gall, the merest drop of honey[3] overwhelmed them instantly. And if, like Homer, I were allowed to compare flies with heroes,[4] I would add that flies are never drowned in sour wine, but often in sweet.

Is there anyone who, upon due reflection, is not truly astonished at how wisely Solomon, the wisest of the Hebrews, persevered with his labor, and how unwisely he succumbed to his lust?[5] Or how bravely Hercules, the bravest of the Gentiles, overcame every danger, no matter how great; yet how weakly he placed his neck under the yoke of pleasure?

Should you enquire why good fortune rather than adversity softens and breaks men's spirits, Philosophy's brief reply would be that prosperity fills men's spirits with the breeze of abundance and that this abundance makes them unrestrained and neglectful; license renders such men weaker, that is more inclined to evil, than all other men.

The truth is that by nature every appetite chooses and pursues the good, while it shuns and drives away evil.[6] Now pleasure appears to carry before it an image of the good, but pain an image of evil. Therefore, when pleasure comes to us, not only do we not shun it, we wantonly pursue it as if it were a mistress, yielding and giving ourselves up to it. And so, as Plato says,[7] we are caught, as if on a fishhook, and then unwittingly we are destroyed by enemies, that is by those evils that lurk beneath the pleasure. But when the hideous face of pain shows itself, the whole strength of our nature is instantly armed within us, as against an enemy; and so we often fight vigorously, overcoming this open foe more easily than the hidden traitor.

Therefore to prosper from prosperity, let us remember that the nature of evil is to offer itself to us daily under the guise of good, that is, pleasure, a snare to deceive and destroy the wretched. As for evil itself, especially corruption of the mind, should it ever come to us undisguised, being even more ugly than ugliness itself, it would be promptly shunned. But when it comes to us covered by pleasure, the image of the good itself, it is very easily taken in by anyone and given lodging as if it were the good; but soon after, it secretly strikes down its unwary host with a sword, as he deserves.[8]

Therefore let us flee from pleasure to escape from pain. Pleasure bought with pain brings destruction.[9] [4.34]

17

Slanderers are to be scorned

Marsilio Ficino to the magnanimous Lorenzo de' Medici.

The laws abhor infamous report and hate slanderers so much that they are particularly severe on those who speak foully, against even a foul man. We have both seen and approved the public observance of this twice—or rather, three times—during our lifetime in Florence. But today I ask no such thing of the laws; for I do not wish the laws to be marshalled on my behalf against fleas,[1] which will perish at the first onset of cold.

So let that little imp bite your Christian priests with impunity, as he was long ago allowed to bite Christ. Let the mob judge at random a teaching that is scarcely known even to the very few. Let little men, who have no sense, pass sentence as they please on my life, which is known to God alone. For these and similar matters I, like Socrates and Zeno,[2] care nothing—or at most, like Aristotle and Theophrastus,[3] very little.

I have surely learnt from Heraclitus and Thales[4] that all the affairs of mortals, whether good or bad, while seeming to rise are falling. I have learnt from Pythagoras and Plato[5] that the soul is asleep in the body, and that whatever we seem to do or suffer here is nothing but a dream. I have learnt from the Master of Life[6] that the whole world is immersed in evil, but that through a good man all things return to good. Thus the lofty ramparts of sacred Philosophy keep all such trifles far from us. Yet today this same Philosophy gives me one bidding, that I should indicate to you the very way to discharge your duty—as you have done most diligently for us at other times. That is, with just the slightest tilt of the head show that you are displeased at what above all displeases God, namely, that something holy, and indeed something of yours, is being given for dogs to tear or for their fleas to bite. [2.5]

18

The desire for vengeance is nothing but the acceptance of another injury

Marsilio Ficino to a man who cannot bear an injury.

You grieve, my friend, because you have received an injury; that I grant.

But you appear to have been injured not so much because someone has done evil to you but because you thought what he did to be evil. To an evil man, indeed, all things, even the good, are turned into evil. To a good man, however, all things, even those which seem very bad, are finally turned into good.

Are you thinking of revenge? I earnestly warn you: have a care. For if you attempt to be avenged, you will suffer a second and a third injury, and through your desire to destroy the other man you will destroy yourself. Bees, provoked, sting with very little injury, and in stinging give up life. Of course, I do not urge you to forget entirely. Perhaps it is worthwhile to remember, so that at least another time you may be wary of malignant men.

He is accustomed never to forgive, who has once injured. Forgive freely, I beseech you, lest you bring trouble on yourself, and he harm you again and again. Of necessity his evils await him. For fortune leaves nothing untouched, nature leaves nothing unharmed, nor does God leave anything unavenged. [2.47]

19

The folly and misery of men

Marsilio Ficino to Riccardo Angiolieri of Anghiari, Oliviero Arduini, and Antonio Serafico, his fellow philosophers: greetings.

What did Democritus[1] laugh at so much? What made Heraclitus[2] weep? The former, I believe, laughed at the folly of men, and the latter wept at their misery. Folly appears to be ridiculous, and misery lamentable. What is folly, but a corruption of judgment? What is misery, but the torment of desire springing from corrupt judgment?

Who will deny that those men are foolish who attend to other people's affairs, but neglect their own? They esteem highly what is absent and what is new, and belittle what is present and familiar. Because of their ceaseless longing for what is to come, they do not enjoy what is present. Although movement has to be stilled for there to be rest; yet those men are forever beginning new and different movements, in order that they may one day come to rest. They accumulate wealth as though they would never die. They misuse pleasures as though they would die each day. Let us have done with further examples for the present, for an endless number occur to us.

I can only judge it the most foolish act of all, that many people most diligently feed a beast, that is, their body, a wild, cruel, and dangerous animal; but allow themselves, that is, the soul, insofar as they have one, to starve to death. We are surprised that while we continue to live, or rather die like this, we are unhappy, as though we could reap a different harvest from the one we have sown. Misery is the fruit of foolishness. How is this? Because we foolishly overfeed the body and neglect the soul, the body becomes fat and robust and the soul thin and puny. So it comes about that the soul, in its meager and feeble state, sees physical things as both large and strong. The soul greatly desires what looks large, but fears what looks strong even more. For this reason, in its misery, it is harassed partly by the passion of greed and partly by the dread of fear.

Let us, I beg you, nourish and increase the spirit with spiritual food, so that it may at length become mighty and have small regard for physical things, as though they were worth very little. Then may no part of the spirit shift from its own seat through the assaults of the flesh.

Let us climb into the high watchtower of the mind, leaving the dust of the body below; then we will gaze more closely at the divine and view the mortal from a distance. The former will seem greater than usual, and the latter smaller. So, cherishing the divine, and disregarding the mortal, we will no longer be foolish or miserable, but indeed wise and happy.

Farewell. [1.57]

20

The folly and misery of men

Marsilio Ficino to Piero Vanni, Cherubino Quarquagli, Domenico Galletti: greetings.

You have seen painted in my academy a sphere of the world; on one side Democritus laughing, and on the other Heraclitus weeping.[1] Why is Democritus laughing? Why does Heraclitus weep? Because the mass of mankind is a monstrous, mad, and miserable animal.

Mortal men ask God for good things every day, but they never pray that they may make good use of them. They want fortune to wait upon their desires, but they are not concerned that desire should wait upon reason. They would like all their household furniture down to the least article to be made as beautiful as possible, but they are hardly ever concerned that the soul should become beautiful. They diligently seek out remedies for bodily diseases, but neglect the diseases of the soul. They think they can be at peace with others, yet they continually wage war with themselves. For there is a constant battle between body and soul, between the senses and reason. They believe that they can find themselves a faithful friend in others, but not one of them keeps faith with himself. What they have praised, they reject; what they have desired, they do not want; and contrariwise. They lay out the parts of buildings to a measure, and tune strings on a lyre to a hair's breadth, but they never attempt to harmonize the parts and movements of the soul. They make stones into the likeness of living men, and they make living men into stones; they despise wise men themselves, but they honor the statues and names of the wise. They claim to know about everyone else's affairs, although they do not know about their own.

What more, my friends? The magistrates forbid murder, and allow instruments for killing men to be made everywhere. They desire an excellent crop of men, yet they do not take sufficient care of the seedling, that is the child.

People always live badly today; they only live well tomorrow. For the sake of ambition they strive against each other with evil deeds, but the path to glory would be easier to tread by doing good to one another. Although they always speak evil, they hope to be well spoken of themselves; although they do evil, they hope to receive good. We proclaim that we are the authors of good, but that God is the author of evil. We blame our faults on the stars.

How many people will you find who value a man as much as money; who cultivate themselves in the same way as they cultivate their fields and other affairs; who bring up their family with as much care as many rear their horses, dogs, and birds; who consider how grave is the waste of time? In spending money we are very mean, in expending time we are extravagant beyond measure. How many can you name who recognize the poverty of their soul? Everyone believes that he abounds in wisdom, but is short of money.

What a sorry state! We seek the greatest in the least, the high in the low, good in evil, rest in activity, peace in dissension, plenty in penury; in short, life in death.

I beg you, my friends, let us seek the same ends that we are already seeking, but let us not continue to seek them in the same place. The man who believes he will find one thing in its opposite is mad and miserable.

Farewell. [1.58]

21

The folly and misery of men

Marsilio Ficino to Cristoforo Landino, matchless in learning and virtue: greetings.

Aristotle raised questions about the nature of things. I am now going to pose you questions about the nature of Man. Come tell me, why do men boast of their reason yet live at the mercy of chance? They desire or fear any number of things before they really know whether such things should be either desired or feared, and they put the momentary and trivial before the eternal and immeasurable. Why will they pay no heed to man, nor be subject to the wise, yet give themselves up most willingly to the service of brutes and of wickedness?

Why is it that we strive to be masters of others, when we are not masters of ourselves? Why in our zeal for mastery do we fall daily into slavery? And why do we strive to gain honors, instead of to be worthy of them? Again, seeing that animals without human protection cannot properly be controlled by an animal, what makes us think that men can happily be ruled by a man without God's counsel and assistance? And how in the midst of such bounteous plenty do we come to be querulous and needy? What makes us envy so many people, when the plight of mortals rather merits pity than envy? Why do we so easily overlook goodness, but evil never? And since qualities are canceled by their opposites, why do we try to cure evils with evils? Why do we often hope to gain honor through infamy? We admire virtue in another, but we ourselves strive rather to seem worthy of admiration than to *be* worthy of it. We are upset by faults in others, but we hardly ever consider how we can avoid upsetting both ourselves and them. We close our ears to truth, but to lies they are open wide. And what shall I say of those made captive by their love for some person or some object, who despise and abandon their own selves to pursue something else? Oh fools! Oh wretches! Since you cannot lay hold of anything by any means but through your own selves, how will you ever come by outer possessions if you have lost the inner? Travelers! Why do you seek treasure far away, when it is nearby, indeed within yourselves?

I am often given to wonder, too, Landino, at the reason why we fear merely that one death, which is clearly the end of dying, but never at all our daily deaths. Undoubtedly at every moment the constitution of the body is changed, and the past life comes to an end. Finally, as it seems to me, seeing that we practice the virtues falsely but the vices faithfully, it is no wonder that to the best of our ability we end up falsely happy, and sincerely miserable. This Democritus ridiculed, Heraclitus bewailed, Socrates sought to cure, and God can cure. Oh what a miserable creature is man, except he sometime rise up above the man, I mean commit himself to God, and love God for the sake of God and everything else for His sake. That is the sole answer to these problems and the end of all ills.

Farewell. [1.59]

THE SOUL

22

On the soul

Marsilio Ficino to Francesco Tedaldi, his friend: greetings.

Lattanzio Tedaldi, as dear to me as a friend as he is to you as a son, has returned to me from you the short work in which the views of the Western philosophers about the soul are set forth. Now Marsilio Ficino is asked what he thinks on this subject.

Although it is not my part to resolve arguments of such importance between them, yet, since they ask what I think, the books I have written on the *Immortality of Souls* will explain this very fully and I hope they will be sent to you shortly. Meanwhile, I will give a very brief reply regarding that part of the discussion that they especially desire.

First of all, I know that my soul is substance; otherwise I could not fully understand and define substance. I would be nothing more significant than a chance attribute, nor could I judge and evaluate how far an attribute falls short of substance. I know that my soul is not corporeal and mortal; for if it were, I would not understand the incorporeal and immortal and distinguish them from the corporeal and mortal. I know that it is rational; otherwise I would not know how to bring reason to bear on the soul and other matters. I know that, although it partakes of reason, yet it is not reason itself, as some think; if it were I could not wander from the truth in ascribing reasons to things, and wander from reason in conducting my affairs. He who declares that the soul is reason departs from reason more than he who denies this.

Similarly reason is either substance or quality. If reason is substance, it is like existence; it is the all, perfect and utterly boundless. The soul is not of this nature; only God is. If reason is a quality, it is clearly an attribute and faculty of the soul rather than the soul itself. But no one would venture to assert that the soul is itself a quality and an attribute, for it freely rules the body by shaping its substance, moving it in opposing directions and making it stand still, and in some way having the power to assume opposing qualities by turns. For how can it be called either an attribute or perishable? It runs impartially through everything, through the classes and kinds of both substance and attributes. It also turns back upon itself, sometimes through desire, sometimes through knowledge, and for that reason it is also life itself, since it cleaves to itself, not to anything lower. It acts without the bodily instrument whenever it reaches toward and chooses the incorporeal, and correctly distinguishes it from the corporeal. It often resists the inclination of the body, and is not at rest there. Moreover, the more it withdraws itself from the body, the more effectively it understands and the better and happier it is. The soul, therefore, is an incorporeal rational substance, fitted to direct the body.

Many of the Platonists think that the soul precedes the body,[1] but the Peripatetics think the contrary. I believe that those Western philosophers whom you commend are Peripatetics even though you do not say so. For, as you say, they discussed the soul after a banquet as if they thought that the body should be refreshed before the soul could be brought into being. For my part, although I created the little soul of this letter before dining, I nevertheless agree with them about the order of creation.

Farewell, and see that you continually take part in these discussions, for in this way you will care for your body at the same time as your soul.

My friend Giovanni Cavalcanti commends himself to you. And please commend me to those philosophers of yours. [1.96]

23

The nature and duty of the soul; the praise of history

Marsilio Ficino to Jacopo Bracciolini, son of the orator Poggio, and heir to his father's art: greetings.

Every year the early disciples of Plato used to hold a city festival in honor of Plato's birthday.[1] In our own times the Bracciolini, his modern disciples, have celebrated the occasion both in the city and the surrounding countryside. Our book on love records the country festivities at the home of the splendid Lorenzo de' Medici at Careggi,[2] while in the city of Florence the festival was celebrated at princely expense by the richly gifted and noble-minded Francesco Bandini.

I was among the company when you, Bindaccio Ricasoli, our Giovanni Cavalcanti, and many other members of the Academy sat down to the feast. Of the many different things we discussed at that gathering, I often reflect especially on the conclusion we reached before the feast, about the nature of the soul. I will gladly remind you of it now, for nothing befits a man more than discourse on the soul. Thus the Delphic injunction "Know thyself" is fulfilled and we examine everything else, whether above or beneath the soul, with deeper insight. For how can we understand anything else fully unless we understand the soul itself, through which everything must be understood? Does not a man abuse the soul by not devoting himself to its study, when it is by means of the soul and for its sake that he wants to understand everything else?

We all agreed there that the reasonable soul is set on a horizon, that is the line dividing the eternal and temporal, because it has a nature midway between the two. Being in the middle, this nature is not only capable of rational power and action, which lead up to the eternal, but also of energies and activities that descend to the temporal.[3] Since these divergent tendencies spring from opposing natures, we see the soul turning at one moment to the eternal and at another to the temporal and so we understand rightly that it partakes of the nature of both. Our Plato placed the higher part of the soul under the authority of Saturn, that is, in the realm of mind and divine providence, and the lower part under Jupiter, in the realm of life and fate. Because of this the soul seems to have a double aspect,[4] one of gold and one of silver. The former looks toward the Saturnine and the latter to the Jovial. But this looking carries both desire and judgment. It is better to love eternal things than to judge them, for they are very difficult to judge rightly but they can never be wrongly loved. They can never be loved too much; indeed they cannot be loved enough until they are loved passionately. But it is better to judge temporal things than to desire them. Usually they are judged well enough, but basely loved. A judge takes within himself the form of the object being judged, whereas the lover transports himself into the form of the beloved. It is better to raise to ourselves inferior things by judging them, than to cast ourselves down through loving them. It is better to raise ourselves to higher things through love than to reduce them to our level by judgment.

Farewell.

But before I draw to a close I beg you, my Bracciolini, not to lose your enthusiasm for writing history, now that you have begun. For historians praise the style of your prose and the subject itself is very necessary for the life of mankind, not only to make it more agreeable but to found it upon tradition. What is in itself mortal, through history attains immortality; what is absent becomes present, what is ancient becomes new. A young man quickly matches the full development of the old; and if an old man of seventy is considered wise because of his experience of life, how much wiser is he who covers a span of a thousand or three thousand years. For each man seems to have lived for as many thousands of years as the span of history he has studied.

Once more, farewell. [1.107]

24

On divination and the divinity of the soul

Marsilio Ficino of Florence to his fellow philosopher Matteo Corsini: greetings.

The father of my mother Alessandra was called Giovanni, and her mother was called Angela. Alessandra was in Figline, Giovanni in the town of Montevarchi, and Angela in Florence. Angela wrote to Giovanni and Alessandra that she was well, and would return on the following day. They read her letters, and while asleep that night they both saw Angela at the same time. She appeared to Alessandra in the entrance of the house, and when the daughter was greeting her mother as if she had returned home, the mother avoided her daughter's embrace. "Farewell," she said, "and take care that the priests pray to God for me." And to Giovanni she said, "My Giovanni, how I grieve at your misfortune! Farewell, and ask that prayers be offered to God for me."

Suddenly aroused by these visions, they both cried out, thinking her to be dead. They sent to Florence. The news came back that she had departed this life that very night.

You may wonder at these things, Corsini, but listen to something equally miraculous. As soon as her son was born, my mother entrusted him to a country woman as a wet nurse. Seventeen days later, while asleep at noon, it seemed to her that she was deeply troubled and was being comforted by her own mother, long since dead, who said "Do not grieve, my daughter." On the following day, the country people brought her the news that her son had been suffocated by the nurse.

I shall omit how she foresaw in a dream that her husband, Ficino the doctor, would fall from his horse, and where it would happen. I shall also omit many other instances of this kind. For the present it is enough to have told you these two stories which seem to confirm two things in particular. First, that the souls of men that are almost separated from their bodies because of a temperate disposition and a pure life may in the abstraction of sleep divine many things,[1] for they are divine by nature; and whenever they return to themselves, they realize this divinity. The second thing these stories confirm is that the souls of the dead, freed from the chains of the body, can influence us, and care about human affairs. Hesiod[2] sang of this; our Plato[3] confirmed it in the *Laws*; and both these men were known as heroes to all antiquity.

Farewell. [1.9]

25

Serious words to Giovanni. The soul perceives
after death, and much more clearly than when in the body

Marsilio Ficino to Giovanni Cavalcanti, his unique friend: greetings.

I have written to you several letters, my dearest friend, in which I have attempted the style of love; which indeed is fitting for our friendship and which in its freedom and purity is no different from that of Socrates and Plato. But now, after loving jests in the Platonic style (for this is how Plato introduces his writings) we must come to serious matters. Listen now to the discussion we had once regarding the mind with those excellent citizens and lawyers Bernardo Giugni and Bartolomeo Fortini.

There are two main questions that people have about the mind. The first is whether the intellect can be separated from the body, and whether it can live and operate once the body has been laid aside. The second is, if it does then understand anything, whether it understands clearly or not. We shall now reply to these questions as briefly as possible, for they and similar ones are discussed at great length in our *Theology on the Immortality of Souls*.[1] We admit that the intellect can apprehend many incorporeal things, such as God, angels, souls, virtues, numerical proportions, ideas, and universal principles. But just as we cannot distinguish the invisible through sight, so neither can we reflect on things incorporeal through any bodily means. Nor can we through a nature confined to body, space, and time, enquire into, seek, discover, or retain those things that are not bound by matter, space, and time. But if the mind, while still in control of the body, becomes collected in itself, so that it may observe some things through itself alone, it follows that when it is separated from the body it is able to observe much more, and much more easily through its own self. If it can function by itself, then it must also be able to exist and to live by itself.

And to take the second question: the mind without the body will observe more clearly what is presented to it for its understanding from within, than the senses now observe what is presented to them from outside to be sensed. And it will do so at least as much more clearly as sight is more acute and faster than hearing and the other senses, and as mind is superior to sense, and the objects of mind to the objects of sense. No one who uses the powers of the mind doubts that mind is superior to sense, for he sees that mind is the judge of the senses, and that being more precious it is granted to fewer beings, takes longer to train and is used less frequently. This shows that the objects of mind also are more sublime than the objects of sense, because they are universal, vast, and eternal, whereas those of sense are particular, limited, and mortal. It may be added that the more we concentrate on external sense, the more is the internal sense withdrawn, and vice versa. For he who looks and listens attentively can scarcely imagine at the same time, and he who imagines a great deal scarcely sees or hears what is happening around him. The same relation exists between the imagination and the intellect.

The soul in this body has two principal impediments. First, it is drawn into many activities and much agitation, and its different activities weaken and obstruct each other, for it is very hard to apply the mind to different things at the same time. Secondly, the soul is engaged in inferior activities much earlier, more attentively, and more often than in higher ones, not only because of the condition of its abysmal dwelling but also because of the corporeal service assigned to men for a time by God. And so it is that when we wish to consider the incorporeal, we function for the most part feebly, and perceive it dimly as though through a cloud. But whenever the actions of eating, accumulating, feeling, or imagining either entirely cease or are greatly reduced, then the vision of the mind will be correspondingly sharpened, so that whatever is observed by the mind is observed more clearly under the power of this light. Then indeed the soul will observe through itself, and it will see that light of the intellect more clearly than it now sees the light of the senses through the glass windows of this bodily prison. Entirely at peace, it will perceive through its own perfect transparency the highest impressions in the light of the divine sun. So bright is that light, that the light of this sun becomes a shadow in comparison, and because it is so clear it is hidden from impure eyes but fully manifest to those that are pure. Nor will the mind then gaze as if at painted images, but rather at real objects, of which all other things are images.

When in sleep the workings and movements of the external senses cease, then the imagination, which is fed by the rest of the senses, gathers so much strength that it paints pictures internally, which seem to represent what is real. What therefore will the intellect, which is so much more powerful than the imagination, do when it has escaped free from impediments to a far greater extent than the imagination of the dreaming man, and in pure truth and reason perceives the true principles of everything? Certainly it will then depict within itself with the greatest precision all that is true; or rather, it will receive the image of all that is true from everywhere. But from where, chiefly? From the mind of minds, from the light of lights. How easily does this come about? Very easily. For because of a natural kinship between the two, visible light instantaneously illumines a transparent substance as soon as this substance becomes still and pure; such light gives this substance its own form, through which it gives it the forms of all things visible. In the same way the intelligible—indeed more than intelligible—light that is God forms that transparent substance of the intellect as soon as that substance becomes still; I say it gives this substance its own form, that is the divine, and through this the forms of all things intelligible.

And just as God has already imparted His bounteous light, so immediately He imparts life-giving warmth and joy, thus bestowing life, free from death. And just as He has shed into physical matter light unmixed with darkness so He has shed light into the mind beyond any limit of time, by which it rises from the currents of time to the stillness of eternity. Moreover, He ever nourishes the mind with goodness, to its content. For God draws the desire of the mind to Himself by filling it with beauty, and by drawing desire to Himself he fulfils it. Where there is good without evil there is fullness without surfeit, and through infinite goodness there arises infinite capacity. Thus infinite goodness and beauty, the source of innumerable forms of goodness and beauty, equally attract and fulfil the mind in eternity. [1.39]

26

On the divinity of the soul and on religion

Marsilio Ficino to Francesco Bandini: greetings.

When others are writing to Marsilio Ficino and his Achates, Giovanni Cavalcanti, they write two letters, assuming that where they see two bodies therein must also be two wills. But Bandini, who so to speak, has eyes like a lynx, perceiving only one, wrote a letter to only one. In his letter he calls Marsilio immortal and divine, since he does not consider the fleshly covering, but sees through to the inner man, to his very soul, which being given from God to man is immortal and divine. O Bandini, how penetrating you are; for, in one moment of insight, you perceive what first took me ten years to discover, by way of long and tortuous paths, and then five years to write about in eighteen books.[1] The opening of this work begins to reveal, step by step, the divine nature of the soul, which you seem to understand already. It starts with these words: "Since Man, with his restless mind, feeble frame, and desire for everything, leads a harder life on earth than the very beasts, then, if nature were to appoint for him exactly the same limit of life as for other creatures, no animal could have a sadder lot than he. But it is not possible that Man, who by worship of God comes nearest of all creatures to God, the source of happiness, could be the least happy of all. Therefore it is only after the death of the body that his greater happiness may be achieved; and it surely follows that when our souls leave this prison some measure of light survives."[2]

But enough of this Bandini; continue as far as you can to look at the inner nature of everything. Then you will never be deluded. Just looking at the surface reveals only shadows and dreams. The center is the pivot and substance of things.

You promise to honor us as soon as you can. Some while ago you honored the divine Plato and his followers in magnificent style. With your promise you honor us already. For when a truthful man, such as Bandini, makes a promise, it is already fulfilled.

Farewell. [1.111]

27

Nothing is more shameful than a man in whose house all things are beautiful before the soul

Marsilio Ficino to Mankind: greetings.

If some farmer were not only to work the land of another for no reward but were also to neglect his own at the greatest loss to himself, he would without doubt be judged to be most dense and pitiable. Therefore, those minds are too far out of mind and pitiable that expend all their labor always in this: that the body and externals be kept as well and as finely adorned as possible; but they neglect to labor inwardly, through which they could be good and adorned in themselves.

Oh how corrupted is the man to whom a dog and a horse are better than the soul! Oh how deformed is he to whom a shoe, whatever its worth, is more beautiful than the soul! Nothing is truly good or beautiful in the house of that man where all things seem good and beautiful before himself, that is before the soul. If some Cynic philosopher were to enter the sanctuary of such a man, in all its adornment, and were compelled by some necessity to spit, certainly he should spit in his face,[1] for clearly he would see each single thing therein clean and adorned, in preference to the man himself.

Nothing is poorer nor more empty than a man whose storehouse is full but whose soul is vacant. Those who would be stationed outside mind, we are wont to call demented. By what arrangement a soul which for so long has been in cooking vessels[2] may be in mind, I do not understand. Say, I beg, O unhappy mind, as careful of what is alien as negligent of what is yours, declare, I say, to which man are all things sound, except to the sound man? Why, therefore, do you ramble about hither and thither so anxiously outside yourself, out of mind? And labor so greatly and so vainly?

Labor so that you may be good and shine with beauty; suddenly all things are good and shining with beauty for you. But, in truth, you will not carry through what I command you, until you desire to come forth good and shining with beauty, just as much as you exert yourself to ensure that the merest household utensil is the best and seems most ornamental.

If we did not allow Man himself, that is the soul, to perish from hunger while we feed the body, the dogs, and the birds, then each man would live content and plenished; just as now no one is content.

Now, in truth, to whom is it a wonder if the soul is never filled, if it is always afflicted? That man abandons his own self who cares only for this: that he may fill his beast. This beast becomes continuously more voracious in its very satiety, and against its Lord, who through neglect is burning up within and is deprived of blood; whereby the beast becomes roused to more ferocity and filled with greater energy. [2.60]

28

The soul is not satisfied by mortal things, for it seeks again the eternal

Marsilio Ficino to the magnanimous Lorenzo de' Medici: greetings.

If I were now to recite to you, Lorenzo, the shortest Lenten oration[1] which my mind delivered to me at dawn, of what value would this be? Perhaps now, just to move you to laughter at my follies, just as in these days very adept orators shake tears out of the multitude. Nevertheless I shall recite it just as it is seen by me, Lorenzo; because I know that a man outstanding for piety, though perchance he may sometimes laugh a little at the words of piety, could not in truth deride piety itself.

He who thirsts for wine, as you observe, Marsilio, quenches the thirst with wine; and more so, if he drains two bowls than one. For such a man the image of wine, whether from seeing or thinking, does not slake the thirst; it stirs it up. For it is of the nature of an image to attract but of a substance to nourish. Wherefore, just as the image of wine feeds thirst, so wine itself feeds the thirstful man. Indeed the torment of Tantalus[2] shows us this; or rather our torment shows us, for we are all Tantali. In fact we all thirst for the good and the true, yet all drink dreams. While, with wide open jaws, we let the lethal waters of Lethe[3] flood down our throats, meantime we scarcely sense the shadowy faint trace of nectar and ambrosia, lapping our uppermost lip. Thence, a panting thirst continuously burns up the wretched Tantali.

If by nature the mind desires certain things, we should acquire them. And certainly, in acquiring them, the soul would at some time be fulfilled by them, either wholly or in greatest part. But the more we acquire mortal things from all sides, by so much the more is the appetite of the soul inflamed. It is therefore clearly established that the mind does not desire to receive again mortal things, which are images of the eternal, but the eternal. Therefore it is plain that the mind is eternal and not devoted to death, because its true food is eternal.

In consequence, it falls asleep inwardly in the body devoted to death, and grows sick, drinking dreams in it through the senses. By drinking, it feeds the thirst, not itself. Sick also on account of unsatisfied appetites, the wretched mind comes to rest nowhere, but wanders vainly and restlessly hither and thither. Where it trusts confidently to lay itself gently down, it drops from a height; where it hopes for health-restoring medicine, it drinks death-dealing poison. Oh wretched fate of mortals, more wretched than wretchedness itself! Whither now shall we wretches fly for refuge? Certainly nowhere, except we fly back from the depths to the heights; except we fly to those things that flee nowhere.

What therefore is to be done, so that we may be of good strength and good vigilance? Life for us should straightway be turned right round in the opposite direction. Those things which we have learned from the many should be unlearned; in having to learn which, we have up to now ignored our own selves. Those things left undone should be learned; the which having been ignored, we cannot know ourselves. What we neglect should be esteemed; what we esteem should be neglected. What we flee from, should be borne; what we pursue should be fled. For us the smile of fortune should bring tears; and the tears of fortune should bring a smile. For by these means, the filth of the multitude will not defile us, nor will carelessness of immortal things harm us, nor desire for knowledge of mortal things torment us. Weakness will not prostrate us, nor desire undo us. Neither will prosperous fortune ensnare us, nor adverse fortune slay us. But, insofar as we shall be cleansed, so shall we be serene; insofar as we shall be serene, so shall we shine. Then, for the first time, we shall go forth full of true beauty, when for the first time we are devoid of dreams. [2.62]

29

A theological dialogue between God and the soul

Marsilio Ficino to Michele Mercati of San Miniato, his beloved fellow philosopher: greetings.

We have often talked together of moral and natural philosophy, beloved

God is the substance of abstractness

Michele, and even more often of divine philosophy. I remember you used to say again and again that morals are developed through practice, natural things discovered by reason and the divine begged of God by prayer. I have also read in the works of our Plato that the divine is revealed through purity of living rather than taught by verbal instruction. When I seriously considered these things I sometimes began to feel sick at heart, for I had already come to distrust reason but still lacked faith in revelation. From this there arose an intimate conversation between the soul and God. Listen to this, if you please, although I think you may already be nearer to speaking with God than I.[1]

GOD: Why do you grieve so much, my unhappy soul? O my daughter, weep no more. Behold, I, your father, am here with you. I am here, your cure and your salvation.

SOUL: Oh that my father would enter into me. If I believed such a grace could befall me, ah! I should go mad with joy. As it is, I do not see how that can come about; for if, as I thought, the creator of the world created me, his offspring, nearer to himself than his own created world, he who is only outside me is not my highest father. Nor could he who was only within me be my father, for my father is certainly greater than I, yet he who is contained in me must be smaller. But I do not know how anything can be both inside me and outside me at the same time. What sorely distresses me, stranger, whoever you may be, is this: that I do not wish to live without my father, yet despair of being able to find him.

GOD: Put an end to your tears, my daughter, and do not torment yourself; it is no stranger who speaks to you but one who is your very own, more familiar to you than you are to yourself. Indeed, I am both with you and within you. I am indeed with you, because I am in you; I am in you, because you are in me. If you were not in me you would not be in yourself, indeed you would not be at all. Dry those tears, my daughter, and look upon your father. Your father is the least of all things in size, just as he is the greatest of all things in excellence; and since he is very small he is within every thing, but since he is very great he is outside everything. See, I am here with you, both within and without, the greatest smallness and the smallest greatness. Behold, I say, do you not see? I fill heaven and earth, I penetrate and contain them. I fill and am not filled, for I am fullness itself. I penetrate and am not penetrated, for I am the power of penetration itself. I contain and am not contained, for I am containing itself. I, who am fullness itself, am not filled, for that would not be worthy of me. I am not penetrated lest I cease to exist, being myself existence. I am not contained lest I cease to be God, who am infinity itself. Behold, do you not see? I pass into everything unmingled, so that I may surpass all; for I am excellence itself. I excel everything without being separate, so that I am also able to enter and permeate at the same time, to enter completely and to make one, being unity itself, through which all things are made and endure, and which all things seek.

Why do you despair of finding your father, O foolish one? It is not difficult to find the place where I am; for in me are all things, out of me come all things and by me are all things sustained forever and everywhere. And with infinite power I expand through infinite space. Indeed no place can be found where I am not; this very "where" surely exists through me and is called "everywhere." Whatever anyone does anywhere, he does through my guidance and my light. Whatever anyone seeks anywhere, he seeks through my guidance and my light. There is no desiring anywhere, except for the good; there is no finding anywhere, except of the truth. I am all good; I am all truth. Seek my face and you shall live. But do not move in order to touch me, for I am stillness itself. Do not be drawn in many directions in order to take hold of me; I am unity itself. Stop the movement, unify diversity, and you will surely reach me, who long ago reached you.

SOUL: How quickly you leave me, O my comforter! Why do you so suddenly leave your daughter thirsting like this? Go on, say more, continue I beg you, venerable deity. By your divine majesty, if it please you, I pray you speak more plainly. Oh may it please you! And because I know it will, tell me more plainly then what you, who are my father, are not, that I may be restored to life; and, O my father, tell me again what you are, so that I may live.

GOD: Your father is not of a physical nature, my daughter. The more you obey your father the better you are, and the more you resist the body the finer you are. It is good for you to be with your father, bad for you to be with your body. It was not some mind that fathered you, O soul; otherwise you would contemplate nothing beyond mind and you would be held in that same changing mind, and not seek an unchanging nature. It was no intellect of many parts that made you, for then you would not attain complete simplicity, and the possession of intellect itself would be sufficient for you; but as it is, you ascend by understanding and love beyond any kind of intellect, to life itself, pure existence, absolute being. And understanding is not sufficient for you unless you not only understand well, but understand good itself. Without doubt only the good itself is sufficient for you, for the only reason you seek anything is because it is good.

Therefore, O soul, good is your creator; not the good body, not the good mind, not the good intellect, but good itself. Good is that which is indeed self-sufficient, infinite beyond the limits of what is beneath it, and it bestows on you infinite life, either from age to age, or at least from some beginning to the end of time. Do you desire to look on the face of good? Then look around at the whole universe, full of the light of the sun. Look at the light in the material world, full of all forms in constant movement; take away the matter, leave the rest. You have the soul, an incorporeal light that takes all shapes and is full of change. Once again, take from this the changeability, and now you have reached the intelligence of the angels, the incorporeal light, taking all shapes but unchanging. Take away from this that diversity by which any form differs from the light, and which is infused into the light from elsewhere, and then the essence of the light and of each form is the same; the light gives form to itself and through its own forms gives form to everything. That light lights without limit, because it lights by its own nature and is not stained by mixture with something else. Nor can it diminish; belonging to nothing, it shines equally through all. Its life is self-dependent, and it confers life on all, seeing that its very shadow is the light of this sun. It alone gives life to the incorporeal. It perceives everything and bestows perception, since its shadow awakens all the senses for all creatures. Finally it loves each single thing, for each single thing is especially its own.

What then is the light of the sun? It is the shadow of God. So what is God? God is the sun of the sun; the light of the sun is God in the physical world, and God is the light of the sun above the intelligences of the angels. My shadow is such, O soul, that it is the most beautiful of all physical things. What do you suppose is the nature of my light? If this is the glory of my shadow, how much greater is the glory of my light? Do you love the light everywhere above all else? Indeed, do you love the light alone? Love only me, O soul, alone the infinite light; love me, the light, boundlessly, I say; then you will shine and be infinitely delighted.

SOUL: Oh wonder, surpassing wonder itself! What strange fire consumes me now? What new sun is this, and whence does it shine upon me? What is this spirit, so powerful and so sweet, which at this moment pierces and soothes my inmost heart? Whence does it come? It bites and licks, goads and tickles. What bitter sweetness is this? Who could think it? This bitter sweetness melts me through and through and disembowels me. After this even the sweetest things seem bitter to me. What sweet bitterness it is which joins together my torn fragments, making me one again, by which even the most bitter is made sweet to me? How irresistible is this will! I cannot but desire the good itself; I may avoid or postpone anything else, but not this longing for the good. How freely chosen is this necessity; for if I want to avoid it, I shall try to do so only because I think the avoidance itself is good. Nothing is more freely chosen than the good; because of it I desire all things; no, rather it is good which I desire in all things everywhere, and desire in such a way that I do not even wish to be capable of not desiring it. Who would think it? How full of life is that death by which I die in myself but live in God, by which I die to the dead but live for life, and live by life and rejoice in joy! Oh pleasure beyond sense! Oh delight beyond mind! Oh joy beyond understanding! I am now out of my mind, but not mindless, because I am beyond mind. Again I am in a frenzy, all too great a frenzy; yet I do not fall to the ground; I am borne upward. Now I expand in every direction and overflow but am not dispersed, because God, the unity of unities, brings me to myself, because he makes me live with himself. Therefore now rejoice with me, all you whose rejoicing is God. My God has come to me, the God of the universe has embraced me. The God of gods even now enters my inmost being. Now indeed God himself nourishes me wholly, and he who created me recreates me. He who brought forth the soul, transforms it into angel, turns it into God. How shall I give thanks to you, O grace of graces? Teach me yourself, O grace of graces; I pray you teach me and be my guide. May that grace be to you which is your very self, O God. [1.4]

30

That the soul is immortal. And why, though
it be divine, it often leads a life similar to that of a beast[1]

Marsilio Ficino to Giovanni Nesi, distinguished by his writings and conduct: greetings.

Were there not within us divine power, and were our minds not of heavenly origin, we could in no way acknowledge the insufficiency of mortal things and we should certainly never reason beyond, or pursue anything above, the physical level. No one would exert himself at all, even in the smallest matter, to resist the body for we should be satisfied with earthly riches. And all men, or certainly the great majority, would rest content with this middle region of the universe[2] as their natural birthplace and home. But as it is, since our condition is very different, I believe—and with no empty faith—that we are of divine origin. Yet, if we are divine, why do we often lead a life similar to that of a beast? It is because the natural condition of this region determines that we use sense like an animal long before we use reason like men. Furthermore, far more numerous and more obvious inducements present themselves to our senses than to our minds. Lastly, the man in us is one, but the beasts are many.

It is worthwhile considering that picture of us which Plato paints in the ninth book of *The Republic*, thus:[3]

"Let us fashion an image of the soul similar to the natures once said to have been possessed by the Chimaera, Scylla, Cerberus and many another, in which, they say, a variety of forms was begotten in one body. So picture a single model of a beast of many forms, having heads facing all directions; some, I say, are the heads of tame beasts and some of wild, all of which it can generate from itself and interchange with each other. Above these add the form of a lion and at the top one of a man. Let the first one described be the largest, the second and third smaller. Then join these three so that they coalesce to make one. Surround them with the form of a single man, so that to one who is unable to look within but only on the surface, who discerns only the covering, the man seems clearly to be one being.

"Thus to him who asserts that it profits this human being to act unjustly, but that it does not profit him at all to live justly, let us point out that he is asserting just this: that it profits the human being to feed the manifold beast and the lion, and to make them both stronger, but to allow the man to starve and to be so weakened that because of his feebleness he is dragged in whatever direction the other two carry him off. He should not make them gentle or friendly with one another; rather should he allow them as separate creatures to savage one another, and their conflicts to devour them alike.

"Accordingly, the man who declares that just actions are profitable will advise what ought to be said and done to enable the man within a being of this kind to achieve complete mastery. He should tend the many-headed monster like a husbandman, cherishing the tame heads, giving them water and food, but instantly cutting off the wild ones, making the lion's nature his ally in this; and in common care of them all, he should reconcile each one with the others in mutual goodwill toward himself.

"And so, from every consideration, he who praises what is just, speaks truth; but he who praises what is unjust, lies. For in relation to pleasure, honor, and advantage, the commender of justice proclaims truth; but he who slanders justice speaks no truth, nor does he know what he condemns." Thus far Plato.

A similar division of our soul is described in Plato's *Timaeus*.[4] There he divides the soul into three powers, as into parts, whose natures are reason, passion and desire. He has appointed the power of reason to the head, queen, as it were, in the highest citadel, chiefly because the head more than anything else seems to exert itself in watching; and it is there that all the senses are most vigorous. Next, he has set the power of passion in the region of the heart, since it is in anger, boldness, and fear that this region is most agitated. Lastly, he has given the power of desire to the liver because its natural vigor lends itself both to the digestion of food and to the growth of bodily craving.

Likewise in *Phaedrus*[5] he calls reason a charioteer, since in the order of nature it is master of the other parts. To the charioteer he links twin horses, one white and one black. As he sees this analogy, the horses are the powers of the heart and the liver because these should submit to reason as to a charioteer. Magnanimity, which is accorded to the heart, is said to be the white horse, for it is closer to reason. But the liver's power of desire is the black horse, since it is farther away from the preeminence of reason.

Then again, reason within us is called Hercules: he destroys Antaeus,[6] that is the monstrous images of fantasy, when he lifts Antaeus up from the earth, that is, when he removes himself from the senses and physical images. He also subdues the lion, meaning that he curbs passion. He cuts down the Hydra with its many sprouting heads; that is, he cuts off the force of desire which, as passion, is borne not into a few things, and those of great importance, but into anything whatsoever, or rather into innumerable things, by means of an insatiable whirlpool. But while our Hercules is cutting down the Hydra of the liver with his sword, heads instantly sprout again because the fuel for new heads is still there. But when he consumes the Hydra by fire, he utterly destroys the fuel and so nothing is born from it again.

In Plato's *Phaedo*, Socrates commands thus: "Do not abstain from one bodily pleasure to gratify another. Otherwise in place of the one, many are instantly reborn."[7] On the contrary, he enjoins us to try to abstain from pleasures for the sake of reason, for only thus is it possible, he says, to root out vices at the source.

Let me now bring this letter to an end, but may I first remind you of this one thing, which clearly we should bear in mind: if the wild beasts within us are many, it is not surprising that according to Plato souls are transmigrating from man to beasts.[8] Certainly we have within us, from the beginning, fuel for desire and something of animal nature. When we have heedlessly nourished these for a long time, reason is either in some way lulled to sleep, or else it is awake under a cloak of passion and desire. Wherefore, under that human skin, the man himself seems to have been transformed into beasts. Hence Socrates says in *Phaedrus*, "Indeed I examine myself, Phaedrus. Am I a monster with more heads than Typhon, more full of fire and fury? Or am I a simpler and calmer being, sharing in some divine and favorable destiny, partaking in a quiet understanding?"[9]

1 July 1477. [3.27]

MUSIC, HARMONY, AND DIVINE FRENZY

31

A man is not harmoniously formed who does not delight in harmony

Marsilio Ficino to Sebastiano Foresi, his beloved fellow priest: greetings.

Our Saint Augustine writes in his books on music that a man is not harmoniously formed who does not delight in harmony;[1] nor is that unjust. Indeed, since pleasure generally arises on account of some likeness, it necessarily follows that he who takes no pleasure in concordant sounds in some way lacks concord within. Let me say, if I may, that this man has not been formed by God, for God forms all things according to number, weight, and measure. Moreover, I would say that such a man is no friend to God, for God rejoices in harmony to such an extent that he seems to have created the world especially for this reason, that all its individual parts should sing harmoniously to themselves and to the whole universe; indeed the universe itself should resound as fully as it can with the intelligence and goodness of its author. Let us add that He has so arranged the spheres and regulated their movements in relation to one another, as the Pythagoreans and Platonists teach, that they make a harmony and melody beyond compare.[2] We have discoursed at length on this subject elsewhere.

It will also help to remember one thing which I have particularly noticed: one is always finding gifted people who by nature are hardly affected by the pleasures and pursuits of the other senses, but we have never found any gifted person who is not moved by the power of music. Furthermore, we have never known anyone who is not moved by music to have much penetration or judgment. There are two main reasons for this: one physical, the other mathematical. The physical reason is that the middle part of the brain, to which the ear is closely connected, seems in some way to act as an instrument or stimulus to the faculty of judgment. But when this part of the brain is not in harmony, it does not respond at all to the universal harmony. On the other hand, when it is in harmony, it is wonderfully moved by the universal harmony as though by something totally similar.[3] The mathematical reason, which the poets have received from the astrologers, is that Mercury is the bestower of intelligence as well as the maker of the lyre. Thus we see that when Mercury looks down on a man's birth without much favor, that man often seems like an ass with both lyre and letters. On the other hand, those who are regarded favorably by Mercury, the master of lyre and letters, have an ability for both.

Farewell, my Foresi, you whom far-seeing Mercury has looked down upon favorably, even if blind fortune[4] has not.

Now, my Foresi, just after I had written farewell, I rose to my feet, and hastened to take up the lyre. I began to sing at length from the hymns of Orpheus. Get up yourself, get up as soon as you have read this second farewell and, if you are wise, willingly take up the lyre, that sweet solace of labor.[5]

8 September 1479.
Careggi. [5.21]

32

He who has blended the serious with the pleasing has satisfied everyone[1]

Marsilio Ficino to Sebastiano Foresi, his dear fellow priest: greetings.

There is no one among all my friends with whom I converse more profoundly and more enjoyably than with you, my sweet Foresi. For I address others with only the tongue or the pen, but you I often address with lute and lyre. In fact, without you my lutes are silent, my lyres mute. Come, I beseech you, my Foresi, whenever you sing to the lyre, sing in harmony with me. But I see that while you are so intent upon constructing one lyre, you are forgetting the music of the other. Among the heavenly beings, Sebastiano, even Phoebus does not both play the lyre and make it, while Mercury makes the lyre but does not play it.[2] Therefore, let no one on earth presume to exercise equally the skills of making and of playing the lyre.

Should anyone object that those obsessed by matters lyrical are driven delirious,[3] I know that you would reply in turn that we play the lyre precisely to avoid becoming unstrung, so to speak. It is no wonder that those who always deal with grave matters are bowed by the sheer weight of gravity, while those forever occupied with light matters are justly blown hither and thither by every light breath of air. But we need to mix gravity with levity, just as nature teaches us, so that gravity may be lightened and lifted, if I may put it thus, with a measure of levity, and levity held steady by the stability of gravity.

But what am I doing? Am I alleging that our music is a light matter? As you know, I have already revealed in a long letter the dignity, or rather the divinity, of music.[4] But lest we seem to be indulging in music too much, we shall conclude briefly as follows: nothing can be conceived that is graver than grave music, lighter than light music or in better proportion than music that is well tempered.[5] So may the well-tempered lyre always be our salvation when we apply ourselves to it rightly.[6] Blessings upon you, provided that you always remember to bless our two eyes: Giovanni Cavalcanti and Pietro Nero.

I, Luca, Marsilio's scribe, having penned this letter, commend myself to you.[7] And if I seem to you worthy of so great a gift, I beg you to love me as much as I see you are loved by Marsilio himself. My master loves you, Foresi, as much as you yourself love to be loved. [4.11]

33

On Music

Marsilio Ficino to Antonio Canigiani, a man both learned and wise: greetings.

You ask, Canigiani, why I so often combine the study of medicine with that of music. What, you say, has the trade of pharmacy to do with the lyre?

Astrologers might relate these two, Canigiani, to a conjunction of Jupiter with Mercury and Venus. They consider that medicine comes from Jupiter and music from Mercury and Venus. Followers of Plato, on the other hand, ascribe them both to one god, Apollo, whom the ancient theologians thought was the inventor of medicine and lord of the sounding lyre.

Orpheus, in his book of hymns,[1] asserts that Apollo, by his vital rays, bestows health and life on all and drives away disease. Furthermore, by the sounding strings, that is, their vibrations and power, he regulates everything: by the *hypate*, the lowest string, winter; by the *neate*, the highest string, summer; and by the *dorians*, that is, the middle strings, he brings in spring and autumn. So, since the patron of music and discoverer of medicine are one and the same god, it is hardly surprising that both arts are often practiced by the same man. In addition, the soul and body are in harmony with each other by a natural proportion,[2] as are the parts of the soul and the parts of the body. Indeed, the harmonious cycles of fevers and humors and the movements of the pulse itself also seem to imitate this harmony.

Plato and Aristotle taught,[3] as we have often found from our own experience, that serious music maintains and restores this harmony to the parts of the soul,[4] while medicine restores harmony to the parts of the body. Since the body and soul correspond with each other, as I have said, it is easy to care for the harmony of both body and soul in the same man. Hence Chiron practiced both arts, while the prophet David is said to have soothed the soul as well as the body of the mad Saul with his lyre.[5] Moreover, Democritus and Theophrastus maintained that this can be done in the case of other diseases, of both the body and the soul. And Pythagoras, Empedocles, and the physician Asclepiades proved this in practice. Nor is this any matter for wonder. For sound and song arise from consideration in the mind, the impulse of fantasy[6] and the desire of the heart, and in disturbing the air and lending measure to it they vibrate the airy spirit of the listener, which is the link between body and soul. Thus sound and song easily arouse the fantasy, affect the heart, and reach the inmost recesses of the mind; they still, and also set in motion, the humors and the limbs of the body. This indeed was shown by Timotheus when, by sounds, he roused King Alexander to fury and then restrained him; not to mention the miracles of Pythagoras[7] and Empedocles who could quickly quell lust, anger, or madness by serious music. Then again, using different modes, they used to stimulate lazy minds. And there are the stories told of Orpheus, Arion, and Amphion.[8]

But let us get back to the matter at hand. The first music takes place in reason, the second in fantasy, and the third in words; thence follows song and after that the movement of the fingers in sound. Lastly the movement of the whole body in gymnastics or dancing. Thus we may see that the music of the soul is led by steps to all the limbs of the body. It is this music that orators, poets, painters, sculptors and architects seek to imitate in their work. Since, therefore, there is such strong communion between the music of the soul and of the body, is it surprising that both the body and the soul may be set in order by the same man?

Finally, anyone who has learned from the Pythagoreans, from the Platonists, Mercurius[9] and Aristoxenus,[10] that the universal soul and body, as well as each living being, conform to musical proportion, or who has learnt from the sacred writings of the Hebrews that God has ordered everything according to number, weight, and measure, will not be surprised that nearly all living beings are made captive by harmony—nor will he blame Pythagoras, Empedocles, and Socrates in his old age, for playing the lyre. Rather will he consider Themistocles ill-educated for refusing a lyre offered to him at a banquet. Our Plato showed in *Alcibiades*[11] how music is the special concern of those men of knowledge who worship the Muses. He said that the Muses engender music, and that music was named after them. Plato does, however, criticize plaintive and light music[12] on the grounds that it leads to lack of spirit, lechery, and bad temper. But he recommends solemn and calming music as the most wholesome medicine for spirit, soul, and body.

For myself, to say something of your friend Marsilio, this is why, after my studies in theology and medicine, I often resort to the solemn sound of the lyre and to singing, to avoid other sensual pleasures entirely. I do it also to banish vexations of both soul and body, and to raise the mind to the highest considerations and to God as much as I may. This I do with the authority of Mercurius and Plato, who say that music was given to us by God to subdue the body, temper the mind, and render Him praise. I know that David and Pythagoras taught this above all else and I believe they put it into practice.

Farewell. [1.92]

34

Medicine heals the body, music the spirit, and theology the soul

Marsilio Ficino to Francesco Musano of Iesi: greetings.

As soon as you were cured of your wrongly diagnosed tertian fever[1] by our medicines, both you and Giovanni Aurelio paid your respects to our Academy, as if it were your own doctor. You then asked for and heard the sound of the lyre and the singing of hymns.

Since then you have gleaned a great deal from our *Theology*. Do not be surprised, Francesco, that we combine medicine and the lyre with the study of theology. Since you are dedicated to philosophy, you must remember that within us nature has bonded body and spirit with the soul.[2] The body is indeed healed by the remedies of medicine; but spirit, which is the airy vapor of our blood and the link between body and soul, is tempered and nourished by airy smells, by sounds, and by song. Finally, the soul, as it is divine, is purified by the divine mysteries of theology. In nature a union is made from soul, body, and spirit. To the Egyptian priests medicine, music, and the mysteries were one and the same study. Would that we could master this natural and Egyptian art as successfully as we tenaciously and whole-heartedly apply ourselves to it! But enough of these things for the present.

You asked me yesterday to transcribe for you that maxim of mine that is inscribed around the walls of the Academy. Receive it. "All things are directed from goodness to goodness. Rejoice in the present; set no value on property, seek no honors. Avoid excess; avoid activity. Rejoice in the present."

Farewell. [1.5]

35

On divine frenzy

Marsilio Ficino to Peregrino Agli: greetings.

On November 29 my father, Ficino the doctor, brought to me at Figline two letters from you, one in verse and the other in prose. Having read these, I heartily congratulate our age for producing a young man whose name and fame may render it illustrious.

Indeed, my dearest Peregrino, when I consider your age and those things that come from you every day, I not only rejoice but much marvel at such great gifts in a friend. I do not know which of the ancients whose memory we respect, not to mention men of our own time, achieved so much at your age. This I ascribe not just to study and technique, but much more to divine frenzy. Without this, say Democritus and Plato,[1] no man has ever been great. The powerful emotion and burning desire that your writings express prove, as I have said, that you are inspired and inwardly possessed by that frenzy; and this power, which is manifested in external move- ments, the ancient philosophers maintained was the most potent proof that the divine force dwelt in our souls. But since I have mentioned this frenzy, I shall relate the opinion of our Plato about it in a few words, with that brevity that a letter demands; so that you may easily understand what it is, how many kinds of it there are, and which god is responsible for each. I am sure that this description will not only please you, but also be of the very greatest use to you. Plato considers, as Pythagoras, Empedocles, and Heraclitus maintained earlier, that our soul, before it descended into bodies, dwelt in the abodes of heaven where, as Socrates says in the *Phaedrus,*[2] it was nourished and rejoiced in the contemplation of truth.

Those philosophers I have just mentioned had learnt from Mercurius Trismegistus,[3] the wisest of all the Egyptians, that God is the supreme source and light within whom shine the models of all things, which they call ideas.[4] Thus, they believed, it followed that the soul, in steadfastly contemplating the eternal mind of God, also beholds with greater clarity the natures of all things. So, according to Plato, the soul saw justice itself, wisdom, harmony, and the marvelous beauty of the divine nature.[5] And sometimes he calls all these natures "ideas," sometimes "divine essences," and sometimes "first natures that exist in the eternal mind of God." The minds of men, while they are there, are well nourished with perfect knowledge. But souls are depressed into bodies through thinking about and desiring earthly things. Then those who were previously fed on ambrosia and nectar, that is the perfect knowledge and bliss of God, in their descent are said to drink continuously of the river Lethe, that is forgetfullness of the divine. They do not fly back to heaven, whence they fell by weight of their earthly thoughts, until they begin to contemplate once more those divine natures that they have forgotten. The divine philosopher considers we achieve this through two virtues, one relating to moral conduct and the other to contemplation; one he names with a common term "justice," and the other "wisdom." For this reason, he says, souls fly back to heaven on two wings, meaning, as I understand it, these virtues; and likewise Socrates teaches in *Phaedo*[6] that we acquire these by the two parts of philosophy; namely, the active and the contemplative. Hence, he says again in *Phaedrus*[7] that only the mind of a philosopher regains wings. On recovery of these wings, the soul is separated from the body by their power. Filled with God, it strives with all its might to reach the heavens, and thither it is drawn. Plato calls this drawing away and striving "divine frenzy," and he divides it into four parts.[8] He thinks that men never remember the divine unless they are stirred by its shadows or images, as they may be described, which are perceived by the bodily senses.

Paul and Dionysius,[9] the wisest of the Christian theologians, affirm that the invisible things of God are understood from what has been made and is to be seen here,[10] but Plato says that the wisdom of men is the image of divine wisdom. He thinks that the harmony that we make with musical instruments and voices is the image of divine harmony, and that the symmetry and comeliness that arise from the perfect union of the parts and members of the body are an image of divine beauty.

Since wisdom is present in no man, or at any rate in very few, and cannot be perceived by bodily sense, it follows that images of divine wisdom are very rare among us, hidden from our senses and totally ignored. Because of this, Socrates says in *Phaedrus*[11] that the image of wisdom may not be seen at all by the eyes, because if it were it would deeply arouse that marvelous love of the divine wisdom of which it is an image.

But[12] we do indeed perceive the reflection of divine beauty with our eyes and mark the resonance of divine harmony with our ears—those bodily senses that Plato considers the most perceptive of all. Thus when the soul has received through the physical senses those images that are within material objects, we remember what we knew before when we existed outside the prison of the body. The soul is fired by this memory and, shaking its wings, by degrees purges itself from contact with the body and its filth and becomes wholly possessed by divine frenzy. From the two senses I have just mentioned two kinds of frenzy are aroused. Regaining the memory of the true and divine beauty by the appearance of beauty that the eyes perceive, we desire the former with a secret and unutterable ardor of the mind. This Plato calls "divine love," which he defines as the desire to return again to the contemplation of divine beauty; a desire arising from the sight of its physical likeness. Moreover, it is necessary for him who is so moved not only to desire that supernal beauty but also wholly to delight in its appearance which is revealed to his eyes. For Nature has so ordained that he who seeks anything should also delight in its image; but Plato holds it the mark of a dull mind and corrupt state if a man desires no more than the shadows of that beauty nor looks for anything beyond the form his eyes can see. For he believes that such a man is afflicted with the kind of love that is the companion of wantonness and lust. And he defines as irrational and heedless the love of that pleasure in physical form that is enjoyed by the senses.

Elsewhere he describes this love as the ardent desire of a soul that in a way is dead in its own body, while alive in another. He then says that the soul of a lover leads its life in another body. This the Epicureans follow when they say that love is a union of small particles, which they call atoms, made to penetrate the person from whom the images of beauty have been taken. Plato says that this kind of love is born of human sickness and is full of trouble and anxiety, and that it arises in those men whose mind is so covered over with darkness that it dwells on nothing exalted, nothing outstanding, nothing beyond the weak and transient image of this little body. It does not look up to the heavens, for in its black prison it is shuttered by night.[13] But when those whose spirit is drawn away and freed from the clay of the body first see form and grace in any one, they rejoice, as at the reflection of divine beauty. But those people should at once recall to memory that divine beauty, which they should honor and desire above all; as it is by a burning desire for this beauty that they may be drawn to the heavens. This first attempt at flight Plato calls divine ecstasy and frenzy. I have already written enough about that frenzy which, I have said, arises through the eyes.

But the soul receives the sweetest harmonies and numbers through the ears, and by these echoes is reminded and aroused to the divine music that may be heard by the more subtle and penetrating sense of mind. According to the followers of Plato, divine music is twofold. One kind, they say, exists entirely in the eternal mind of God. The second is in the motions and order of the heavens, by which the heavenly spheres and their orbits make a marvelous harmony. In both of these our soul took part before it was imprisoned in our bodies. But it uses the ears as messengers, as though they were chinks in this darkness. By the ears, as I have already said, the soul receives the echoes of that incomparable music, by which it is led back to the deep and silent memory of the harmony that it previously enjoyed. The whole soul then kindles with desire to fly back to its rightful home, so that it may enjoy that true music again. It realizes that as long as it is enclosed in the dark abode of the body it can in no way reach that music. It therefore strives wholeheartedly to imitate it, because it cannot here enjoy its possession. Now with men this imitation is twofold. Some imitate the celestial music by harmony of voice and the sounds of various instruments, and these we call superficial and vulgar musicians. But some, who imitate the divine and heavenly harmony with deeper and sounder judgment, render a sense of its inner reason and knowledge into verse, feet, and numbers. It is these who, inspired by the divine spirit, give forth with full voice the most solemn and glorious song. Plato calls this solemn music and poetry the most effective imitation of the celestial harmony. For the more superficial kind that I have just mentioned does no more than soothe with the sweetness of the voice, but poetry does what is also proper to divine harmony. It expresses with fire the most profound and, as a poet would say, prophetic meanings, in the numbers of voice and movement. Thus not only does it delight the ear, but brings to the mind the finest nourishment, most like the food of the gods; and so seems to come very close to God. In Plato's view, this poetic frenzy springs from the Muses; but he considers both the man and his poetry worthless who approaches the doors of poetry without the call of the Muses, in the hope that he will become a good poet by technique.[14] He thinks that those poets who are possessed by divine inspiration and power often utter such supreme words when inspired by the Muses, that afterwards, when the rapture has left them, they themselves scarcely understand what they have uttered.[15]

And, as I believe, the divine Plato considers that the Muses should be understood as divine songs; thus they say "melody" and "muse" take their name from "song."[16] Hence divine men are inspired by divine beings and song to imitate them by employing the modes and meters of poetry. When Plato deals with the motion of the spheres in the *Republic*,[17] he says that one siren is established within each orbit; meaning, as one Platonist says,[18] that by the movement of the spheres song is offered to the gods. For "siren" rightly means in Greek "singing in honor of God." And the ancient theologians maintained[19] that the nine Muses were the musical songs of the eight spheres, and in addition the one great harmony arising from all the others.

Therefore, poetry springs from divine frenzy, frenzy from the Muses, and the Muses from Jove. The followers of Plato repeatedly call the soul of the whole universe Jove, who inwardly nourishes heaven and earth, the moving seas, the moon's shining orb, the stars and sun.[20] Permeating every limb, he moves the whole mass and mingles with its vast substance.

It is thus that the heavenly spheres are set in motion and governed by Jove, the spirit and mind of the whole universe, and that from him also arise the musical songs of these spheres, which are called the Muses. As that illustrious Platonist says, "Jove is the origin of the Muses;[21] all things are full of Jove, and that spirit which is called Jove is everywhere; he enlivens and fulfils all things." And as Alexander Milesius, the Pythagorean, says, "touching the heavens as though they were a lyre, he creates this celestial harmony." The divine prophet Orpheus[22] says, "Jove is first, Jove is last, Jove is the head, Jove is the center. The universe is born of

Jove, Jove is the foundation of the earth and of the star-bearing heavens. Jove appears as man, yet he is the spotless bride. Jove is the breath and form of all things, Jove is the source of the ocean, Jove is the movement in the undying fire, Jove is the sun and moon, Jove, the king and prince of all. Hiding his light, he has shed it afresh from his blissful heart, manifesting his purpose." We may understand from this that all bodies are full of Jove; he contains and nourishes them, so that truly it is said that whatever you see and wherever you move is Jove.

After these follow the remaining kinds of divine frenzy, which Plato considers are twofold. One is centered in the mysteries, and the other, which he calls prophecy, concerns future events. The first, he says, is a powerful stirring of the soul, in perfecting what relates to the worship of the gods, religious observance, purification and sacred ceremonies. But the tendency of mind that falsely imitates that frenzy he calls superstition. He considers the last kind of frenzy, in which he includes prophecy, to be nothing other than foreknowledge inspired by the divine spirit, which we properly call divination and prophecy. If the soul is fired in the act of divination he calls it frenzy; that is, when the mind, withdrawn from the body, is moved by divine rapture. But if someone foresees future events by human ingenuity rather than by divine inspiration, he thinks that this should be named foresight or inference. From all this it is now clear that there are four kinds of divine frenzy: love, poetry; the mysteries, and prophecy. That common and completely insane love is a false copy of divine love; superficial music, of poetry; superstition, of the mysteries; and prediction, of prophecy. According to Plato, Socrates attributes the first kind of frenzy to Venus, the second to the Muses, the third to Dionysus, and the last to Apollo.[23]

I have chosen to describe at greater length the frenzy belonging to divine love and poetry for two reasons: first, because I know you are strongly moved by both of these; and second, so that you will remember that what is written by you comes not from you but from Jove and the Muses, with whose spirit and divinity you are filled. For this reason, my Pellegrino, you will act justly and rightly if you acknowledge, as I believe you do already, that the author and cause of what is best and greatest is not you, nor indeed any other man, but immortal God.

Farewell, and be sure that nothing is dearer to me than you are.

1 December 1457.

Figline. [1.7]

36

Poetic frenzy is from God

Marsilio Ficino to Antonio Pelotti and Baccio Ugolini: greetings.

When my good friends, Antonio Calderini and Bindaccio da Ricasoli, and I were reading together what you each wrote in praise of Carlo Marsuppini, that child of the Muses, we agreed that Plato was right in his view that poetry springs not from technique but from a kind of frenzy. Although it is not necessary to give reasons where the matter is self-evident, I shall nevertheless mention the reasons Plato gives. In *Phaedrus* and *Ion,* he discusses divine frenzy,[1] of which he claims there are three principal signs.

Firstly, without God, one man can scarcely master a single art, even after a long time; but the true poets, such as he holds Orpheus, Homer, Hesiod, and Pindar to have been, included in their poems signs and evidence of every art. Secondly, those who are in a frenzy utter many wonderful things, which a little later, when their frenzy has abated, they themselves do not really understand, as if they had not spoken them, but God had sounded through them, as though through trumpets. Thirdly, neither prudent men nor those learned from their youth have proved to be the best poets. Indeed, some were out of their minds, as Homer and Lucretius were known to have been, or unlettered, as Hesiod testifies of himself, and as Plato describes Ion and Tynnicus of Calchis. Passing beyond the limitations of skill, these men suddenly produced astonishing poetry.

Plato adds that some very unskilled men are thus possessed by the Muses, because divine providence wants to show mankind that the great poems are not the invention of men but gifts from Heaven. He indicates this in *Phaedrus* when he says that no one, however diligent and learned in all the arts, has ever excelled in poetry unless to these other qualities has been added a fiery quickening of the soul. We experience this when we are inflamed by God's presence working in us. Such force carries the seed of the divine mind.[2]

Farewell.

4 March 1474. [1.52]

37

There are four aspects of divine frenzy, and love is the foremost of all

Marsilio Ficino and Giovanni Cavalcanti to Naldo Naldi, the poet: greetings.

Your fine letter was delivered to us at the very hour in which the Moon was in direct alignment with Mars.[1] Insofar as it is lawful to interpret the heavens, would one not have expected your letter to ramble with lunar instability and to be full of the fury and hatred of Mars?

In fact, it is quite the opposite; for it does not wander at random with the base movement of the Moon but is marvelously regulated by the sublime harmonies of Urania and Calliope.[2] It burns, not with the fire of Mars, but with that of Venus. It is afire not with hatred but with love. Hence we see clearly that what the poets and astronomers say is true. Mars is indeed overcome and tamed by Venus.[3] It is also true what the theologians say, that divine frenzy is, as it were, above the movements of the heavens and is in no way subject to the stars but commands them. For according to our Plato, there are four aspects of divine frenzy: love, prophecy, the mysteries, and poetry. Love is attributed to Venus, prophecy to Apollo, the mysteries to Dionysus, and poetry to the Muses.[4] Foremost of these is said to be divine love, by which you have been possessed and from which you write to us. For this there are two reasons: first, without love's impulse, the other frenzies are never united with that truth toward which the soul is driven by frenzy, not without love's impulse are these frenzies sustained. Secondly, when love carries the lover into the beloved and as long as that love is directed to the sublime, it unites the mind more closely with God than do the other frenzies.[5]

And now, were we to begin praising your frenzy of love as it deserves, we should need a poetic frenzy, but since the Muses are not inspiring us now, in that we are unable to give praise to your frenzy with poetry, we confirm it beyond doubt through our mutual love, and we shall always do so. [5.35]

38

They who abuse the Muses bring back from their fountain not honey but gall

Marsilio Ficino to the distinguished citizen, Angelo Manetti: greetings.

My friend, there are a number of writers, both Latin and Greek,[1] who compare to bees men who are totally devoted to study. For, like bees, they gather here and there from many authors, as from flowers, and store what they have gathered in the capacious hives of their memory. They then let it ripen by reflection, to bring forth the mellifluous liquid of learning and eloquence. If anyone should deny this comparison, which is made by the best authors, he would seem to me to deserve to bring back gall rather than honey, even from the fount of the Muses. I shall therefore subtract nothing at all from this simile, but rather add to it.

You must have heard, my friend, that when bees suck from too many wormwood flowers they very often produce honey that, tasted on the lips, seems quite sweet but immediately afterward, when swallowed, proves to be not sweet at all but bitter, almost like gall. We know full well that something very similar often happens to gluttons for study and devourers of books, who have neither measure nor discrimination. Indeed, the more greedily they seem to drain the sweet liquor of the Muses, the more bitterly do they take into their heart I know not what! Perhaps this is what the Latin authors call bile, the Greeks melancholy: a disease, as Aristotle shows, peculiar to men absorbed by study.[2] For this reason Solomon calls study a most onerous occupation; and he adds that the companion of knowledge is sorrow.[3]

What therefore shall we say of Aristotle's remark:[4] "The tree of knowledge indeed has bitter roots but the sweetest fruit"? We shall certainly grant this to Aristotle, but add that such a fruit is perhaps the peach, in which a bitter kernel lies within the sweetness.[5]

What then? Should we denounce the Muses? Let us never think that the fount of celestial nectar and ambrosia pours forth bitter and deadly streams. Therefore, much as we praise the true use of the Muses, so we condemn their abuse. Who then makes the greatest abuse of the Muses? Surely one who heedlessly and importunately presses on their tracks; or one who impudently involves them with the common Venus;[6] or who separates them from their lord Apollo. Ignorant little men do not attain knowledge when they grasp unwisely at wisdom herself. The Muses do not sing well when the wanton son of Venus molests them; either they are silent or they shriek. The chorus of the Muses does not dance becomingly, but limps and falters, whenever its lord Apollo is far away.[7]

One who believes that he will perceive the sun's light without the sun's aid deservedly falls into darkness; he is not raised into light. So one who pursues this truth and that truth, separated from the highest truth, without doubt does not light upon truth but upon falsehood. No wonder that whoever searches for the nectar of heaven in the Stygian marsh deservedly drinks the genuine gall of opinion beneath the illusory honey of knowledge. [4.15]

39

Prose should be adorned with
the rhythms and numbers of poetry

Marsilio Ficino to the rhetorician Bartolomeo della Fonte: greetings.

You ask, most discriminating Fonte, by whose direction I am principally compelled, or on whose support I mainly rely, when on occasion I weave poetic rhythms and numbers into my prose. So let me give a brief answer to a most perceptive man: heaven commands me and the heavenly Plato also teaches the same. For if you look up to heaven, there you see Mercury, both the master of eloquence and inventor of the lyre. Were we, therefore, ever allowed to hear him speak, we should frequently hear him mingling the melodies of his lyre with his words; particularly since he is always totally united, or at least closely linked, both with Phoebus, the father of serious music, that is, the father of poetry, and with Venus, the mother of lighter music.

If you hear the celestial Plato you immediately recognize that his style, as Aristotle says, flows midway between prose and poetry.[1] You recognize that Plato's language, as Quintilian says, rises far above the pedestrian and prosaic, so that our Plato seems inspired not by human genius but by a Delphic oracle.[2] Indeed the mixing or tempering of prose and poetry in Plato so delighted Cicero that he declared: "If Jupiter wished to speak in human language, he would speak only in the language of Plato."[3] I might also mention that Moses, Job, Solomon, Isaiah, Jeremiah, Daniel,

and Ezekiel and almost all the other Hebrew prophets have given beauty
to their prose with the rhythms of poetry. So did Mercurius, wisest of
the Egyptians, and in Greece, Gorgias, Isocrates, Herodotus, Aristides
and a great many others. Finally, of the Romans, Cicero in some passages, and Livy in many, followed the same practice; so did Apuleius,
Saint Jerome and the great philosopher Boethius.

Clearly they did this so that, insofar as the language is prose and free
of restrictions, it should reach its point more swiftly, as prose often moves
with greater freedom and ease; and that, insofar as it is poetry and has
number, it should delight, soothe, and enrapture through the blending of
harmonies and imagery; assuredly, inasmuch as individual things are born
of music, by a natural impulse they are wonderfully enraptured by it. I
would rather follow these men haltingly than not follow them at all.
Therefore, my friend, you will forgive a Platonist, even if he be inept, and
pardon his mixed style of speech. First of all, his very source implanted
this in him, then continual reading of the poetic Plato nourished it and,
finally, frequent practice with the lyre confirmed it. However, I do not
break into poetic strains in some places by chance, but particularly when
what underlies the subject or form is poetical; every note has its corresponding string.[4]

All antiquity, indeed, teaches us to combine poetry with philosophy.
This was always done, particularly before Aristotle, mainly so that the
sacred mysteries of Minerva should be honored and loved by all and should
be understood by the few who are indeed pure. We are taught the same
thing by the Divinity itself which, rejoicing everywhere in poetic form,
adorned the heavens with innumerable lights, as flowers in a meadow,
and ordered the diverse orbits of the spheres so that, in perfect concert,
they make a marvelous harmony and melody. Then, in the sublunar regions the same God, with a similar delight in poetry, arranged discordant
forms of things into exquisite concord. Finally, in a variety of ways, he
graced the earth, which seemed as though it would be the least beautiful
of all creation, with the wonderful shapes and images of minerals and
stones, plants and animals. He willed the very fruits of the earth to be
covered with leaves and decorated with flowers. What more? He tempered both the individual and the universal with the numbers of music
and the measures of poetry. [2.3]

KNOWLEDGE
AND
PHILOSOPHY

40

An exhortation to pursue knowledge

Marsilio Ficino to Niccolo degli Albizzi: greetings.

You have heard that proverb, my dear Niccolo: Nothing is sweeter than profit. But what man does profit? He who takes possession of that which will be his. What we know is ours, everything else depends on fortune. Let small-minded men envy the rich, that is those whose coffers are rich but not their minds. You should emulate those wise and good men whose mind is like God. Warn your fellow students to beware of Scylla and Charybdis; that is, the attractions of pleasure and the noisome fever of the mind given to opinion rather than knowledge.[1] Let them remember that one day the highest delight for each will be that which is experienced in the highest part of the mind, in the supreme treasury of truth itself, when they discard the shadow of worthless pleasures for the sake of knowledge. The tree of knowledge, even if it seems to have rather bitter roots, brings forth the sweetest possible fruit. Let them remember too that there will never be too much of this fruit because there is never enough.

He who still doubts has not yet learnt enough, yet we doubt as long as we live; and so as long as we live we should learn. Indeed we should imitate the wise Solon, who even when dying sought to learn something, for he was nourished by the food of truth and to him death was no more than rebirth. A man can never die who enjoys immortal nourishment. Socrates was first called the wisest of all men by Apollo,[2] when he began to say publicly that he knew nothing. Pythagoras told his disciples that they should look at themselves in a mirror, not by the light of a lamp, but by the light of the sun. What is the light of a lamp, if it is not a mind as yet too little instructed by knowledge? What the light of the sun, if not the mind totally under its instruction?

When, therefore, anyone wants to know about the state of his mind, he should compare it not with the ignorant, but on the contrary with the wisest; thus he may see more clearly how much he has gained and how much remains. In feeding the mind we ought to imitate gluttons and the covetous, who always fix their attention on what is still left. What is there further?

The Lord of Life says, "No man, having put his hand to the plough, and looking back, is worthy of reward."[3] You have heard too of that woman who, because she turned back, was changed into a pillar.[4] You have also heard how Orpheus, when he looked back, lost Eurydice; in other words, his depth of judgment. Ineffective and empty-handed is the hunter who goes backward rather than forward.

Farewell. [1.22]

41

Knowledge and reverence of oneself are best of all

Marsilio Ficino speaks of mankind's salvation, which is knowledge and reverence of oneself.

Know yourself,[1] offspring of God in mortal clothing. I pray you, uncover yourself. Separate the soul from the body, reason from sensual desires; separate them as much as you can; and your ability depends on your endeavor. When the earthly grime has been removed you will at once see pure gold, and when the clouds have been dispersed, you will see the clear sky. Then, believe me, you will revere yourself as an eternal ray of the divine sun and, moreover, you will not venture to contemplate or undertake any base or worthless action in your own presence. Nothing at all can be hidden from God, through whom alone is revealed everything that is revealed. Nothing of yours lies hidden from the mind, the everliving image of God who lives everywhere.

If the venerable countenance of a monarch of old inspires awe, you should always and everywhere reverence the wondrous presence of God, the king over all; and of mind, the queen over the body. Rightly therefore did divine Pythagoras give the instruction, "Honor thyself."[2] But he who, in the presence of himself, is not ashamed to think of worthless things and suffers the soul, which is by nature divine, to serve its servant the body, and plunges this divine pearl into the mire, such a man surely seems ignorant of his own worth and has not considered that divine saying: "Thou hast made him a little lower than the angels";[3] and the words that follow. Again: "I have said, Ye are gods, and all of you are children of the most High."[4] Alas most ignorant minds! Alas blind hearts! I beseech you, arise now from this deep slumber; come to yourselves one day, I beg you. For if you come to yourselves you will live happily. Why have you been looking at the ground for so long, divine men? Look up, citizens of the heavenly country, denizens of the earth. Man is an earthly star enveloped in a cloud; but a star is a heavenly man.

O soul, you are mighty if small things do not satisfy you. You are most virtuous when evil displeases you; most beautiful when you shun what is base. When you set small value on the transient you are indeed eternal. Since your nature is such, if you wish to discover yourself I pray you seek yourself where such things are. Truly the great is only found in that place where no limit is imposed; the best where no adversity reaches; the beautiful where exists no disharmony; and the eternal where there is no flaw.

Therefore seek yourself beyond the world. To do so and to come to yourself you must fly beyond the world and look back on it. For you are beyond the world while you yourself comprehend it. But you believe yourself to be in the abyss of this world simply because you do not discern yourself flying above the heavens, but see your shadow, the body, in the abyss. It is as if a boy leaning over a well were to imagine himself at the bottom, although it is only his shadow he sees reflected there, until he turns his gaze back to himself. Or it is as if a bird flying in the air and watching its shadow were to believe it flew on the earth.

Therefore leaving behind the narrow confines of this shadow, return to yourself; for thus will you return to spaciousness. Remember that there is immeasurable space in the spirit, but in the body one could say infinite constriction. This indeed you can see from the fact that numbers, which are akin to the nature of spirit, increase without limit, but do not so diminish; whereas there is a limit to the expansion of the physical, to its contraction[5] there is no limit. [1.110]

42

A speech of Marsilio Ficino in praise of philosophy[1]

Most noble gentlemen, at this moment my mind is pulled in contrary directions, as has often happened to those about to give an address on serious subjects. For the ancient custom of this venerable school and the weighty authority of its founders, both of which rightly have the strongest possible influence upon me, urge me to speak today in praise of philosophy.

But when I inwardly consider the power and nature of this subject, it appears to me to be so noble and excellent that I despair of its being understood by the human mind or expounded by the human tongue. The loftiness of the subject, the lowliness of my talent, and furthermore your awesome aspect, all now make me frightened to speak. So I falter between silence and speech. Yet, noble gentlemen, as far as I am able, I shall speak, having concluded that it is preferable for the subject of my speech not to appear to Marsilio than for Marsilio not to appear at the behest of his superiors. So you will forgive me if I fail utterly to express any outstanding praises of philosophy in accordance with her worth; and everything I say you will ascribe directly to the divine light by whose illumination we perceive, by whose rays we understand, and by whose splendor we reveal everything.

Most excellent gentlemen, the age-old view of the theologians, confirmed by the reasonings of many philosophers, by which we have been well taught and in which we have been raised, is this: the more perfect and worthy of honor each being appears in the natural order, the closer it approaches the perfection and worth of the first cause of all, and the more nearly and clearly it represents the image of this cause within itself. The ancient theology of the Egyptians and Arabs handed down this: God is the source of being, knowing, and acting.[2] Whence Pythagoras, Heraclitus, and Plato, conveying that theology into Greece, declared that the beginning of creation, the truth of the teaching and the joy of life are from this selfsame God. To this Plato bears witness in *The Republic, Parmenides,* and *Timaeus,*[3] as do Iamblichus and Proclus in their theologies.[4]

Following those ancient writers, Dionysius the Areopagite,[5] initially a Platonist and then a Christian, gave very extensive expression in his books to the same view, which was also held much later by St. Hilary[6] and St. Augustine, the principal Latin theologians. And so Augustine,[7] in his books on *The True Religion* and *The City of God,* calls God Himself "The Maker of All Things," "The Illuminator of Truth," and "The Bestower of Happiness"; and he confirms that this had been systematically treated, albeit in different words, by the Platonic philosophers many centuries previously. Furthermore, that in these three titles of God, first introduced by the ancient philosophers, the Christian Trinity is also comprehended in some way; and lastly, that the three aspects of philosophy[8] discovered and disseminated by Plato correspond to this trinity of ours in all its particulars.

Let that branch of philosophic discourse that sets forth the causes and development of things correspond to God, their source. Let the next branch, in which the origin and method of setting things in order are treated, correspond to God, the illuminator of truth. Let the last part of philosophy, by whose precepts and on whose foundations we lead our lives and direct ourselves, the family, and the state in the pursuit of happiness, also be compared in some measure to God, the bestower of happiness.

From this it can now be quite clear that philosophy in every part accords, as I have said, with the Godhead whole and perfect, and contains, so far as it is revealed to us, a full and complete image of the power, wisdom, and goodness of Father, Son, and Spirit. Thus it is, that of all the faculties of men none appears closer or more similar to the Godhead than philosophy, and so nothing available to us, save God Himself, is seen as more perfect or more excellent. For which reason Hermes, wisest of the Egyptians, seems, through godlike power, to have explained this, when he declared that men become gods through the light of philosophy.[9] Pythagoras also sounded the same note in the *Golden Verses;*[10] and Plato, in his books on *The Republic,* appointed for philosophers at their death the sacred rites and mysteries that are accorded to the gods.[11] Again, Empedocles of Agrigentum said that philosophy is a gift of the gods that brings anyone it has touched to such a state that from a lofty mind he holds in contempt everything that is set in motion; from the innermost point of the mind he is illumined by divine rays, and awaits future blessedness with steadfast purpose.[12]

But what is nobler than the declaration made by Aristotle? Whereas the other arts and sciences, aghast at the size and difficulty of the matter, have moved a long way from the search for truth, philosophy alone has never shirked laborious work; she has considered that she is not unworthy of the richest treasures, and that knowledge of these befits her and is of the same birth. And since it is impossible to approach the heavenly regions through bodily strength, the soul, having acquired the power of mental discernment as guide by the gift of philosophy, transcends the nature of all things through contemplation. So said Aristotle.[13]

Finally, to be brief, since she is a gift from heaven, philosophy drives earthly vices far away; firmly subdues fortune; marvelously softens fate; uses mortal gifts most rightly; and bestows immortal gifts according to desire. O treasure, of all things most precious, in no way produced from the bowels of Earth and Pluto, but descending from the topmost point of heaven and from the head of Jove! Without possession of this treasure we cannot make right use of other treasures nor possess anything fruitfully. O surest guide for human life who, firstly, with club of Hercules, puts the monsters of vice to headlong flight! Then, with the shield and spear of Pallas she averts or overcomes the perils of fortune. Lastly, supporting men's souls with the shoulders of Atlas, she frees them from this earthly exile and restores them to their celestial homeland in the fullness of truth and happiness. May what Plato said be justified: that there was once a golden age when wisdom reigned, and that if ever philosophy reigns again the Golden Age will return.[14] But what are we doing, noble gentlemen? Why do we vainly seek to measure eternity in, so to speak, a moment of time? Not merely a day, but very many years, would be insufficient, were we directly to undertake to adorn blessed philosophy with all her praises.

So there remains nothing more to be said or done, but having left behind all that is set in motion, all that is lifeless, in which there is nothing to be found beyond shadows and phantoms, we should devote ourselves with whole mind and ardent spirit to the study of this divine gift.

For, lower than the human race, those who have no part in philosophy degenerate rapidly, as it were, into beasts. Those, however, who give moderate service to philosophy will without doubt go forth as men fit to teach the learned and rule the rulers. Yet he who, throughout an entire life, devotes himself wholly to her alone, once the body has been laid aside, as it were, will go straight and free to the upper regions and will ascend beyond human form, having become a god of life-giving heaven.[15] [3.13]

43

In praise of those who expound Plato

Marsilio Ficino, the Florentine, to Bessarion, the Greek, Cardinal of Sabina: greetings.

You are well aware, venerable father, that when our Plato discoursed on beauty in the *Phaedrus*[1] with such insight and at such length, it was beauty of soul he sought from God, which he called wisdom and most precious gold. When this gold was given to Plato by God, it shone in him most brilliantly, because he was so pure in heart.

Neo - P

Although this great brilliance is revealed in his words and writings, yet the treasure became enveloped by darkness in the mind, and difficult to see, as if covered with a cloak of earth. It lay hidden from any man who did not have eyes like a lynx. For this reason some men of narrow learning[2] were once deceived by the outer crust and, since they could not penetrate to the core, they despised the hidden treasure.

But when that gold was put into the workshop first of Plotinus[3] then of Porphyry,[4] Iamblichus,[5] and eventually of Proclus,[6] the earth was removed by the searching test of fire, and the gold so shone that it filled the whole world again with marvelous splendor. But some night owls, it seems, were upset by such bright rays of light, and not only despised the sacred treasure of our Plato, as some had before, but sinfully even began to abuse it, which was much worse than the first error!

But Bessarion, the light of the Academy swiftly applied an effective medicine for these dim and feeble eyes, so that the gold would be not only pure and shining, but malleable for the hands and harmless to the sight. This Plato foretold; he said to King Dionysius[7] that a time would come after many generations, when the mysteries of theology would be purified by penetrating discussion, as gold is purified by fire. This time has come indeed, Bessarion! May the spirit of Plato, we, and all his followers rejoice at this exceedingly!

Farewell. [1.13]

44

Theologians are awake; the rest dream

Marsilio Ficino to Giovanni Cavalcanti, his unique friend: greetings.

Some people wonder why we follow Plato with such respect, when he continually seems to be involved with paradoxes and myths. However, in my opinion, they would cease to wonder if they were to consider that divine things alone truly exist, because those things are not impaired by contact with any outside influence, nor do they ever change their state. Physical bodies are not in the least real, but they seem to be since they are afflicted by opposing forces and are constantly undergoing change. However, this is the very reason why they are not true, but are images or shadows of what is true.

Now, while nearly all other philosophers were devoted to natural studies alone and were asleep in these images as if they were true, our Plato, attending to the divine, was the only one awake; or at least was much more so than anyone else. That is why I believe it is so much better to follow Plato as a theologian than other philosophers; just as it is better to entrust oneself to helmsmen[1] that are awake, rather than to those that are asleep.

Farewell. [1.41]

45

No one who lacks self-restraint can be wise

Marsilio Ficino to philosophers and teachers of sophistry: greetings.

Of all the powers of the soul that are concerned with knowing, the highest are intellect and reason, and the lowest are taste and touch. The last two for the most part lead down to bodily nature, while the first two lead up to divine substance, which is not of the body. Therefore, not surprisingly, whoever strives to serve all the powers of the soul at once, strives in vain. For whoever completely submerges himself in the darkness of the lower world will not be illuminated by the rays from the higher. Similarly, a man does not heed the ridiculous attractions of the lower world once he has tasted the true goodness and joy of the higher. The mind will not rise to the truest causes of things, which are separate from the bodies, unless it has separated itself from the body, first by cleansing itself of its habits and then by the effort of contemplation. He who already possesses heaven and appraises eternity itself, so to speak, will reckon as nothing those things that are subject to time on earth. I need not say how people suffering from a bloody inflammation of the eye[1] see everything as red, and those with a bitter taste on the tongue taste everything as bitter. In the same way the mind, which from a long-standing desire and indulgence in physical things has become physical, so to speak, will believe the divine to be completely nonexistent, or will regard it as physical.[2] I shall not discuss the peace, freedom, or length of time necessary to investigate the hidden causes of things. Nothing can be conceived as more enslaving, giving rise to more agitation and anxiety, than the worried life of the man who serves the senses as though they were many mad masters. And while he is in bondage to foolish tyrants, he is professing allegiance to wisdom as well.

So if you catch anyone foolishly serving the body you will know he is not wise. But you will find those whom you know to be wise are not slaves but masters of the body, which is their servant. Troubled indeed are they who live only to serve the desires of the body. But in much greater trouble are those who mistakenly try to couple the pleasures of the lower world with those of the higher. For since they labor so hard in contrary directions, they can enjoy the pleasures neither of the mind nor of the body. God condemns none more than those who expect to drink nectar and ambrosia out of the filthy vessels of vice. As Aristotle says,[3] God values and loves none more than those who cultivate above all a mind in the very likeness of God and who set it apart from this body of decay, so unlike Him. These men take care not to obscure the divine light with clouds of vice but to perceive it in pure peace of mind.

This principle, we think, led Socrates to offer men primarily a moral training,[4] and Pythagoras to drive the ungodly far from his sacred schools.[5] For if you pour liquid into a tainted vessel, the vessel will turn even the finest liquid foul by its contact. In the same way, an evil mind on receiving knowledge produces not wisdom, but evil. Furthermore, as the sky is to the light of the sun, so is the mind to the light of truth and wisdom. Neither the sky nor the intellect ever receive rays of light while they are clouded, but once they are pure and clear they both receive them immediately. Plato's letter to the Syracusans refers to this.[6] It says that the divine cannot be spoken or learned as other things are. However, from continued application and a matching of one's life to the divine, suddenly, as if from a leaping spark, a light is kindled in the mind and thereafter nourishes itself.

Why, therefore, do you burden yourselves with so much night study, O philosophers? What need for such long, tortuous arguments, O sophists? Do you not see the one way? The one way to that light for us is serenity. Alas, to attain the pure, you often vainly put your trust in the impure. This Socrates condemns.[7] Learn from Galen the Platonist that it is impossible for a soul stifled by blood and fat to contemplate anything heavenly.[8] Learn from Pythagoras and Plato that wisdom of mind is nothing but the light of the highest good, diffused everywhere through minds that are truly good, like mirrors of spotless purity. Therefore, as soon as you have become wholly good, you will shine forth with the splendor of the highest good, that is, with wisdom.

The sun in the heavens gives birth to the eyes in creatures and the colors in objects, and the same sun shows those colors to eyes that are open and pure.[9] The sun that is above the heavens, that is truth itself, is the father both of minds and of true things. That same sun reveals true things to minds that are pure and turned toward it. Cleanse the eye of reason of all the dirt from this noxious body. Turn the keen edge of the mind away from the shadow of base matter. Turn the gaze of the inner intelligence to the light of the supernal form. From here substance, when it is fully ready, is instantly given bodily forms. From here the mind, when it is ready, is instantly impressed with incorporeal forms. And as the mind is illumined with the brilliant rays of truth, so does it overflow with true joy without limit.[10] [4.7]

46

On the Platonic nature, instruction, and function of a philosopher[1]

Marsilio Ficino to Giovanni Francesco Ippoliti, the distinguished Count of Gazzoldo.

A long time ago I wrote rather a lengthy letter to Bernardo Bembo of Venice in praise of philosophy,[2] and lately, something also on the same subject to the distinguished orator, Marco Aurelio.[3] What remains, it seems, is for me to write something about the Platonic nature, instruction, and function of a philosopher, so that it may be more clearly revealed how that precious treasure of philosophy may be most easily rediscovered by us; and, once it is found, by what principle it may lawfully be possessed and measured out.

Since philosophy is defined by all men as love of wisdom (the very name introduced by Pythagoras[4] supports this) and wisdom is the contemplation of the divine, then certainly the purpose of philosophy is knowledge of the divine. This our Plato testifies in the seventh book of *The Republic*, where he says that true philosophy is the ascent from the things that flow and rise and fall, to those that truly are, and always remain the same. Therefore philosophy has as many parts and ministering powers as it has steps by which it is climbed from the very lowest level to the highest. These steps are determined partly by the nature and partly by the diligence of men. For, as Plato teaches in the sixth book of *The Republic,* whoever is to become a philosopher[5] should be so endowed by Nature that, in the first place, he is willing and prepared to enter upon all manner of disciplines; thereafter that he is truthful by nature, completely opposed to all falsehood; in the third place that, having scorned all that is subject to corruption, he directs his mind to that which remains always the same. He must be magnanimous and courageous, so that he neither fears death nor longs for empty glory. Over and above this, he should be born with something of an even temperament, and from nature he should receive already under control those parts of the mind that are usually carried away by the feelings. For whoever longs for the truth turns his mind to contemplation of the divine and sets little value on the pleasures of the body. Beyond this, a philosopher should be of liberal mind. And in fact the prizing of worthless things is opposed to this and completely counter to the way of a man intending to contemplate the truth of things. Above this his will chooses justice, since he is utterly devoted to truth, moderation, and liberality. But most of all, it seems that he needs sharp insight, memory, and magnanimity.

What is more, these three gifts of nature, namely, sharp insight, memory, and magnanimity, when discipline and a proper education have been added, produce a man perfect in virtue. But if they are neglected, they are said by Plato to be the cause of the greatest crimes.[6] Therefore, this nature must be given man's greatest care, so that he who is thus shaped by Nature, from his childhood, learns letters, the elements of all knowledge. And indeed the unordered mind of this person must be put in order by use of the lyre; the body must be exercised by gymnastic games, so that, coming into a good condition itself, it offers service to the studies of philosophy. Meanwhile the precepts of the best laws should be heard by him and fixed in his mind. Thus the mind of the young man should be formed by honest encouragement, so that it is rendered temperate and peaceful. This moral education men in fact call Ethics.

In truth, when the mind is freed from the disturbance of desire by these means of which we have spoken, it will already have begun to be loosed from the body; then it must be given knowledge of mathematics,[7] which concerns number, plane figures, and whole forms, and their manifold movements. Indeed, since numbers and figures and the principles of movement belong to the faculty of thought rather than the outer senses, the mind, by the study of these, is separated not only from the appetites of the body, but from its senses also, and applies itself to inner reflection. This is indeed to meditate on death which, Plato writes in *Phaedo*,[8] is the duty of one practicing philosophy. Through this we are restored to the likeness of God, as is taught in *Phaedrus* and *Theaetetus*.[9]

However, according to the Platonists, in the thorough understanding of these things there is this order:[10] Geometry follows Arithmetic; Stereometry, Geometry; Astronomy follows this, and lastly Music follows Astronomy. For numbers are before figures, plane figures are before whole forms, but bodies are whole before they are set in motion. The order and ratios of sounds follow movement. Therefore let Arithmetic, which concerns number, come first. Let Geometry, which deals with plane figures, follow. Let Stereometry, which considers whole bodies, follow after this. Let the fourth place be held by Astronomy, which raises the sight to the movements of whole bodies, that is, the movements of the spheres. Let Music, which investigates the order of sounds born out of motion, be last.

When these have been thoroughly understood, Plato gives dialectic,[11] that is, knowledge of how truth is made manifest. But he means by dialectic not only that logic that teaches the first and most detailed rules of reasoning, but also the profound skill of the mind freed to comprehend the true and pure substance of each thing, first by physical, then by metaphysical principles. Thus the reason for anything can be made known and finally the light of the mind may be perceived beyond the nature of senses and bodies; and the incorporeal forms of things, which we call ideas, may be understood. By means of these, the same one source of all species, the origin and light of minds and souls, the beginning and end of all, which Plato calls the good itself, may be inwardly perceived. The contemplation of this is wisdom, love of which is most correctly defined as philosophy.

In truth, once the mind of a man practicing philosophy has contemplated the good itself, and thence judges what things in human affairs are good, what bad, what dishonorable or honorable, harmful or useful, he organizes human affairs as a model of the good itself. He leads them away from evil, directs them to the good, and by this wise governance he manages personal, family, and public affairs, and he teaches the laws and principles of good management. From this laws have their beginning.

For this reason in *Timaeus* Plato asserts that philosophy is a gift of God, and nothing more excellent has ever been granted us by God than this.[12] For the good itself, which is God, could bestow nothing better on a man than a complete likeness of its own divinity, as near as possible. Indeed, who would doubt that God is truth unconfined by the body and providing for all? But the philosopher, by moral instruction and that early education of which we have spoken, frees the mind from desire and the sense of the body, attains truth by dialectic, and makes provision for men by teaching them citizenship. Thus it comes about that philosophy is a gift, a likeness, and a most happy imitation of God. If anyone is endowed with philosophy, then out of his likeness to God he will be the same in earth as He who is God in heaven. For a philosopher is the intermediary between God and men; to God he is a man, to men God. Through his truthfullness he is a friend of God, through his freedom he is possessor of himself, through his knowledge of citizenship he is a leader of all other men. Indeed it is said that the golden age once existed because of such a ruler and Plato prophesied that it will return only when power and wisdom come together in the same mind.[13]

According to Plato, the minds of those practicing philosophy, having recovered their wings through wisdom and justice, as soon as they have left the body, fly back to the heavenly kingdom. In heaven they perform the same duties as on earth. United with God in truth, they rejoice. United with each other in freedom, they give thanks. They watch over men dutifully, and as interpreters of God and as prophets, what they have set in motion here they complete there. They turn the minds of men toward God. They interpret the secret mysteries of God to human minds. On this account the ancient theologians justly honored the minds of those practicing philosophy as soon as they were released from the body, just as they honored the thirty thousand divinities of Hesiod[14] as demigods, heroes, and blessed spirits.

Thus philosophy, to express it in a few words, is the ascent of the mind from the lower regions to the highest, and from darkness to light. Its origin is an impulse of the divine mind; its middle steps are the faculties and the disciplines that we have described; and its end is the possession of the highest good. Finally, its fruit is the right government of men.

I have communicated these matters to our Francesco Berlinghieri, as a philosopher friend. For the same reason you will also communicate them to our Giuliano Burgo. [3.18]

47

On the life of Plato[1]

Marsilio Ficino to his own Francesco Bandini: greetings.

In the last few days I have tried to paint the ideal form of a philosopher in Platonic colors. However, if I had brought Plato himself into our midst, I would assuredly not have pointed to some picture of that ideal form of a true philosopher, but to the ideal form itself. Therefore, let us look closely at our Plato, so that we may see equally philosopher, philosophy, and the ideal form itself, at one and the same time.

Genealogy and birth of Plato[2]

Plato of Athens, the son of Ariston and Perictione (or Potone) traced his descent on both sides from Neptune. For Solon was descended from Nereus and Neptune. The brother of Solon, Dropides, had a son, Critias the elder, from whom Callaeschrus is descended. He had two sons, Critias the younger, who was one of the thirty rulers of Athens, and Glaucon, who was the father of Charmides and Perictione. Perictione married Ariston and gave birth to Plato, Adeimantus, Glaucon, and a girl, Potone, who married Eurymedon and gave birth to Speusippus. Plato's father, Ariston, in turn, was descended from Codrus, the son of Melanthus, who again trace their descent back to Neptune, as does Solon. It is said to have been well known in Athens that Ariston tried to approach Perictione, as she was very beautiful, but his attempts were in vain; then he saw Apollo in a dream and was commanded by him to keep her free from conjugal intercourse until she had given birth. Both Laertius and Policrates[3] write of this.

Plato was born either in Athens or on Aegina seven hundred and fifty-six years after the capture of Troy, three hundred and thirty-three years after the founding of Rome, and four hundred and twenty-three years before the coming of Christ.[4] In my book *On Love* I describe the position of the planets at Plato's birth, as I heard of them in my youth.[5] But now I shall draw your attention to their position as described by Julius Firmicus,[6] the astronomer, whose opinion on this matter I consider to be more correct. And it is as follows: Mars, Mercury, and Venus are in Aquarius, which is in the ascendant. In the second house the Sun is in Pisces; in the fifth the Moon is in Gemini; in the seventh Jupiter is in Leo, and in the ninth Saturn is in Libra.

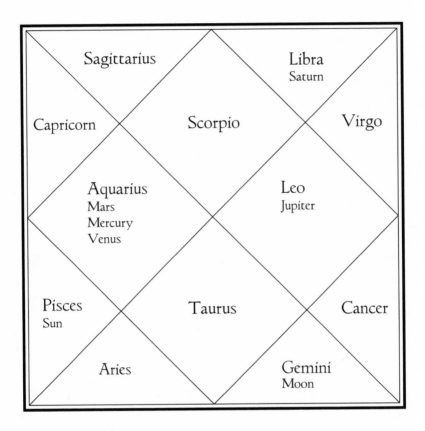

Julius Firmicus claims that such a nativity signifies a man who has the power of wonderful eloquence and approaches all the secrets of the Godhead with divine genius.

The upbringing, natural qualities, learning and even-mindedness of Plato

It is related that while he was in the cradle some bees cast honey onto his infant lips, as a presage of future eloquence.[7]

They say that Socrates in a dream saw on his knee a fledgling cygnet; all at once it grew its feathers and, spreading its wings, flew into the sky, sending forth the sweetest songs. The next day Plato was presented by his father to Socrates who said, "This is the swan I saw."[8]

In Plato's youth his poetry came to flower. He composed elegies and two tragedies, which he himself consigned to the flames as soon as he had applied his mind to philosophy.[9] His first learning was imparted to him by the teacher Dionysius; then at the age of twenty he received instruction from Socrates; after the death of Socrates he attached himself to Cratylus, a disciple of Heraclitus, and to Hermogenes, an upholder of the philosophy of Parmenides. When he was twenty-eight he and other disciples of Socrates betook themselves to Euclides at Megara; from here he set out for Cyrene to hear Theodorus the mathematician. Next he went to Italy to the Pythagoreans: Philolaus, Archytas of Tarentum, and Eurytus. From them he withdrew to the prophets and priests in Egypt. He had intended to go on to the Magi and the Indians but because of wars in Asia he gave up this plan. Finally he returned to Athens and lived at Academia.[10] It is said (and St. Basil and St. Jerome confirm this)[11] that he chose this unhealthy place in Attica so that the over-fine condition of his body, like the excessive growth of a vine, might be cut back; for he was very strong and handsome. And because of this, his broad shoulders and ample forehead, the outstanding condition of his whole body, and also his richness of speech, he was called Plato, although he had previously been named Aristocles.[12] He was without flaw except perhaps that he had rather a soft voice and some kind of lump just below the neck which marred him a little. Through living at Academia he suffered a quartan fever for eighteen months, but with temperance and care he gained greater strength after his fever than he had had before.

The three military expeditions and sea voyages of Plato[13]

The first voyage. He went on military service three times, first to Tanagra, secondly to Corinth, and thirdly to Delium, where he also gained the prize for valor. He sailed to Sicily three times; the first time to see the island, the marvels of Mount Etna, and the craters. He was then in his fortieth year and it was at this time too that Dionysius, the son of Hermocrates, urged Plato to come and talk with him. Here Plato was discoursing on absolute rule, saying it was not the best because absolute rule would only profit itself alone, unless it were also distinguished by virtue. The story goes that the tyrant, offended and angry, said, "Yours are the words of idle old men," to which Plato rejoined, "And yours smack of tyranny." At these words the enraged tyrant at first actually wanted to kill him, but on the entreaty of Dion and

Aristomenes he did not carry this out. However, he did hand him over to Polis of Sparta—who at that time had come to Dionysius as an ambassador—so that Plato might be sold as a slave. Polis took him to Aegina and sold him, whereupon Charmandrus too arraigned him on a capital charge; for, indeed, according to a law passed there it was a capital offence for any Athenian to go to that island. On the other hand, when someone put forward the argument that Plato, thanks to his training, had risen to become a philosopher, and that law spoke of men and not philosophers (who are above men), they acquitted and dismissed him; and they decreed that he should not be killed, but sold. Anniceris the Cyrenian happened to be there, and he redeemed him for twenty *minae* and sent him back to his friends in Athens.

But Polis was defeated by Chabrias and a little later he was drowned in Helice,[14] being told by a spirit, so the story goes, that he was suffering these things on account of the Philosopher. Nor did Dionysius rest; indeed, when he learned what had befallen Polis, he wrote begging Plato not to put a curse on him. Plato wrote back to him that the study of philosophy left him little leisure for thinking about Dionysius. When some other people disparagingly remarked that he had been forsaken by Dionysius, Plato replied, "On the contrary, Dionysius has been abandoned by Plato."

The second voyage.[15] On the second occasion he went to Dionysius the Younger, having been invited by him and by Dion to expound philosophy. He was also led by the hope that through his counsels he would bring it about that there a republic or kingdom would evolve from a tyranny; and that he would see something he had been ardently desiring for a long time, namely, a most philosophical form of government, in which either the philosophers govern or the rulers study philosophy. For he believed that in no other way could states avoid misery. He wanted all this to be brought about not by force or deceit but, once Dionysius had been won over, by philosophical reasoning. But about four months after Plato's arrival, Dionysius was persuaded, by false accusations of plotting against the tyranny, to banish Dion. Nevertheless he gladly continued to show favour to Plato. But Plato returned to his own country.

The third voyage.[16] On the third occasion Plato came intending to reconcile Dion with Dionysius, after he had been implored again and again by both of them; he was asked by Archytas also. On that occasion Dionysius sent a well-provisioned trireme, Archidemas the Pythagorean orator and many noblemen to meet Plato, and he himself also welcomed him ashore with a chariot drawn by four white horses.[17]

Plato asked for the promised recall of Dion, and in addition for land and men, so that they all might live there in accordance with the constitution of his Republic. Although Dionysius had promised this he drew back from fulfilling it. But when Plato publicly accused Dionysius of having broken faith—first with Plato himself over the reinstatement of Dion, and then with Plato's Theodotus over the protection of Heraclides—he had Dionysius as an enemy from that moment. Hence he continually lived in great danger of being killed by Dionysius' soldiers. But Archytas of Tarentum sent Lamiscus the orator to Dionysius with a ship, asking him to let Plato go. Dionysius released him, giving him provisions, and Plato returned home.

Shortly afterwards Dionysius paid the penalty for his crime committed against philosophy, being driven from his seat of tyranny by Dion and the people. Plato was welcomed back to his own country in high honor. There he was invited to enter the service of the state, but was unwilling to accept, as the people had accustomed themselves to evil ways.

Those to whom Plato gave laws

It is said that the Arcadians and Thebans, who had established a state of respectable size, asked him to set it up as a republic; but when he understood that they were unwilling to pursue the ideal of equality, he did not proceed.[18] However, he did give laws to the Syracusans when the tyrant had been driven out;[19] and for the Cretans he wrote Laws, arranged in twelve books, soon after the city of Magnesia had been founded.

From those closest to him he sent Aristonymus, to instruct the Arcadians in the laws; he sent Phormio to the Ilians and Menedemus to the Pyrrheans.[20]

Plato's self-restraint, dignity and affability

He lived single. His life was wholly temperate and, as St. Augustine asserts, chaste. Hence in old age he is said to have made sacrifice to Nature to free himself, in the view of the people, from the charge of childlessness.[21] As a young man he had such a sense of propriety and such composure that he was never caught laughing except modestly.[22] But no one saw him angry. Hence, when a boy who had been educated under Plato, returned to his parents and saw his father shouting, he said, "Never did I see this with Plato."[23] Only once was he inwardly somewhat angry with a boy who was doing serious wrong, but he said to Xenocrates, "You beat this boy, for I cannot, as I am angry."[24]

No matter what the day he would eat only once or, if twice, very sparingly. He used to sleep alone. He would strongly condemn a contrary way of life.[25]

Like his own Socrates too, he seemed somewhat inclined to the loving of youths; but, in the same measure as both were disposed to the sensuous, they were restrained by reason. How spiritual was their love and how what they said about love may be expounded, we have dealt with adequately in our book *On Love*.[26]

Plato chose to bequeath a memorial of himself, both in his books and in his friends.[27] Although as Aristotle writes[28] he was melancholy and of a profound nature, yet he used to make many jests, and he frequently reminded the rather austere Xenocrates and Dion to sacrifice to the Graces so that they would be made more agreeable, and gracious.[29] Plato's affability, however, was combined with dignity.

The leading pupils of Plato[30]

His pupils were: Speusippus of Athens, Xenocrates of Chalcedon, Aristotle of Stagira, Philip of Opus, Hestiaeus of Perinthus, Dion of Syracuse, Amyclus of Heraclea, Erastus and Coriscus of Scepsis, Timolaus of Cyzicus, Euaeon of Lampsacus, Python and Heraclides of Aenus, Hippothales and Callippus of Athens, Demetrius of Amphipolis, Heraclides of Pontus, and several others, among them two women, Lastheneia of Mantinea and Axiothea of Phlius, who both wore men's clothes. It is said that Theophrastus, too, heard him speak, as did Hyperides, the orator, and Chamaeleon and Lycurgus; Demosthenes and Mnesistratus too were devoted to him.[31]

At the entrance to the Academy was inscribed: "No one lacking geometry may enter here"; which indeed, he wished to be understood as not only the due measurement of lines but the due measure of the state of mind as well.[32]

Plato's books[33]

He wrote a book, *Euthyphro*, on holiness; he wrote *The Apologia* of Socrates; *Crito*, on what Crito discussed with Socrates in prison; *Phaedo*, on the immortality of the soul; *Cratylus*, on the proper consideration of names; *Theaetetus*, on knowledge; *The Sophist*, on being; *The States-man*, on government; *Parmenides*, on the single origin of all things and on the ideal forms; *Philebus*, on the highest good; *The Symposium*, on love; *Phaedrus*, on beauty; *Alcibiades* I, on the nature of man; *Alcibiades* II, on prayer; *Hipparchus*, on the desire for gain; *Amatores*, on philoso-phy; *Theages*, on wisdom; *Charmides*, on temperance; *Laches*, on cour-age; *Lysis*, on friendship; the refutative dialogue *Euthydemus*; *Protagoras*, on ethics; *Gorgias*, on rhetoric; *Meno*, on virtue; *Hippias Maior*, on beauty; *Hippias Minor*, on falsehood; *Menexenus*, on ancient Attica; ten books on *The Republic*; *Timaeus*, on the nature of the universe; *Critias*, on ancient Attica; *Minos*, on law; twelve books on *The Laws*; *Epinomis*, called The Philosopher; and thirteen *Epistles*.[34] We ourselves have trans-lated all these books of Plato from Greek into Latin.

There are three kinds of Platonic dialogue; that is to say, in one he refutes the sophists, in another he encourages the youth, and in the third he teaches adults.[35] What Plato himself says in his letters or his books on *The Laws*, and in *Epinomis*, he wishes to be taken as completely true; whereas what he discusses through the mouths of Socrates, Timaeus, Parmenides, and Zeno, in other books is to be taken as probable.[36]

The eloquence, wisdom, and authority of Plato

The style of Plato (as Aristotle says) flows midway between prose and poetry,[37] and is of such sweetness and fullness that Cicero said that Plato was the greatest authority and master, both in understanding and teach-ing.[38] He added that if Jupiter had wished to speak with a human tongue he would have spoken with none other than the tongue of Plato. Indeed such great teaching was in him that whereas before him all enlightened Greeks had travelled abroad to foreign peoples for wisdom's sake, after the time of Plato all nations streamed as one into Athens; even Aristotle, endowed with such wonderful natural abilities and eager for a new way of thinking, listened to Plato's words for twenty years continuously, although he was nearly adult when he came to him.[39] Added to which, before he came to Plato he was already advanced in his studies; from then on he had only Plato as a teacher. Let me quote what Cicero writes: "I prefer to err with Plato than to feel I am right with everyone else."[40] Further, with Panaetius, he calls him the God of philosophers.[41] And Quintilian writes, "Who doubts that Plato is foremost both in the penetration of his argument and in the divine and Homeric eloquence of his speech, for his language rises so far above the prosaic and what Greeks call 'pedestrian' speech, that to me he seems to be instinct not with human genius but with Delphic utterance?"[42] Through godly wisdom and uprightness he seems to have obtained for himself a wonderful authority, even in his own country, which very rarely happens.

When on his return from Sicily, Plato arrived at that most magnificent assembly of the Olympic Games, which seemed like a gathering of the whole world, he was received with such joyful greetings from all it was as though a god had been sent from heaven to mortal men.[43] You would have seen the games deserted, the athletic contests abandoned, the boxers left to themselves; and what is more remarkable, people who had come such long journeys over land and sea to feast their eyes, ears, and minds on the Olympic games, forgetful now of all pleasure, were coming to Plato and gazing upon him. In Plato, as in a most delightful hospice, they found their rest.

When a man was reciting a tragedy with no one present but Plato, some objected that it was degrading for him that only one person should be there. He replied, "But this one man is more than the whole Athenian people."[44]

The charity, magnanimity and holiness of Plato

How great and constant he was in spirit, particularly in the cause of his friends, is shown by his letters, his contempt for a tyrant, and his defense of Dion. Often Plato argued boldly with the tyrant, even in the presence of witnesses, since he said the tyrant governed unjustly and deceived his own friends;[45] so far was Plato from flattering him. Let me add some minor details, thus: at a feast, Dionysius had ordered everyone to dance dressed in purple. Aristippus promptly danced but Plato declined, saying that women's things did not become a philosopher.[46] Further, the corrupt accuser Crobylus had laid an accusation against the courageous general Chabrias and had threatened him with sentence of death. In these circumstances, when the general, deserted by all the other citizens and fearing danger, went up into the fortress, only Plato stood by him all the time, ready to give help. The slanderer Crobylus, to prevent him from defending Chabrias, said threateningly, "You press forward to assist the defense of other people, not heeding that the poison of Socrates awaits you too." Plato replied, "In days gone by, Crobylus, when I fought for the honor of my country, I was not slow to face dangers that had to be borne. Now, for duty and for the safety of a friend I will not turn from any crisis, even though you may threaten sword, poison, and fire."[47]

When Socrates had been imprisoned most unjustly, Plato collected money to buy the release of the innocent man, and while the trial was in progress, he ascended the platform and began to speak thus: "O men of Athens, although I am younger than all those here who have mounted the tribunal . . ." then the tyrannical judges, fearing that his authority and eloquence might move the citizens, suddenly interrupted and shouted "Get down!"[48] Plato left for home. For he was then suffering from some bodily sickness, just as they were suffering from sickness of the mind. In fact, Socrates' persecutors paid the penalty soon afterwards.

One of the fellow disciples of Xenocrates was pricked by jealousy that Xenocrates was so favored and so close to Plato. In order to arouse hostility against Xenocrates, he reported many malicious sayings of Xenocrates against Plato. Plato listened but rejected the charge as he was speaking. The malicious critic stood his ground, with hardened countenance, affirming the charge. At length, Plato, to free himself from the tenacity of the man who was calling on all the gods and goddesses to bear witness, said, "Be it so: but Xenocrates is so strong in faith and is of such dignity that unless he had judged it to be useful he would never have said these things."[49]

Diogenes' *Life of Xenocrates*[50] bears witness that Xenocrates, the beloved disciple of Plato, imitated his dignity and magnanimity; and Xenocrates' life is indeed an example of fortitude and devotion. Plutarch is a witness that Dion too imitated Plato.[51] Further, Philiscus,[52] describing the life of the orator Lycurgus, says, "Lycurgus was a great man, and many things were brilliantly accomplished by him which no man could have done who had not been a pupil of Plato."

When fleeing from Antipater, Demosthenes said to Archias, who was promising to save his life with fawning words, "Far be it from me that, after I have heard both Xenocrates and Plato discoursing on the immortality of the soul, I should prefer to live with shame rather than to die with honor."[53] The same man, writing to a certain Heracleodorus, his fellow student, reproached him because, after he had listened to Plato, he neglected good studies and led a life of little honor. He said, "Do you not feel ashamed to be neglecting what you have learned from Plato?"[54]

Dionysius, writing to Speusippus, says, "Plato used to teach without charge those who frequented his house, but you exact fees, and take them from those who are willing to pay and those who are not."[55] Laertius also criticises Speusippus for not, in contrast to Xenocrates, imitating Plato's purity, fortitude and gentleness.[56]

I cannot be silent about Xenocrates' courage when Dionysius said to Plato, "Someone will take off your head." Xenocrates, who was there, said, "No one cuts off that head without first cutting off mine!"[57]

Maxims and sayings of Plato [58]

Plato used to say this about Aristotle and Xenocrates, "Oh! What have I taken on to be yoked together! A horse and an ass! Aristotle needs the bridle, but Xenocrates needs the spur."[59]

There was among his disciples an over-fastidious young man, too concerned about his external appearance: Plato asked him, "How long will you go on building a prison for yourself?"

As often as he might see a man ensnared by love he used to say, "That man is dead in his own body; he lives in another's." He would add, "He who deserts his own self for the sake of another is of all men the most miserable, since he no longer possesses either himself or the other."

A certain close friend of Plato, a learned man, was pleading with Plato to listen for a while as he was intent on reading a paper he had produced. Whereupon, asked by Plato what was the title of the work, he answered, "Do not contradict." Plato said to him, "Why then are you doing so yourself? Why contradict contradictors? Why consult me since you do not allow yourself to be contradicted?"[60]

A powerful citizen, Leo, was publicly criticized for making a loud and excessive uproar in the senate. Plato said, "This is truly being a lion."

To Diogenes the Cynic who maintained that he certainly saw mortal things but ideas not at all, Plato said, "What a marvel! For you have eyes with which these mortal things are seen, and you use them, but you do not use the mind by which alone ideas are discerned."[61]

To some disciples, marveling that Xenocrates, throughout his life a grave man, had said something intended to be received with laughter, Plato said, "What? Do you wonder that among thorns sometimes roses and lilies are born?"

To young men he often used to say, "Put work before leisure, unless perhaps you think rust better than brilliance."

He used to fire the young with enthusiasm for a happy life, very often with this reasoning: "Consider the contrary nature of virtue and pleasure: for the momentary sweetness of the latter is followed by sudden remorse and perpetual sorrow; but the brief toils of the former are followed by eternal delight."[62]

When he saw someone playing at dice Plato rebuked him, and when the man said, "What small matters you find fault with!" Plato replied, "On the contrary! Habit is no small matter."[63]

He used to advise drunkards and those prone to rage to observe themselves attentively in a mirror; they would immediately turn their backs on such foulness.[64] Drunkenness and idleness he abhorred.

He used to say that in the education of the young what is of most importance is that children should become accustomed to delight only in those things that are honorable. "Otherwise," he used to say, "pleasure is a bait for evils."[65] He would add that true health of mind is love of wisdom. In truth other powers seem to be not so much love of wisdom as embellishments. Nothing is sweeter for a healthy mind than to speak and hear true things; for there is nothing better or more enduring than truth.[66] To some people who asked what kind of possessions then should one chiefly provide for one's children, he said, "Those that would dread neither hailstorm, nor the violence of men, nor even Jove himself."

To Demodocus, taking counsel about the instruction of his son, Plato said, "There should be the same care in the begetting and rearing of children as there is in the planting and training of young trees. The rearing is work, the begetting pleasure; but beware lest we seem deeply asleep at the work yet more than awake in the pleasure."

To a certain Philedon, who was carping at Plato because Plato was no less zealous and assiduous in learning than in teaching, and who was asking him how long he wished to be a student, Plato said, "For as long as I have no cause to repent being better and wiser."

Asked what was the difference between a wise man and an ignorant man, he replied, "The difference between a doctor and a sick man."

He used to say that for princes there was no more excellent kind of surety for men in their position than to have retainers to whom trade was unknown.[67]

He said, "To the prince wisdom is as necessary as breath to the body. States will be most blessed if either philosophers rule or at least, by some divine destiny, those who govern study philosophy; for nothing is a greater scourge than power and boldness that are accompanied by ignorance.

Also, subjects are usually such as they see their princes to be.[68]

"A magistrate should consider not his own but the public good; not some part only, but the whole of the state, should be his care."

How lightly Plato regarded the human; how much he delighted in the divine

Every day he used to repeat, "The eternal alone is true, the temporal only seems to be. The soul sleeps in the body and those things that the senses desire or fear are nothing but dreams. Thus all such things are to be thoroughly condemned, and to avoid the evils that are plentiful in the world we must flee to the eternal for refuge. For in no other way can evils be avoided."[69]

And he put into practice what he taught. For when, both by a hereditary right and the support of the citizens, he would have been a leader in the state, he totally rejected all public honor. When by inheritance from his father he became very rich, he showered all on his brothers, except for a small suburban estate, called Academia.[70] With this alone he lived content. Although he came to be the teacher and the friend of princes, yet he accepted no riches from them. King Dionysius used to say, "Aristippus is always asking for money, Plato is always asking for books."[71] In addition he neither took a wife nor lived in the city. Free from all things, he served truth alone.

Whence, St. Jerome says, "Despite great difficulties Plato travelled throughout Egypt, and to Archytas of Tarentum and to that coast of Italy formerly called Magna Graecia. So that he who in Athens was a master and a man of power, with whose teaching the halls of the Academy resounded, became a pilgrim and a disciple, preferring humbly to learn from the words of others rather than, without modesty, to hold forth himself.

"Finally while pursuing learning which seemed to flee before him round the whole globe, he was captured by pirates and sold into slavery; furthermore he served the cruelest tyrant. Captive, bound, and enslaved, yet, because a philosopher, he was greater than the man buying him."[72] Thus Jerome.

The piety and gratitude of Plato

He was filled with gratitude to God, from whom, he used to say, the beginning of thinking, speaking, and acting in all matters ought to be made;[73] and he himself always put this into practice. Moreover, he gave thanks daily to God that he was born a man and not a brute, that he was born a Greek and not a barbarian, and that he was born in the time of Socrates.[74] His dialogues, in which he wonderfully honors his teachers and all his friends, are testimony to how grateful he was to them all. And he ascribed his books to Socrates; for not only does he introduce him as disputant in almost all his dialogues, but also writes that everything he had set down was not his but Socrates'.[75]

What Plato affirmed and those who supported him

In matters subject to the senses he used to support the views of Heraclitus. Then in that which pertains to the intellect he would rest mainly with Pythagoras. But in matters affecting the community he embraced his own Socrates.[76]

These are the things that he asserted everywhere: God provides for all; the souls of men are immortal; there will be rewards for the good, punishments for the wicked.[77]

Augustine, in his book *Against the Academics,* says, "The authority of Christ must be put before everything." However, if there is something to be done requiring the use of reason, he says he finds himself with the Platonists, for this is not contrary to the sacred Christian writings.[78] Dionysius the Areopagite[79] pointed out the same; later Eusebius and Cyril[80] explained it more fully. Hence Augustine, in his book *On True Religion* says, "If a few things were changed, the Platonists would become Christians."[81] And in *The Confessions* he relates that he has found nearly all the opening words of John the Evangelist in the works of the Platonists.[82] Therefore in the second book of *The City of God* he says, "Labeo the pagan theologian thought that Plato should be numbered with the demigods, like Hercules and Romulus. Furthermore, he places demigods above heroes. But both he sets among the divine powers. Nevertheless I have no doubt that Plato, whom he calls a demigod, should be preferred not only to the heroes but even to the gods themselves."[83] Whence he says that he chose the Platonists before other philosophers as they had a much truer understanding of divine and human matters than the rest. Also Marcus Varro[84] had earlier come to this conclusion and Apuleius regarded Plato as not merely superior to the heroes but equal to the gods, since he had evidently penetrated the inmost secrets of divine matters.[85]

Plato was endowed with such modesty that, although he had won himself marvelous authority above others, even so, when he was asked by someone for how long his precepts should be obeyed he replied, "Until someone holier appear on earth to uncover the fountain of truth for all; whom in the end all will follow."[86]

He added that he had discovered nothing by his own light but much by divine light. However, what he observed in philosophy we have discussed adequately in our books, *On Love* and *The Theology*.

Plato's return to his celestial land and praises of him

It was on his birthday that he departed life, when he had fulfilled eighty-one years and not a day less. For this reason the Magi who were then in Athens made sacrifice to Plato; they reckoned his lot to be greater than that of a human being since he had fulfilled the most perfect number, which is the product of nine times nine.[87] And, what is a marvel, he was still writing at that age and on that very day; about which Cicero says, "There is also the calm and gentle old age of a quiet and pure life lived with good judgment; such we are told was that of Plato who died while writing at eighty-one years of age."[88] Seneca also affirms that Plato reached this age by means of even-mindedness and care.[89] Some affirm that he returned to the gods above while writing, others that he returned in middiscourse, while reclining after the meal had been cleared at a wedding feast.[90]

Aristotle consecrated an altar and a statue to Plato in a temple with this inscription: βωμον Ἀριστοτελης ἱδρυσατο Τονδε Πλατωνος ὁν ἐπαινουν Τοισι Κακοισι θεμις, that is, "Aristotle has dedicated this altar to Plato, a man whom it is sacrilege of bad men to praise."[91] Aristotle added, "By his life, his teaching, his conduct and his speech, he alone gave guidance to all men, and handed on his writings, so that through virtue they might be able to lead a happy life. No future age will bring forth such a man."[92] And other wise men have added many verses to the praise of Plato, but above all three epitaphs.[93] This is the meaning of the first: "He excelled all men in temperance and justice, but was so far above them in wisdom that he completely overcame all envy." This is the sense of the second: "Plato has been removed from the world to be numbered among the gods; distant nations honor him, for he had knowledge himself of the divine life, and showed it to others." The third sentence is like this: "Phoebus begat Aesculapius and Plato—Aesculapius to heal bodies, Plato to heal souls."[94]

Furthermore, Mithridates, the king of the Persians, placed in the Acad-

emy a statue of Plato with this inscription: "Mithridates, the Persian, son
of Orontobates, has dedicated this image of Plato (the work of Silanion)
to the Muses."[95]

From all this Plato attained such a reputation that, although the Greeks
placed Aristotle among the spirits, they named Plato divine; because it is
clear that, in the main, Aristotle's life was earthly, and his knowledge
natural; whereas Plato, at once by knowledge and by his life, devoted
himself above all to the divine.

An Apologia on the character of Plato

I shall now draw to a close, once I have added a few more words.

There are some common rhymesters who without meriting it, usurp
for themselves the name of poet. Roused as much by the difference in
conduct as by the malice of envy, they mock shamelessly any man of
excellence. And to these men a certain supreme license is allowed against
good men rather than bad, especially in our time.[96] But let me not be
mindful of our times, which are as incapable of pursuing virtue as they
seem to be well capable of persecuting it. Accordingly, in former times,
such petty poets did not hesitate to sink their teeth into the divine Plato,
considered by the Greeks to be the son of Apollo, and also into Socrates,
considered by Apollo to be the wisest of Greeks. Diogenes Laertius utterly detested the impiety of these poets. And, as Diogenes declares,
Aristippus of Cyrene, the most wicked man of his time and an adversary
of the best one of his time, also added to the facetious abuse of the comic
poets.[97] Just as Aristippus slandered many other very virtuous and learned
men with false stories, so he even slandered Socrates his teacher and his
fellow pupils, Xenophon[98] and Plato. He made up certain lascivious poems in their names about harlots and young boys,[99] evidently so that, by
falsely using the great philosophers as examples, he might procure a freer
license to sin himself.

But Aristotle, to whom truth was more dear than Plato,[100] could not
tolerate such false calumny against a holy man. For in his elegies to Eudemus
he recites those words about Plato that we have quoted above, paying him
the greatest tribute: that profane men not only must not slander Plato in
any way, but even, under the pretext of praise, they should not dare to
utter his holy name through their profane mouths.[101] And he was not
content with an elegy, but also, according to Olympiodorus, composed a
brilliant oration in praise of Plato.[102]

Therefore let the hounds of hell be silent in the world of the living; rather let them howl in company with Cerberus in the world of the dead. But, for our part, let us venerate Plato's life and wisdom, in the judgment of the wise regarded as the best, and together with Apuleius of Madaura let us freely proclaim: "We, the family of Plato, know nothing except what is bright, joyful, celestial, and supreme."[103] [3.19]

48

Oratorical, moral, dialectical, and theological praise of Philosophy

Marsilio Ficino to Bernardo Bembo, lawyer and knight, the Venetian orator distinguished for his learning and authority: greetings.

You ask why it is that, although I have praised the arts and many other things, yet I have never praised philosophy, which I have always studied with such devotion. Giovanni Cavalcanti, my Achates, happened to ask the same question some days ago. My reply is: first, that what has been discovered by men may at any time be duly praised by them, but that Philosophy, the invention of God, is far beyond human eloquence; secondly, in singing the praise of each of these arts and activities, I have indeed been honoring Philosophy, inventress and mistress of them all. Indeed it is only by her power and eloquence that we give each art its due honor, and we consider each worthy of praise in so far as it shares the virtue and dignity of Philosophy. But because she is our mother and nurse, it seems that sometimes with perfect justice she demands her due honor from us, so if it find favor, let our praise begin.

Oratorical praise of Philosophy

Oh Philosophy, guide of life, seeker of virtue, scourge of vice! What would we be, what would the life of men be, without you? You have begotten cities, called scattered men into the fellowship of life, brought them together first within dwellings, then in marriage, then in communion of tongue and letters. You were the inventress of laws, mistress of men's conduct and of discipline. But where is this unfamiliar digression leading? I do not know how I started this Ciceronian[1] oratory and song. Such melody may be sweet, but since Philosophy is as much the principle of song as of the subject which is sung, we must sing philosophically. So let us start this game afresh.

Moral praise of Philosophy

Philosophy is defined by everyone as love of truth and devotion to wisdom. But truth, and wisdom itself, are God alone, so it follows that lawful Philosophy is no different from true religion, and lawful religion exactly the same as true Philosophy. If the properties of words derive partly from the properties of things and partly from those of ideas, as Plato, Aristotle, Varro, and Saint Augustine have shown in great detail;[2] then certainly Philosophy, the explorer and discoverer of the conception of things, brought forth Grammar, the measure of correct speech and writing.

If only Philosophy, or Philosophy above all, knew the nature of souls, the power of actions, the form of works, the arrangement of places, and the fitness of times, then it is she, above all, who taught the orators what to say, and how, whom they should persuade, and when. She also taught the poets what to describe, how to move the emotions and delight the soul. From this it follows that without her assistance historians could not serve their office.

Philosophy endowed states with souls when she made human laws on earth reflect the divine laws of heaven. She brought forth the body of the state and made it grow by providing agriculture, architecture, medicine, military skill, and every other art that gives nourishment, elegance, or protection to a state.

Then, above all, Philosophy removes misery from mortals, and bestows happiness upon them. For she discriminates good from evil and shows us how to avoid evil so that it does not hurt us, or how to bear it with strength so that it hurt us less. Furthermore, she shows us how to find goodness more easily, and how to use rightly the gifts that have either been bestowed on us by nature or fortune or acquired through work, so that they may be profitable.

I intended to end this letter here, dear Bernardo, and not make it longer than usual, for you know how much we dislike length, except in Plato, our fountainhead of divine eloquence; but the divine mother, whom we revere above all, protests too strongly. Listen, therefore, if you will, to the words she now demands from me, or rather that she presents to me.

Dialectal and Theological praise of Philosophy

Philosophy uses the tools of dialectic,[3] created by her own hand, to discover the truth in things through contemplation, the virtue in them through use, and the goodness in them through both. She thus suggests many principles for contemplation, many precepts for action, and much instruction for both. But of the many things she teaches I shall mention one in particular. The end is superior to those things that are related to it, just as a master is superior to his servants; so it is quite right that external, mortal, and bodily things should serve the body, the body should serve the soul, the senses should serve reason, active reason should serve contemplative reason, and contemplation should serve God. Hence, all the arts that relate to outer things, to the body, to senses, and to action, should be subject, and give place to contemplation as their queen. This is God's own activity. It does not need a special place or special instrument, nor does it serve outer things; of all things it is the most enduring, in fact it is everlasting. Its object is eternal. Everywhere it freely embraces that which is everywhere present.

If life is a kind of activity and the finer the activity the finer the life, then surely contemplation, being the most excellent of all activity, both because of its worth and its permanence, is also the greatest and most distinguished life; and, I would add, the sweetest of all. For unlike sense it does not deal with the impure, false and fickle delights arising from external images but, possessing within itself the true and eternal causes and nature of everything, it purely, truly, and permanently feeds on and rejoices at that which is pure, true, and permanent. I say it takes boundless joy in the boundless and, what is most important of all, such a life, being most near to the life of God, is transformed into his perfect image.

So God is at once the light and eye of human contemplation and contemplation is the light and eye of action. Although this eye appears to be inactive, without it inactivity is bad but activity is worse; both are utterly dark and miserable. But at its command we work successfully in every activity. For mortals, wise philosophy points to this most blessed life, established at the summit of all things, revealing it now with her own eye, now with the finger of dialectic. As I judge, she also leads us to it in four main stages: moral conduct, natural studies, mathematics, and metaphysics.

The divine Plato considers that the heavenly and immortal soul in a sense dies on entering the earthy and mortal body and lives again when it leaves it. But before the soul leaves the body by the law of nature, it may do so by the diligent practice of meditation, when Philosophy, the medicine of human ills, purges the sickly little soul, buried under the pestilent filth of vice, and enlivens it with her medicine of moral conduct. Then by certain natural instruments she raises the soul from the depths, through all that is compounded of the four elements, and guides it through the elements themselves to heaven. Then step by step on the ladder of mathematics the soul accomplishes the sublime ascent to the topmost orbs of Heaven. At length, what is more wonderful than words can tell, on the wings of metaphysics[4] it soars beyond the vault of heaven to the creator of heaven and earth Himself. There, through the gift of Philosophy, not only is the soul filled with happiness but since in a sense it becomes God, it also becomes that very happiness. There all the possessions, arts, and business of mankind have their end, and of their number holy Philosophy alone remains. There, nothing else is true happiness but true Philosophy, when it becomes in fact the love of wisdom, as it is defined by the wise. We believe that the supreme bliss consists in a condition of the will that is delight in and love for divine wisdom. That the soul, with the help of Philosophy, can one day become God, we conclude from this: with Philosophy as its guide, the soul gradually comes to comprehend with its intelligence the natures of all things, and entirely assumes their forms; also through its will it both delights in and governs particular forms, therefore, in a sense, it becomes all things. Having become all things through this principle, step by step it is transformed into God, who is the fount and Lord of them all. God truly perfects everything both within and without.

The mind of the truly philosophic man, like God, also conceives within itself the true and eternal causes of all things. But can we say that the human mind is able to create particular things outside itself? Let me leave aside the fact that the philosophic spirit imitates, and expresses exactly, the secret works of Almighty God, making them manifest in thought, words, and letters, through different instruments and materials. But I think one thing, especially, should be appreciated:[5] not everyone can understand the principle or method by which the marvelously fashioned work of the all-skilled creator has been constructed, but only he who has the same genius for the art. No one could understand how the philosopher Archimedes put together bronze spheres, and gave them movements similar to those of the heavenly bodies, unless he were gifted with the same genius. And he who does understand, because he is so gifted, after recognizing them may construct similar ones, provided that tools and material are available. Since the philosopher has seen the order of the heavenly spheres, whence they are moved and whither they proceed, how these movements can be measured, and what they give rise to, who can deny that his mind is virtually one with the author of the heavens himself? And that in a sense he would be able to create the heavens and what is in them himself, if he could obtain the tools and the heavenly material. For he does now create them, albeit of another material, nevertheless on the same design.

Oh most wonderful intelligence of the heavenly architect! Oh eternal wisdom, born only from the head of highest Jove! Oh infinite truth and goodness of creation, sole queen of the whole universe! Oh true and bountiful light of intelligence! Oh healing warmth of the will! Oh generous flame of our heart! Illumine us, we beg, shed your light on us and fire us, so that we inwardly blaze with the love of Your light, that is, of truth and wisdom. This alone, Almighty God, is to truly know You. This alone is to live most blessedly with You. Since those who wander far from the rays of Your light can never see anything clearly, they are misled and frightened by unreal shadows, as though by terrifying nightmares, and are wretchedly tormented everywhere in perpetual night. Since they alone who live zealously with You see, love, and embrace beneath Your rays those things that are true, eternal, and immeasurable, they alone will regard anything limited by time or place as a shadowy dream of no importance. Thus they cannot be dislodged from the highest citadel of heavenly bliss, either by desire or fear of earthly things.

My Bernardo, I think that your Marsilio has already written as much as a letter can bear. So farewell, and fare fortunately, patron of philosophers; and as you have done hitherto, live continually in the blessed arms of holy Philosophy. I beg you live also ever mindful of Giovanni Cavalcanti, the heart of Marsilio.[6] [1.123]

49

The principle of learning and of speaking

Marsilio Ficino to Luca Fabiano, his scribe: greetings.

Nature endows us with many instruments through which we may learn:

eyes, ears, noses, taste, and touch. But she gave only a single instrument by which we may teach, namely, the faculty of speaking. She has certainly warned us that we should use the service of learning more often than the office of teaching, in the same measure as she has provided more instruments for learning than teaching. Therefore no man who is verbose and talkative can be wise, for he has always taught but never learnt. Now whoever lacks wisdom and learning must be considered not only poor, but also blind and dumb. I pray you be swift and diligent to hear and see, but slow to believe, slower to judge, and slowest of all to speak. So that you can speak what is good, listen to what is good, and so that you may hear well of yourself for your part speak well of others. For it cannot be that he who speaks maliciously does not hear maliciously.

Moreover, in speaking beware of a lie no less than a navigator is wary of a rock. For boundless is the light of truth, boundless its power. The lie swiftly betrays and ruins the liar. Remember that flattery is a servile vice, indeed more vile than servile. For however skillfully a man fawns, he is far surpassed by small dogs. Remember besides, loud scolding is either rash or bigoted; or dangerous or completely useless. Our Plato bids us speak only when we may be useful or else keep silent.[1] Furthermore, if anyone be a disciple of Paul the Apostle in prudence, way of living, and purpose, only he can "be instant in season, out of season."[2]

But especially we must beware lest, while in words we are denouncing the behavior of others, meanwhile our own behavior denounce our words. You have begun well, as I hear, therefore continue in the way you have begun. And, to journey successfully, do not cease to restrain with reins and bit your steed, that is your senses. [2.46]

50

Precepts for memory

Marsilio Ficino to Banco, the arithmetician: greetings.

If you want memory of good things to be strong, try to forget the evil. It is worth sinking useless thoughts into the river of forgetfulness so that you retain those of value.

Avoid the onslaught of the passions, Banco, and the tumult of much activity and many thoughts. Do you wish to think usefully? Then have very few thoughts, and those of a kind that very few think. This is what Pythagoras meant when he said: "Turn aside from highways and walk by footpaths."[1] Why do people wander around so heedlessly? Shrewdness and discrimination are needed, for the hare lies hidden in a small clump of grass. Evils lie everywhere, while the good is reduced to narrow limits.

Do you want to have a powerful memory for what is good? Then take care to learn the reason behind what has to be learnt. For reason is the indissoluble bond between truth and memory. This is perhaps why our Plato said that what has once been well understood can never be entirely forgotten.[2] You should commit things to memory that are not just useful, but also agreeable. Foods that are most pleasant to taste pass more easily into our nature and become part of it. And the more eagerly anything is drunk, the longer it is retained.

In addition it should be especially noted that Aristotle and Simonides[3] think one should always remember that there is a definite order present, or at any rate an order that may be deduced, in what has to be learnt. The order consists in a particular proportion and sequence. When things have been arranged in an ordered sequence, if one thing comes to mind the rest immediately and necessarily follows, either by a natural or a deduced connection. And if the mind's attention is directed either to one thing, or to a few things as if they were only one, it acts more powerfully than if it is divided among many things. Just as the complete order and connection of the parts bring to unity the whole composed of those parts, so they also bring to unity the attention of the mind itself.

We must, moreover, take care that we often reflect on what we have learnt. For in this way the food of the mind is digested and, as it were, turned into mind. Indeed it is of the greatest assistance if what has been committed to memory is often repeated in fine language and sweet song. For enjoyment is the seasoning of things: it is the food of love, the kindling of genius, the nourishment of will, and the strength of memory.

A sense of wonder, too, is very important, for through it the mind is made more attentive and deeply imprints the features of things on its own inner substance. Thus, as boys experience greater wonder because things are new to them, they also retain the memory of them longer. Perhaps they also have fewer thoughts than men, and let us add, much clearer ones. But more of this another time.

If one is to believe the medical profession on this subject, the brain should often be purged with aloe and tended with the scents of cinnamon and marjoram. I certainly do not dispute this, but I recommend far more the cleansing of the soul. For this must first be purged of evils in order to be filled with good.

Farewell: that is to say, give your soul good fare. But you fare well if you feed it, not on great quantity but on the best quality.

13 August 1458.

Fighini. [1.105]

FORTUNE, FATE, AND HAPPINESS

51

For evil men good fortune is bad,
but for good men evil fortune is good

Marsilio Ficino, the Florentine, to the illustrious Venetian knight, Bernardo Bembo: greetings.

Tell me, man of constancy, why it is that fortune often hates and indeed casts down a man whom the people deservedly love and, conversely, even more often loves and raises up one whom they justly hate? Is it perhaps because fortune is not only opposed to reason but, since the world began, has also been hostile to the people? Thus they are always unfortunate and in misery. Perhaps she is also vain and, so that any great action should be ascribed to her alone and not to human virtue or grace, she raises up in wonderful ways a man whom most men would rightly wish suppressed, but sinks into the abyss one who is exalted.[1]

What if she be blind, as they say, or would emulate nature? For if nature has established that you live as an animal before you live as a man, then certainly you sense before you comprehend; if fortune strives to make a man great, she first creates a huge beast puffed up with poisonous pride. And so a tyrant is born, both in nature and in countenance, before he gains tyrannical power. These men without worth, established in high office, render these very offices no longer worthy of upright men. They even cause a belief, from time to time, that the universe is not moved by divine providence, nor mankind by human prudence, but by chance. In fact, divine providence, on occasion, in defiance of fortune's fullest favor, suddenly hurls some men from the highest pinnacle down to the depths; others, in spite of fortune's malign attack, she wonderfully raises on high.

On the other hand, if she permits the proud to stand for a long while, or the humane to fall for a time, she also suffers this to be, so that the former are in as dejected and miserable a mind as in lot they are high, and the latter in as exalted a mind as in fortune they are humble and cast down. And so, for the evil, good fortune becomes evil; but for the good, evil fortune becomes good. For my part, if I were given the choice, I would prefer to be Hercules rather than Sardanapalus.[2] The one overcame as many monsters as overwhelmed the other; Hercules, having vanquished savage beasts, rose up as a god, while Sardanapalus was destroyed by beasts and made lower and more wretched than they.

Where wisdom abounds, there is very little work for dice. Where there is very little wisdom, chance dominates most things. And if at times fortune is joined to wisdom, nevertheless they do not both reign at the same time. For either chance is in no way joined to reason or she is subject to it. Wherefore chance is envious of upright men and obstructs them with all powers, lest straight reason should reign anywhere; for, if reason ruled, chance would lose her glory and her power. Chance often gives much to the man to whom nature or virtue has given very little, and she does not readily enrich a man endowed with gifts of nature or virtue.

In certain ages there are great and powerful men, gods in the guise of humans, or humans who are as gods, but they are rarer than the Phoenix, and have been made great not by fortune but by divine providence. They are distinguished by a certain mark: for they are such that surrender nothing to chance for their prosperity, and very little to human virtue, but as much as possible to divine virtue. Inasmuch as they appear to be human to all men, by so much are they above all men in mind, godlike. If where there is inflation with wind there is no health, certainly no man inflated in mind is sane; no man insane and profane is other than bestial; no divine man is not human: no man fully human is not divine. Certainly a divine man does not wish fortune to be his guide, for fortune is blind and often by chance suffers a fall. He does not rejoice in the promises of fortune, for she is faithless even to her own, whom, without honor, she has exalted to the highest summit of honor. For she rejoices in the reversal game between height and depth, and delights in alternate hap and mishap. He does not even fear the threats of fortune, because they are empty. Fortune, you cannot do anything to us that we ourselves do not wish whenever we make you a goddess and set you in heaven.[3]

No one is more pitiable than he who places true happiness in fortune. No one is happier than he who does not judge fortuitous prosperity truly to be happiness. That man is thought by Hippocrates[4] to be prudent who either laughs with Democritus at the ridiculous tears of fortune or, with Heraclitus, laments over her lamentable laughter. He who with Socrates spurns her childish games is esteemed wise and divine by Apollo.[5] Finally, he who endures adversities, alone with Aeneas preserves himself for favorable times. He looks up at a sky clear after rain and at length becomes Lord of the chosen Italy. Therefore, my Aeneas, do not give way to evils; on the contrary, move forward more boldly. Whatever the situation, all fortune is to be overcome by being borne.[6] Be of good cheer, my Aeneas; one day, safe in port, you will rejoice in as many blessings as the storms you have braved at sea. [2.61]

52

No one can be envied, who can see how many times
we all are driven both inwardly and outwardly by the Furies[1]

Marsilio Ficino of Florence to Lorenzo Franceschi, the son of Domenico.

Pythagoras charged his disciples not to eat brain or heart.[2] That is, they should not consume the brain with empty thoughts, nor burn out the heart with excessive cares. If all things happen by chance, they labor in vain who presume to control completely, and to manage by fixed principles of reasoning, affairs that in countless ways happen beyond reason. If all things come from fate, those who strive to avoid what is an unavoidable necessity fall more heavily into fate, for to it they are adding their own labor. Lastly, whether our affairs are said to come from chance or fate, divine providence, by reason, puts unreasonable chance in order, and gently tempers stern fate in accordance with the good. Thus all things become ordered and good to those who willingly unite with the divine will.

For these men alone, what is within the mind accords with external events; but for everyone else, at every point they are at variance. These men alone make what is necessary voluntary and what appears evil good.

Just as the pure mind rejoices in universal good, so the impure mind is afflicted with every evil. Just as the greatest light plunders and appropriates to itself all other lights, so the greatest evil on earth, an evil man, draws from all quarters every evil to himself. He brings much more onto himself than he would receive from elsewhere. Just as we are insatiable for what is good, so, in some strange way, are we almost insatiable for evil. Present evils we do not so much experience as strengthen; past evils we seek again; future evils we seize in advance; those not in the future we invent. I need not mention the perversity of mind from which we suffer adversities; do we not so misuse prosperity that happiness itself becomes our greatest unhappiness? External success for us is no more than the point of departure from reason and law, and what is soundness of body for us but an unsoundness of mind? Also, beauty and bodily strength often lead to deformity and weakness of soul. Oh, how deformed we are! How often in our deformed state do we set upon that which God makes beautiful. Alas! How ungrateful we are to God, the giver of all good things! How frequently we condemn his works and his governance! The more our stores abound with his good fruits, the more do we produce thorns and weeds within ourselves and sow them at home and abroad. And although we produce and sow bad things, we are nonetheless astonished if we then reap the worst and we blame the stars or God and not our own husbandry. Therefore no one can be envied, who can see how many times we all are driven both inwardly and outwardly by the Furies. In your homeland it would be difficult for you to perceive who is happier than anyone else. Outside it, it would be harder still to see who is most miserable. In both cases the reason is almost the same: in your own country each rejoices with the greatest joy, here each of us is afflicted with the greatest pain. Unless we are completely blind, we should see clearly from this that since our sowing does so badly on earth, it is not earthly but heavenly and, if rightly cultivated, will bear heavenly fruit. [3.1]

53

On constancy in the face of fortune

Marsilio Ficino to Giovanni Cavalcanti, his unique friend: greetings.

In Plato's book *Theaetetus on Knowledge*,[1] Socrates strengthened his friend Theodore the Geometer to resist boldly the blows of fortune, not, as was usual, with iron arms, but with arms of gold.

"It is impossible, Theodore," he said, "to eradicate evils altogether, for there must always be that which opposes goodness. Amongst the gods evil cannot exist, but of necessity it surrounds this mortal nature, this lower region. We must therefore endeavor to escape as quickly as possible from the latter to the former. But by escape I mean to render ourselves, as far as we can, similar to God. Now a man is rendered like God through prudence, piety, and justice."

How this divine principle of our Plato ought to be truly understood you shall hear in a few words. Just as God, who is the Creator of our souls, also regulates them, so is the universe both the begetter and controller of our bodies. Since the soul is the son of God and the body is a limb of the universe, our souls are moved gently and easily by God, as though by a father, through the laws of providence; but our bodies are dragged by the universal body through the forces of fate, as a single particle is dragged by the total mass of which it is a part, under some violent movement. Yet the force of fate does not penetrate the mind unless the mind of its own accord has first become submerged in the body, which is subject to fate. For this reason no one ought so to trust in his own opinion and strength as to hope he may entirely avoid disease of the body and the loss of possessions. Every soul should withdraw from the encumbrance of the body and become centered in the mind, for then fate will discharge its force upon the body without touching the soul. The wise man will not struggle pointlessly with fate. He will rather resist it by flight. You cannot rout misfortune, so flee yourself. That is why Plato advises us to retreat from "here" to "there"—that is, from attachment to the body and involvement with worldly affairs, to the cultivation of the soul. Otherwise we cannot avoid evil.

He adds "as quickly as possible"—I suppose for this reason, that we should from a tender age begin to separate the soul from intercourse with the body before it is submerged by daily habit. Be sure that by this escape the soul is deservedly restored to divine likeness, for it becomes like God, free from bodily taint.

Such freedom we gain principally through the three virtues of prudence, justice, and piety. Prudence recognizes what we owe to God and what to the world. Justice gives its due to the world, and piety its due to God. Thus the man of prudence yields his body, as a limb of the world, to the turmoil of the world wherever it happens to move it. But his soul, the offspring of God, he removes from all dealings with the body and freely commits to the guidance of divine providence.

My dearest Giovanni, if we follow this golden rule of our Plato, with the wind of heaven behind us we shall circumnavigate successfully this vast whirlpool of fortune, and quite untroubled, sail safely into harbor.

Farewell. [1.50]

54

*All the good things of the world are evil to the man
who leads a corrupt life in the world*

Marsilio Ficino to the human race: greetings.

Man, why have you for so long accused the world of being inwardly
corrupt and evil? Although certainly the world is ordered most beautifully and caused to move most excellently, for you, nevertheless, it is
corrupt and evil, because you live corruptly in the pure world and wickedly in the good. The first cause of worldly evils for you is too great a
hunger for worldly goods. You love the small world more passionately
than the great; and you wonder also at this great world that you see,
more greatly than at the boundless world that you perceive by understanding, in which the great world is contained just as the small world is
contained in the great.

O mind that belongs to the heavens, you love your earthly shadow—
that is the body—more than the heavenly splendor, your own light, more
than the light that is above the heavens.

Since in truth love is the beginning of all motion, whether of nature or
soul, for this reason, while you love the body ardently it is on account of
the body that you strive after, or fear, all things. And, in pursuit of these
things, you fill with troubles; and in fearing, you suffer pain. O mind out
of mind, why do you love so hotly those things that can so easily be put
beyond reach before you attain to them, and as easily be taken away
after you possess them?

Alas, fleeing from yourself, why do you follow under such pressure
those things that flee from you so swiftly? Wretched mind! Why for so
long have you vainly tried to keep hold of fleeting, earthly things, as if
they were good; those things, which have power indeed to keep you far
from the good? In fact, these things cannot be held by you in any way.
Why do you so rashly believe that you can check your feet in their rapid
motion? Why be filled with emptiness? Why grasp for the wind? Have
you no wish fully to quench this burning thirst that so torments you?
Awake and drink the true water; and not the image of water in dreams.
Furthermore, know that only those things stand out as true that belong
to the judge of truth, intelligence. As sense is ignorant of truth, those

things that reach toward it, though seeming to be true, are not. Do you want to get rich quickly? Study to withdraw from avarice as much as you have studied to add to your possessions up to the present.

Live, I beg you, by the law of nature, which is content with very few and very small things, and not according to opinion, which always compels you to be poor. Assuredly, necessity is confined within narrow limits, opinion within none. What is necessary is revealed and provided for us at every step; we labor for what is superfluous. For a man going on a journey necessity presents useful and suitable provision; opinion offers useless burden and toil. If you desire rest, do not search for it in movement; stop the movement. If you desire to rule, rule yourself by reason; if you desire freedom, subject yourself to reason. If you desire to avoid suffering, flee from pleasure, the bait of evils.[1] Spurn pleasure; for, being paid for by pain, pleasure inflicts injuries. It is the pleasure of the body, which seems to be the greatest of all pleasures, that most gives rise to pain. The theory and practice of medicine teach that gall is made from nothing more readily than from honey. The sweeter the foods, the more bitter the bile they create. Why has nature determined that in laughing excessively we often weep, but in weeping we seldom laugh? Is it not to admonish us that there is more true pain in the senses than pleasure, for pain is experienced more in pleasure than pleasure in pain?

If you desire to please yourself, take care to please not the multitude but the wise man—or, rather, wisdom; of necessity, you will displease yourself if you want to please anyone against reason. If you desire to live wisely, remember there is this alternation of good and evil, so that good things ought not to be accepted without apprehension nor evil things endured without hope. Therefore we should rejoice in good things with moderation; and sorrow in evil things with even greater moderation.

From the past learn the present. In the present, as far as you are able, look about you at individual things and discern their end. You ought never to launch upon anything that has to be said or done in the present until, as far as possible, you have discerned its future. Nor ought you to do or say anything for which you are unable to give a valid account. Finally, when in each action you have committed yourself humbly to God, and done everything in the light of reason and according to the counsel of the wise, live at peace; and whatever follows accept for the best. [2.40]

55

On the desire for happiness

Cosimo de' Medici to Marsilio Ficino: greetings.

Yesterday I went to my estate at Careggi, but for the sake of cultivating my mind and not the estate. Come to us, Marsilio, as soon as possible. Bring with you Plato's book on *The Highest Good*,[1] which I suppose you have translated from Greek into Latin as you promised. I want nothing more wholeheartedly than to know which way leads most surely to happiness.

Farewell. Come, and bring your Orphic lyre with you. [1.1]

56

The way to happiness

Marsilio Ficino to Cosimo de' Medici: greetings.[1]

I shall come to you as quickly as I can, most willingly. What could be pleasanter than to be in Careggi, the land of the Graces,[2] talking with Cosimo, the father of the Graces. Meanwhile, please accept in these few words what the Platonists say about the most convenient way to happiness. Although I do not think it is necessary to show the way to a man who has already nearly reached the goal, I think your desire must be obeyed, in your absence as well as your presence. All men want to act well, which is to live well. But they live well if they are endowed with as many good things as possible. Now these good things are said to be riches, health, beauty, strength, nobility of birth, honors, power, prudence, as well as justice, fortitude, and temperance, and above all else wisdom, which indeed comprehends the whole essence of happiness. For happiness consists in the successful achievement of the desired goal, but wisdom does this for every activity.

Thus skilled flautists get the best out of their instruments, and learned grammarians best understand what relates to reading and writing. Wise helmsmen also reach a good harbor in their voyage before others do, and the wise general conducts warfare with least danger. The wise doctor can best restore the body's health. Thus with all her strength wisdom gives us mastery of every human activity according to our desire. She never wavers, nor is she ever led astray; otherwise, in truth, she would not be wisdom. Since wisdom is the cause of attaining the goal, necessarily she is all powerful where happiness is concerned.

It is also said that only they are happy who are endowed with many gifts. But they are not happy before those gifts benefit them, and they never benefit from them unless they use them. Possession without use does not contribute to happiness. Nor is use alone enough; for one can use them badly, and thus be injured rather than helped. So as we have added use to possession, we must add rightfullness to use, for we must not only use our gifts but we must use them rightly. Wisdom alone ensures that we do so. This one can see in the arts, in which only those who are skilled in their art make right use of their material, no less than they do of their tools. So also, wisdom makes sure that we rightly use riches, health, beauty, strength, and the other things that are called good. For this reason knowledge is the cause of good and successful action in the possession, use and working of every gift. The man who possesses many gifts and uses them without intelligence is injured the more, the more he possesses, since he has more to misuse. Certainly, the less someone does who is ignorant the fewer mistakes does he make. The fewer mistakes he makes, the less is the harm he does. The less harm he does the less miserable is he. Certainly he does less if he is poor than if he is rich, if he is weak than if he is strong, if he is timid rather than bold, if he is sluggish rather than alert, slow rather than quick, dull rather than clever. Thus none of those qualities that above were called good are good in themselves, for if they are dominated by ignorance they are worse than their opposites, in so far as they can plentifully supply the means of crime to an evil leader. If on the other hand, prudence and wisdom govern these qualities, then they are so much the better. Thus they are not good or bad in themselves. To the wise man both advantages and difficulties become useful, because he makes good use of them both; but the opposite applies to the ignorant.

Of everything that is ours, wisdom alone is good in itself. Only ignorance is bad in itself. Since therefore we all wish to be happy, and happiness cannot be obtained without the right use of our gifts, and since knowledge reveals their proper use, we should leave all else aside and strive with the full support of philosophy and religion to become as wise as possible. For thus our soul becomes most like to God, who is wisdom itself. In this likeness, according to Plato, consists the highest state of happiness. [1.2]

57

Fortune can neither benefit the wicked nor harm the good

Marsilio Ficino to Antonio Ivani of Sarzana: greetings.

If you see someone suffering from incurable physical illness, tormented by a variety of pains in different parts of the body, will you envy him his dainty feasts, his throng of attendants, soft pillows, robe of purple and gilded bedchamber? Of course you cannot, unless you too are sick; as sick in mind as he in body. But those who are slave to pleasures or riches, the pursuit of fame or power, are beset by incurable sickness of mind and by manifold suffering. So whoever looks enviously at such people sees nothing. That is why the most blind of all seems to me to be those who say that fortune is blind, because she benefits the wicked, for whom in truth nothing is good, or because she harms the good, for whom finally nothing is bad. For as a man is in himself, so for him is that which he receives.

Among men, only those who have been deprived of the eye of reason do not see with what wondrous reason each and every part of the universe is put in place and set in motion. Only those men, I would say, seem to be at the mercy of fortune and the greatest injustice, who, when the precise ordering of things points to the infinite power, wisdom, and justice of the Author, still either believe that unreasoning fortune is in command, or else complain of divine governance as if it were less than just. [3.33]

58

As soon as we strive to oppose fate, we overcome it

Marsilio Ficino to Francesco Marescalchi of Ferrara: greetings.

You ask, my excellent fellow philosopher, four questions. Firstly how am I? Indeed, Marescalchi, I am as I wish to be, since I now wish to be as I am. Secondly, why do I practice philosophy? I practice philosophy chiefly for this reason: since events themselves do not otherwise follow my will, at least I by my will shall follow events, for it is to a will which follows them that events conform. Thirdly, how much do I love you? If there be any measure to love, or rather if there be any fixed measure to free will, measure your love toward me, Francesco; thus perhaps you may measure my love toward you. Fourthly, what am I working on? I am preparing a book on the providence of God and the freedom of human judgment,[1] in which a case is moved against the predetermination of the stars and the prophetic utterances of the astrologers.

But perhaps someone may say it is foolish to wish to contend against unassailable fate. I, however, reply that it can be opposed as easily as one may wish to oppose it, since by that very opposition one may immediately overcome what one wishes. Surely the movement of the heavenly spheres is never able to raise the mind to a level higher than the spheres. But he who puts them under examination seems already to have transcended them, to have come near to God Himself and the free decision of the will. It is as if he is not constrained by heavenly fate, but guided, now by the providence of God that is above the heavens, and now by the freedom of the mind. Furthermore, although any adverse and, as I might say, fatal action habitually proceeds from one contrary position of the stars to another, no one dares to assert that will itself and reason, resisting the assumed force of the stars, arise from the force of the stars; but rather we understand that they flow from providence and freedom itself, by whose grace we have spoken against fate.

28 June 1477.
Florence. [3.29]

59

What happiness is; that it has degrees; that it is eternal

Marsilio Ficino to the magnanimous Lorenzo de' Medici: greetings.

At Careggi recently, when you and I had discussed at length many aspects of happiness, we eventually arrived through reason at the same conclusion. You then perceptively discovered fresh proofs why happiness lies in action of will rather than the action of intellect. You wanted to set down that discussion in verse, and wished me to do so in prose. You have just fulfilled your duty with an elegant poem,[1] and so, God willing, I will now carry out my task as briefly as possible.

There are reckoned to be three kinds of human good.[2] These are of course the benefits of fortune, of the body, and of the soul. The benefits of fortune consist in wealth, honor, favor, and power. And so to begin at the beginning; wealth is not the highest good, as Midas believed, for it is sought and acquired not for its own sake but for the convenience of the body and soul. Nor are honor and favor the highest good, as Augustus used to say, since they are at the discretion of another and are often not experienced by us; and very often, they are bestowed or withdrawn irrespective of merit. Nor is power the highest good, as Caesar maintained, since the more people we control, the more acutely are we harassed by worries, the more dangers we are subject to, the more men and the more business we have to serve, and the more enemies we have.

The benefits of the body consist in strength, health, and beauty. Strength and health are not the supreme good, as Milo of Crotona seemed to think, for we are cast down by the most trifling discomforts; nor is beauty, so much honored by Herillus the Skeptic. No one, however beautiful, could live content in this alone, and beauty is a benefit for others rather than for the beautiful themselves.

Some benefits belong to the irrational and others to the rational part of the soul.[3] The benefits of the irrational part are the keenness of the senses and their enjoyment. Aristippus thought that the highest good lay in both of these. We believe that Happiness lies in neither; not in keenness of sense, for in this we are surpassed by many animals and a keen sense generally disgusts as often as it delights; nor does the highest good consist in the enjoyment of the senses, for this is preceded by longing, accompanied by doubt and followed by regret. One short pleasure is purchased by much prolonged pain. And the intensity of this kind of pleasure lasts only as long as the demands of the body; consider how drink is sweet only as long as one is thirsty. But every demand of the body is a kind of annoyance. Sensual pleasure, therefore, because it is frequently mixed with its opposite, that is pain, is neither pure nor true, nor does it satisfy. And if anyone says that there are some sensual pleasures that do not spring from the demands of the body, I reply that these are so weak that no one finds any happiness in them. Indeed, let no one venture to ascribe happiness to that state that consists of the keenness and delight of the senses, since this state is false, fleeting, and anxious. Trifling amusements do not satisfy the soul, which by natural inclination seeks finer things.

Some good qualities of the rational part of the soul are said to be natural, such as a keen intellect, memory, and a bold and ready will.

Happiness is not in these, for used well they are indeed good, but badly used they are evil. Other good qualities of the rational part of the soul, such as the moral and reflective virtues, are acquired. Is happiness found in moral conduct, as the Stoics and Cynics believe?[4] Certainly not, for the practice of moral virtues such as moderation and endurance is full of toil and difficulty. We will not find the goal we seek in toil, but in rest, for we are endlessly busy to enjoy leisure, and wage war to live in peace. Besides, right conduct is never sought for its own sake but put to use, like a medicine, for cleansing and calming the mind. Neither is Epicurean peace[5] the ultimate goal. For the use of a still mind is the contemplation of truth, as the use of a clear sky is to admit sunlight.

Does happiness then reside in the virtues of reflection, such as the contemplation of truth? Certainly it does. But there is, so to speak, contemplation of different kinds: subcelestial, celestial, and supercelestial. Democritus set as his goal[6] the first of these. Anaxagoras was not satisfied with this, because the celestial is higher than the subcelestial, but he was willing to be content in the contemplation of the celestial for, he said, he was born to contemplate that, and heaven was his homeland. But Aristotle disagreed with this[7] because the consideration of the supercelestial seemed to him altogether more deserving. He thought happiness consisted in the highest activity of the highest power directed to the highest purpose. The soul trapped in a body is able to consider these things in one way, and the soul that is free in another. Aristotle believed that man in the first state is happy, but our Plato denied this, since consideration of the divine in this life is always mixed with uncertainty of intellect and unsteadiness of will. So, according to Plato, true happiness is the property of the soul that, when freed from the body, contemplates the divine.[8] Both angels and God are accounted divine. Avicenna and Al Ghazzali seem to maintain that the soul will be happy in contemplating angels. The Platonists refute this for two reasons. The first is that it is the nature of our intellect to look for the cause of things, and then the cause beyond this cause. For this reason, the search of the intellect never ceases, except it discovers the cause behind which there is no cause, but is itself the cause of causes, and that is God alone. The second reason is that the desire of the will cannot be satisfied by any good so long as we think that some other good remains beyond; therefore it is only satisfied with that good beyond which there is no other. What else is this but God? Therefore in God alone may the search of the intellect and the desire of the will come to rest. The happiness of man therefore consists in God alone, from which it follows that nothing can rest except in its own cause. And since God alone is the real cause of the soul it rests in God alone. But we discussed these things more fully in the *Theology of the Immortality of Souls*.[9]

However, there are two activities of the soul in its relationship to God, for it sees God through the intellect and it rejoices in the knowledge of Him through will. Plato calls the vision ambrosia, the joy, nectar, and the intellect and will, twin wings by which we may fly back to God, as though to our father and homeland. This is why, he says, when pure souls ascend to heaven they feed at the divine table on ambrosia and nectar.[10]

In that happiness the joy surpasses the vision. For as we find more merit with God in this life by loving Him than by searching for Him, so the reward in the next life is greater for loving than searching. We find far more merit by loving than by searching for many reasons. First, because no one in this life truly knows God. But a man truly loves God, no matter how he understands Him, if he despises everything else for His sake. Second, just as it is worse to hate God than to be ignorant of Him, so it is better to love Him than to know Him. Third, we may make ill use of the knowledge of God, for instance, through pride. We cannot misuse the love for Him. Fourth, the man who looks for God pays Him no tribute, but he who loves Him yields to God both himself and all he possesses. So it is that God gives Himself to the lover rather than the investigator. Fifth, in investigating God, we take a long time to make very little progress, but by loving Him we make much progress in a very short time. The reason love unites the mind with God more swiftly, closely, and firmly than cognition is that the power of cognition lies mainly in making distinctions but the power of love lies in union. Sixth, by loving God, not only do we experience greater joy than by seeking Him out, but we are made better people. For these reasons we may conclude that the reward of loving is greater than that of human enquiry.

It befits the lover to enjoy and rejoice in the beloved for that is the aim of love, but it befits the seeker to see. Thus joy in a happy man surpasses vision. Besides we desire to see in order to rejoice; we do not seek to rejoice in order to see. We can find the cause for our desire to see, but we cannot find the cause for our desire to rejoice, other than the very joy itself, as though it is desired for its own sake. We do not desire simply to see, but to see those things that make us rejoice, in a way that makes us rejoice. Nature herself never rejects any joy, but she sometimes rejects cognition, and indeed she rejects life too if she thinks that it will be very burdensome; so that delight is not only the seasoning of cognition but also of life itself. When this is removed everything seems tasteless. Joy is richer than cognition, for not every man that knows rejoices, but those who rejoice necessarily know. Just as nature considers it worse to suffer misery than ignorance, so it is better to rejoice than to know. And just as nature always and everywhere avoids pain on its own account and everything connected with it as being the greatest evil, so she pursues pleasure on its own account, and other things connected with it, as being the highest good. Since the power of cognition, as I have said before, lies mainly in making distinctions, but the power of love lies in union, we are united more closely with God through the joy of love than through cognition, for joy transforms us into beloved God. Just as it is not the man who sees the good, but he who desires it, that becomes good, so likewise the soul becomes divine, not by considering God but by loving Him; as timber becomes fire because it draws heat, not light from the flame. Hence, since the soul is not goodness itself what is good for it must be sought outside its own nature. It follows that a turn of the will, so that will is directed toward what is outside, is more truly based on goodness itself than an intellectual concept that remains something purely internal. For the intellect grasps the object by a kind of imagery, but will strives to transfer itself to its object by natural impulse. Desire, which is wide-ranging and continual, is rooted in being since all created things are always desiring something. Cognition acts through images that are received; it is the property of few beings and is intermittent. Therefore the enjoyment of goodness is more substantial through the medium of desire than through the vision of cognition.

If God were to separate the mind from the will and keep the two apart, the mind might seem to retain its previous form, for it would still be a form of reason; but the will might change its form since it would be a desire lacking the power to choose, a property of reason. But the mind would not enjoy any further good at all; it would be like a creature without taste; nothing would please it; it would find nothing good, nor would it be agreeable to itself or anything else. But will would continue to enjoy to the full some goodness of its own. Therefore enjoyment of the highest good seems to be the property of will rather than intellect. The end of movement, that is, happiness, rightly pertains to will, since that is the aim of movement at its outset. The intellect, understanding things, not so much through their nature but rather through its own, seems to draw things toward itself and for that reason it cannot really be said to move the soul. Since will desires to perceive things as they are in themselves, it draws the soul to things outside itself; and therefore it is will that is the origin of movement. Moreover the end of all movement is outside the soul but is finally connected to the soul as form. Through will the soul greatly rejoices in this end, for the laborer is worthy of his hire. The concern and impulse to attain the good and to avoid evil are based on desire. The will receives a greater reward from God than the intellect, not only because it enjoys Him more fully, but also because the discovery of happiness belongs to will. The more ardently a man loves, the happier he becomes in that he approaches the very substance of happiness itself. What shall we add to this? Since far more people can love God ardently than can know him clearly, the way of love is safer to mankind and far more suitable for the infinite good, which wishes to impart itself to as many as possible.

So it is through will that happiness is attained. Again, what more? Free movement is the property of reasonable beings, and because it is free a man may therefore advance beyond any finite limit whatever, to achieve all that he deserves, so that he can rise above the bliss of many of the angels; indeed, we can rise above them by loving and rejoicing rather than by apprehending. Therefore, by cognizing God, we reduce His size to the capacity and understanding of our mind; but by loving Him we enlarge our mind to the immeasurable breadth of divine goodness. By the first we bring God down to our own scale, by the second we raise ourselves to God. For our cognition is measured by our capacity to understand; but we love Him not only as far as we perceive Him but also as far as we may conceive His divine goodness extending beyond what we can clearly see. When dimly and feebly we look into the depth of God's infinity, our love burns warmly and eagerly and so does our joy. Vision is not the measure of joy as some believe, for he who sees little may love much and vice versa.

Finally, the highest good for the soul is what satisfies it, but it is not really satisfied with its own vision of God. For the vision perceived by the eyes of the soul is a created thing and limited by degrees of perfection, just as the soul is. Yet the soul is never satisfied with any created or finite good. So vision is not the highest good. The soul is satisfied by the God who is seen, rather than by the seeing of Him. The enjoyment of the good in sensual perception arises not because the good moves sense but because sense is reflected, turned toward, and diffused in the good that is presented to it. This spiritual turning and diffusion is delight, as we explained in our book on delight.[11] Thus, even for the mind which has been separated from the body, so to speak, the enjoyment of God does not primarily arise because God reveals Himself to the mind, which in any case is an act of God rather than our own, but it arises because the mind turns to God, and this is joy.

It should not be thought that the soul turns to the vision of God to rest in that, but turns rather to the God who is seen; it desires the vision for what is seen that becomes joined to the soul as form. In the same way there is no relish in the tasting of a flavor, but in the flavor that has been tasted. A craving does not have an imaginary object but a real one; otherwise the desire might be appeased by remembering or imagining the good when it is absent. The vision of God is imaged within us and, as I said before, is limited. For this reason an act of will, which is the turning toward and diffusion of the substantial into the infinite God, partakes more of the infinite than an act of intellect, which is conception of God according to the mind's capacity. Therefore God is the greatest good. Bliss is the enjoyment of God and we enjoy God through will. Through will we move toward God by loving Him, and by being joyful we are enlarged and turned toward Him.

Different souls enjoy different virtues and different ideals of God, and each excels in that virtue in which he particularly delights in this life and which he has followed to the best of his ability. All men, however, enjoy God in His fullness for in these many ideals He remains one. The men who best possess God are those who have the best ideal of Him. Each man understands the wholeness of God according to his capacity and enjoys Him according to his love. For this reason, as Plato said, there is no envy in the choir of Heaven.[12] Because the happiest thing of all is to possess the object of one's love, whoever lives in the possession of what he loves, lives content and satisfied. For if two lovers share their enjoyment with one another, each will rest content in the possession of the beloved and neither will worry that the other may love someone more beautiful. Moreover, although in that respect some have more capacity than others, yet each finds fulfilment according to the limit of his capacity, so that he desires nothing beyond that. Let me add that any man who yields by loving desire to the will and order of divine justice, yields most willingly.

The blessed soul can never be removed from God. For that cannot be done by force. Where is the force that can be inflicted on a soul enveloped in the infinite power of God? Nor will the soul leave willingly, for the will is not moved to anything except by reason of the good, and once it has cleaved to that which is the principle of all goodness and understands it it is never moved from there to anything else. And since it is the nature of goodness to direct the force of desire toward itself, it follows that infinite goodness does so everlastingly. Again, since will finds rest in anything according to its measure of goodness, in infinite goodness it finds infinite rest. But if the soul, even while involved in the movement of the body, chooses the happiness that is free from all change, it will do so far more when it is beyond movement. Nor can the lower parts of the soul divert the higher ones from this state, since the lower will yield to the higher for ever, when the soul turns toward the infinite existence of God.

Lastly, if ever the soul had to be separated from this state, either the soul would not realize it, in which case being ignorant of God it could not be happy; or else it would know, in which case it could not be happy either, for it would be sick and afraid. Therefore, he who once finds happiness in God finds it forever. Read happily, happy Lorenzo, what your Marsilio Ficino has written here about happiness, much of which you discovered yourself. The subject is treated briefly here as befits a letter, but more thoroughly in the books on *Love* and on *Theology*.[13]

The end. Praise be to God.

Farewell. [1.115]

DIVINE PROVIDENCE AND THE GOOD

60

Since all things are well governed by God, all things should be accepted for the best

Marsilio Ficino to Bishop Campano, the poet: greetings.

Tell me, Campano, do you ever laugh at the arrogance of mortals? I often do. I ridicule it in the hope that I may avoid it. Boys cannot understand the counsel of their elders, nor peasants the thoughts of the wise. However, with unbecoming arrogance, the earthly creature Man often presumes to fathom the reasons of divine nature, and to search into the purpose of its providence. And, what is worse, men of all ages blasphemously discuss the divine mysteries at banquets, and even in brothels. Pythagoras justly prohibited speaking of these mysteries without divine insight.[1] No man, but the divine, Campano, perceives the divine. For Paul the Apostle rightly said: "The things of God knoweth no man, but the spirit of God."[2] Again, no man speaks more falsely about divine matters than he who measures them to a hair's breadth. In Isaiah,[3] God speaks thus: "He taketh the wise in their own craftiness." And again "The Lord knoweth the thoughts of the wise, that they are vain."[4]

It should therefore be enough for man to know that the beautiful working of this single universe is governed by the wise architect, on whom it depends. From goodness itself only good can spring. And what proceeds from that can only be ordered well. Therefore, everything should be accepted for the best. Who thus understands the divine, and loves it, is divine by nature, good in practice, joyful in hope, blessed in reward.

Farewell, O blessed man. [1.68]

61

Ideas, according to Plato, exist in the divine mind

Marsilio Ficino to Giovanni Cavalcanti, his unique friend: greetings.

Our Plato in the *Timaeus*, following and supporting Timaeus, the Pythagorean,[1] tells us that the world is begotten of God. He shows us the threefold cause of this creation;[2] its efficient cause, its final cause, and its formal cause. He has it that the world was made by God's power through the grace of His goodness, as a model of divine wisdom. As the design of a whole building and of its parts exists in the mind of an architect, so the design of this whole world and of its parts exists in the divine intelligence beyond the world. That world beyond he calls the world of intelligence, and eternal; this world he calls the world of senses, and temporal. The models of things in this world he calls ideas in the divine intelligence, and the resemblances of the divine intelligence in this world he calls images and shadows.

And so we may by all means ridicule those ignorant people who so foolishly proclaim that Plato wrongly asserted that universal ideas and principles are separated not only from physical bodies, but also from the divine intelligence and even from each other, like little clouds scattered through the air by the wind. But since we produced many arguments against these people in the books we wrote at your house in Regnano, let it suffice for now to follow what Plato says in the *Timaeus*.

Let us first consider,[3] he says, what is usually asked before anything else in questions about the universe—whether it has always existed without beginning or whether it had an origin. Clearly it can be seen and touched and is physical. All things of this kind affect the senses, and are known through them. It is agreed that such things are being and have been created. Now that which is created must, as we affirm, of necessity be created by a cause. It is indeed difficult to find the maker and father of the world and, when you have found him, it is impossible to describe him to ordinary people.

Let us consider again whether the maker of the world followed a model that is always one and always the same, or whether we should say he followed one that has been created. If the world is beautiful and its creator is good, he would have preferred to follow an eternal model; if otherwise, which would be blasphemous to admit, he would have followed a finite model in place of the eternal. Since in truth the world is the most beautiful of all things that are begotten and its author the best of all causes, there is no doubt that he followed a model without beginning or end. So the creation is brought forth according to that model that may be understood by reason and wisdom alone, and that abides unchanging. Thus it must follow that this world is an image of the other.

A little later on Plato adds:[4] And now we may explain for what reason the author of all things willed creation and this universe. He was good,

and the good is never touched by any shadow of envy. Since envy was so
foreign to him, he wished all things to become as like him as they could.
Should anyone accept this from prudent men as the first cause of the
creation of the world, he would be quite right to do so.

A little further on Plato adds:[5] It should also be said that this world is
a living and intelligent being created by divine providence. Let us see what
follows from this. What being did God make the world like? We do not
think that he made it like any particular species of being. For if it had
been made like an imperfect being, it would certainly not be beautiful; but
on the contrary we believe it was made like that being of whom other
beings both individually and by kind are parts. The world of divine intelligence certainly encompasses within itself every living being that can be
perceived by the mind alone, just as this world contains us and all other
creatures perceived by the senses. Now God, wishing to make this world
in every way like the most beautiful and most perfect of all beings, containing within its limits all creatures appropriate to its nature, caused it to
be brought under His gaze.

Are we right to say that there is one world? Would it not be more
correct to say that there are many, or indeed innumerable worlds? In
truth there is one, since it is formed in the image of one. Because it contains all living beings that may be comprehended, it can have no companion. For otherwise there would have to be another being which contained
these two, and to whom these two parts belonged. And then this world
could not rightly be said to be a copy of such worlds but of this third one.
So that this world should be most like that Absolute Being in its unity,
neither two, nor an infinite number of worlds, were created, but one only-
begotten world has ever been, and ever will be.

Listen to Timaeus, the Pythagorean and master of Plato, who said in
similar words that ideas exist in God. "The world," he said, "is the best
of all things that have been created, since it proceeded from the most
perfect creator, who looked to no handmade models, but to an idea and
to intelligible substance. The creation, made in exact and perfect accord
with this idea, is without blemish and of matchless beauty. This world is
at all times complete as far as the senses are concerned, since its model,
which contains within itself all intelligible beings, leaves nothing outside.
For it is the absolute measure of what is intelligible, just as this world is
of what can be sensed." Thus said Timaeus.

We have heard how the ideas of all things exist in a living and eternal model which is the most excellent of all that is intelligible, absolute and omnipresent, outside which nothing intelligible can exist. Such a model can be none other than God himself. What could be clearer than that?

When Plato said that God made all sense objects in the likeness of intelligible ones, he added that He made them in the likeness of Himself, the original model and God being almost the same. For truly, however many kinds of creature there are in this world, there are at least as many ideas in God. These ideas are intelligible principles through which all things are made. Created forms, which are in matter not in itself alive, either do not live or scarcely do so, but ideas have life because they are in the living God. Therefore Plato says in the same book that the divine mind by the power of thought has created with his own substance as many forms in this world as he has seen ideas in his living self. This is what Plato held, Giovanni, as you have been hearing. His predecessors and those that followed him also held this. Believe Marsilio, that whoever holds otherwise does not hold to the truth. [1.43]

62

The cause of sinning; hope; the remedy

Marsilio Ficino to Giovanni Cavalcanti, his unique friend: greetings.

Since souls are divine, why do they live such unholy lives? Because they inhabit an unholy house in an unholy land. Some go astray through lack of care or knowledge, and there is nothing to wonder at in that, insofar as we live in the murky sediment of this world. Others err through too great a love for the body, and that is not strange either, since the body is the companion and child of the soul. Yet others fail through lack of trust, either in immortality or in divine mercy—and what wonder, since they live their lives in a region of death and cruelty? Others again fail because of overconfidence in the divine mercy, or that all will be put right tomorrow. Both lack of trust and overconfidence are very dangerous: the first torments a man, the second deceives him.

The essence of prudence, therefore, is always to use the present moment as well as we can, and our sole refuge is to commit ourselves constantly to God. This done, the best hope is to remember that God understands how difficult and dangerous is the province which he has given us to live in and govern. Infinite goodness rises far above finite evil. God has ordained various degrees of chastisement and penance, for the particular good of the individual, and for the common good. But he has also established many degrees of rich reward. [1.44]

63

Vainly and to excess we strive for our satisfaction in those things which in no wise satisfy themselves

Marsilio Ficino to Mankind: greetings.

You seek satisfaction everywhere, on the principle that after you have found this one thing, you will search for nothing further. But you are always seeking anew as many things as possible, for the very reason that nowhere do you attain this one thing. So do you wish me to say why you attain satisfaction nowhere? Perhaps because it is outside yourself that you are seeking. If, therefore, mortal possessions cannot satisfy the immortal soul, at least take care that the soul itself may give satisfaction to mortal things. Mark what I say. I do not say that the soul should satisfy itself, for how can that which is formed and perfected by another satisfy itself? Alas, pitiable creatures, how much wasted effort! We seek our satisfaction in those things that in no wise satisfy themselves. In truth, only that which satisfies itself, satisfies all things wholly. Nothing, however, can satisfy itself, but the immeasurable good that comes from itself and returns to itself. Here alone then, here, I say, we should seek that which will satisfy us. Nor would this bring regret, for no one ever follows the good in vain, who follows it truly. For the good itself being without measure, blooms and comes forth in abundance from every point; and our desire to follow it truly is without doubt something good. But he alone truly desires and follows the good who, by grace of the supreme good itself, through which individual good things have their being and are preserved, follows at every step individual things that are good. [3.25]

64

Faith in divine law is confirmed by knowledge[1]

Marsilio Ficino of Florence to his most reverend friends: greetings.

Human laws are accepted from the outset or, once accepted, are kept in being in these ways only: through arguments from common custom based on human and natural principles; through some dictatorial authority or the force of arms; or through ease and convenience of living and the allurements of pleasure. Not even the disposition of the stars[2] can ever establish laws among men by any means other than these. For this reason, if we see that any law has at any time arisen among reasonable men and been widely disseminated, even though the convincing arguments of many men are opposed to it, even though the force of the powerful rages against it, and even though it is clear that all anticipation and enjoyment of human pleasure are completely removed by it, we are forced to conclude that such a law is not a human law nor does it depend on heavenly fate, but is wholly divine and has its origin in some power higher than heaven.[3]

Now what is concluded from inescapable proof is understood with certain knowledge. Therefore whoever trusts in such a law for such a reason will have both knowledge as the mother of his faith, and faith made sure by knowledge. He who does not take account of this cannot take account of himself. He who does take some account of this but does not trust in it, trusts nothing. What others choose, I do not know. For myself, I would rather trust with divine faith than know with human knowledge. Since divine faith is far more certain than human wisdom, such trust is always confirmed by true knowledge, while human knowledge sometimes wavers through lack of trust.

Therefore, so that we can trust something somewhere that is true, let us now trust truth itself which, since it admits no ignorance or deception, certainly keeps no one in ignorance and deceives nobody. Furthermore, so that we can place our hope in something somewhere that is good, let us place our hope in the good itself which, since it does no evil and suffers no injustice, never disappoints those who hope for it and never abandons those who love it. It has given them light that they may hope and set them afire that they may love; for the movement toward the good can depend on no other source than the good itself, and can return[4] there by no other means than that by which it came forth. [4.1]

65

He who by his own will cuts himself
off from God, who is all good, inevitably cuts
himself off, even against his will, from every good

Marsilio Ficino to Leone Michaeli, the Venetian nobleman: greetings.

Were one of us to love the good itself, which is wholly good, as eagerly as we all habitually love one good thing after another, though none of these is good without the good itself, such a man would undoubtedly always experience at least as much good and joy as we now constantly all experience evil and pain. In fact, his joy would be far stronger than this real anguish of ours and sweeter than our unreal pleasure; just as the substance of the good itself is more powerful than evil and truer than the image of goodness, and as the pure mind is more clear-sighted than the impure.

Now why should we be surprised if all evils pursue us, when we ourselves, abandoning the first good, namely God, wrongly pursue individual things as good, when all these things, without the first good, are evil? We deservedly fall into every evil, albeit against our will, every time we willfully fall from that which is wholly good. Why do we mindlessly and miserably stray hither and thither for so long? Certainly, all the time that we are pursuing merely one thing after another, we are running away from the One itself, which is everything. But he who simply pursues the One itself, in that One soon attains everything.[1] Without a doubt the mind, which depends solely upon that which is above all things, can attain all things. Thus man alone among living beings has received the power to achieve whatever he wishes, provided that he desires above all to pursue in whatever he wishes that which alone is good.

Therefore, lion-hearted Leone, I have a high regard for you because you are no longer troubled about many things; but, as our most trustworthy witness Carlo Valguli testifies, you have long since chosen that good part,[2] which, since it not only flows forth from the fullness of its own fountain but also flows back into the same, satisfies the whole thirst of those who taste it and will never be taken away from that mind that has once experienced it. [4.18]

66

Those who are blessed, those who are nearest to the blessed,
those who are further away, and those who are furthest away

Marsilio Ficino to his fellow philosopher Lotterio Neroni: greetings.

Blessed are those celestial beings who never perceive anything but the Good.[1]

Nearest to them come those who, even though they cannot but perceive evils on every side, being placed in the most evil of realms, never join with those evils, since they never depart from the Supreme Good.

In the third place are those who have fallen, but after a time rise again to the Supreme Good and thus realize that what was evil was to have yielded to evils.[2] They realize that they surrender to evils only when they themselves desire that the greater good within them should give way to the lesser. They realize that where the Good of all good is found, there only is the remedy for all evils discovered.

Lastly, those must be considered the lowest and most wretched who have shut their eyes to the rays of the Supreme Good shining everywhere. So shut are their eyes that, although they are within this very light, apart from which nothing good is seen, they can never see how great an evil it is to be forever separate from that Good, without which everything perceived is evil. Indeed, however deep their misery outside the divine happiness, these men still do not look up within the divine brilliance lest by looking up they become happy. But in their own darkness they imagine and perceive through faint glimmers of that brilliance, as though they were under a delusion, so that by such imagining and perceiving they are miserable.

The world, as Christ the Master of Life says, "lieth in wickedness,"[3] principally because we lie in the world and we are wicked. To unsound and unquiet minds nothing appears sound and nothing still.[4] Why do we so often unjustly blame this iron age? As soon as man, preferring iron to gold, became iron, then the age, which till that time had been naturally golden, turned wholly to iron for him, as he deserved.

Is it any wonder that all manner of evils pursue us from every quarter when we ourselves, having abandoned the first Good, namely, God, wrongly pursue individual things as though they were good? For without the first Good they are evil. It is not unjust that we fall into every evil against our will every time we wilfully fall from that which is wholly good. So we should never bewail the times, but rather the times should bewail us, and that most bitterly!

Let us therefore gain for ourselves, let us gain with our whole heart that burning gold that the heavenly eagle[5] shows us: the pure light of truth, ablaze with the love of goodness. But we shall not easily obtain fire from light; rather the reverse, we shall obtain light from fire. For even gold does not burn when struck by rays from a distant fire; but when permeated by heat from one nearby, then indeed it shines. And it is because it does not really shine from the fire but becomes hot from the fire that it becomes completely incandescent. Thus only if we are afire with the love of the Highest Good, God alone, shall we at once shine with His splendor, and we shall be divine.

God is light, God is love.[6] For him who loves God before all else, God shines before all else. When that Sun shines for a man, that Sun through which all things shine, then for him all things everywhere naturally reflect Its light. Furthermore, everything becomes extraordinarily sweet to him who never tastes anything except within that sweetness without whose quality nothing sweet can be produced or experienced.

To what purpose all this? Clearly, Lotterio, to answer your letters on theological subjects as well as I may. For of late you have stirred me by your magnificent writing to raise my thoughts to these considerations. So please accept them, such as they are, for they are yours. I return them to you.

1 August 1479.
Careggi. [5.20]

67

In the midst of evils there is no refuge, unless it be with the highest good[1]

Marsilio Ficino to his friends: greetings.

Tragedies truly lament the wretched fate of mortals; but fate also brings about their truest tragedy. A tragedy is an imaginary life of men; but the life of men seems to be their truest tragedy. Leaving aside for the moment those utterances of orators, poets, and philosophers in which every single evil and trouble of mankind is enumerated, let me now briefly express the full misery of our human race with a single instance: those who are commonly regarded as the happiest of men are usually the most miserable.

According to philosophers there are three kinds of life:[2] the first is dedicated to study, the second to action, and the third to pleasure. Those who in any one of these lives are thought to be at the height of happiness are generally in the depth of misery. Certainly those who in the eyes of the world appear to excel in the study of truth are often more than anyone else locked in an insoluble dilemma of uncertainty. For while they have been inquisitively eager to learn every single thing and to make bold public statements on each, they have quite rightly learned to have doubts about all this; and since they believe they have no one superior or equal to them, they have no one left whom they may trust or consult. O foolish wisdom, O knowledge more confusing than all ignorance! Solomon, the wisest of all men according to divine authority, says that such knowledge brings toil and diappointment.[3] Paul the Apostle asserts that God holds this wisdom to be unwisdom.[4] The prophet Isaiah declares that the thinking based on this wisdom is judged by God to be vanity.[5] This seems properly to apply to those who hope to see true things in something other than the light of truth itself, like someone who, captivated by the light of the mind, believes he sees the colors of things not in the splendor of the sun but by the light of the eye alone.[6]

Next, those who are considered to have reached the highest rank in active life really hold that position in suffering, and when they are said to have most power, then are they most in servitude. Finally, those who too readily yield to pleasures often fall into torments, and when they seem to be gorging themselves as much as they can, they are desperately hungry and thirsty. O miserable fate of mortals, fate more miserable than misery itself! Where shall we wretches flee, if we are ever to escape from our misery? To the philosophy of the Sophists,[7] ever eager for new knowledge? Or to power? Or pleasure? Alas, we already fly far too often to these but in vain. The proud philosophy of the Sophists entangles us in most troublesome questions. Power casts us into the most acute and perilous bondage. Lastly pleasure, which is brief and false, afflicts us with suffering, which is long and real.

Perhaps it would be worthwhile, if we wish to attain what we are seeking, to flee only to that which does not flee anywhere. But that alone cannot flee anywhere which cannot be moved anywhere, since it fills the universe. However, is there any need even to be moved to that which is not moved anywhere, which is present everywhere in every single thing? Then let us not be moved or distracted by many things, but let us remain in unity as much as we are able, since we find eternal unity and the one eternity, not through movement or multiplicity, but through being still and being one. But what is that one, friends? Come on, then, say what it is. Is it not that selfsame good that fills the universe? For nothing can be found that is not good in the presence of the good itself. It is the good itself, do you not see? It is the good itself that all things seek, since all things are from that good. And for this reason every single thing is perfected through that good to the extent that each strives to hold to it. But we can hold fast to the good, it seems to me, only through love of the good, since it is the very nature of the good to be sought after; and the reason for its being sought after is that it is good. Moreover, as soon as we love what is wholly good for us, we cleave to it, since love itself is something good, nearest of all to the highest good, as it is the flame of the good; and wherever the flame of the good burns most fiercely, there its light shines most clearly.

What more? If God is the good itself, and the light of the good, and the love of the light of the good, I beg you, friends, let us love, let us love before all else the good that is light and the light that is good. For thus we shall not merely love our God: we shall delight in loving Him, for God Himself is love, love itself is God. Therefore first and foremost let us burn with that love, without whose heat nothing has heat, that we may reflect, according to our desire, the blessed light of Him without whose splendor nothing has light! Come, friends! Let us rest in that which never recedes and there we shall ever remain. Let us serve the one Master of all, who serves no one, so that we are not enslaved by anything, but are the masters of everything. Let us delight in God if we can, and we can if we will, for through the will is the delight and the delight is in the will. Let us delight, I say, in that which alone fills the infinite; thus alone shall we be completely filled, thus alone shall we rejoice fully and truly. For where the good abounds without defect, there delight is experienced without pain, and everywhere joy to the full.[8] [4.5]

68

Prayers are not to be despised

Marsilio Ficino to Francesco Marescalchi of Ferrara, his distinguished fellow philosopher: greetings.

I have not yet finished the book about the Christian religion, Francesco, because during August, while I was still correcting it, I caught a fever and diarrhea. Perhaps this year Saturn threatened me with this. At the time of my birth, it was in the ascending sign of Aquarius and was then in Cancer, my sixth house.

But now let us leave the heavenly bodies, for there are those who make light of such subjects, and let us come to something beyond the heavens. Listen to what has happened to me during this illness. There were times when I became so weak, Marescalchi, that I almost despaired of recovery. I then turned over in my mind those great works I have read during the last thirty years, to see if anything occurred to me that could ease a sick heart. Except for the Platonic authors, the writings of men did not help at all, but the works of Christ brought much more comfort than the words of philosophers. What is more, I offered prayers to the divine Mary and begged for some sign of recovery. I felt some relief immediately, and in dreams received a clear indication of recovery. So I do not owe a cock to Aesculapius,[1] but my heart and body to Christ and His mother. One must always accept everything as leading to the good, Marescalchi. Could it be that God wished to warn me by a sign during this illness that I must in future declare the Christian teaching with greater zeal and depth? A few days later, with a similar prayer, I was freed of the heat of my urine.

Listen, if you will, to another thing that is wonderful and true. My father, Ficino, who was a surgeon in Florence and outstanding among his contemporaries, was once called by a countryman named Pasquino to heal his son Tommaso whose head had been most gravely wounded. After the doctor had examined the incurable wound he felt sure that the boy would soon be dead and left without expecting to return. The parents of the sick child whom the doctor had abandoned offered prayers to the divine Mary to heal their son. Now, at the very time that they were praying Ficino was in a light sleep resting under an oak tree on his journey when there appeared to him a woman whose countenance was worthy of reverence, and she rebuked him thus:

"Why are you ungrateful toward God, Ficino? You do not give freely what you have freely received from Him." He replied, "I give bread daily to those in need." She rejoined: "Give generously also to those who need the gifts of your art."

Three days later, the countryman came to the doctor again asking him to come back and treat his son. Ficino was utterly astonished as he had been convinced the boy would be dead. He returned, without charge, mindful of his recent dream and the prayers of the parents, for the countryman had related what prayers he had offered and at what hour. Eventually the boy, who had been beyond the hope of the doctor and the art of healing, fully recovered. From that time on, Ficino frequently offered prayers to Mary, with fortunate results for the health of those entrusted to his care. So warn your friends not to despise prayers, for even Aristotle did not scorn them during the illness of his son-in-law.

6 September 1474. [1.80]

69

A theological prayer to God

Marsilio Ficino to a dear friend, and admirable man, Bernardo Rucellai: greetings.

Above men, nothing is dearer to me than to speak with God. Among men nothing is dearer to me than to speak with you. God, our guide in life and source of our friendship, always hears what I say to you. You will now hear what I often say to God. I make use of this prayer to God each day, Rucellai, so that he may enlighten my mind and strengthen my will. Use it yourself too, sometimes, unless you happen to have a better one, for there is no one whom I would rather God favored than you. On occasion I have heard our Lorenzo de' Medici, moved by divine frenzy, sing similar prayers to the lyre.[1] But now hear the prayer itself.

O boundless light, observing yourself, seeing all things in yourself!
O infinite sight, shining from yourself, illuminating all!
O spiritual eye, whom alone, and by whom alone, spiritual eyes see!

O immortal life of those that see!
O all goodness of the living!

You fulfill the whole desire of Your lovers. You alone, God, kindle within us the desire for everything which is good. You alone are everything good. I beseech You, most pure light, I beseech You, through Yourself clear the clouded vision of the mind that I may see You, for You fire my frozen heart, whereby I thirst for You. Enlarge my narrow vision that I may see You, as You raise my downcast eye so that I look up.

For You penetrate my inmost being, O deep of the deeps, as You also raise me aloft, O highest of the high. What is it that penetrates my inmost being? What is it that lifts the highest in me? Certainly it is the miraculous rays of Your amazing goodness and beauty, that wonderfully pour through minds, souls and bodies, everlastingly. By these You work in me, though I do not know it; by these, I say, sole majesty, You attract me, compel me, consume me utterly. See, already, see! I hasten breathless toward You, O matchless beauty. But ah! this lover of Yours limps haltingly. Alas! unhappy man, he limps! Stretch out Your holy hand to one who limps, O my hope, I entreat You. I beseech You, lead him You attract, welcome him You capture, cool him You burn, bring joy to him You torment. May You gladden him, O wonderful joy, source of all joys. For I know that whatever we desire is contained in Your unity, or rather it is Your unity we desire. If we like this or that good thing, it is clearly not because of this or that. In reality we want each good thing because of the quality of goodness in it. If the river of life, which runs through all things, flows from one spring of goodness, that is its own perpetual and abundant source, assuredly we long to drink from that source of goodness itself.

O eternal fount of all that is good, we thirst for You everywhere. And so our thirst is not quenched by this good or that good, or by both together, if we really see that goodness itself is above them both. And may You, our God, may You alone quench this burning thirst, You, I say, the goodness in all, lest You make all Your worshipers thirst so long in vain. O supreme mind, so far from forgetfullness, O supreme wisdom, without trace of folly. Nothing that You have made in Your wisdom is hidden from You. You despise none of those things that You create by Your bountiful will. And You create everything. Do You not care for the least of earthly things? Most certainly You do, and for those things that do not care about You. Do You not care for the least of them, feed them and fulfil them? Do

You despise us alone, who alone on earth do not despise Your majesty? Do You allow us always to wander without rest, we who alone trust that we can find rest only in You? Mean ingratitude is far from the highest good. Deception is far from the highest truth. Alas! You deceive us wretches, indeed You deceive us, if You wound us with Your arrows, and compel us to sigh restlessly for You every day. Nor do You ever heal our wounds if You make us leave temporal things to serve You yet do not replace them with things eternal. You deceive us if You have ordained that those who zealously worship You should lead a life more wretched than beasts on earth, and yet do not reserve for them a happier life hereafter. But this You do reserve for us, so that we are all filled with hope, O savior of the world, sole security and refuge of the human race, within whom all that is good for man exists, without whom nothing is good.

The perfect clarity of Your intelligence enlightens our intelligence so that it may gaze on You and take form within You; Your burning love kindles our desire to love You and unites us to You. And so Your eternal life continually renews our life within itself. And we, who are endowed with the intelligence of immortals and a will capable of ruling mortals, are first and foremost made for immortal life. By virtue of this, the mind, united with eternity, is separated from temporal suffering. It partakes of the eternal to the extent that it subdues desires for the temporal. So every activity of the soul connects with eternity in its own way; will through willing, intelligence through understanding, life through living. Eternity, which encompasses the lesser activities of the soul, has already embraced it in its first action, as life. And so, O best Father, both by law of inheritance and by Your gift we shall one day share Your bliss.

But, we beg You, let us share it now. We beseech You, if it be Your will, let us share it now. If it is not yet Your will, because we are not yet worthy, at least let us not be enmeshed by the false allurements of this world, nor succumb to its threats and blows. Have pity on us, most tender Father, have pity on Your children, care for those that are Yours. We beg You care for Your own and restore those whom You have created; of You alone are we born, since You alone can satisfy our mind and heart by Your pure truth and goodness. So have pity on Your children, banished in this forest full of woe, so far from their heavenly country. We beseech You have pity on us, who are Yours, who long for You both day and night, as for our father and country; for in one's own country there is peace and true good, in exile there is anxiety, false good, and real evil. In life, then, we seem to be separated from evils only for a short time, and for a short time only taste something of true goodness and peace. For a short time, only through resolution of mind or devotion we cleave to You.

Rid us, dear Father, of what has separated us from You for so long: distrust, despair, and indifference. Give back to us, dear Father, what unites us to You: true faith, firm hope, and burning love. Give these back to us, O light of lights and life of the living, lest separated from You and left to ourselves we should, like the dead, at once sink into outer darkness. May we who have lived for You devotedly now live for You spiritually, as far as we are able. May we dwell in Your very being forever. In You may we shine and burn, may we blaze and be made joyful. May we rejoice in bliss without end, beyond the measure of our desires.

May we, without distraction, infinitely love Your infinite beauty. May we without surfeit eternally enjoy Your infinite good. [1.116]

70

The usefulness of the leisured life

Marsilio Ficino to Andrea Cambini, Guardian of the fortress: greetings.

When strolling in the marketplace with our friend, the distinguished Francesco Casato, your fine letter was delivered to me, in which you say that you have now organized a life of leisure for yourself in charge of that fortress, and that in this position everything is available according to your desire; except the divine, which is missing. For this reason you ask me to give my book on religion to Francesco, the son of Berlinghieri, a man of learning and character, so that he can send it on to you.

First, I am indeed glad that you say you have found leisure in the heights of your fortress; certainly, only in the high watchtower of the serene mind does one find that heavenly and joyous peace. The deep valley of the senses is buffeted on every side by the currents of Acheron, Styx, Cocytus, and Phlegethon.[1]

But I can only wonder, when you add that in this leisure you are provided in abundance with human things, but with the divine not at all. For, as you know, since other things are outside us and only in particular places, they are sought in movement, activity, and effort, but the divine, being within us and everywhere, is comprehended in stillness, leisure, and peace. Thus if, as you say, you are truly at leisure it is only the human things you lack that all require excessive activity, but the divine you have in abundance, whose infinite light shining everywhere is reflected in the clear and penetrating eye of the mind as often as that eye turns toward it aright. But the eye of the mind, as if divine by its own nature, turns toward that light once it is not distracted by the anxieties of human affairs. In fact to be turned toward the divine sun is simply not to be turned away from it.

But why are you asking for our *Religion*,[2] dearest companion? In my opinion you are already sufficiently religious if, through leisure, you have been freed from cares about lower things and by your nature have been reunited with the peace of the highest.

But ah! While I write I see what my companion wants. Everyone knows why handsome men take much more pleasure in mirrors than ugly ones do; thus my Cambini, being a man who has already become thoroughly religious, desires my book on divine matters as a mirror in which he may perceive his religion as his own reflection. I shall send this mirror of mine, as soon as I can. Or rather, to put it more correctly, I shall direct the pupil of my eye toward you. Looking into this pupil, you will clearly see both yourself and me at the same time. For those who live with a single heart can also see with a single eye, and in a single eye are seen.

But lest I should now go on longer than usual, farewell. Though I see that because of your great love for Marsilio you do not want me to say farewell so promptly, so that you may fare better. Do you indeed wish for a slightly longer letter as is usual for those who love from a distance? Then accept a greeting from a mutual friend of ours, with which you may fare better! That man of letters, Paolo Saxia, bids me greet you.

So now farewell indeed. [1.126]

71

*The medicine for worldly maladies
is adoration of God who is above the world*

Marsilio Ficino to Bernardo Bembo of Venice, the illustrious knight.

Since man's heavenly Father has ordained that our homeland will be heaven, we can never be content while we dwell on earth, a region far removed from our homeland. Yet such a fate is common, not only to men, but to all created things without exception, so that nowhere do they seek rest save at their own source; and for the sake of rest they try to set their end where they had their beginning. Thus water and earth descend to the depths; fire and air seek the heights; moles and suchlike hide themselves in the bowels of the earth; most other creatures tread the surface of the earth; fish born in the sea, swim in the sea. Even so the souls of men, by a common, natural impulse, continually seek heaven, whence they are created, and the King of heaven, beyond. But since the natural desire for God, instilled in us by God, ought not to be unfulfilled (otherwise supreme reason, which does nothing in vain, has bestowed it upon us in vain), it follows that the souls of men are eternal, in order that one day they may be able to reach the eternal, divine good that their nature desires.

From what we have said it follows that, as our souls are never fulfilled with earthly food, nor while they gorge on earthly things can they enjoy the heavenly feast, so in this life they strive with all their might to cling to the King of heaven. For the less they are tainted by the bitter tastes of earth, and the more they are refreshed by the sweet waters of heaven, the more eagerly are they drawn toward the spring of sweetness that is above heaven. The nearer we approach the Lord of the world, the further we depart from worldly slavery. And, as in our homeland we hold fast to Him by beholding and rejoicing, so, away from that homeland, we hold fast to Him by total loving and adoring.

For this reason, nowhere is there found a medicine adequate for earthly diseases, except divine love and worship. Nor is that wrong. For in any illness, where the medicine does not overcome the condition of the evil humor, it is transformed into the humor, disorders the body, saps the strength, and thus increases the burden upon them. Therefore, as all our infirmity and adversity is of the body, and worldly, undoubtedly anyone who tries to help an ill of this sort with bodily and worldly medicines labors in vain. Believe me, the need here is for a far stronger medicine; a medicine, I say, that is spiritual and above the world, whence it may drive out bodily and worldly illnesses.

Were we suffering only from one ailment or another, then perhaps any doctor would suffice. But our plague is everything evil. Therefore our antidote is everything good. Our disease is insatiable desire and continual turbulence, therefore our doctor is immeasurable good and eternal peace. Should anyone deny that our medicine is the true adoration of God, there is no remedy left for his ills, and all hope of health is removed.

But in truth, he who trusts in divine remedies, grows strong as soon as he trusts. [3.4]

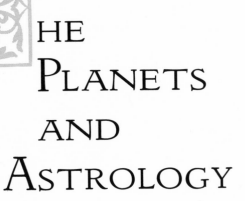

HE
PLANETS
AND
ASTROLOGY

72

Venus subdues Mars, and Jupiter Saturn[1]

Marsilio Ficino to Rinaldo Orsini, Archbishop of Florence.

A few days ago the illustrious Papal Commissary, Pietro Placentino, having been requested in your name, first by letter and then very strongly by word of mouth, not only most generously promised what I had sought concerning the obligation of revenue, but also confirmed it in writing. Then, when I wished to thank you personally for the favor granted at your behest, ill health detained me for many days. At last I determined to make the attempt the day before yesterday, but my breath so failed me in mid-journey that I was scarcely able to walk back home. Soon it was reported to me that your favor[2] had been suspended. I was utterly astonished.

When I looked most carefully for the cause of this reversal, I could not find it on earth; but at last I discovered it in heaven. Do you wonder at this, reverend father? But when Thales of Miletus fell upon earth, did he not rise in heaven, so that he might there perceive those things that he had not seen here?[3] So I observed what had recently prevented my coming to you; and found that it was a malign aspect of Saturn, which was square to the Moon. Whence I concluded that your favor to me had been intercepted by the wiles of a certain Saturnine man. At first, I abandoned almost all hope of remedy, for I considered that perhaps Saturn was the most powerful, as well as the highest, of the planets. But then I recalled what the ancient sages say, not without very good reason, in their fables about Saturn and Jupiter, Mars and Venus; they say that Mars is bound by Venus, and Saturn by Jupiter.[4] This simply means that the benignity of Jupiter and Venus holds in check the malignity of Saturn and Mars. I believe, therefore, that an injury inflicted by a Saturnine man may be effectively cured by one of a Jovial disposition. Now, in whom do I see the full reflection of Jupiter, his power and his gifts? At present I find no one in Florence except you.

People will perhaps laugh at a priest who heeds astronomy. But I, relying on the authority of the Persians, Egyptians, and Chaldeans, considered that while earthly matters were indeed the concern of others, heavenly matters in truth were the sole concern of the priest; so that while human affairs might be left to human counsel, matters for supreme authority should be referred to the ruler of heaven. But do you wish us now to set heavenly matters aside? Let us do so. What therefore shall I ask? This one thing; that since you are above Caesar himself in everything else, you should not allow yourself to seem beneath even Pilate[5] in this one point. But may it be your will that what was written in the first place by the Commissary with your authority, in my presence and on my behalf, may remain written. This, reverend father, is what I ask so that there may be time for philosophy. Nevertheless, may your will be done. [2.10]

73

Evils are not really from the stars, but from a defect in material or understanding

Giovanni Cavalcanti to Marsilio Ficino, the Platonic Philosopher.

In my opinion you sometimes esteem certain things very highly, and because you so esteem them, on that account you fear them. Although such things should be valued a very, very little, nevertheless, I think that by so great a man as you they should be valued even less. So, my Marsilio, you will not complain to me of Saturn's malice any more. By Hercules, the stars can do us no harm; they cannot, I say, because they do not wish to. Moreover, for heavenly beings, to wish is to be able. Again, under what law might they harm us, the sons of the highest Good? For they are led by those who draw their origin solely from that same highest Good. And those most fortunate ones impel the stars in their circuits entirely in accord with the principle of the Good itself.

If we see, and those with experience know, how greatly the second and earthly father cherishes his sons (which father may scarcely be called father when compared to the heavenly Father), then how greatly may we suppose the first and true Father loves us? Certainly, in marvelous measure. So, we are never harmed by those who live together in our Father's most desired home. Henceforth, beware of transferring your blame to that supreme star that has caused you to be heaped up with almost infinite and very great gifts. Lest vainly I attempt to enumerate them one by one, consider: when you were sent to be an ornament to the floral city,[1] already through you filled with flowers, did not that star purpose to look down on you with the same aspect as he looked down on the divine Plato's arising,[2] so that Athens might be made illustrious?

Reply to me, I beg. Whence that wonderful intelligence, by which you know what Saturn is, who completes his course in thirty years? You know what effects he causes on earth by his position in relation to this or that place; and you do not ignore them. Come, tell me, whence that robust and healthy body[3] by which you have made your way by disused and over-grown paths through the whole of Greece, even penetrating into Egypt, to bring to us those most wise men of old on your shoulders? Certainly a bold undertaking. For this posterity will owe very much to you, so much as will be difficult to repay. Your initial concept has not deceived you. Certainly, you have borne away those whom no one dared to touch, and shown them in Western regions where formerly they were only known by name; yet those names were greatly venerated. And you have removed from them all obscurity that used to surround them. You have cleansed our eyes of all mists, in such a way that even their heart may be seen, except we be totally blind. Finally, through you, this age has looked deeply into those whom Italy had never seen. All these things were given to you by that same star.

To this also I wish you to reply: whence that most capacious memory of so many things, which is so tenacious that, at any moment whatso-ever, all things are present for it, whatever you have seen or heard? Not only does it hold these things, but it remembers by whom they were done and also the times and places.

Will you therefore accuse Saturn, he who purposed that you should rise above other men as far as he himself rises above other planets? Where-fore, believe me, a hymn of recantation is necessary which, if you are wise, you will sing without delay. [2.23]

74

All praise of all things should be given back unto God, the beginning and the end of all

Marsilio Ficino to Giovanni Cavalcanti, his unique friend: greetings.

You command me, my Giovanni, to sing a hymn of recantation to Sat-urn, about whom I have recently complained a great deal.[1] Indeed you command most justly. Certainly, no one commands more justly than he who, commanding what is just, himself does just what he commands. But, although you admonish justly, yet you commit to my charge what is most void. To be sure, if my heart be singing, then, of necessity, the hollows of my breast resound. It follows that while you, my heart, sing, I sing. Indeed, in your letter you seem to have sung a hymn of recantation for me to Saturn and the other stars; or rather, to God, the cause of their movements. Therefore your letter to your Marsilio shall be the hymn of recantation; he freely accepts the praises sung to him in it, on this condition, that your praises are for one part attributed to your very ardent love for him and for the other part truly to the gifts of Saturn. But praises of love, of Saturn and finally of all things should be given back unto God, the beginning and end of all. I praise God within myself especially on this account: that, because of a certain eternal gift of His, I have very little desire for mortal goods, since I am in truth too fearful of the surrounding evils, which you reprove in me from time to time. I accuse a certain melancholy disposition, a thing which seems to me to be very bitter unless, having been softened, it may in a measure be made sweet for us by frequent use of the lyre.

Saturn seems to have impressed the seal of melancholy on me from the beginning; set, as it is, almost in the midst of my ascendant Aquarius, it is influenced by Mars, also in Aquarius, and the Moon in Capricorn. It is in square aspect to the Sun and Mercury in Scorpio, which occupy the ninth house. But Venus in Libra and Jupiter in Cancer have, perhaps, offered some resistance to this melancholy nature.

But where have I so heedlessly fallen? I see that you are again, not unjustly, urging me to sing another hymn of recantation to Saturn. So, what shall I do? I shall seek a shift; either I shall say, if you wish, that a nature of this kind does not issue from Saturn; or, if it should be necessary that it does issue from Saturn, I shall, in agreement with Aristotle,[2] say that this nature itself is a unique and divine gift. [2.24]

75

The Orphic Comparison of the Sun to God and the setting forth of causal forms

Marsilio Ficino and Giovanni Cavalcanti to Lotterio Neroni, their fellow philosopher: greetings.

According to the Orphic tradition,[1] the whole sphere of the Sun has a life-force far excelling that of all other spheres. It is this which causes life and movement to course through the entire body of the sphere and then to pour out through everything. But through the actual globe of the planet Sun it first brings about understanding and sight: it brings about understanding through the light of consciousness ruling in the very center of the Sun, as it were in the head; and it brings about sight through the visible light that shines everywhere within the full circuit of the Sun, as it were in the eye.[2] It is certainly in the Sun that visible light is created from the light of consciousness, and there also sight is created from understanding. For there understanding is no different from the same light of consciousness, nor sight from visible light itself. For the Sun, to be is to shine, to shine is to see, and to illuminate is to create all that is its own and to sustain what it has created. Of its very nature, by being it shines effortlessly within; just as effortlessly, by shining it illumines without, and by that illumination creates and sustains all that is its own.

But setting aside for the present all other properties of the Sun, let us consider only the visible light, the very power of sight, coming from deep within it. There sight is perfect, as is what is seen. It is the sight through which all other sight sees; what is seen is that through which all things seen are seen. For where does that sight first turn to see anything, except to itself, into which all else looks, as far as it can, in order to see? But what essentially does sight see when it sees itself? Surely it sees visible light, the source and origin of all visible things and of all colors. If in the sun sight is perfect and what is seen is perfect, then the seeing is perfect and undivided. And what we hastily reckon as three are in truth one and the same. For if this kind of sight and what is seen are one, as we have said, it follows that seeing, which is considered as an action intermediary between these two, is the same as them both. Therefore if that light sees itself perfectly, certainly it looks into itself to see what potential it has within and how much it can create from itself. But without mentioning all the countless other things, there is no doubt that it creates and sustains all the colors. For as it pours out in different ways in all directions through the manifold creation, so does it bring forth varied colors everywhere, and in seeing itself it sees all colors in itself.

But if that light is single and, so to speak, single-colored, how can it possibly become so manifold and many-colored?[3] Clearly for this reason: because it is single, within its order it is first and universal. If this is so, then of course it embraces within itself all the levels of its order.[4] For in any order the only form which has every form is the form which has only one form. Moreover, the multiplicity of forms, which leads to mixture and diversification in the objects formed away from the center, expresses the outstanding richness and the singular and most mighty potency within the creative principle.

But to come to the point: that light sees as many causal forms of color in itself as there are kinds of color in composite objects. For insofar as it sees itself partaking of the lowest level only, it is the causal form of the color black; at the next level it becomes the causal form of dark brown; at the third, of reddish yellow; at the fourth, of blue and green; at the fifth, of silver gray; at the sixth, of deep red; at the seventh, of bright red; at the eighth, of saffron yellow; at the ninth, of white; at the tenth, of transparent or shining; at the eleventh, of brilliant; and finally, at the twelfth, of brilliance itself.[5] Levels of this kind, which are many in the many objects formed outside the Sun, in the one creative principle of them all are one level, and that the highest; just as innumerable numbers are one in their origin, which is unity, and innumerable lines are one and undivided in their one and undivided center. Nevertheless, while that light looks into the highest level of its own self, it likewise observes into how many successive levels the highest level can extend in all directions, or how many kinds of color it can thereby create. It is the threefold cause of colors: their generator, their model, and their fulfilment.[6] It is their generator insofar as it brings them forth from itself by its own power. It is their model insofar as it forms them in its own likeness. It is their fulfilment insofar as it raises them up and leads them back to itself, insofar as the colors themselves strive to reach the fullness of the light by a natural impulse that it has implanted in them, and to the extent that a specific can attain its original.

The colors in objects are differentiated according to quality, place, and time, but in their cause they are fully united in these three respects. Furthermore, in objects they are often combined and mixed together in mutual opposition, but in their cause and creative power they are distinct without any confusion. They are distinct both because of the clear insight of the faculty that distinguishes one thing from another and because of the will of the one choosing multiplicity. Finally, in objects the colors are imperfect because they are everywhere incomplete; but in their cause they are fully perfect because they are totally pure and complete. Therefore, just as they are more differentiated from each other in objects, so they are more real in their cause, since there they suffer no loss in their essence and nature.

How, you will perhaps ask, are they distinguished in their cause? By way of example and still keeping to the Orphic Mystery, I answer that the colors within light itself are considered in three ways: the first, according to the absolute essence and nature of light; the second, according to its power of seeing; and the third, according to its influence and will. They are in no way differentiated through the absolute essence, for there all colors are a single, pure light; but they are distinguished through the power of seeing and through the will, for the light sees and wills the pouring out of the one light in many ways through many objects.[7]

Does that light therefore shine forth compounded and multiple because it sees that many things within itself can be created from itself and this is what it wills? Not at all, since it does not see these many things through many forms but through one form, that is, the one light, the origin and model of the various colors. Nor does it make use of numerous powers of seeing and choosing, to see and choose multiplicity, but it sees multiplicity through a single power of seeing, and likewise chooses with a single will. Therefore it seems that multiplicity is perceived by intelligence alone, that is, by the clear insight that discerns innumerable things and by the will that judges them. It is not, of course, by the intelligence of our eyes, which look up from here and see multiplicity in another realm, but by the intelligence of the light's own eye, which observes and judges things there in itself.[8] Thus those observations by which the causal forms of colors are individually distinguished are not occasioned by these colors or by these eyes but by the light itself, which is all-discerning and totally transparent; by the light itself, which imparts itself to the different kinds of color. There are as many colors seen and chosen in this way as there are observations made by the light into itself. Multiplicity of this kind in that which sees and chooses does not negate the simplicity of its own nature.[9]

But enough, my Lotterio, enough of fixing our gaze with such exertion, like the eagle, upon the celestial Sun.[10] So, to avoid the misfortune of going blind, let us now turn our keen sight back to what is our own, what is really our own, that is, to our causal form and that supercelestial Sun that does not permit its ardent lovers and contemplatives to go blind through recklessness.[11] But the more it flashes in their eyes, the more it strengthens and invigorates their sight. For this reason, even if we are not prepared to admit the Orphic Mystery as true, let us at least for now pretend that it is true, so that by looking up at the celestial Sun in this way we may descry in it, as in a mirror, that supercelestial One who has set His tabernacle in the Sun.[12]

19 December 1479.
Florence. [5.27]

76

A disputation against the pronouncements of the astrologers by Marsilio Ficino of Florence

Marsilio Ficino to Francesco Ippoliti, the distinguished Count of Gazzoldo: greetings.

I have written a book opposing the empty pronouncements of the astrologers.[1] I am sending you the preface, and will send the rest as soon as our scribe has copied it.

These astrologers, in declaring that every single thing is necessarily brought to pass by the stars, are themselves involved in three highly pernicious errors, and they involve the public in them too. For insofar as they are able, they take away from God, Almighty and Supreme, his own providence and his absolute sovereignty over the universe. Next, they deny the justice of the angels; for according to them, the angels move the celestial bodies in such a way that from thence come forth all the crimes of men, all evil events for good men, and all good events for evil men. Lastly, they take away from men their free will and deprive them of all peace of mind, for it seems to the astrologers that men, no less than beasts, are driven hither and thither.

If they predict good events, which they usually do infrequently, uneasily and in complete obscurity, they commonly envelop them in the greatest difficulties, whence it happens that we benefit very little. But if, very occasionally, they foretell that these events will happen without great exertion, we are thereby rendered idle, arrogant, and careless. And if by some chance it turns out as they have foretold, the long-awaited pleasure proves after all to be not so pleasing. If, however, they threaten evils, which happens much more often, either we long anticipate events that will come much later, or we miserably imagine things that will never come, and by imagining suffer.[2]

Then if the Fates cannot be avoided, they are foreseen and foretold to no purpose. Yet if they can be avoided by some method, the inevitability of fate is falsely maintained by the astrologers. They will probably say, I suppose, that this also is in the Fates, that once in a while one thing out of many may be foreknown and guarded against. Thus it follows that among the Fates there will be contention, so that one will be determined to harm a man and another to protect him. However, let us, for the present, concede this to the astrologers, lest perhaps we appear to anyone to be too stubborn. But we shall never concede that it also stands in the decrees of the Fates that many people should disbelieve them and many besides contradict them. For how does fate now impel Marsilio to pit all his strength in fighting fate? He now inveighs against fate, certainly not with the strength of fate itself, but rather with the power of something contrary and even superior in virtue. For necessity can in no wise fight against her own self, thereby denying that necessity exists and annihilating herself at her own instigation, and by her own sting.

What then is the meaning of that common saying, "We are moved by the Fates; believe in them"?[3] But if we consider the matter more carefully, we are moved not so much by the Fates themselves as by the foolish advocates of the Fates. Believe me, you will not yield to the Fates provided you do not believe these fools who veil in obscurity not the truth, as it is said the Sybil did, but falsehoods. Besides, they do not predict particular things for individuals, but things common to all.

These wordmongers bring so many things before the public that it is no wonder if among the multitude of lies they occasionally stumble by chance on something true! They want to be wise for others since they know so little for themselves.

It is worth reflecting on how destitute they are, how mean, how unfortunate in their business dealings, how inept and imprudent in their affairs. If perchance they engage in commerce, they have much less foresight regarding the turn of the market than other merchants; if in medicine, their foreknowledge of the course and outcome of an illness is much less than that of other physicians, and their care of the body is worst of all. And although they profess divination, yet they appear to live and die according to chance.

So pray arise, philosophers. Arise all who yearn for freedom and most precious peace. Come, gird yourselves now with the shield and spear of Pallas. War is impending for us against those petty ogres. By foreknowledge of the future they presume to equate themselves with God, who is infinite. By upholding heavenly fate, they presume to take away freedom of direction from God, who is above the heavens, and who is the highest freedom. But those who aspire with such arrogance to climb to the world of the gods will in humiliation be cast down headlong to the infernal regions.

Almighty God, extend your hand to us from on high. Give your soldiers strength; for now we are undertaking to defend your sovereignty. Hasten to our aid, O divine powers who revolve the heavenly spheres; help us as we defend your justice against the wicked enemies, who accuse you of extreme injustice. You too, O human race! Give us your unprejudiced support, for it is your most precious freedom and peace, the freedom and peace of all men, that we are protecting. So may we triumph over the diviners, albeit not divine but mightily profane, who have for so long been shackling us to their illusions; so at last may we be able freely to exclaim, "Wickedness is once more trampled underfoot, and victory elevates us to the heavenly kingdom."[4] [3.37]

77

The good man will rule over the stars

Marsilio Ficino to the magnanimous Lorenzo de' Medici: greetings.

Lorenzo, today and also tomorrow, be on your guard; for Mars, passing into Capricorn, your ascendant, is seen to look with square aspect, today at Saturn and tomorrow at the Sun. Besides this, Saturn himself, the lord of your ascendant, has still not quite passed through the rays of the Sun. For this last reason I, too, should take care.[1]

I was coming to you the other day to tell you all this, but on the way it occurred to me that it would be better to wait until now, so as not to burden you with fear and unease any longer than necessary. For by our predictions we often anticipate evils that are in the far distant future, or sometimes imagine evils that will never come to pass. While all who at any time are subject to fear are considered wretched, those are certainly less wretched who are troubled by fear for a shorter time.

I certainly trust, and my faith is not unfounded, that the one ruler of the stars and of men, who has till now miraculously saved you time and again from the threats of the stars and from the heinous hands of men,[2] will of his mercy likewise save you in the future.[3]

26 September 1480 [5.37]

78

Good fortune is in fate; true happiness in virtue[1]

Marsilio Ficino of Florence to Lorenzo de' Medici, the Younger: greetings.

My great love toward you, excellent Lorenzo, has long bidden me give you great gifts. Among all the things that he sees with the eyes, the observer of the heavens considers nothing to be great except the heavens. Therefore, if I were to give you the heavens themselves today, Lorenzo, what would be their price? But let me not bring price to mind just now, for love born of the graces gives or receives all things freely, nor can anything under heaven itself be weighed in balance with the heavens.

Astrologers say that he is born most fortunate of all men, for whom fate has so apportioned the signs from the heavens that the Moon firstly has no unfavorable aspect with Mars or Saturn, and secondly has favorable aspects with the Sun and Jupiter, Mercury and Venus. Just as astrologers account him to be fortunate for whom fate has favorably disposed things celestial, so equally theologians count him to be blessed who has similarly disposed the same things for himself. But, you will say, surely this is far too much! Much certainly; nonetheless, approach the task with good hope, free-born Lorenzo; far greater than the heavens is He who made you; and you yourself will be greater than the heavens as soon as you resolve upon the task. For these celestial bodies are not to be sought by us outside in some other place; for the heavens in their entirety are within us, in whom the light of life and the origin of heaven dwell.[2]

First, what else does the moon in us signify other than that continuous movement of our mind and body? Next Mars signifies swiftness, and Saturn tardiness; the Sun signifies God; Jupiter, law; Mercury, reason; Venus, human nature.[3] Come! Gird yourself now, noble youth, and together with me apportion the heavens for yourself in this way: let your Moon, that is the continuous movement of mind and body, avoid the excessive speed of Mars and the tardiness of Saturn; that is, let it deal with every single thing as it arises and as it requires, neither hastening more quickly than is meet nor postponing it till later. Furthermore, let this Moon within you continually turn toward the Sun, that is God Himself, from whom it always receives life-giving rays, so that in all places you may worship Him before all others; Him, from whom you have that Self by which you too are worthy of worship.

Also let your Moon observe Jupiter, that is, laws divine and human, which it should never transgress, since to depart from the laws on which all things are established is surely to perish. Again, let this Moon be directed to Mercury, that is, to counsel and reason, knowledge and discernment. And let it not attempt anything without the counsel of the wise, nor do or say anything for which it could not render good reasons. Again, let it consider a man without knowledge and education as, in a way, blind and dumb.

Lastly, let this Moon fix its gaze on Venus herself, which is human nature, by whom it is, of course, warned to remember that nothing great can be possessed by us on earth, unless we men, for whose benefit all earthly things were created, possess ourselves; and to remember that men can be taken by no other bait whatsoever than their own nature.[4] Beware that you never despise it, perhaps thinking that human nature is born of earth,[5] for human nature herself is a nymph with body surpassing. She was born of a heavenly origin and was beloved above others by an ethereal god. For indeed, her soul and spirit are love and kinship; her eyes are majesty and magnanimity; her hands are liberality and greatness in action; her feet, gentleness and restraint. Finally, her whole is harmony and integrity, honor and radiance.

O excellent form, O beautiful sight! My Lorenzo, a nymph so noble has been placed wholly in your power. If you yourself unite with this nymph in marriage and call her your own, she will bring sweetness to all your years and make you progenitor of beautiful offspring.[6]

Finally, to sum up: if by this reasoning you prudently temper within yourself the heavenly signs and the heavenly gifts, you will flee far from all the menaces of the fates and without doubt will live a blessed life under divine auspices. [4.46]

79

You may neither seek pure things in an impure way nor,
after you have found them, may you reveal them to impure men

Marsilio Ficino to the magnanimous Lorenzo de' Medici: greetings.

When, on the Kalends of November last, I had composed one letter to Giovanni Cavalcanti on the rapture of Paul into the third heaven and another to Febo Capella on the celestial and supercelestial light,[1] I soon afterwards unhappily contracted that disease of the eyes to which doctors give the name cataract[2] and which, they affirm, betokens the onset of blindness. Although I have tried practically everything that is employed by doctors who are the heirs of Apollo, the shining father of doctors, Apollo himself has not yet restored to me the light I once had.

Alas! How different is the nature of all other things from that of light, my Lorenzo! Those who shun noises, smells, or tastes, certainly escape such things; and those who particularly search for things of this kind are chiefly the ones who obtain them. But, alas, he who with all his strength seeks out light itself, is apt to lose it, as much as he who seeks to flee far away from it. Paul of Tarsus, while fleeing with precipitate steps from the true sun and pursuing the light of the very same sun with impious arms, was deprived of all light, as it is recorded.[3] Marsilio, on the other hand, while seeking to serve the sun and tend its light, has also nearly been deprived of it. Hence, yesterday, while the moon was in conjunction with the sun, a prayer to the divine sun came to me. Perhaps the prayer is somewhat obscure, but in time it will become clearer, I hope, when my human sun has illumined this moon of mine (and his) at least once with the rays of his eyes. Farewell.

O, Sun! purging all men's hearts with your flames, do you wish so very much to be inaccessible to any mortal when, in fact, you are of all things most accessible to everyone? O, Sun! Source of Justice! Sun! Model of generosity! As urgently as you incite me to seek you out, so shine back on me; with just such brilliance, with just such healing. Have I, perhaps, dared to raise eyes that are too impure to the purest light? In this event, I confess, I have perhaps been Phaeton.[4] Nevertheless, Phoebus, I have been and I am, yours, so cleanse me with your heat, I pray, and cherish me. As you can cast your rays through everything, Phoebus, so can you heal everything with your health-giving flames; for, unlike Julian, the Platonist[5] and former, but apostate Christian, I have not, being sunless, yet hymned the very sun himself. Nor, in company with Claudian,[6] have I impiously sung of your dear sister, Proserpine, snatched, as the story goes, into the underworld. But rather, with Luke, Hierotheus, and Dionysius,[7] I have honored your son, a certain Aesculapius, that doctor of souls from Tarsus,[8] who was carried off into the world above. And I have not, like Stesichorus and Homer, depicted the ill-fated seizure of Helen,[9] that is earthly appearance, but, as is the way of true Platonists, I have depicted the sublime upward soaring of the heavenly mind. Nor have I, like Numenius,[10] indiscriminately made public the Eleusinian mysteries; nor, like Pherecydes of Syros,[11] disclosed to any earthly man the secrets of heavenly beings; nor, like Hipparchus the Pythagorean,[12] have I ever made common to everyone the Delphic mysteries of the sacred Seer, which are proper to very few. Nor, as was the way with Dionysius of Syracuse,[13] have I attempted to lay before the impure senses of the crowd the Apollonian[14] sense of Plato. I have not spoken openly of that about which men are not permitted to speak; I have not given what is holy to dogs or pigs[15] for it to be torn into shreds. On the other hand, it certainly seems to me that I have revealed to men like Oedipus as many secret things as I myself have seen; however, to all the ignorant[16] I have given them completely veiled.

What now, Phoebus? What do you most want me to do? You will send me, I suppose, to Ananias[17] at Damascus, whither you once sent the blind Saul, where he immediately regained his lost sight. However, I wish that Ananias for me, Phoebus, might be that child of yours, victorious Medici, once born in your morning rays.[18] I have just set out for Damascus, my guide for the journey being that very son of the Platonic sun. To him who is indeed your child, but my Ananias, I have made a little offering in pledge of a greater sacrifice, the remainder of which I will shortly give him.

Therefore, Phoebus, now give back to me, if it is your will, give back to me I beseech you, the light I have long desired.

14 April 1477. [3.10]

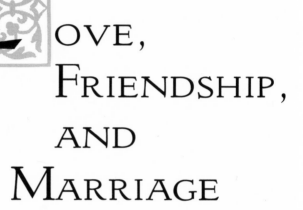

Love, Friendship, and Marriage

80

The lawful end of love is union

Marsilio Ficino to Giovanni Cavalcanti, his unique friend: greetings.

You ask what chiefly caused me to write letters about love. There are very many men, Giovanni, who in speaking or writing on matters of love stray a long way from its law. But a mistake of this kind is as harmful as lawful love is useful; and love has as many forms as there are lovers. In truth all men love; men, I say, Giovanni, for he who loves no one is not a man. So not only in the book which I have written on love[1] but also in my letters, I have pointed out for those who love the mark to which they should advance. Since the man who oversteps this mark is his own real enemy, he can be no true friend to others. He alone will keep to the right mark in speaking or writing, who first keeps to it in thinking. But he will keep to it in thinking who knows both what true beauty is and what is not true but its imitation. The right end of loving is union, which consists in these three: thinking, seeing, and hearing.

Certainly, love (as all philosophers define it) is the longing for beauty.[2] The beauty of the body lies not in the shadow of matter, but in the light and grace of form; not in dark mass, but in clear proportion; not in sluggish and senseless weight, but in harmonious number and measure. But we come to that light, that grace, proportion, number, and measure only through thinking, seeing, and hearing. It is thus far that the true passion of a true lover extends. However, it is not love when the appetite of the other senses drives us rather toward matter, mass, weight, and the deformity that is the opposite of beauty or love, but a stupid, gross, and ugly lust.

But why do I, like Socrates and Plato, consider for so long the populace rather than myself? For perhaps the more I strive to prevent the people from loving basely all the more will these insane and ungrateful people suspect my love is excessive. This is said to have happened also to those heroes, Socrates and Plato, our divine guides. So let that be enough on this subject; indeed it is more than enough for now.

Farewell. [1.47]

81

Whence the reciprocity of love is born

Marsilio Ficino to Amerigo Corsini: greetings.

That proverb, Corsini, "If you want to be loved, then love"—from where principally do we think it derives its power? If we ask love himself the reason for this proverb, he will perhaps reply that he is so free and so precious that neither does he wish, nor is he able, to be bought or sold at any price but that of himself. However, should we question anyone who is a true lover and friend, I think he will reply thus: Whoever loves passionately in some way takes himself from himself and gives himself up to his beloved, so the beloved, if he be right minded, cherishes the lover as his own. For everyone should hold dearest what belongs to him. The beloved also knows that if like is to be rendered for like, man must be given for man, and of course, will for will.

Now the lover fashions in his mind the image of the one he loves, and so his mind becomes, as it were, a mirror in which the form of the beloved is reflected.[1] Since the beloved recognizes himself in the lover, he is compelled to love him. But if we seek the truth of that proverb from nature, she will perhaps teach us this: likeness always begets love.[2] But likeness is a quality that is the same in more than one person, for if one man is like another the other is necessarily like him. And so the same likeness that compels one man to love another also leads the other to love him. For, as we experience every day, when two strings or lyres are tuned to the same pitch, whenever one is plucked the other vibrates.

If such teachers are not adequate or not clear enough, then let us turn to the philosophers, my Corsini, and hear to what they chiefly attribute the cause of this mutual emotion. Astrologers[3] consider there is mutual attraction between those at whose birth the sun and moon were in complementary positions; for instance, if at my birth the Sun was in Aries and the Moon in Sagittarius, and at your birth the Sun was in Sagittarius and the Moon in Aries. Such attraction also occurs in those born under the same sign or a similar one, and with the same planet or a similar one in the ascendant; or again if the benign planets make a similar aspect to the ascendant or if Venus was placed in the same house and degree at birth.

Followers of Plato add that the same spirit or a similar one guides the life of those men. Natural and moral philosophers believe this attraction is caused by similar temperament, upbringing, education, behavior, and way of thinking. Finally, where many causes coincide we find the mutual attraction much stronger. Where they all coincide, there springs again the love of Pythias and Damon, Pilades and Orestes.[4]

What more? A principle of this kind, Amerigo, a long time ago united Giovanni Cavalcanti and Marsilio Ficino in divine love; happily the same principle now joins a third to us: Amerigo. And what shall I say about Bernardo Bembo, the Venetian? Not only has this principle united him with us, but so has divine providence. [1.129]

82

Nothing is frailer than human love, nothing stronger than divine love

Marsilio Ficino to Girolamo Amazzi: greetings.

How different is the nature of love from that of almost everything else, my most loving and best loved Amazzi.[1] For the bigger other things are, the stronger they are thought to be; but the more extreme love and friendship appear, the frailer they seem to be. For often extreme love is injured by a succession of little things, more so than moderate love. Either the heat of the desire itself arouses fiery choler which, fanned by something trivial, sometimes floods out in a great surge of anger;[2] or preoccupation with one fixed idea begets melancholy, which is full of groundless fears.[3] More precisely, when a man thinks that he has given everything to another and therefore demands everything in return from his beloved, his avarice never obtains what it was seeking with the whole force of his mind.[4]

But the desire of the erring mind, essentially weak or self-seeking, suffers these frustrations deservedly. Since this desire feeds on the winds of the world, just when it seems to be growing most it is not so much growing as swelling; thus the stronger it appears, the weaker it is. Therefore human love is a thing full of anxious fear.[5]

Divine love, however, kindled by the flames of the virtues and growing strong from celestial rays, seeks to return to the sublime heights of heaven that no fear of earthly ills can ever trouble. Of such a kind is our mutual love, Amazzi. Therefore, as you are sure of your love toward me, so be just as sure of my love toward you. Far be it from us that one human heart should fail to respond to another that is always calling. Even strings seem to respond to strings that are similarly tuned, and one lyre resounds in answer to another;[6] indeed a solid wall may echo to one who calls. [4.25]

83

Grace, love, faith, and friendship

Marsilio Ficino to Naldo Naldi, poet: greetings.

I wanted just now to call you the delight of Phoebus, and to honor your poetry, as is just, with abundant praise, but it came to mind that it is quite unfitting to praise the Muse except by the Muse, or to praise poetry except by poems. However, I cannot be entirely silent about your works, O Love and Faith, for something rouses me to speech; therefore I will praise you. Grace moves Love, Love begets Faith. Faith embraces her father Love, and through the heat of this embrace, by Love gives birth to Friendship. Then Faith feeds this infant Friendship, allowing her to grow daily, and completely protecting her from destruction.

Why do we think this happens? Because when other things grow older they become weaker, but Friendship as it grows older grows stronger. Is it fostered by the frequent exchange of many favors? No, certainly not. For since the will is free, Friendship is obtained by free will and not at a price. Faith, made firm by time, confirms Friendship, and by Faith alone Goodwill becomes at the same time most ancient and most strong.

It is Faith above all else I delight in praising. For the learning of anyone belongs to one only, but Faith belongs to at least two; for what you know, you know for yourself, but you are faithful both to yourself and to me.

Farewell, my Naldo, more faithful than faith and oldest friend of all. Continue to be in the company of that learned and upright man, Bernardo Rucellai. Remember, whenever we used to seek an example of a just citizen or a happy man, from a hundred thousand men, with my full agreement, you would put Rucellai first.

Once more farewell.

8 April 1474. [1.56]

84

A friendship is lasting that is forged by God

Marsilio Ficino to Giovanni Cavalcanti, his unique friend: greetings.

My dear Giovanni, the Platonic philosophers defined true friendship as the permanent union of the lives of two men. But I think that life is one only for those men who work toward one end, as it were treading the same path toward a common goal. I believe their fellowship will only be permanent when the aim that they have set themselves as a common duty is not only single but also permanent and sure.

Now the whole study and business of Man is always to strive for what is thought to be good. Since there seem to be three kinds of good for mortals, which are those of the soul, body, and external objects, man seeks the virtue of the soul, the pleasures of the body, or abundance of riches. The first of these is sure and everlasting. The other two are transitory and mortal. Therefore that permanent union of lives, which is true friendship, can only exist for those who neither seek to accumulate riches nor to satisfy sensual pleasures that change and perish. It is possible only for those who apply themselves with common zeal and determination to acquire and exercise the single and permanent virtue of the soul.

Our Plato, the master and guide of all philosophers, called this virtue of the soul wisdom. He held wisdom to be the understanding of the divine.[1] In the *Republic*[2] he shows how the divine can only be manifest to our mind if God reveals it, just as the eyes only perceive physical forms when they are illuminated by the sun.[3] Likewise it is God, whom we long to see, who illuminates the eye of the mind, so that we can understand. To the enlightened mind He then reveals Himself, delighting us by that revelation. Therefore God is for us the way, the truth, and the life:[4] the way because by His rays he turns us, leads us to Him and gathers us up; the truth, because when we have turned toward Him, He reveals Himself to us; and lastly the life, since by that blessed vision He constantly nourishes and gives joy to our soul which contemplates Him. Therefore let all who desire to taste the sweetest waters of wisdom thirst for Him, the everlasting fountain of all wisdom. All who hope to acquire the virtue of the soul must fervently seek wisdom. Thus whoever resolves to cultivate his soul must also cultivate God.

We have now defined friends as those who strive for virtue with equal zeal, and who help one another to cultivate their souls. The cultivation of the soul is established in virtue alone, virtue is wisdom, and wisdom is understanding the divine. Divine light bestows knowledge of this kind upon us. Therefore, to cultivate the soul is to cultivate God Himself.

And so friendship, as it endeavors through the single aim of two men to cultivate the soul through virtue, is clearly nothing but the supreme harmony of two souls in the cultivation of God. And as God loves those who cultivate Him with devoted minds, there cannot be the two friends on their own, but there must always be three, the two men and God; God, or in other words Jupiter, the patron of hospitality, protector of friendship, and sustainer of human life, worshiped at all times by Plato and honored by Socrates. He is the guide of human life; He unites us as one; He is the unbreakable bond of friendship, and our constant guardian.

The theologians of antiquity, whose memory we revere, are said to have entered into a sacred bond of friendship with one another, having God as their mediator. We are told that among the Persians Zoroaster, by divine inspiration, adopted as his constant companion Arimaspis in his search for the holy mysteries of religious philosophy. So also among the Egyptians, Hermes Trismegistus chose Aesculapius. In Thrace, Orpheus chose Musaeus, and Aglaophemus, Pythagoras. Plato of Athens at first chose Dion of Syracuse and after his death, Xenocrates. So wise men have always thought it necessary to have God as their guide, and a man as companion for the safe and peaceful completion of the heavenly journey.

And although I have little confidence in being able to follow the footsteps of these men through the heavenly regions, there is one thing I do seem to have acquired in full measure for the study of sacred philosophy, the exercise of virtue and the search for truth; that is, the fitting and joyful company of the best of men. For I hold the friendship of Giovanni Cavalcanti and Marsilio Ficino worthy of being numbered among those I have just mentioned. With God to guide us, who has so fortunately established and quickened this bond, our friendship will serve us well in our necessary tasks, in leading a tranquil life and in discovering the divine.[5]
[1.51]

85

To throw away money appears to be serious indeed, but to cast aside a man is most serious

Marsilio Ficino to Andrea Cambini, an excellent fellow citizen.

Now what is pitiable in love? For it not to be requited. What is impious? To love on account of oneself what should be cherished for the sake of another; and contrarily, to cherish for the sake of something other, that which should be loved for its own sake. What is most disgraceful? To hate someone you have loved. In this respect we are much at fault, for although we do not abandon other things, however trifling, unless compelled to do so for a serious cause, yet we forsake and abuse a friend, a priceless treasure, led into it by any cause, often a very light one.

Pythagoras commands that we should not lightly discard a friend,[1] whatever the cause; rather we should bear with him for as long as we are able; and we are able until we are compelled to leave him wholly against our will. To throw away money appears to be serious indeed, but to cast aside a man is most serious. Nothing in human life is more rarely acquired, or more dearly possessed. No loss bodes more ill or is more perilous than that of a friend. [2.51]

86

A vow; a sign; a wonder

Marsilio Ficino of Florence to Bernardo Bembo, the illustrious Venetian ambassador, scholar and knight: greetings.

Good health to you always, heavenly and divine friend. Of my other friends, some were presented by chance and the rest were of my own choosing; but the heavens joined Bernardo Bembo to me from the beginning, and then divine providence confirmed this in a wonderful way. I say "heavens" because we were born in the same year, on the same day, under the same star.[1] Further, I maintain that divine providence has bound us fast together principally on these grounds: in the year that you first came as ambassador to Florence, almost four months before your arrival, I was seriously ill and had just made a vow in prayer to God and the blessed

Mary for my recovery,[2] when you instantly appeared to me. Hitherto you were quite unknown, but then became known to me for the first time, in a dream, promising me an early return to good health. Waking up, I was almost well, and in a short time I recovered completely.

Five months later to the very day, I fulfilled that vow, and in the same hour you first came, quite of your own accord, to our Academy at the head of a large company, and by divine inspiration greeted me, exactly as I had seen before in the dream. Then much took place and was spoken between us, exactly as I had dreamt.

In the same year, restored to life as if by religious vows, I wrote the book *On the Christian Religion*. So enjoy reading this book, heavenly and divine friend, bound to us from the beginning by the heavens, and since bound doubly fast by that religion beyond the heavens.

Your Marsilio, in his own hand.

15 July 1479.
Careggi. [5.17]

87

The greatest care should be taken about marriage and marriage arrangements

Marsilio Ficino to his fellow philosopher Francesco Berlinghieri, the son of Niccolo: greetings.

If you intend to entrust someone with the protection of your house, the safekeeping of your finances, the feeding of your sheep, or the care of your fields, will you look for someone very rich and powerful? Or will you choose above all a man endowed with the particular ability that your circumstances require? You will entrust at least the protection of your house and the safekeeping of your finances, if you are wise, only to a man who is prudent, strong, just, and trustworthy. Likewise, you will entrust the feeding of your sheep to a skilled shepherd and the care of your fields to the best farmer. Moreover, if you wish to adopt someone as your son, will you consider his external circumstances rather than his inner character and virtue? When taking on a servant, will you value his clothes more highly than the strength of his body, or the loyalty and diligence of his character? When you buy a horse, will you look more closely at its ornamental trappings and beautiful bridle than at its limbs and the way it moves? When building a house, will you lay the foundations on sand rather than on rock, even if the sand is golden?[1]

Your daughter, I hear, has reached the age for marriage; a daughter dearer and more precious to you by far than all these things that I have mentioned. I beg you, consider carefully what you do. The gravest errors we make are those that can be openly and permanently condemned but that cannot be corrected. The most dangerous fall for us is one from which there seems to be no chance of rising. We grieve most bitterly when we grieve for our own errors, and when we believe that our grief will be with us forever.

What is giving one's daughter in marriage? Is it not entrusting her to a husband's protection, safekeeping, support, and care? A husband's fortune may promise all these things, but only his virtue will provide them. No one is more blind than he who follows blind fortune as his guide. No one is played false more often than he who believes the promises of false fortune. Furthermore, is not choosing a son-in-law almost the same as adopting someone as your son? Would you acquire such a man just to gratify your whims, or, worse still, just for show when occasion demands it? Would you strengthen the family bond for your own material gain, as if it were some kind of building? These examples show clearly the sort of son-in-law that a prudent man should be seeking; and also the sort of wife that he should take in marriage.

Now I shall conclude this letter with the words of Themistocles and Plautus. If you are choosing a son-in-law, the wise Themistocles gives this advice: "I would rather have a man who needs money, than money which needs a man."[2] Whether you are about to gain a daughter-in-law or give away a bride, or if you are about to take a wife, Plautus gives this shrewd advice: "She comes with sufficient dowry if she comes with good character."[3]

Farewell. [5.39]

88

In praise of matrimony

Marsilio Ficino to Antonio Pelotti, poet and excellent friend: greetings.

I cannot but highly approve, my Pelotti, of the fact that you have long been applying your mind to matrimony. By matrimony, man, as if divine, continuously preserves the human race through succession.[1] As though in gratitude, he returns to nature what he has received on loan, often with interest. Like a true and generous sculptor he carves in his offspring a living image of himself. Moreover, it is only, or principally, through these means that he obtains loving companionship for life and faithful guardianship of his affairs. He also has a domestic republic, in the governing of which he may exercise the powers of prudence and all the virtues. At the same time, he provides the greatest protection for his old age, which he may spend more serenely in the bosom of a beloved wife, or in the arms of sons or grandsons, or in the care of relatives by marriage. Finally, a wife and family offer us sweet solace from our labors, or at least the strongest incentive toward moral philosophy: wherefore Socrates used to confess that he had learnt much more moral philosophy from his wives than natural philosophy from Anaxagoras or Archelaus.[2]

Who would deny that from the time man was created nothing has been ordained or established for him by God which is more important and more ancient than matrimony, and that it is numbered among the sacred mysteries and held in the highest regard among all peoples? The powerful have always respected it and the wise have not disdained it, having seen that it is conducive to the ordering of society and does not hinder learning, provided one lives temperately and spends one's time carefully.

Although in youth our Plato rather neglected matrimony, yet finally in old age, moved by repentance, he made sacrifices to the Goddess of Nature, thereby to absolve himself publicly from the charges, first, of having ignored matrimony and, second, of being barren.[3] And he proclaimed in his *Laws* that a man who did not take a wife ought to be kept well away from all public duties and offices, and at the same time be burdened with public taxes more heavily than other citizens.[4] Hermes Trismegistus says that men of this sort are judged to be wholly unfruitful by human law, and like dry and barren trees by divine law.[5]

Under divine law only two kinds of men seem to be exempted: those who are quite unsuited to matrimony on account of some disability in their nature, or those who have devoted themselves to Minerva alone, as though they had pledged themselves to a wife. Nature herself excuses the former, while chaste Minerva would perhaps reproach her devotees if they were to pursue Venus.

Nature, which brought forth our Pelotti strong and handsome, would certainly have disapproved had he by chance neglected matrimony. And if Minerva, whom he has long served, tries to reprove him for mixing Venus with the Muses, Apollo and Mercury will come at once to his defense. They will surely say that Pelotti has dedicated to the sacred Muses more and better songs after his wedding than before it. Finally, these sublime beings will bid one raise one's eyes to the stars. There Phoebus, lord of the Muses, and their companion Mercury, move as escorts on either side of Venus, mother of love and of music, and walk with her almost step for step, so to speak, and never go far from her.

But let us now leave the stars and return to mankind. I see you in the future, Antonio, frequently declaring in the following manner, within your own household, the benefits of taking a wife: "Man alone, or man most of all, is a social being, as the philosophers say,[6] and for this reason the power of speech and of formulating laws is bestowed by nature on him alone. One who has lived alone may see himself as somewhat greater than man, but more probably as something less, since he who transcends human powers while among men is rarer than the phoenix. He will play his part better than the rest of mankind if he has entered into a permanent and indissoluble family union. In this fellowship let him strive to serve and to learn how to guide the society of mankind itself.

"Surely, just as the state consists of households, so skill in state affairs consists of the judicious handling of family affairs. He who has not learnt to govern his household will never know how to rule the state. He will never love his country while he believes that its blessings and its woes hardly apply to him. He will not care to instill more serious conduct in himself who, by living alone, does not provide a model of good conduct to a family. Anyone who is not occupied in family matters will each day become more neglectful and degenerate through idleness and license. He will never know how to love anyone truly and steadfastly if he does not experience the true and imperishable love of wife and children. He will never learn to endure the world, and by enduring to conquer, if he has not had a family to teach him patience. He will not learn to feel compassion for men if he has never experienced a weeping wife or child, for indeed, if the mind is not unacquainted with misfortune, it learns how to succor the afflicted.[7] But worst of all is the man who does not know how to watch over his family, nor that God should frequently be invoked for their welfare. For the most part he ignores the laws of mankind, men themselves, and the worship of God. In short, it will be exceedingly difficult to avoid stripping man bare, unless we clothe him with the lawful mantle of matrimony.

"Wherefore, friends, if you wish to be men and lawful sons of God, increase the human race legitimately, and, just as you are like God, so in the fashion of God, beget sons like yourselves. Nourish them, rule them, direct them. And remember! In family affairs, which need to be so carefully directed, have due regard to yourselves: gain skill and acquire authority in the earthly commonwealth; be worthy of office in the heavenly commonwealth." [3.34]

WORLDLY THINGS AND CIVIC DUTY

89

By discord are all worldly things held together in place, by discord are all things held in opposition both to themselves and to others

Marsilio Ficino desires peace for his Pace[1] but fears war.

You wrote to me recently, my Pace, as is your custom, a very kind and elegant letter; but I wrote nothing to you because I considered that no-where was there peace, since I regarded all things to be inwardly filled with discord. But now I have just found my Pace[2] where I have long been finding my peace. Jove, as they who understand heavenly things declare, is the author of human peace. Rinaldo Orsini, child of Jove, nourishes both my Pace and my peace. As you request, I will earnestly commend you to the child of Phoebus.[3] But I beseech you, in your turn commend me to the child of Jove. However, before bringing this letter to a close, unless perhaps you think it absurd, after peace, I want to philosophize with you a little about war.

The evil spirits are in opposition to the blessed angels, the signs of the Zodiac to each other, planets to planets, elements to elements, plants to plants, animals to animals. Furthermore, movement is set against still-ness, deprivation against possession, light against darkness, the white and clear against the black, sound against silence, high notes against low ones, the fragrant against the fetid, the salty against the insipid; and as the Aristotelians[4] believe, sharp and bitter against sweet, hot against cold, dry against wet, light against heavy, dense against fine, rough against smooth, and finally, hard against soft.

Fortune and fate are opposed to the body, the bodily humors to one another, limbs to limbs, the body itself to the soul, the senses to reason, one emotion to another, vice is set against virtue and the vices against each other, opinion is opposed to opinion, and finally, desire to desire.

Of all things, the virtues alone, if they are found anywhere, so accord that the man who pursues but one of them acquires them all. Other things, however, nowhere more accord than in their very discord. Who should therefore wonder that mankind is driven by its own unceasing discord. By discord all things are held together in place. By discord all things are held in opposition both to themselves and to others.

All things sound in consonance outwardly only where inwardly nothing is in dissonance; furthermore nothing is inwardly dissonant where either pure truth holds sway, or the splendor of pure truth shines forth in abundance, or the heat of that same splendor glows. First is God, second is the contemplation of God, third is the love and adoration of God. These things are able to give us that peace, my Pace, which the world, being everywhere full of discord, cannot give. But lest perhaps by reasoning any more about war, I should seem by this lengthy discourse to have declared war on your eyes and ears, I will say farewell.

13 April 1478.[5] [3.8]

90

Three guides for life, and the one best principle for living

Marsilio Ficino to Lorenzo Franceschi: greetings.

There are three guides for the life of man. First is principle, which has been long and carefully tested; the second is experience, strengthened by long practice; and third, the authority of those ancients who could not have been easily deceived by anyone, and who appear not to have wished to deceive others. Attend more to what a man has done than to what he has said, for many speak well but few act well.

The best principle for living is to think, and to do your utmost to live in harmony with the mind, for this is to live forever and to live happily. For it is in the mind that stability and peace are found. The man who falls from the mind sinks into hell. Do not set your heart upon a long life in the body, for a long time in the physical world is nothing if you compare it to eternity. Besides this, in the life of the body we are a prey to a host of trivial vexations. The life of the body is a penance, worthy to be called the death of the soul. Strive for this one thing before all else, as our Plato counsels in *Gorgias*,[1] so that during the time God allots to you here, you may live as well as possible. In this way the torments of everlasting misery are avoided, and with divine help the foundations of eternal and blissful life are laid. [1.108]

91

The principle of teaching, praising, and blaming

Marsilio Ficino to Lorenzo Lippi, the rhetorician: greetings.

Since you have studied the Greek and Latin orators, I take it that you teach your pupils always to remember that their audience must be swayed not by what is pleasing, but by what is right. For he who urges what is just will win his case most easily, for of course he has Justice as his patron. Let them be mindful of their own integrity, because if a man's life is a lie, his speech will give him the lie. Facts carry greater weight than words, and the speaker who is most deeply moved himself will move others most deeply, whereas the man who sings one tune and plucks another from his lyre totally offends the ear. Divine music is the true harmony of thought, word, and deed.

When about to praise or blame anyone, your pupils should remember that the nature of matter, time, and space is vast; hence nobody is so wise and good that none wiser or better may be found, nor on the other hand can anyone be so foolish and evil, that there is no place for someone more foolish and more evil. Praise, therefore, should be sparingly given, and blame more sparingly still; further, by praising they should encourage and instruct. No one is more deadly a murderer than the flatterer, who does everything in his power to kill the soul. Therefore, rather than praise persons let them praise virtues, and God, the fount of all virtues. Such is the part of the true philosopher. The other is the way of the flatterer. Let them censure the fault, which is the act of a friend, not blame the man, which is the act of an enemy. It is evil they should loathe, not men. Let them study, not how to injure men but how to remove vice.

Let them study to be good rather than learned, for learning begets envy which goodness destroys. Goodness is both more useful to men and more pleasing to God than learning. It is also more enduring. We forget more quickly some fact that was quickly learned than we lose principles of conduct that we have attained by arduous daily practice. Learning in itself brings little of value, and that for only a short time, while goodness is eternal and leads to the realization of God. Therefore, following the example of Socrates, advise your pupils to use human learning to dispel the clouds of the senses, and to bring serenity to the soul. Then will the ray of truth from the divine sun illumine the mind, and never in any other way. That is the only useful study. A man who acts otherwise labors vainly and miserably.

Thus, Lippi, shall your pupils bring you honor. It is not their books, but their disciples, that have brought glory to the divine teachers, Pythagoras and Socrates; or rather it is books, but living ones, for a book is a disciple without a soul, but a disciple is a living book. And, Lorenzo, what you have freely learned from God, the master of all truth, freely teach. It is utterly wrong that knowledge, which is by nature free, should bear a price. All praise to him who has learned without reserve, and who teaches without jealousy. Whatever flows out from the pupils, flows back to the teacher. I beseech you, teach without stint. We may count our pupils as our spiritual sons. And if fathers beget their bodily children with pleasure, why should not teachers also beget their spiritual offspring with joy?

Show in yourself an example of good conduct. Purity of life engenders reverence for the teaching. The young eagerly take up the example of their elders. Those who corrupt a younger man, or indeed the mind of anyone at all, whether by words or conduct, must be held guilty of sacrilege. Finally, do according to Pythagoras[1] and Apollonius of Alabanda[2] who, in the tradition of the Indian philosophers did not admit any young men to their discipline except those of fortunate birth and the best education. For it is not fit that the Muses become either ministers of wantonness or the tools of iniquity. Farewell, and convey my good wishes to Albertino of Cremona, a true philosopher, that is, a model of learning and honesty. [1.109]

92

Concerning duties

Marsilio Ficino to the learned Cherubino Quarquagli: greetings.

Although, as is customary for those occupied in the study of philosophy, I am perhaps sometimes less dutiful than is appropriate, I cannot now refrain from writing to the most dutiful of men something about duty.

If I were as dutiful in discourse as you are in action, I should be as subtle as Panaetius[1] and as abundant as Cicero on this subject. But I shall deal with it with my native bluntness since I cannot now do otherwise and, so that I may for once do my duty, I shall send to the most dutiful of friends the duties of everyone.

Duty is the action proper to each man, which keeps to what is fitting and honorable as circumstance, person, place, and time require.

The virtue and duty of the priest are a wisdom that glows with piety, and a piety that shines with wisdom. The duty of the prince is to watch over all; mercy in justice, humility in greatness and greatness in humility. The duty of the magistrate is to remember that he is not the master but the servant of the law, and the public guardian of the state; furthermore, that while he is judging men he is being judged by God. The duty of the private individual is to obey the magistrates' commands so willingly that he seems not to be compelled by the necessity of the law but to be led by his own will. The duty of the citizen, whether he be a magistrate or private individual, is to care as greatly for the public interest as he greatly cherishes his own. The duty of the knight is bravery in war and noble action in peace; of the merchant, with true faith and diligence to nourish both the state and himself with good things from abroad; of the tradesman, honestly to distribute the provisions received from the merchant to each member of the state. Merchants, craftsmen, and others should so seek wealth that they harm no one. For whatever arises from evil in the end falls back into evil. Let them keep their wealth in such a way that they do not seem to have acquired it in vain, nor just for the sake of keeping it. Let them so spend that they may long be able to spend, and may prove to have spent honestly and usefully. The duty of the farmer is to consider the weather, and to consult older farmers on when to cultivate the land, and also to offer the fruits of the farm to his guests with trust and liberality equal to that of the farm that yielded those fruits to him with interest.

The duty of the master is to serve law and reason, so that he can rule his servants lawfully and reasonably; to consider the servant to be a man as much as the master, and always to combine humanity with authority. The servant's duty is to regard his own life as his master's, and his master's interest as his own; the husband's to love his wife as his own body and faculty of perception, and most carefully to lead her; the wife's to honor her prudent husband as if he were her mind and reason, and to follow him most willingly. The duty of the father is to cherish his sons as branches of his own life that have taken root, and to keep them upright by his own best example as if they were parts of himself; of the sons, to follow their father as their root and head, and to revere him as a second God; of a brother, to be disposed toward his brother as to a second self; of blood relatives, mutually to love each other as members of the same body; of those related by marriage, to remember that they have been joined by law as if it were by nature, and that they should share their possessions and labors.

The duty of friends is to seek the truth by taking counsel together, and to pursue the good by helping each other; of the teacher, by his instruction and his own goodness, to beget a learned and good disciple as if he were bringing to birth a child of his own mind. I desire, if I may, to warn teachers not to forget that Aristotle spurned the divine Plato.[2] The duty of the pupil is to honor his teacher as if he were the father of understanding, but to beware of unknowingly absorbing the teacher's faults; that of the lawyer to be the most venerable of men, and to know that a man who corrupts the sacred law should be punished as for a sacrilege by a more severe penalty than a man who debases the coinage.

The duty of the doctor when he visits the sick is to realize that a life is at stake, so that he dare not attempt anything without a reason nor without a purpose; of the orator, to have already convinced himself of those matters of which he would persuade others. The duty of the poet, so that he be able to depict nature and character, is to have observed them both. The duty of the musician is to portray the beauty of song in sound, and the fineness of speech in song. It is also his duty to remember that harmony in the motions of the soul is far more needful than harmony in voices. For ill-proportioned and a stranger to the muses is the musician to whom, while voice and lyre sound harmoniously together, mind sounds discordantly. David and Hermes Trismegistus command that, as we are moved by God to sing, of God alone we should sing.[3]

The philosopher should seek most diligently for divine things so that he may enjoy them, and investigate natural things so that he may use them. Let him give aid to human affairs but not be buried in them. The philosopher is unique in this: that he is rightly not pressed by Plato and Aristippus to hazard his life for his country.[4] Indeed, this pleases me also, because, as it seems to me, a philosopher is a philosopher against the will of the state in which he is born and in spite of its active resistance; and he is a son of heaven, not of earth. Moreover, it seems to be wholly without reverence or respect for God, and full of affliction, to lose an all-seeing man to save the blind who, perhaps, can never be made whole.

A man should beware of being effeminate in any way. A woman should strive to have the spirit of a man in some measure, but above all to be modest. As magnanimity becomes a man, so modesty becomes a woman.

Let the old man watch that he be not childish; let him remember that he has been a young man himself. The adolescent should take care to be like the old man. He should admit that he can age, and should honor his elders.

A man's duty to the country of his birth is to care for it as the father of his father and the mother of his mother; and, when he has dealings with travellers from abroad, to bear in mind that he will at some time be a wanderer himself. It is the duty of both native and foreigner to know he is himself alone, to honor all men, and scarcely to touch—let alone manage—the affairs of others.

The fortunate man should understand that the good things of fortune are good only to the good man; and that after fair weather comes the rain. The unfortunate man should reflect that the evil that fortune brings is evil only to the evil man, and after days of rain he should expect fair weather. For we see that Spring restores to the trees the leaves that Winter took away.

Since man cannot live content in earth, he should realize that he is indeed a citizen of heaven, but an inhabitant in earth. He should therefore strive to think, say, and do nothing that does not become a citizen of the kingdom of Heaven. [2.53]

93

On the duty of a citizen

Marsilio Ficino to Piero del Nero: greetings.

Tell me, Piero, why did the fever suddenly strike me after it had attacked your uncle Bernardo? Is it that, as we are so close to each other, when the Dog Star belches its flames on one of us it also sets fire to the other? May your uncle quickly recover so that Marsilio may too, or rather so that Florence may enjoy better health. If she always had such medical men as she has in this Medici, she would never be seriously ill. Such men properly perform the function of a citizen, without which the good health of the country is not preserved.

It is the duty of a citizen to consider the state as a single being[1] formed of its citizens who are the parts; and that the parts should serve the whole, not the whole the parts. For when the profit of the part alone is sought, there is no profit at all for either part or whole. When, however, the good of the whole is sought, the good of both is assured. Therefore because of this connection the citizen ought to remember that nothing good or bad can touch one limb of the state, without affecting the others and indeed the state as a whole. And again, nothing can happen to the whole body of the state without soon affecting each limb.

Let no one, then, in this household of city say, "This is mine," and "That is yours," for everything in this vast organism belongs in a way to everyone in common. Rather let him say, "Both this and that are mine," not because they are his personal property, but because he loves and cares for them. Let each man love and reverence his country as he would the founder of his family. Let the ordinary citizen obey the ancient, well-tried laws, just as he would obey God, for such laws are not established without God. Let the magistrate remember that he is subject to the laws in just the same way as the ordinary citizen is subject to the magistrate. Let him understand that when he passes judgment he is himself being judged by God. Let him always have before him the injunction of Plato, to have regard not for himself, but the state; and not just some part of the state but the whole. In short, he should know that Heaven's highest place is reserved for the man who has done his best to model his earthly country on the heavenly one. For nothing pleases the universal ruler of the world more than the universal good.

I think that you know these and similar precepts relating to the true citizen, and I hope that you will abide by them since you lack neither instruction nor prudence. Besides, you have at home a competent teacher in this subject, about whose merits I will write another time.

Farewell. Our Giovanni Cavalcanti commends himself to you. [1.78]

94

On law and justice

Marsilio Ficino to the magnanimous Lorenzo de' Medici: greetings.

I promised Lorenzo, on his return to Florence from Pisa on the seventh of March, if I remember rightly, that I would write to him when he next went to Pisa. Usually I write to friends because I wish to; on the present occasion I shall write because I must. It is just to keep a promise, for law ordains it so. So accept a just and lawful letter. No! To speak more truly, whenever I wish to write, then write I must, by the law of love; when I must write, then I also wish to, for the love of law. So today you will receive a letter written of my own accord and in accordance with the law. To separate the voluntary from the just or the just from the voluntary is not lawful for anyone and is unpleasant for friends. So Marsilio, you now both must, and wish to write to Medici.

Of what can you principally write, and which god will be your guide? Oh salvation of mankind! Oh Justice, Queen of the world! For a long time you have given me cause to write; now, I beseech you, provide material so that I may fulfil my promise as successfully with your aid, as I gave it gladly when you commanded.

That divine law[1] by which the universe abides and is governed, kindles in our minds at their creation the inextinguishable light of natural law, by which good and evil are tested. From this natural law, which is a spark of the divine, the written law arises like a ray from that spark. Moreover, these three laws, divine, natural, and written, teach each man what justice is, so that there is scarcely any room left for sinners to plead complete ignorance as an excuse for their faults.

These three lights show the eye of the mind that justice is really a quality of will, which is directed and strengthened by reason, so that despising threats and enticements, it decides to act only as divinity, nature, and citizenship dictate. What does divinity instruct but to give back to God, from whom we receive everything, every insight of the mind, every desire of the will, the energy of every action, and the reward of work? What else does nature teach, if not that we should make wealth subject to the body, the body to the soul, the soul to reason, and reason to God?

Finally, citizenship seems to teach that each citizen should remember that he is a member of the state.[2] Therefore it is right for men to love their country as if it were one body,[3] and fellow citizens as members of that body. And so a man will be considered indisputably just who reverences God as his Father and Lord with utmost piety. He will carefully restrain his feelings and emotions; he will love all men as his brothers; he will love himself in God and all men in himself; he will cleave to God with all his strength and, so far as he is able, he will unite others with himself in the divine nature. Therefore it is the duty of a just man to render each his due;[4] to those above, honor and respect; to equals, family companionship; and to those below, support and advice.

Furthermore, when he is appointed an officer of the government, he will have the law always in view as if it were God. He will not, indeed, consider himself a master of the law, but its faithful interpreter and devoted servant.[5] In administering it he should punish offences impartially and with even temper. Without envy he should reward virtuous actions according to their worth. He should not give thought to his own interests but rather to those of the community. Neither should he trust in his own ability, but he should seek advice in all matters from elder men, those who are prudent and god-fearing. That, too, should remain deeply impressed on his mind.

Lay aside your proud and pompous looks, you to whom the ruler of the sea and land has given the great jurisdiction of life and death. Whatever a lesser man dreads at your hands, with that a greater Lord threatens you. Every authority is subject to a greater authority.[6] Let that be enough about what justice is; what a just man is; and what is his duty.

Moreover, how important the fruit of just action is, is very clear, because neither home, state, army, nor business of any kind, whether of good or bad men, can endure without a just distribution, made according to merit. In fact, if it is so vital to the structure of the world that its removal would mean the world's immediate destruction, its importance for the life of men cannot be expressed. Indeed, if justice were not present among men either they would herd together in one place and quickly perish at each other's hands or they would live scattered to be separately torn to pieces by wild beasts. Oh eternal bond of the human race! Most wholesome cure for our sickness! Common soul of society! Justice that is blissful life! Justice that is heavenly life! Mother and Queen of the golden age, sublime Astrea[7] seated among the starry thrones! Goddess, we beg you, do not abandon your earthly abode, lest we miserably sink into the iron age. Heavenly goddess, we beseech you, ever live in human minds, that is, in citizens who belong to the heavenly country, so that for the present we may imitate the divine life as well as we can, and that in the time to come we may live it to the full.

Farewell. [1.95]

95

A plea from the Christian flock to its shepherd
Sixtus, urging him to say to his sheep, "Peace be with you"[1]

The Christian flock humbly commends itself to Sixtus, its most blessed shepherd.

Good shepherd, it is not easy to see where best to begin. For while I am moved to praise by the wonderful blessings of your holiness, I am equally moved to complaint by the deplorable evils of my wretched condition.[2] So what shall I do? Shall I sing your praises? Or shall I recount our troubles? We seem to achieve nothing by praising you; for rare excellence does not depend upon popular praise. Laying bare our wounds to our doctor because he will cure them is therefore better than enumerating his countless well-known praises to no avail. And if, compelled by dire necessity, we make our pleas to him in unsuitable terms, yet trusting in his compassion rather than in those pleas, we hope that he will entirely purge his flock of all disease.

Even if I were all tongue, blessed Father, I would not be able to express the magnitude of the misfortune that now oppresses me, nor of the sorrow that consumes me; but it would also be impossible to describe the immensity of the joy with which I was filled long ago when God Himself appointed you as my shepherd. I had heard that you were the phoenix of philosophy[3] and the foremost guardian of the lofty citadel of Minerva.[4] Indeed, this is so obvious to all that it cannot be denied. I was in fact hoping that, since the highest power was joined to the highest wisdom, that golden age would return that Plato foretold would occur when power and wisdom came together in the same man.[5] In short, I had for a long time heard as many truths about your wisdom as I have had false hopes about my happiness. I only fear that one day someone lacking due respect and patience may have the temerity to exclaim: "Alas! How far have I been deceived in this hope, wretch that I am! For me, joy has turned to sorrow; not the golden age I was hoping for but, even under the wisest Pontiff, an age of iron. Who would have believed it? The iron age has returned.[6] I see nothing anywhere except arms made for my destruction. I hear nothing except the clash of weapons, the neighing of horses, the thundering of cannon. I feel nothing anywhere except weeping, looting, burning, and slaughter; added to which I am racked by hunger, and everyday I am more and more wasted by disease.[7] And, as if these things which endlessly torment me within were not enough, my life is continually threatened from without by the most ravenous wolf of all, a roaring lion, a monstrous elephant, a noxious dragon: the Turk, that savage enemy of the Church. And now, even now, unless you are at hand to resist, he is about to devour this wretched flock of yours, and indeed you first."[8]

Upon you alone, as upon the head, depends the whole body of the Church. To you alone redounds all the glory, or all the infamy. For you awaits the greatest reward of all, or the greatest punishment. So to prevent occasion for misfortune to befall or for patience to give way, look first to your own interests, most holy Father, and take care of us. First, protect your own safety for us, we beg you, and in turn keep us safe for you, most blessed Father. Forgive your children, we beseech you, most forbearing Father and source of all forbearance if, partly forced by pressing evils and partly taking advantage of our love for you and relying on your love for us, we approach your Holiness to advise you, as swine might approach Minerva.[9] Charity believeth all things, hopeth all things, endureth all things. Charity never faileth;[10] so it is not possible for supreme benevolence to take anything unkindly.

Remember that you are the Vicar of Christ,[11] who is most mild and most merciful. Forget injury, as you have done in the past; for remembrance of injury is forgetfulness of oneself. If you have any hatred toward your flock, put it aside, so that you may regain, if you have ever lost it, your accustomed charity,[12] which, being wholly innate, you cannot lose without losing yourself. That is why you will hold to your former charity—we know you will—because otherwise you will be forced to give up your true spirit. You will not allow anyone to savage the flock any further with your weapons or, through the crime of another, you will become a wolf instead of a shepherd; or at least you will be thought one. Whoever uses arms against your sheep undoubtedly harms you before anyone else. For there is no shepherd without a flock, and he who disowns or loses any part of the flock at once ceases to be shepherd of the whole. If you are shepherd of no particular part, you will be shepherd of all. If you are shepherd of a part, you will be shepherd of none. In the first place Christ granted you divine rule, not so much over arms as over souls. Then he gave you keys, not a helmet or sword; keys with which you may close the doors of Janus and Pluto and open the gates of the kingdom of heaven.[13] Three times he called out to you, "Lovest thou me?

Lovest thou me? Lovest thou me?" Then he added, "If ye love me, feed my sheep."[14] If any have erred seventy times seven, forgive them.[15] Leave for a time the ninety-nine obedient ones to redeem the hundredth who has gone astray, and when you have redeemed him, rejoice more in this one than in all the others.[16] He did not say pursue this sheep with curses but follow him with gentle coaxing. He did not give you a rod to beat the straying sheep but he did give you mild words to call them back kindly to the folds, and keys to keep them safe. A hireling sometimes harshly beats sheep that have gone astray, for they are not his own, but a shepherd always forgives his sheep and watches over them. The Lord did not appoint you as a hireling but as a shepherd.[17]

But I see how you will accuse us: you will say it is one thing to stray from the path away from the shepherd, another to butt him with one's horns. And so perhaps you will complain of a certain ram among us.[18] We have looked around everywhere, good shepherd; we have not found this ram. No violence is intended, nor is there such arrogance in the sheep, penned as they are in the celestial and indestructible fold.[19] But because you are angry with some unknown ram, you are somehow destroying almost all your flock or driving them away from the fold. O shepherd, for some reason your flock lies hidden from your eyes, scattered to the woods and crags. Oh, if only you were to look at your flock for a while, you would not be able to look at so great a ruin of your own ones with dry eyes. Oh the sorrow! The whole of your flock is being afflicted from all directions by every sickness and evil.

Far and wide the shepherd is blamed, far and wide he is criticized, while grave difficulties press upon me in my wretchedness from every side. I grieve for your dishonor, yet I bewail my own distress. If you could borrow Rumor's ears[20] just for an hour you would hear your own ill fame and my weeping, and certainly you yourself would weep no less over your fate than I do over mine. O my shepherd, how unfortunate for you, one could say! But how ruinous for the flock! How utterly wrong! Do you not hear?

Against you, O supreme Pontiff, against you, mordant satirists[21] everywhere are sharpening their knives but the grim tragedians are turning their attention to me. No satire more bitter will ever be read, even if it be false; no tragedy more true or more sad. If you remove the material for tragedy you remove the material for satire at the same time. Strike out your name from the book of infamy; it has long been written in the book

of life by God. Rise up, our guardian, before it is too late. Rise up now, O
lawful guardian. Speak as one with your Lord; say, I entreat you, "Peace
be with you." He spake, and it was done.[22] There will be peace and at
once glory both to you and your flock. The golden age will be brought in
for you and us together. The iron sword, in the hands of the soldiers of
Constantine,[23] will be turned away from your fold and against the barbarian wolves. Without any doubt, the shepherd will be praised when the
wolves have been slaughtered or subdued, as much as he is now univer-
sally blamed while the sheep are being hurled to destruction. A thousand
warriors shall fall beside you, even though you are unarmed, and ten
thousand at your right hand, but almighty God Himself will fight for
you.[24]

But look, you are rebuking that ram again. Rebuke him perhaps, if he
seems to you to need it. But let your rebuke be Christian rather than
hostile. Let it not lead to damnation but rather to salvation. Your Lord did
not come to destroy anyone but to save.[25] He wished you to be a healer,
not a murderer. But I wish I had not mentioned in the presence of your
most Holy Majesty that terrible word "murderer." Let no one, even a
murderer, dare to suspect your Holiness of that crime. Almighty God has
not given you physical weapons but spiritual and divine ones, as Paul the
Apostle says.[26] Indeed, He has commanded you to provide for the sheep
in your charge and at the same time to be merciful to them but to van-
quish the arrogant wolves, that is the barbarian enemies of the faith, with
the forces of Constantine; not for the sake of war but of peace. With the
beasts tamed and the sheep protected under one shepherd, there may at
last be but one fold. First, however, spare your sheep, gentle shepherd.
Spare your own sheep, lest, while there is strife between us about wool
and pasture, the wolves find it easier to make savage attacks on the very
lives of both sheep and shepherd. It will be no dishonor to you even if you
spare any of your erring sheep seven times, since the command to you
from the Lord was that you should forgive them even seventy times
seven. Your duty, as you well know, is to recognize each sheep so that
you may pardon it and to cleanse the sick so that you may restore them
to health.

Your victory rests not in war but in peace. Even if you do prevail over
Christian men in war, demons will prevail over you (may it never befall
you) and you will be overwhelmed by public disgrace. If you gently correct and are forbearing, you conquer all and preserve your sway intact

over all your own. Let your strength be shown in forbearance, not in aggression; your highest quality lies in being lowly. You most make all men gentle when you are the most gentle of all. You will easily move everyone wherever you please if you yourself are not moved at all. Do you want to gain an immediate victory, and a most happy one? Do not conquer your own people in war, but conquer war itself. Govern by divine providence rather than by the movements of the heavens. By the goodness in your nature subdue malign and savage Mars and unyielding Saturn.[27] It is no great victory to overcome small things. What, tell me, is great on earth, seeing that the whole earth itself is a very small thing? Therefore, celestial bishop, having put aside the earth, conquer heaven, for you will conquer earthly things effectively if you have conquered the heavenly. Where your kingdom is, there is your victory. But, as Jesus says, your kingdom is not of this lower world but of the higher and divine.[28] Consider, most holy Father, which of these would you prefer, and both are within your choice: on earth to be considered a soldier or a pontiff? In heaven to be rejected by Christ as different, for He is completely unarmed, while you yourself are laden with arms; or laying your arms aside, to be accepted by Him as the same?

Perhaps you will say: the flock is not allowed to admonish the shepherd. That is granted; for we acknowledge that our Father, made supreme by providence, needs no correction. But at least allow us to make fitting petitions or even unfitting petitions when necessity compels. Again, allow us to fear for him whom alone we fear and love and whom we reverence as an image of God.

Look up to heaven for a while, we beseech you, as you used to once, before you turned your mind to these earthly battles. You will see Peter, the first pontiff, clearly seeing these wounds of mine, which perhaps you do not yet see yourself. You will see Peter, full of compassion, grieving deeply at my suffering. Perhaps, unless you take heed, it is inevitable that he, while pitying us so much, will be angry with you. But far be it from us, far be it that either Peter be angry with Sixtus or Sixtus displeased with his flock. It is a sin to predict anything bad for a good shepherd or to expect anything in the end from him except good. For our Pontiff, the most far-sighted of all men, has not forgotten himself. He did not lose his own wisdom when he began to be wise for all. He did not cast off his natural generosity when he put on the mantle of the most generous Peter.

Therefore, what shall we say? Perhaps it seems right for a skilful ruler sometimes to threaten his people rather sharply, lest his continual silent forbearance be thought to be slackness, and so that after some severity his incomparable sweetness might taste even more sweet. Perhaps, too, he has till now allowed his flock, unused to war, to fight among themselves for a certain time so that by this training they may become more prepared for the battle that must be joined against the barbarian wolves.

O our Sixtus, stop this great conflict now. We have practiced enough, more than enough, inasmuch as we are now completely exhausted. Kind Sixtus, have pity on your own. Come speak, blessed Father; of your own goodwill say now to your sheep, "Peace be with you." So in turn your sheep may proclaim together with you, "Glory to God in the highest and on earth peace to men of good will."[29] [5.1]

96

Affairs of state cannot be properly and successfully conducted without divine help

Marsilio Ficino to Francesco Berlinghieri: greetings.

While most men usually congratulate their friends on attaining offices and honors, I pray to God on such occasions, craving divine grace for my friends. For I have learned from Plato that those arts that are concerned with personal welfare may sometimes be adequately directed by human wisdom; but that in the art that looks after the good of the state, the director is God Himself and should be acknowledged as such. I have learned that to God belongs the care of all things, but especially of public and state affairs, and that human wisdom is not the governess, but rather the handmaid and servant of divine government.

The Platonic myth in *Protagoras* alludes to this: Prometheus, or human providence, discovered all the arts except care of the state.[1] For this, he says, is given to us by Jupiter through Mercury; that is, it is granted by divine providence through angelic inspiration[2] day by day. Plato also alludes to this by means of comparison: just as without man one beast cannot be successfully and rightly guided by another, so without God man cannot be guided by man. What else could this prophecy mean: "The king's heart is in the hand of the Lord and He turneth it whithersoever He will"?[3] Likewise, this saying from the gospels: "Thou couldest have no power except it were given thee from above";[4] and again: "There is no power but of God: the powers that be are ordained of God."[5] Dionysius the Areopagite made archangels teachers and guides to the leaders of men.[6] David used the Psalms as reins to regulate the government of his kingdom. For he knew that "except the Lord keep the city, the watchman waketh but in vain."[7] Solomon represents divine wisdom as proclaiming: "By me kings reign and lawgivers decree what is just. By me princes rule and the mighty decree justice."[8] The religion of the Romans ordained that no affairs of state be undertaken either in peace or in war without sacrifices and augury.[9] Scipio would never proceed with any state business until he had attended to divine sacrifices.[10]

Orators and poets wisely say that those who hold public office are like the helmsmen of ships and, like those who are forever tossed among rocks by wind and wave, they are perpetually in need of protection by divine powers.[11] Thus, my very dear friend, as with my other friends who have attained office, I now feel moved in the first place to pray to God for your happiness. Then rather than congratulate you I shall make a wish; I wish for you divine aid, so that you may undertake and fulfil this and all other offices dutifully, with prudence, justice, and mercy, and finally with success. Indeed, knowing your spirit, I expect that with divine grace you will achieve this.

Farewell. [5.30]

97

A picture of the evil mind and the good;
of the ignorant and the enlightened

Marsilio Ficino to Lorenzo de' Medici: greetings.[1]

Long ago, Lorenzo, I heard that men of evil conduct were utterly distasteful to you, and recently I have heard that good men approve of you precisely because you disapprove of evil men. For the one I thoroughly commend you, and for the other I heartily congratulate you. For there is no shorter, no easier way to the good than to hate evil; no surer sign of good taste than to reject those tastes that are harmful to health. There is no life more secure, no surer glory, than to be loved by good and discerning men; for even the wicked are finally compelled to honor those loved by the upright and discerning. Yet in order that evil men may not only be hateful to you but fill you with horror, I wish, if I may, to observe for a while the utterly repulsive and wretched life of those ruled by passion and, as it were, to point it out to you.

Lorenzo, the soul corrupted by evil conduct is like a wood dense with tangled thorns,[2] bristling with savage beasts, infested with poisonous snakes. Or it is like a swelling sea, tossed by battling winds, waves, and wild storms; or like a human body misshapen without and tortured within by excruciating pains in every joint. On the other hand, a mind endued with fine principles is like a well-tended and fertile field, or a calm and peaceful sea, or the body of a man that is both beautiful and strong.[3]

My friend, we have now seen the shadow of the evil mind and its opposite, the image of the good mind. As soon as we perceive the first clearly, we cannot but loathe it; but when we see the second, we cannot but love and venerate it. How else can one become a good man except by resolutely seeking the company of a mind that is good and shunning one that is evil?

In the same way as we have been considering the evil soul and the good soul, please tell me, excellent Lorenzo, do you now wish to look more closely with me into the ignorant mind and into the mind that has been enlightened? I believe you do desire this very strongly, and I, for my part, wish to show it to you briefly. The mind ignorant of truth is just like the moon when the earth is between it and the sun and it undergoes an eclipse: it is deprived of the sun's splendor. Or again, it is like the cold and foggy air of night, or like a human body with blind eyes, deaf ears, and mute tongue. On the other hand, we can compare the mind that has knowledge of reality and the full power of speech to the full moon shining in the light of the sun; or to the clear air of day with its abundant light and gentle warmth, or to the body whose senses are alert and whose tongue is free to speak. But whoever sees the mind ignorant of truth and does not flee immediately from its foul appearance or shadow, will flee from nothing; while whoever does not eagerly follow the mind that does know the truth, wherever such a mind appears, will not, I see, follow anything anywhere.

So press on, my Lorenzo, press on, I beg you. Flee, as you once began to, flee far from that loathsome shadow, from that miserable image of the impure and ignorant mind. Bestir yourself, and every day with all your strength pursue more and more closely, as you do, the form of the good and wise soul, full of light and bliss. Just as nature endowed you at birth and fortune enriched you thereafter, may you by your own efforts enrich yourself in the same measure, so that you may not consider yourself lacking in anything; for nature as well as fortune has provided you with everything else that you could wish for. All your possessions—your lands, houses, furnishings, clothes, and even the limbs of your body—shine around you, each of them, like stars. May you also shine out like the Sun itself among those stars, with your soul resplendent in the radiance of your actions and your writings.[4] [5.44]

98

The nobility, usefulness and practice of medicine

Marsilio Ficino to Tommaso Valeri, an outstanding physician: greetings.

I have read in Homer that one man of medicine is worth a host of other men,[1] and justly so; for the sacred writings of the Hebrews teach that the power of healing is the gift of God, rather than an invention of men. Let us honor the man of medicine because the Almighty created him of necessity. Furthermore, the Gentiles regard the masters of this art as gods. They bestowed divine honors upon Isis, Apollo, and Aesculapius,[2] and also upon outstanding doctors. For they dedicated temples to Chiron, Machaon, Podalirius, Hippocrates, and Hermagoras. Hippocrates confirms this in his letter to the Abderites,[3] when he says that medicine is a gift of the gods, that it is free, and that he has never accepted a reward for practicing it. Also in a letter to Philemon[4] he says that medicine is related to prophecy, because our ancestor Apollo is the father of both arts; he foretells future illness as well as curing those already ill. Hence Pythagoras,[5] Empedocles, and Apollonius of Tyana are said to have cured diseases with chants rather than with herbs.

The Magi thought that the mind of the sick should first be cleansed with sacred teachings and prayers before they attended to the body. For clearly such an art as this has been received and is practiced through divine grace, because the soul is dependent on God, and the body on the soul. Do not the Hebrews consider that the Archangel Raphael practiced this art? Quite apart from other doctors, Christ Himself used to cure all the sick and ailing who were brought to Him, as though He were the doctor of mankind, and He entrusted the power of healing to His disciples. So it is that kings have never scorned to study and practice this most noble art, such as Sapor and Ginges, kings of the Medes, Sabid, king of the Arabs, Mithridates,[6] king of the Persians, Hermes, king of the Egyptians, and Mesues,[7] nephew of the king of Damascus. Some believe that Avicenna was the prince of Cordova. Such famous philosophers as Democritus, Timaeus of Locris, Plato, Aristotle, and countless others of note have written about this art.

This letter has said almost as much as a letter can about the nobility of medicine. We can see how useful it is, from the fact that the arts that are directed toward the good life seem to be of little benefit without its assistance. We cannot live well if we are not alive! In this short span of life, little can be achieved in any skill without good health; and we cannot easily attain great merit among men or with God unless we live a long and temperate life. The careful application of medicine gives every opportunity to lead such a life. But in the practice of this art there must be the utmost devotion to God, and charity toward men, as Luke the Evangelist and the divine physicians Cosmus and Damian[8] have taught us by their example. For God is the source of all good and so the true doctor is like a god among men. He restores them from death to life and so he is worshiped as God, even by kings and wise men when they are ill.

All agree that a doctor needs a keen mind, knowledge, and experience. It is clear that his consideration needs to be profound and full of care. But as Hippocrates[9] says to the Abderites, when a case has been properly considered, delay may be more harmful in this art than in any other. However, in Galen's words to Glaucon,[10] it is even more dangerous to anticipate and interfere with the course of nature. For he says that many lives are lost daily as a result of this error, that is to say, the presumption of doctors who either hinder or hasten nature. The man who does not rely solely on his own skill is less likely to fall into such an error. Hippocrates[11] writes to Democritus that even though he is now very old he has not yet reached the final aim of medicine. Galen also says that it was not until he was ninety that he finally grasped the nature of the pulse. Above all the doctor should remember that the creator of health is God, that nature is God's instrument for establishing or maintaining health, and that the doctor is the servant of both. So he does not provide the strength, but prepares the ground and removes obstacles for the master craftsman. If he rashly wants to change or check the physical condition he often does both badly, and impedes nature which would do both well.

But let us listen to our divine Plato, as he speaks with the authority of the Pythagoreans on this subject in the *Timaeus*.[12] In truth the best of all movements is that which arises naturally by itself, as it is most akin to the motion of the mind and of the universe. Movement caused by an outside agency is of a lower order, but the lowest movement of all is when parts of the body are moved by outside agencies, while the body as a whole is at rest. So, of all the ways of cleansing and regulating the body, exercise is the most healthy. Next is the gentle motion of being carried in a ship or some other form of transport. The third sort of movement is only useful under the compulsion of extreme necessity. In no other circumstances should a man of sound mind undertake it, namely, the remedy of doctors who are in the habit of using drugs as laxative medicines. Diseases, unless they are very dangerous, should not be irritated by drugs. For the whole constitution of diseases is rather like the nature of living beings. In fact the structure of living beings is bounded from the very beginning of their own generation by a set length of time. The whole genus is subject to this, and each being contains within itself its allotted life span from its birth, unless unavoidable events intervene. For the triangles, that is to say the proportional qualities, from the very beginning hold the life force of every one, and hold together for the purpose of life up to a certain time. Life is not prolonged for any one beyond this fixed time. The same rule of nature applies to diseases. If anyone tries to shorten them by drugs before they have run their allotted course of time, illnesses that were minor or rare usually become serious or widespread.

Therefore diseases should be treated and controlled by attending to diet insofar as each person has leisure for this, lest a difficult and dangerous disease be aggravated by drugs. So says Plato. The Florentine people often commend our Galileo because he observes this rule. For this reason I, too, am full of praise for Lorenzo Martellini, a true doctor, and would also praise Tommaso Valeri—except that I am writing to him!

Farewell, and send my greetings to Antonio Benivieni, the skilled physician. Girolamo Amazzi, our delightful companion in the study of medicine and the lyre, sends his to you.

Once more farewell. [1.81]

99

Men should not be admitted indiscriminately to holy orders

Marsilio Ficino to Leonardo of Perugia, the theologian: greetings.

Our pupil, through excessive love and zeal for the Muses, last autumn fell into a morbid state of melancholy. Consequently, he asserted that he saw black phantoms by day and night, and that he was tormented by a great fear of hell. He added many other things which, as you may have heard, have happened before. Thus driven by anguish, he turned to the monks of St. Mark, and said that he wished to serve God according to their rule. But since he promised to bestow upon them his inherited possessions, the greedy men, wishing to ensnare the melancholy young man, more quickly than was fitting at once clad him in religious habit.

Foolish and corrupt rulers of religious orders do similar wrongs every day. Wrongdoing of this kind is as evil as religion is good. It concerns me, since I am a priest, a follower of Peter, to point out to you the faults of religious people; but it concerns you, since you are a leader of those people, to correct these faults, lest in future a similar fate befall young men being rashly brought to take their vows. But if the Brahmins and Pythagoreans used to admit no one at all to their human teaching unless examined and proved for two years, why is anyone at all admitted so rashly to the divine teaching? For this very reason religion is held in contempt by many; because, since people are accepted indiscriminately, there are huge numbers of men in holy orders, some of whom are corrupt, some ignorant and some mad. God, however, demands from men that which is of greatest worth. [vol. 1 app.][1]

NOTES ON THE LETTERS

Where translations are used in the notes to the letters, they are taken from the following sources: for the dialogues of Plato, from Jowett's version (Oxford, 1892); for the Orphic Hymns, the Greek text in E. Abel, *Orphica* (Leipzig, 1885, reprint, Hildesheim, 1971) and the English translations of Thomas Taylor first published in 1787, and reprinted in *Thomas Taylor the Platonist: Selected Writings*, ed. K. Raine & G. M. Harper (London, 1969). The following abbreviations are used in the notes.

Cosenza	M. E. Cosenza. *Biographical Dictionary of Humanism and Classical Scholarship.* 5 vols. Boston, 1962.
Della Torre	A. Della Torre. *Storia dell' Accademia Platonica di Firenze,* 1902.
De amore	M. Ficino. *In convivium Platonis de amore.*
De vita	M. Ficino. *De vita libri tres.*
Diog. Laert.	Diogenes Laertius. *Lives of Eminent Philosophers.*
Diz. biog. Ital.	*Dizionario Biografico degli Italiani.* Rome, 1960–.
Gentile, *Un codice*	S. Gentile. "Un codice Magliabecchiano delle epistole di Marsilio Ficino." *Interpres* 3 (1980), pp. 80–157.
Gior. stor. della lett. Ital.	*Giornale storico della letteratura Italiana.*
Iter Ital.	P. O. Kristeller. *Iter Italicum: A Finding List of Uncatalogued or Incompletely Catalogued Humanistic Manuscripts of the Renaissance in Italian and Other Libraries.* 3 vols. London and Leiden, 1963, 1967, 1983.

Kristeller, *Studies*	P. O. Kristeller. *Studies in Renaissance Thought and Letters*, 1956, 1969.
Letters	*The Letters of Marsilio Ficino.* Trans. School of Economic Science, London. 5 vols. 1975, 1978, 1981, 1988, 1994.
Macrobius, *Commentary*	*Commentary on the Dream of Scipio, De republica*, Cicero. Trans. W. H. Stahl. New York, 1952.
Marcel	R. Marcel. *Marsile Ficin.* Paris, 1958.
Opera	Marsilius Ficinus. *Opera omnia.* Basel, 1576.
Pat. Graec.	J. P. Migne. *Patrologiae Graecae.* 1857–66.
Pat. Lat.	J. P. Migne. *Patrologiae Latinae.* 2nd ed., 1878–.
Platonic Theology	M. Ficino. *Theologia Platonica sive de immortalitate animorum.*
Sabbadini	R. Sabbadini. *Le Scoperte dei Codici Latini e Greci ne' Secoli XIV e XV.* Florence, 1905.
Sermoni morali	M. Ficino. *Sermoni morali della stultitia et miseria degli Uomini.*
Sup. Fic.	P. O. Kristeller, *Supplementum Ficinianum.*
Vespasiano	Vespasiano da Bisticci, *Lives of Illustrious Men of the XVth Century.* Trans. W. George & E. Waters.

1

1. Aristippus was founder of the Cyrenaic school of philosophy, which made pleasure the highest good. For a time he was a disciple of Socrates.
2. Lucretius, in his poem *De rerum natura*, also accords an important place to pleasure.

2

1. Cf. Horace, *Ars poetica*, 361.
2. Copies of this letter were sent to Lorenzo de' Medici and Bernardo Bembo.
3. This passage echoes Cicero, *De officiis*, 1.5. Cf. also Cicero, *De finibus*, 2.16.52. See also Plato, *Phaedrus*, 250D. This passage from Plato is quoted by John of Salisbury, *Policraticus*, 8.121.
4. Compare this to Cicero, *Tusculan Disputations*, 5.24.68-69, where Cicero says that in the quest for the good the reader must set before his eyes certain tangible images to enable him more readily to understand the good: "Let us assume a man preeminently endowed with the highest qualities and let our imagination play for a moment with the picture."

3

1. See Ficino, *Platonic Theology*, 8.3.1 (ed. Marcel, p. 296); also *De amore*, "Oratio Sexta," 18 (ed. Marcel, p. 237). In Plato, definitions of virtue are found in *Republic*, 4.427E-433, *Laws*, 1.631-32, *Phaedo*, 69BC.
2. For a distinction between the reflective and moral virtues, see Aristotle, *Ethics*, 2.1. See *Republic*, 7.518E.
3. The freedom to choose between good and evil; see *Republic*, 10.617E-618.

4

1. Augustine, *Confessions*, 10, chap. 23.

5

1. Raffaele Riario was made a cardinal at the age of sixteen by Pope Sixtus IV on 10 December 1477.
2. This letter was written on 27 January 1477 (1478 new style), according to the MS Magl. VIII 1441. The letter was therefore written three months before the Pazzi conspiracy (26 April 1478).
3. See Horace, *Odes*, 1.24.7, for the image of naked truth.
4. Virgil, *Eclogues*, 2.29: *Humilis habitare casas*.
5. Colossians 3:10. These words are used in the ordination ceremony.

6. Cf. Horace, *Odes*, 2.10.9–10: "The wind most oft the highest pine tree grieves; the stately towers come down with greater fall; the highest hills the bolt of thunder cleaves" (trans. Sir Philip Sidney).

7. The Latin word *cardo* means a pivot; *cardinalis* is the adjectival form.

8. *Humanitas* is used by Ficino here to convey the love of mankind. He probably used this word as an equivalent for the Greek *philanthropia*. See Plato, *Euthyphro*, 3D.

9. See Plato, *Epistles*, 4.321B.

10. For this simile of the head and its members cf. John of Salisbury, *Policraticus*, 4.1 (*The Statesman*, trans. J. Dickinson, p. 3).

11. Argus, called "the all-seeing," had eyes in the whole of his body. Only two were closed at any one time. See Apollodorus, 2.1.3; Hyginus, *Fabulae*, 145. Oedipus solved the riddle: "What walks on four legs at sunrise, two legs at midday, and three legs at sunset?" The answer is man. Apollodorus, 3.5.8; Diodorus Siculus, 4.64.3; Hyginus, *Fabulae*, 67. This indicates that a prince should be always watching (like Argus); he should be able to see through the outer mask (like Lynceus) and understand the nature of a man at all stages in his life (as Oedipus did).

12. Quintus Curtius Rufus, *De rebus gestis Alexandri Magni*, 6.3.

13. See Iamblichus, *Life of Pythagoras*, 31.196–98.

14. Cf. Seneca, *De ira*, 3.13.3: "In the case of Socrates it was a sign of anger if he lowered his voice and became sparing of speech."

15. Diog. Laert., 3.39 (Life of Plato).

16. See Plato, *Laws*, 5.731E: "The lover is blinded about the beloved so that he judges wrongly of the just, the good, and the honorable." Horace, *Satires*, 1.3.38: "The lover in his blindness fails to see his lady's blemishes." For a study of this idea see Panofsky, "Blind Cupid" in *Studies in Iconology*, 4.

17. Matthew 16:18.

6

1. In Latin *humus* means "earth" or "soil."

7

1. See Ficino, *Opera*, p. 1979 "Symbola Pythagorae" and Iamblichus, *Protrepticos*.

2. See Virgil, *Aeneid*, 6.128–30.

8

1. Cf. Virgil, *Georgics*, 1.393.

9

1. See Kristeller, *Philosophy of Marsilio Ficino*, pp. 299–300, for a discussion on this letter.

2. A king of Mycenae who imposed upon Hercules his twelve labors.

10

1. "Many-footed," from the Greek, πολύπους.

11

1. This letter is published in *Sup. Fic.*, vol. 2, pp. 293-94. Salvini argues that there are different degrees of changeability and that God alone is truly unchangeable.
2. See Ficino, *Platonic Theology*, 2.5. Cf. Boethius, *The Consolation of Philosophy*, 5.6, and St. Augustine, *Confessions*, 11.11 seq.
3. For the function of will in the enjoyment of the divine nature, see letter 59; also *Platonic Theology*, 18.8.3-8 (Marcel, vol. 3, pp. 209-20).

12

1. Aristotle, *Physics*, 8.7.261b.
2. Plato, *Phaedrus*, 230A: "Am I a monster more complicated and swollen with passion than the serpent Typho, or a creature of a gentler and simpler sort, to whom Nature has given a diviner and lowlier destiny!"
3. Plato, *Timaeus*, 69C-72C; also, letter 30, where Ficino summarizes this description of the soul in *Timaeus*, 89D-E.
4. Ficino is probably referring to a previous letter from Cavalcanti (letter 73) in which he commends the benefits that the planet Saturn brings.
5. Iamblichus, *Protrepticus*, 27. In Ficino's notes to *Protrepticus* in MS Vat. Lat. 5953, and *Sup. Fic.* vol. 2, pp. 99-101, he gives the meaning of this metaphor: one should not be distracted by bodily concerns on a spiritual occasion, but should purge oneself of the superfluous before approaching the divine.

14

1. Plato, *Laws*, 1.643BC. "To be good at anything one must practice that thing from one's youth upwards"; *Republic*, 10.618. "Let each one of us leave every other kind of knowledge and seek and follow one thing only, if peradventure he may be able to learn . . . to discern between good and evil."
2. Porphyry, *Life of Pythagoras*, 49-50.
3. This idea of the spirit or *pneuma* that penetrates all the parts of the body was formulated in detail by the Stoics and developed by Galen. It was considered as threefold: πνεῦμα φυσικον, *spiritus naturalis;* πνεῦμα ζωτικον, *spiritus vitalis;* πνεῦμα ψυχικον, *spiritus animalis.* The breath or pneuma was thought to enter through the left side of the heart where it was converted into natural, vital, and psychic force. The pneuma then went to the brain whence it was distributed throughout the nervous system. See Galen, *De Hippocratis et Platonis Placitis*, in *Works*, ed. Kühn, vol. 3, p. 288 seq.

15

1. A manuscript copy of this letter is preserved in the Bodleian Library, Oxford: MS Lat. misc. d. 85, which originally belonged to Bartolomeo della Fonte. See Gentile, *Un codice*, p. 108.

2. Cf. passage in *Asclepius:* "God does not will anything in vain for he is full of all things and all things that he wills are good. He has all that he wills and wills all that he has." Hermes, *Asclepius*, 26b (ed. Scott, p. 347).

3. Sassetti's original villa has been substantially altered, but the late owner, Sir Harold Acton, informed us that it did once contain two chapels.

16

1. Aristotle, *Nicomachean Ethics*, 3.9.

2. This moral point concerning Hannibal is effectively made by John of Salisbury, *Policraticus*, 8.6.260, who draws on Valerius Maximus, 9.1; Mark Antony's conduct is described in Macrobius, *Saturnalia*, 3.17.15-17, and John of Salisbury, *Policraticus*, 8.7.265. According to one classical tradition Achilles was fatally wounded in the heel by an arrow from Paris as he was seeking the hand in marriage of Paris' sister Polyxena in the temple of Minerva in Troy.

3. Honey and gall are frequent images of pleasure and pain in Ficino; see letter 38.

4. Homer, *Iliad*, 17.570. "She (Athene) put strength into his (Menelaus') knees and shoulders and made him as bold as a fly which, though driven off, will yet come again and bite if it can, so dearly does it love man's blood—even so bold as this did she make him" (trans. Samuel Butler).

5. See 1 Kings 11:1-10.

6. Aristotle, *Nicomachean Ethics*, 1.1094.

7. Cicero, *De Senectute*, 13.44: "The divine Plato calls pleasure the bait of evil because evidently men are caught by it, like fishes on a hook." He is referring to Plato, *Timaeus*, 69D: "Pleasure a mighty lure to evil."

8. Virgil, *Aeneid*, 1.350.

9. Horace, *Epistles*, 1.2.55: *Nocet empta dolore voluptas* (from Plato, *Timaeus*, 69D).

17

1. This refers principally to Luigi Pulci (1432-84), *pulci* being Italian for "fleas." He was the poet and wit who, in his poem *Morgante*, held up to contempt religious belief, as well as lampooning Ficino and the Platonic Academy. In spite of Ficino's letters to Lorenzo, Pulci continued to enjoy the favor and friendship of Lorenzo, who was also a poet. (For a full account see Marcel, *Marsile Ficin*, pp. 420-33).

2. See Diog. Laert. 2.36 (Life of Socrates). "'We ought not to object,' he used to say, 'to be subjects for the comic poets, for if they satirize our faults, they will do us good, and if not they do not touch us.'" Also see Diog. Laert. 7.117 (Life of Zeno). Zeno was the founder of the Stoic school of philosophy.

3. See Diog. Laert. 5.18 (Life of Aristotle). "On hearing that someone abused him, he declared, 'He may even scourge me as long as it be in my absence.'" See also 5.41 (Life of Theophrastus).

4. See Diog. Laert. 9.7-8 (Life of Heraclitus); and 1.27 (Life of Thales).

5. See Plato, *Phaedo*, 81, 83, and *Cratylus*, 400C for the Orphic and Pythagorean doctrine that the body is the grave *(σῆμα)* of the soul *(σῶμα)*.

6. 1 John 5:19.

19

1. Greek philosopher of the fifth century B.C. Some of his doctrines, including that of atoms, and pleasure (i.e., tranquillity of the soul) as the supreme good, influenced Epicurus. In ancient times he was known as "the laughing philosopher."

2. Heraclitus was a fifth century B.C. philosopher of Ephesus. Maintaining that "everything is and is not," he held that fire embodied most perfectly the principle of "becoming," and thus the harmony of the universe. The soul approached most nearly to perfection when most like the fiery vapor out of which it was created and to which it will return. Thus "while we live our souls are dead in us, but when we die our souls are restored to life."

   He was known as the "dark" or "weeping" philosopher in ancient times from the lonely life he led, as well as from the nature of his philosophy.

   Artists in the Renaissance often juxtaposed the two philosophers. See E. Wind, "The Christian Democritus," *Journal of the Warburg Institute* 2 (1938–39).

20

1. See letter 19, notes 1 and 2.

22

1. Plato, *Timaeus*, 34E; *Laws*, 10.892A.

23

1. Ficino writes in the prologue to *De amore* (ed. Marcel, p. 136): "Plato died at the age of eighty-one at a banquet on 7 November, his birthday. This banquet, which commemorated both his birthday and the anniversary of his death, was renewed every year by all the first followers of Plato down to the time of Plotinus and Porphyry. But for twelve hundred years after Porphyry, these solemn feasts ceased to be celebrated, until in our time Lorenzo de' Medici, wishing to restore the Platonic Symposium, appointed Francesco Bandini as master of the feast *(archytriclinum)*."

2. The feast at Careggi was held on 7 November 1468. Ficino wrote his commentary on the *Symposium* between November 1468 and July 1469.

3. See Plato, *Timaeus*, 34B, 36E, seq., describing the creation of the soul.

4. "Like Janus having two faces" in the Italian manuscript.

24

1. Cicero, *De divinatione*, 1.129.

2. Hesiod, *Works and Days*, 120–25.

3. Plato, *Laws*, 11.927.

25

1. See Ficino, *Platonic Theology*, 9.1–5 (ed. Marcel, vol. 2).

26

1. The *Platonic Theology on the Immortality of Souls*, written between 1469 and 1474.
2. This is the opening paragraph of Ficino's *Platonic Theology*, 1.1.1 (ed. Marcel, vol. 1, p. 38).

27

1. See Diog. Laert. 6.32 (Life of Diogenes): "Someone took him [Diogenes] into a magnificent house and warned him not to spit, whereupon, having cleared his throat, he spat into the man's face, being unable, he said, to find a meaner receptacle."
2. Terence, *Eunuchus*, 4.4, 7.

28

1. This sermon or *Declamatiuncula* formed part of a collection of such sermons that were translated into Italian by Ficino and sent to Jacopo Guicciardini in June 1478 under the tile *Sermoni morali della stultitia et miseria degli uomini.*
2. Tantalus was the legendary king of Lydia said to have stolen the secrets of the gods, for which he was punished in Hades with an insatiable thirst, being placed up to the chin in a pool of water that flowed away as soon as he tried to taste it. Hyginus, *Fabulae*, 82. Fulgentius, *Fabulae*, 2.15.
3. Lethe was one of the rivers of the underworld from which souls drank in their journey through Hades. It had the power of making them forget whatever they had done, seen, or heard before. See Plato, *Republic*, 10.621.

29

1. The style of this dialogue is inspired by St. Augustine's *Soliloquies* and refers to a period in Ficino's life when he experienced "a bitterness of spirit," *spiritus amaritudine distractus.* See Corsi 8 in Marcel, p. 683.

   The passage beginning "Your father is not of a physical nature . . ." was inserted later, as the early manuscripts show. It is similar to one in Augustine, *De trinitate,* 8.3-5, which treats of the search for God by the intellect. Both it and other parts of the dialogue are also found in the *Platonic Theology* of Ficino, 9.3.14, and 10.8 (ed. Marcel, vol. 2, p. 88).

30

1. This letter was translated into Italian by Ficino and included in his *Sermoni morali della stultitia et miseria degli uomini* addressed to Jacopo Guicciardini. See letter 52, note 1.
2. Ficino's universe, which is based partly on the Neoplatonic system, is divided into four hierarchies: (1) the Cosmic Mind or Nous, the Supercelestial Realm, which is incorruptible; (2) the Cosmic Soul or Anima Mundi, the Celestial World of Pure Causes; (3) the Realm of Nature, compounded of form and matter, which is connected to the Celestial World by the Spiritus Mundanus or Humanus; (4) the Realm of Matter,

which is formless and gross. The "middle region" in this letter would seem to refer to the Realm of Nature and Spiritus Mundanus. See Panofsky, *Studies in Iconology* (Oxford, 1939), chap. 5, "The Neoplatonic Movement in Florence and Northern Italy."

3. Plato, *Republic*, 9.588C–589C.

4. Plato, *Timaeus*, 69C–72C.

5. Plato, *Phaedrus*, 246, 253DE.

6. The giant Antaeus, symbolizing desire, was invincible so long as he remained in contact with his mother earth. He forced strangers to wrestle with him and then slew them. Hercules, lifting him from the earth, crushed him to death in the air. Fulgentius, *Mythologiae*, 2.4.

7. Plato, *Phaedo*, 84A.

8. Cf. ibid., 81B–82A and Ficino, *Platonic Theology*, 17.4 (ed. Marcel, vol. 3, pp. 167–74), where transmigration and the soul's appetites are discussed.

9. Plato, *Phaedrus*, 230A.

31

1. St. Augustine, *De musica*, 6.1.3.

2. Pythagoras is credited with the discovery of the numerical rations of harmony by listening to a blacksmith beating different lengths of iron. Plato's world soul is based on harmonic rations. See Macrobius, *Commentary*, 2.1–4; Plato, *Timaeus*, 34–37; and Ficino's commentary on Timaeus (*Opera*, pp. 1438–66).

3. Modern medical opinion confirms that the auditory nerve passes from the ear via the brain stem to the auditory cortex on the temporal lobe of the brain, which being neither anterior nor posterior could be described as middle. This temporal lobe is also responsible for memory. If it becomes diseased, disorders of memory, behavior, hearing, and other senses occur.

4. Cicero, *De amicitia*, 15.54.

5. Horace, *Odes*, 1.32.

32

1. Horace, *Ars poetica*, 343.

2. Mercury (Hermes) is said to have invented the lyre from the shell of a tortoise, bestowing it as a gift upon Phoebus (Apollo), who played it with consummate skill. See *Homeric Hymns* (to Hermes), 40–55, 470–503; Orpheus, *Argonautica*, 381.

3. *Lyrare ne deliremus*: A rhetorical figure of speech (paranomasia) that transfers into English.

4. See letter 33.

5. The qualities of gravity and levity and the combination of the two *(temperatio)* were associated by Ficino with the music of Jupiter, Venus, and Mercury, respectively. *De vita*, 3.2; *Opera*, p. 534. See also Quintilian, *Institutes* 1.10.24.

6. An allusion to Horace, *Odes*, 1.32.15, *salve rite vocanti*, in which the poet invokes his lyre to grant him the song that he desires, if he invokes her rightly.

7. This last paragraph is a postscript written by Luca Fabiani, Ficino's scribe (Della Torre, p. 102).

33

1. Abel, *Orphica*, hymn 34, to Apollo, p. 76; and Thomas Taylor, *The Orphic Hymns*, 33, to Apollo, pp. 246–48; also see his footnote about the lyre of Apollo being an image of celestial harmony.

2. See Plato, *Timaeus*, 87C–88, and also 35B–36C, for the ratios of the tetrachord that according to Plutarch represent the harmony of the four elements in the soul. Plutarch, *De musica*, 1138D–1139B, *Moralia*, Loeb, vol. 14, pp. 399–403.

3. See Aristotle, *Politics*, 8.7, for purification by music.

4. Plato, *Republic*, 3.401E–402.

5. 1 Samuel 16:14–16 and 23.

6. Fantasy *(phantasia)* was distinguished from imagination *(imaginatio)* in that the latter signified the retention of images whereas the former dealt with them by "separating and putting together." Albertus Magnus, quoted in C. S. Lewis, *The Discarded Image* (Cambridge, 1964), p. 163.

7. One such story of Pythagoras is told in Quintilian, *Institutiones*, 1.10.31–33.

8. Arion was a lyric poet from Lesbos who lived in the seventh century B.C. In legend he escaped from sailors who meant to murder him by jumping overboard, and getting to shore on the back of a dolphin that had been attracted by his playing on the lyre (Herodotus 1.23, 24). Amphion in mythology was a son of Jupiter, who was said to have raised the walls of Thebes with the sound of his lyre (Homer, *Odyssey* 2).

9. See Hermes Trismegistus, *Pimander*, 1.16–19.

10. Aristoxenus, a Pythagorean philosopher and musician who wrote on the principles of harmony. See Cicero, *Tusc. Disp.* 1.10.19, and Quintilian, *Institutiones*, 1.10.22.

11. Plato, *Alcibiades*, 108C.

12. Plato would only have allowed the Dorian and Phrygian modes to be played to the guardians of his republic—"which will best express the accents of courage in the face of stern necessity and misfortune, and of temperance in prosperity." Plato, *Republic*, 3.399, trans. Cornford.

34

1. A fever that recurred every other day. According to Plato it was caused by an excess of water in the system. See Plato, *Timaeus*, 86.

2. The source for the doctrine of *spiritus* as a substance that linked body and soul is Plato's *Timaeus*, 43A. Ficino describes the *spiritus* at length in his work on medicine and astrology, *De vita libri tres*, *Opera* 1.493. In *De amore* he defines it as "a kind of very thin and clear vapor created through the heat of the heart from the purest part of the blood, and diffused through all the parts." *De amore*, "Oratio Sexta," 6 (ed. Marcel, p. 207). See D. P. Walker, *Spiritual and Demonic Magic from Ficino to Campanella* (London, 1958); and C. S. Lewis, *The Discarded Image*, pp. 165–69.

35

1. Plato, *Ion*, 533D–536; *Phaedrus*, 245. For Democritus, see Cicero, *De oratore*, 2.46. 194. *De divinatione*, 1.37.80.

2. *Phaedrus*, 250.
3. Hermes Trismegistus, *Pimander*, 1.6–8.
4. In the *Republic*, 5.476 seq., Plato describes ideas as the unchanging forms of justice, goodness, beauty, etc., of which the manifestations we perceive are shadows. They alone are the objects of real knowledge. See also Plato, *Timaeus*, 28, seq. The substance of this letter is drawn from Plato's *Phaedrus*, 244–56, and *Phaedo*, 81–83, 66–68.
5. *Phaedrus*, 247.
6. *Phaedo*, 66–68, 82.
7. *Phaedrus*, 249.
8. Ibid., 244–45.
9. This Dionysius was, in the fifteenth century, wrongly believed to be Paul's Athenian convert (Acts 17:34). He was in fact a Christian Neoplatonist of the fifth century A.D., whose writings were much studied by Christian theologians.
10. Romans 1:20; Dionysius the Areopagite, *The Divine Names*, 4.4.
11. *Phaedrus*, 250.
12. For this and the following passage see *Phaedrus*, 251–56, and *Phaedo*, 81–83.
13. Virgil, *Aeneid*, 6.734: "*Clausae tenebris et carcere caeco.*"
14. *Phaedrus*, 245.
15. *Ion*, 534.
16. According to Macrobius the muses are the song of the universe. The Etruscan name for them, "Camenae," a form of "Canenae," is derived from *canere*, "to sing." Macrobius, *Commentary*, 2.3.4.
17. *Republic*, 10.617.
18. Macrobius, *Commentary*, 2.3.1.
19. Ibid. See Porphyry, *Vita Pythagorae*, 31; Proclus, ed. Diehl, 203E; Plutarch, *De procreatione animi in Timaeo*, 32.1029C.
20. Virgil, *Aeneid*, 6.724–27.
21. Virgil, *Eclogues*, 3.60.
22. From the Orphic theogony, quoted also by Plato, *Laws*, 4.715E—"God, as the old tradition declares, holding in his hand the beginning, middle and end of all that is . . ." See Abel, *Orphica*, p. 167, verse 46. Quoted also in Eusebius, *De praep. evang.*, 3.9.
23. *Phaedrus*, 265. In *De amore*, Ficino describes the four kinds of divine frenzy as means by which God draws the soul back to unity and to Himself (*De amore*, "Oratio Septima," 13.257, 14.258, ed. Marcel).

36

1. Plato, *Phaedrus*, 244, seq.; *Ion*, 533–54.
2. Ovid, *Fasti*, 6.5–6: "*Est Deus in nobis agitante calescimus illo impetus ille Sacrae semina mentis habet.*" This text is also repeated in Ficino's *Platonic Theology*, 13.2; *De poetis*, 2 (ed. Marcel, p. 203).

37

1. When the Moon and Mars are 180⁰ apart, i.e., opposite in the zodiac, the negative aspects of each planet could be strong. Ficino, seeing the whole situation, was aware

that the Moon and Mars were both favorably aspected by Venus (608 and 1208) so that negative effects were neutralized. This allowed the positive effects such as fruitfullness and courage to be revealed by the beauty and harmony of Venus.

2. The Muses presided over the nine principal arts. Urania, meaning "the heavenly one," was associated with the art of astronomy; Calliope, meaning "she of the beautiful voice," was associated with the art of heroic song, and said by Hesiod to be the most glorious of the Muses. Ficino expounds the character of the Muses in his commentary on Plato's *Ion* (*Opera*, p. 1283): Urania is the voice of the starry heaven; Calliope is the harmony arising from all eight spheres. See also Plato's *Republic*, 10.617; Macrobius, *Commentary*, 2.3; and letter 35.

3. See *De amore*, 5.8. Botticelli's painting in the National Gallery in London depicts the taming of Mars by Venus.

4. In letter 35 Ficino follows Plato in describing as divine ecstasy or frenzy that ardent desire of the soul to return to its own true nature from its imprisonment in the body. This desire is stimulated by the reminders that come from the contemplation of visual beauty, and from love (Venus); from music and poetry of the highest quality (the Muses); from participation in the sacred mysteries (Dionysus); or from the divine rapture of prophecy (Apollo). See Plato, *Ion*, and Ficino's commentary thereon (*Opera*, p. 1283).

5. See *De amore*, 7.15, and Plato, *Symposium*, 195–97.

<h1 style="text-align:center">38</h1>

1. Latin and Greek authors, known to Ficino, who used this simile were Seneca, Plutarch, Isocrates, Basil, John Chrysostom, Macrobius, John of Salisbury, and Petrarch.

2. Aristotle, *Problemata*, 30.1. See also Cicero, *Tusculan Disputations*, 1.33. In *De vita libri tres*, 1.4, Ficino lists the three causes that produce melancholy in scholars. The first cause is heavenly: "Mercury, which invites us to pursue learning, and Saturn, which makes us persevere in the pursuit of learning, are said by the astronomers to be somewhat cold and dry . . . in the view of the doctors this is the melancholic nature, and this nature Mercury and Saturn impart to the students of letters." The second cause is natural: "To pursue studies that are particularly difficult it is necessary for the mind to betake itself from the outer to the inner, as if from the circumference to the centre. . . . But to be established in the centre is principally the property of the earth itself, to which black bile has a very close resemblance. . . . Contemplation produces a nature very similar to black bile." The third cause is human: the brain turns dry and cold through excess of thought, and the man's spirits are depleted. The finer parts of the blood are utilized in the work of replenishment, leaving the blood thick, dark, and cold. The powers of digestion are weakened, while lack of exercise leads to accumulation of poisons in the body.

    To relieve the melancholic condition Ficino (*De vita*, 1.10) recommends "the frequent sight of shining water and of the colour green or red, the enjoyment of gardens and groves, walks by the riverside and delightful rides through pleasant meadows . . . gentle sailing . . . easy occupations and various harmless activities, and the constant companionship of agreeable men." See *Opera*, pp. 496–502.

3. Ecclesiastes 1:18.
4. Diog. Laert., 5.18 (Life of Aristotle).
5. Pliny, *Natural History*, 15.34 (110-11).
6. Ficino, following Plato, distinguishes two Venuses, a heavenly Venus and a "common" or natural Venus. The heavenly Venus, ᾿Αφροδίτη οὐρανία (Venus Caelestis), daughter of Uranus, has no mother and dwells in the world of causes as a divine idea; she represents the intelligible beauty that cannot be seen by the eyes. The second Venus, ᾿Αφροδίτη πάνδημος (Venus Vulgaris), the daughter of Jupiter and Dione (a sea nymph), gives life and shape to the things in nature and thereby makes the intelligible beauty accessible to our perception and imagination. The higher Venus draws the mind to the contemplation of divine beauty, while the lower draws the mind to recreate that same beauty in bodies. See Ficino, *De amore*, 2.7 and 8 (*Opera*, pp. 1326–27). The origin of the idea is in Plato, *Symposium*, 180DE, and is elaborated in Plotinus, *Enneads*, 3.5.2; see Panofsky, *Studies in Iconology*, chap. 5, "The Neoplatonic Movement in Florence and Northern Italy."
7. Ficino in his commentary to Plato's *Ion* writes, "Jupiter is the mind of God from which come Apollo, the mind of the world-soul and the soul of the whole world, and the eight souls of the celestial spheres, which are called the nine Muses; because as they move the heavens harmoniously they produce musical melody which, distributed into nine sounds, namely, the eight notes of the spheres together with the one harmony of them all, gives rise to the nine Sirens singing to God. Wherefore Apollo is led by Jupiter and the Muses by Apollo, that is, the chorus of Muses is led by the mind of the world-soul." *Opera*, p. 1283. See also letter 35.

39

1. Diog. Laert. 3.37.
2. Quintilian, *Institutio Oratoria*, 10.1.81.
3. Cicero, *Brutus*, 31.121. See also Cicero, *Orator*, 19.67 for Plato's poetic language.
4. The Pythagorean concept of celestial harmony expressed by Cicero in the *Somnium Scipionis* (Cicero, *De republica*, 6.18.18) and by Macrobius (*Commentary*, 2.1.8-13) was derived from Plato's *Timaeus* and *Republic*, 7.529-30.

40

1. Knowledge and thinking are concerned with "true being," while "opinion" and "imagining" constitute the apprehension of appearance in the world of becoming. See Plato, *Republic*, 7.534A.
2. See Plato, *Apology*, 20E-21A.
3. Luke 9:62.
4. Genesis 19:26.

41

1. One of two famous inscriptions in the temple of Apollo at Delphi; the other is "Nothing to excess."

2. Pythagoras, *Golden Verses* (*Aurea Verba* in *Opera*, vol. 2, p. 1978.)

3. Psalm 8:5.

4. Psalm 82:6.

5. This passage is also quoted in Ficino, *Platonic Theology*, 6.2.1 (ed. Marcel, p. 227).

42

1. This speech is an early work of Ficino, written probably when he was a student. See Kristeller, *Sup. Fic.*, vol. 1, p. c.

2. Compare this with a passage in Augustine, *City of God*, 8.9 (trans. H. Bettenson, p. 311): "There are philosophers who have conceived of God, the supreme and true God, as the author of all created things, the light of knowledge, the final good of all activity, and who have recognized him as being for us the origin of existence, the truth of doctrine and the happiness of life. They may be called most suitably Platonists." Augustine would seem to be Ficino's main source for this idea.

3. This idea does not appear to occur in the three dialogues mentioned, but see Plato, *Philebus*, 65: "If we are not able to hunt the good with one idea only, with three we may catch our prey; beauty, symmetry, truth are the three . . ."

4. Cf. Iamblichus, *On the Egyptian Mysteries*, 8.2–3 (paras. 261–3); 1.5 (18): existence, power, activity. See also Ficino's epitome of Iamblichus' *De mysteriis*, *Opera*, p. 1873. Cf. Proclus, *Elements of Theology*, 101–103 seq.: being, life, intelligence.

5. See Dionysius the Areopagite, *The Divine Names*, 5, on Deity as existence, life, and wisdom. See also Ficino's commentary to the *Mystical Theology* of Dionysius, *Opera*, p. 1013.

6. Hilary (A.D. 300–367), Bishop of Poitiers, who was a convert from Neoplatonism, wrote a work on the Trinity, *De Trinitate* (*Pat. Lat.*, 10).

7. *De vera religione*, 55.112 (*Pat. Lat.*, 34); *City of God*, 8.5.

8. The three divisions of philosophy: natural, rational, and moral, corresponding to the threefold conception of God as the cause of existence, the principle of reason and the rule of life. Augustine, *City of God*, 8.4. See also chaps. 6–8.

9. Hermes Trismegistus, *Pimander*, 10.6.

10. Pythagoras, *Golden Verses*, 36 (final verses). See *Opera*, p. 1979.

11. Plato, *Republic*, 7.540.

12. See Plotinus, *Enneads*, 4.7.10, on the immortality of the soul, (McKenna, p. 354), which also quotes a line from Empedocles describing the soul that has ascended to the pure intellect: "Farewell: I am to you an immortal God." Diels, *Frag. der Vorsok.*, 31, B112.

13. For this quotation see Pseudo-Apuleius, *De mundo*, proem. The Greek original (Περι Κόσμον) is by an unknown Platonic writer of the first century A.D., not by Aristotle.

14. See Plato, *Statesman*, 271D–272A for a description of the age of Cronos or the Golden Age; see Plato, *Republic*, 5.473D for the belief that the ills of the human race will end only when power and wisdom are united in the same man.

15. Pythagoras, *Golden Verses*, 36 (final verses). See *Opera*, p. 1979.

43

1. See Plato, *Phaedrus*, 249–56.

2. The *"philodoxi"* in Plato, *Republic*, 5.479 (ed. Cornford). They "set their affections on the objects of belief"; as opposed to philosophers, "whose affections are set, in every case, on the objects of reality."

3. Plotinus (A.D. 204–270), the founder of Neoplatonism, described the fundamental ideas of his philosophy in the *Enneads* (translated by Ficino into Latin), in which he treats of the immortality of the soul.

4. Porphyry (A.D. 233–305) studied under Plotinus, interpreted his works, and wrote his life.

5. The Syrian Iamblichus (died *c*. A.D. 330). In his writings Neoplatonism was further developed.

6. Proclus continued the development of Neoplatonism in his *Platonic Theology* and the *Elements of Theology*, which were both much studied in the Middle Ages and the Renaissance. (Ficino borrowed Proclus's title for his own work on the immortality of the soul, and also many of his views on mythology.)

7. Plato, *Epistles*, 2.314. Dionysius was king of Syracuse. Plato corresponded with him and visited his court.

44

1. Plato, *Republic*, 488.

45

1. Translation of the Greek *ophthalmia*. It is mentioned in Plato, *Gorgias*, 495E, where Plato uses similar arguments to show that the good and the pleasant are incompatible.

2. See *Phaedo*, 81B.

3. Aristotle, *Nicomachean Ethics*, 10.8.1179a.

4. See Augustine, *City of God*, trans. H. Bettenson, 8, chap. 3 (p. 301): "He (Socrates) saw that man had been trying to discover the causes of the universe, and he believed that the universe had its first and supreme cause in nothing but the will of the one Supreme God; hence he thought that the causation of the universe could be grasped only by a purified intelligence. That is why he thought it essential to insist on the need to cleanse one's life by accepting a high moral standard, so that the soul should be relieved of the weight of the lust that held it down, and then by its natural vigour should rise up to the sphere of the eternal and behold, thanks to its pure intelligence, the essence of the immaterial and unchangeable light where dwell the causes of all created things in undisturbed stability."

5. See Iamblichus, *Life of Pythagoras*, 32: "Pythagoras showed favor to just and good men, while rejecting the company of the violent and malevolent."

6. Plato, *Epistle*, 7.341C.

7. Plato, *Phaedo*, 67B.

8. Cf. Jerome, *Contra Jovinianum*, 2.11 (*Pat. Lat.*, vol. 23, p. 313). See Ficino, *De vita*, 1.7, *Opera*, p. 499. See also John of Salisbury, *Policraticus*, 8.6.256. These passages may have their origin in Plato, *Republic*, 9.586.

9. Plato draws an analogy between the visible sun perceived by the eye and the Good perceived by the enlightened mind. See *Republic*, 6.508E–509B; also Plotinus, *Enneads*, 1.6.9.

10. See Kristeller, *Philosophy of Marsilio Ficino*, p. 301, for a translation of parts of this letter. Kristeller says: "Philosophy is here conceived as an active and living force guiding men by means of knowledge toward their real goal. We must go back to antiquity to find such a sublime yet concrete conception of philosophy."

46

1. This essay, together with the *Life of Plato* (see letter 47), originally formed the introduction to Ficino's *Philebus Commentary*, which was written before 1474 (according to Corsi before 1469) and delivered in a series of public lectures, possibly in the former church of Santa Maria degli Angeli in Florence, prefaced with these words: "Since we are going to interpret the sacred philosophy of the divine Plato in this renowned place at the request of the leading citizens, I thought it appropriate that we should first briefly consider what philosophy is." In 1477 the essay was added to the fourth book of letters (see *Sup. Fic.*, vol. 1, pp. c–ci). The original version is preserved in MS Vat. Lat. 5953; see *Sup. Fic.*, vol. 1, pp. 30–31 for variants.

2. See letter 48.

3. See letter 42.

4. See Augustine, *City of God*, 8.2, (trans. Bettenson, p. 299): "Pythagoras . . . is credited with the coinage of the actual name of philosophy."

5. Plato, *Republic*, 6.485 seq. The passage that follows, down to "greatest crimes" agrees in part with Ficino's epitome of Alcinous, *De doctrina Platonis*, chap. 1 (*Opera*, p. 1946).

6. Plato, *Republic*, 6.495.

7. On the importance of mathematics, see Plato, *Republic*, 7.522 seq.

8. Plato, *Phaedo*, 67.

9. Plato, *Phaedrus*, 249C; *Theaetetus*, 176.

10. See Plato, *Republic*, 7.526–31 for the order of the studies. The Latin word used by Ficino here is *stereometria* (solid geometry). The Greek στερεομετρια is used to describe three-dimensional forms in Plato (*Epinomis*, 990D, but see note 33 to letter 47) and in Aristotle. Plato also uses στερεομετρια to designate cubic numbers (Theaetetus, 148B).

11. For the hymn on dialectic see Plato, *Republic*, 7.532–34: "When a person starts on the discovery of the absolute . . ."

12. Plato, *Timaeus*, 47B.

13. Plato, *Republic*, 5.473D; *Laws*, 713: "There is said to have been in the time of Cronos a blessed rule and life, of which the best ordered of existing states is a copy."

14. Hesiod, *Works and Days*, 120 seq.

47

1. An earlier version of this *Life of Plato* originally formed the first chapter of Ficino's *Philebus Commentary*, and was written between 1469 and 1474. It is preserved in MS Vat. Lat. 5953 (See Kristeller, *Sup. Fic.*, vol. 1, pp. 30–31). This final version was written at the end of 1477, and in a number of MSS (L. 12, L0 1, etc.) it forms an

introduction to the dialogues of Plato translated into Latin by Ficino. Contemporary with this *Life of Plato* is one by Guarino Veronese (Vat. Lat. 8086).

Ficino's life of Plato is drawn mainly from Diogenes Laertius, *Lives of Eminent Philosophers* (third century A.D.). A medieval version of this work, *De vita et moribus Philosophorum* by Walter Burley, is found in Vat. Lat. 3081. A large number of other sources are also used, notably Apuleius, Cicero, Plutarch, and the *Epistles* and *Dialogues of Plato*. The earliest extant life of Plato is Apuleius' *De Platone et eius dogmate* (Concerning Plato and his Teachings, second century A.D.). Plato's disciples Speusippus, Aristotle, and Xenocrates all wrote accounts of his life that have been lost. Olympiodorus of Alexandria (sixth century A.D.) wrote a *Life of Plato* that is extant. Many of the anecdotes mentioned by Ficino are outside the mainstream tradition of Plato's life. For more detailed information on the sources, see Alice S. Riginos, *Platonica: The Anecdotes Concerning the Life and Writings of Plato* (Leiden, 1976).

2.   Diog. Laert., 3.1 (Life of Plato). The same story of Plato's divine birth is given in Apuleius, *De Platone et eius dogmate*, 1.1 and Olympiodorus, *Life of Plato*, 1. A similar story concerning the birth of Pythagoras is given in Iamblichus, *Life of Pythagoras*, 2.4-5, who was said to be descended from Apollo.

3.   John of Salisbury, *Policraticus*, 7.5. The legend of Plato's divine birth from Apollo is justified by Plutarch on the grounds that Plato was the healer of men's souls as Apollo was the healer of their bodies. Plato came to be permanently associated with the divine physician Asclepius: Plutarch, *Quaestionum convivialium* (Table Talk), 8.1; *Moralia*, 9. Plato was also associated with Apollo by the fact that the Academy celebrated his birthday on the seventh day of the month of Thargelion, Apollo's birthday. Thargelion corresponds roughly with May. Julius Firmicus's horoscope quote in note 6, however, would place his birthday in January or February.

4.   Apuleius, *De Platone*, 1, states that Plato was born the day after Socrates' birthday. This would make Plato's birthday the seventh day of Thargelion of the first year of the eighty-eighth Olympiad, i.e. 427 B.C.

5.   Ficino is possibly referring to the first version of *De amore*, written between 1467 and 1469, which is not extant. The second version does not contain this description. See *Sup. Fic.*, vol. 1, p. cxxv.

6.   Julius Firmicus Maternus, *Matheseos*, 6.30.20. Ficino has paraphrased the original words. "If the ascendant is in Aquarius, and Mars, Mercury, and Venus are in conjunction in that degree; Jupiter is on the descendant in Leo; the sun is on the anaphora of the ascendant in Pisces; the moon is in the fifth house in Gemini, in trine to the ascendant; and Saturn is in the ninth house in Libra—this chart produces an interpreter of divine and celestial matters. He possesses a combination of learned speech and divine intelligence and is trained by some kind of heavenly power to give true expression to all secrets of divinity. This chart is said to have been that of Plato." J. F. Maternus, *Matheseos: Ancient Astrology, Theory and Practice*, trans. Jean Rhys Bram (Park Ridge, N. J., 1975), p. 209.

7.   Cicero, *De divinatione*, 1.36. A longer version of this story is recounted in Olympiodorus, *Life of Plato*, 1, where the event takes place in the hills of Hymettus

while a sacrifice is being made to Apollo and the gods by Plato's parents on his behalf. See *Prolegomena to Platonic Philosophy*, 1.2, ed. Westerink (Amsterdam, 1962).

8. Diog. Laert., 3.5; Apuleius, *De Platone*, 1.1, the longer version of the story. The swan was a bird sacred to Apollo.

9. Diog. Laert., 3.5; Ficino also admitted burning some of his early compositions on pleasure (*Opera*, p. 933, 3, letter to Martinus Uranius).

10. Academia (*Ἑκαδημεια*) was a piece of land near Athens, originally belonging to the hero Hecademus that Plato purchased for his school, from which the word "academy" derives. Cf. Diog. Laert., 3.8.

11. Basil, *Sermones*, *De legendis libris Gentilium*, 7 (*Pat. Graec.*, 31). Jerome, *Adversus Jovinianum*, 2.9 (*Pat. Lat.* 23).

12. Diog. Laert., 3.4. A pun on the word *πλατων* (platon), which in Greek means "broad."

13. Diog. Laert., 3.8; 3.18–21. Diogenes Laertius, on whom Ficino relies at this point, would appear to be inaccurate. The battle of Tanagra took place in 457 B.C. about thirty years before Plato was born. The battle at Delium took place in 424 B.C. when Plato would have been about four years old. It is possible that Diogenes has mistaken the presence of Plato at this battle for that of Socrates. The latter certainly fought there. It is uncertain to which campaign at Corinth Diogenes is referring, but none is known at which Plato could have been present. Diogenes gives as his source Aristoxenus, who wrote, *inter alia*, many biographies, now lost, among which was one of Plato.

14. Helice in Achaia in the Bay of Corinth was overwhelmed by a tidal wave in the great earthquake of 372 B.C. Pliny, *Nat. Hist.*, 2.92.

15. Diog. Laert., 3.21–22; see Plato, *Epistles*, 7.327–33, and Plutarch's *Life of Dion* for an account of Plato's friendship with Dion and his voyages to Sicily.

16. Diog. Laert., 3.23; Plutarch, *Life of Dion*, 18–20; Plato, *Epistles*, 7.338 seq.

17. Pliny, *Nat. Hist.*, 7.30 (110).

18. Diog. Laert., 3.23. Aelian, *Varia historia*, 2.41. Plato also declined a similar invitation from the Cyrenaeans because they were so prosperous; Plutarch, *Ad principem ineruditum*, 779 (*Moralia*, 10). Cf. Plato, *Epistles*, 7.330D–331D for the idea that a philosopher should only give advice where there is a reasonable likelihood that it will be heeded. He may never use force to bring about a change in a constitution.

19. See Plato, *Epistles*, 3.316A, where Plato is described as having worked on the preamble to the laws of the Syracusans.

20. For this group of Plato's followers who were described as lawgivers, see Plutarch, *Adversus Colotem*, 32 (*Moralia*, 14).

21. Augustine, *De vera religione*, 3.5 (*Pat. Lat.*, 34).

22. Diog. Laert., 3.26.

23. Seneca, *De ira*, 2.21.10; 3.12.6.

24. Diog. Laert., 3.39.

25. See Plato, *Epistles*, 7.326B for a reference to Syracusan banquets, with men eating twice a day and never sleeping alone.

26. See especially Ficino, *De amore*, 7.2, "Socrates the true lover," and 16 (ed. Marcel, pp. 242–45, 260–62).

27. Diog. Laert., 3.40. Cf. Plato, *Epistles*, 2.311, on the great importance that men of

superior virtue attach to the memorial of themselves to be left after their death, in the minds of men.

28. Aristotle, *Problemata*, 30.953a; quoted by Cicero, *Tusculanos*, 1.33.80.
29. Diog. Laert., 4.6 (Life of Xenocrates); Plutarch, *Life of Dion*, 17.1.
30. Diog. Laert., 3.46.
31. The Greek text of Diogenes gives "Chamaeleon *adds* Lycurgus . . ." Chamaeleon was a peripatetic writer of the third century B.C., not a member of Plato's Academy. Mnesistratus is mentioned only by Diogenes as an authority for the statement that Demosthenes was Plato's pupil. See Diog. Laert., 3.47.
32. This is Ficino's interpretation.
33. See Diog. Laert., 3.57–60. *Ion* is missing from this list, although it was translated into Latin by Ficino. The following works, once attributed to Plato, are now considered to be spurious: *Axiochus, De Justo, De Virtute, Demodocus, Sisyphus, Eryxias, Epinomis, Hipparchus, Amatores, Theages, Minos,* and the *Definitions*. The following works are of dubious authenticity: *Alcibiades* 1 and 2, *Hippias maior & minor, Menexenus,* and *Cleitophon.*

    Of the dialogues now regarded as spurious, Ficino translated *Epinomis, Hipparchus, Amatores, Minos, Theages,* and *Cleitophon.* Of these only the last he considered was possibly not by Plato. Ficino also translated *Axiochus,* which he considered to be the lost dialogue on death by Xenocrates, and the *Definitions* which he attributed to Speusippus.

    Of the *Epistles*, seven and eight are generally regarded as genuine, while one and twelve are thought to be spurious. The authenticity of the rest is dubious. The only one questioned by Ficino was thirteen, which he did not translate. See *Sup. Fic.*, vol. 1, p. cxlvii seq.
34. See note 33 above.
35. Cf. Diog. Laert., 3.49 for other classifications.
36. Cf. Diog. Laert., 3.52: "Where he has a firm grasp, Plato expounds his own view and refutes the false one, but if the subject is obscure, he suspends judgment. His own views are expounded by four persons, Socrates, Timaeus, the Athenian Stranger (in the *Laws*), the Eleatic Stranger (in the *Statesman* and *Sophist*)."
37. Diog. Laert., 3.37.
38. Cicero, *Brutus*, 31.121.
39. Diog. Laert., 5.9 (Life of Aristotle). He was seventeen when he came to Plato.
40. Cicero, *Tusculanos*, 1.17.39.
41. See Cicero, *De natura deorum*, 2.12.32.
42. Quintilian, *Institutio oratoria*, 10.1.81.
43. Diog. Laert., 3.25: "The eyes of all the Greeks were turned toward him." The tradition concerning Plato's life has it that Plato, before joining Socrates, had been an athlete (a champion wrestler) and had participated in all four of the major Panhellenic games, including the Olympic. This story, however, relates to his return from the third Sicilian voyage, when he met Dion at Olympia. Compare Aelian, *Varia historia*, 4.9, where Plato visits the Olympic games incognito and associates freely with people assembled there, who are delighted by the company of this "stranger." A fuller source for this anecdote has not been found.

44. This story is told of Antimachus of Colophon, author of a long epic poem on the Theban cycle. See Cicero, *Brutus*, 51.191.
45. Diog. Laert., 3.18; see Plato, *Epistles*, 3 and passim. Cf. *Epistles*, 7.334D: "Despotic power benefits neither rulers nor subjects, but is an altogether deadly experience for themselves, their children and their children's children."
46. Diog. Laert., 2.78 (Life of Aristippus).
47. Ibid., 3.24.
48. Ibid., 2.41, (Life of Socrates); Olympiodorus, *Life of Plato*, 1.3. See *Prolegomena to Platonic Philosophy*, 1.3 (op. cit., p. 8).
49. The sole source for this anecdote is Valerius Maximus, *Factorum et dictorum memorabilium*, 4.1.2.
50. Diog. Laert., 4.6–15.
51. Plutarch, *Life of Dion*, passim.
52. Philiscus of Miletus (*c.* 400–325 B.C.), a rhetorician who studied under Isocrates. Only fragments of his writings survive including the *Life of Lycurgus* (*Frag. Graec. Hist.*, 3.496F9).
53. For this anecdote see Pseudo-Lucian, *In Praise of Demosthenes*, 47.
54. Demosthenes, *Letters*, 5 (to Heracleodorus), now regarded as spurious.
55. Diog. Laert., 4.2 (Life of Speusippus). The Dionysius referred to is Dionysius the Younger of Syracuse.
56. Ibid., 4.1–2 (Life of Speusippus).
57. Ibid., 4.11 (Life of Xenocrates).
58. Many of the following anecdotes are outside the mainstream tradition of Plato's life, and come possibly from a *florilegium* or *gnomologium* accessible to Ficino.
59. Diog. Laert., 4.6. Xenocrates was slow and clumsy.
60. Ibid., 3.35. The friend was Antisthenes.
61. Ibid., 6.53 (Life of Diogenes).
62. Plato gives advice to students in *Stobaeus*, 2.31.62; and in MSS Gnom. Vat. 433, 449; Cod. Vat. Graec. 742, f. 67ᵛ and 633, f. 121ᵛ.
63. Diog. Laert., 3.38.
64. Ibid., 3.39.
65. Plato, *Timaeus*, 69D, *voluptas esca malorum;* quoted in Cicero, *De Senectute*, 13.44.
66. Diog. Laert., 3.40; Plato, *Laws*, 2.663E. For Demodocus see Plato, *Theages.*
67. See Plato, *Statesman*, 275B et passim, where a distinction is made between the function of a true statesman and that of other callings such as merchants, husbandmen etc: "He alone of shepherds . . . has the care of human beings."
68. Cf. Plato, *Statesman*, 275C: "The statesmen who are now on earth seem to be much more like their subjects in character, and much more nearly to partake of their breeding and education."
69. Cf. Plato, *Phaedo*, 66B–67, for the condition of the soul in the body, and Plato, *Theaetetus*, 176B for the instruction to fly from evil in order to become like God.
70. See note 10 above.
71. Diog. Laert., 2.81 (Life of Aristippus).
72. Jerome, *Letters*, 53.1 (to Paulinus).

73. Plato, *Timaeus*, 27C: "All men . . .who have any degree of right feeling, at the beginning of every enterprise, whether small or great, always call upon God."

74. Lactantius, *Divine Institutes*, 3.19 (*Pat. Lat.*, 6). The same story is told of Socrates and Thales. See Diog. Laert., 1.33 (Life of Thales).

75. See Plato's assertion that there are no writings of his own; all are those of an idealized Socrates: Plato, *Epistles*, 2.314C.

76. Diog. Laert., 3.8 (Life of Plato). Cf. the threefold division of philosophy into physics, ethics, and dialectic described by Diogenes in the prologue to his *Lives* (Diog. Laert., 1.18). Plato is credited with dividing philosophy into three parts—natural, moral, and rational. Previous to this the division was twofold, the active represented by Socrates and the contemplative represented by Pythagoras. See Augustine, *City of God*, 8.4.

77. Cf. Plato, *Meno*, 81CD, the "sacred words"; Plato, *Laws*, 10.903B-905C; *Epistles*, 7.335.

78. Augustine, *Contra academicos*, 3.20.43.

79. Dionysius the Areopagite in the *Divine Names* introduces a Plotinian concept of the godhead into his exposition of the Trinity.

80. Cf. Eusebius, *Praeparatio evangelica*, 11-13; Cyrillus Alexandrinus, *Contra Julianum*, 1.29 passim. (Eusebius of Caesarea, historian and theologian c. A.D. 260-340; Cyril of Alexandria, patriarch and theologian, d. A.D. 444).

81. Augustine, *De vera religione*, 4.7 (*Pat. Lat.*, 34).

82. Augustine, *Confessions* 7.9: the Word or Λόγος, John 1:1-5.

83. Augustine, *City of God*, 2.14. (Cornelius Labeo, pagan writer, A.D. 300, works not extant).

84. Marcus Varro: Roman historian (116-27 B.C.), whose lost encyclopaedia of learning, the *Antiquities*, is quoted by Augustine in the *City of God*, passim.

85. Apuleius, *De Platone*, 1.2.

86. For this, see Aeneas Gazaeus, *Theophrastus* (dialogue on the immortality of the soul). This work was translated into Latin by Ambrogio Traversari in 1456. Gazaeus was a Platonist and later a Christian of the fifth century A.D.

87. Seneca, *Epistles*, 58.31; Olympiodorus, *Life of Plato*. See *Prolegomena to Platonic Philosophy*, 1.6.

88. Cicero, *De Senectute*, 5.13.

89. Seneca, *Epistles*, 58.31.

90. Diog. Laert., 3.2.

91. Ammonius Hermiae (attrib.), *Vita Aristotelis*, 2.5, quoted in G4. D. L. Stockton suggests this translation:

> *This altar Aristotle did to Plato raise,*
> *a man whom Heav'n forbids the base should praise.*

92. Olympiodorus, *Commentarium in Georgia Platonis*, 41.9.

93. For these epitaphs see Diog. Laert., 3.43-45.

94. A similar description of Ficino as a healer of men's souls is said to have been given by Cosimo: see Ficino, *Opera*, p. 493 (dedicatory letter to *De vita libri tres*) and Corsi, *Life of Marsilio Ficino*, 5. See *Letters*, vol. 3, p. 138.

95. Diog. Laert., 3.25.

96. The reference is undoubtedly meant to include the contemporary burlesque poet Luigi Pulci who had lampooned Ficino and Plato in his poem *Morgante.*
97. Diog. Laert., 3.29 seq.
98. See Diog. Laert., 2.49 (Life of Xenophon).
99. Ibid., 3.29.
100. See Ammonius Hermiae, *Vita Aristotelis,* 1.43, relating Aristotle's description of himself as "the friend of Socrates but more the friend of truth."
101. See note 91 above.
102. Olympiodorus, *Commentarium in Georgia Platonis,* 41.9.
103. Apuleius, *Apologia,* 64.

The first and shorter version of the *Vita Platonis* (V10) ends with these words: "Let that be sufficient on the life of Plato. To you, most noble gentlemen, who have thought fit to honor this speech of mine with your presence, I render great thanks. Immortal God, would that I might bring back the immortals." *(De vita platonis iam satis dictum sit. Vobis autem viri praestantissimi, qui meam hanc orationem vestra praesentia honestare dignati estis, ingentes gratias habeo. Immortalis deus immortales referam).*

48

1. The first sentences of this paragraph are Cicero's own words in praise of philosophy. See Cicero, *Tusculan Disputations,* 5.2.5, Loeb, p. 429.
2. See Plato, *Cratylus,* and Varro, *De lingua Latina.*
3. A technique of philosophic conversation carried on by means of question and answer that seeks to elicit "an account of the essence of each thing." See Plato, *Republic,* 7.534; and Plato, *Philebus,* 58 seq.
4. Here "and theology" occurs in the Italian manuscript.
5. Quoted from Ficino, *Platonic Theology,* 13.3 (ed. Marcel, vol. 2, p. 226).
6. This essay appears to have been written about the beginning of 1476, to judge from a letter to Francesco Gazolti. See letter 46.

49

1. Plato, *Epistles,* 7.330D.
2. See 2 Timothy 4:2.

50

1. Iamblichus, *Life of Pythagoras,* 18.83; Porphyry, *Life of Pythagoras,* sec. 42.
2. For a description of how the soul receives lasting impressions, see Plato, *Theaetetus,* 194C.
3. See Cicero, *De oratore,* 2.86.353–54 seq. Simonides of Ceos (556–468 B.C.), the lyric poet, was said to have invented mnemonics.

51

1. Bembo appears to have suffered some misfortune, either an injury at the hands of

someone in high office, or failure to secure some position. To what precisely this letter refers is uncertain.

2. Sardanapalus: Assur Banipal, fortieth and last king of Assyria, celebrated for his effeminacy and luxury, which led to his downfall. Cicero, *Tusculanos*, 5.35.101; Augustine, *City of God*, 2, chap. 20.

3. Juvenal, *Satires*, 10.365.

4. See Hippocrates, *Works*, ed. Littré, vol. 9 (epistles), p. 349 seq.

5. Plato, *Apology*, 21B, 23.

6. Virgil, *Aeneid*, 5.710.

52

1. Written in the spring of 1477. This letter is one of eleven letters comprising the *Sermoni morali della stultitia et miseria degli uomini*, translated into Italian by Ficino in June 1478 and addressed to Jacopo Guicciardini. See *Sup. Fic.*, vol. 1, p. cxi.

2. Iamblichus, *Life of Pythagoras*, 24.109; Porphyry, *Life of Pythagoras*, 42.

53

1. Plato, *Theaetetus*, 176AB. See also Ficino, *Platonic Theology* (14.2, ed. Marcel, p. 251).

54

1. Plato, *Timaeus*, 69D. Quoted in Horace, *Epistles*, 1.2.55.

55

1. The *Philebus*, one of the ten dialogues of Plato that Cosimo asked Ficino to translate in 1463. The illuminated manuscript (*Canonicianus Latinus* 163) of the ten dialogues is in the Bodleian Library, Oxford.

56

1. The substance of this letter is drawn from Plato's *Euthydemus*, 278–82.

2. A pun on the Greek word for the Graces, χαριτες, and γῆ, meaning "land."

58

1. *Disputatio contra iudicium astrologorum*. See *Sup. Fic.*, vol. 2, pp. 11-76.

59

1. The *Altercazione* of Lorenzo de' Medici in *Opere volgari*, vol. 3, *Scritti spirituali*, ed. Rizzoli (1958).

2. For a classification of "good" in Plato, see *Laws*, 1.631; and in Aristotle, *Ethics*, 1.8. See also Plato, *Euthydemus*, 279.

3. Aristotle, *Ethics*, 1.13; 10.7-8.

4. See Cicero, *De finibus*, 3.8 seq. (Loeb, p. 245) for Stoic and Epicurean definitions of the "good."

5. To Epicurus and his school pleasure was the highest good. The test of true pleasure was the removal and absorption of all that gives pain to the body or trouble to the mind. Virtue he valued, as it led to the health of the body and tranquillity of the mind.

6. Cicero, *De finibus*, 5.23.

7. Aristotle, *Ethics*, 10.7-8.

8. See Plato, *Phaedo*, 67, and *Phaedrus*, 247D.

9. Ficino, *Platonic Theology*, 18.8 (3-8) (ed. Marcel, pp. 209-20).

10. *Phaedrus*, 247D.

11. *De voluptate*, Ficino, *Opera*, 1.986.

12. *Phaedrus*, 247A.

13. Ficino, *De amore* and the *Platonic Theology*, 18.9 (ed. Marcel, pp. 220-26).

60

1. Iamblichus, *Life of Pythagoras*, 17.75-77.

2. 1 Corinthians 2:11.

3. The reference is to Job 5:13.

4. 1 Corinthians 3:19-20.

61

1. Timaeus of Locris, who wrote *De anima mundi*, a treatise on the nature of the world soul.

2. See Aristotle, *Physics*, 2.3.194, 7.198a, where four causes are enumerated: *efficiens, finis, materia*, and *forma*. And see Ficino, *Platonic Theology*, 5.5 (ed. Marcel, p. 181).

3. Plato, *Timaeus*, 28.

4. Ibid., 29.

5. Ibid., 30-31.

64

1. This letter is given as a summary *(argumentum)* of Ficino's *De Christiana religione* in the Sarzana MS (Cod. S). It was also translated into Italian by Ficino to make it available to a wider audience and included in the *Sermoni morali della stultitia et miseria degli uomini* dedicated to Jacopo Guicciardini (*Sermone decimo*, preserved in MS Riccardiana 2684).

2. Ficino discusses whether the laws of Christianity could be influenced by the stars in *De Christiana religione*, especially chapter 4 (*Opera*, p. 12), entitled *Auctoritas Christi non ab astris sed a Deo*, "The authority of Christ comes not from the stars but from God." It was a commonly held belief among the astrologers of the Middle Ages, such as Alkindi and Albumasar, that major changes in religion were brought about by planetary conjunctions.

3. The first paragraph is almost identical with a passage in Ficino's *Praedicationes*, (Sermons) *Opera*, p. 479. The composition of the *Praedicationes* is of uncertain date (*Sup. Fic.*, vol. 1, pp. lxxxii).

4. This idea is beautifully expressed in the words inscribed around the walls of Ficino's

Academy mentioned in *Letters*, 1.5 (see letter 34): "All things are directed from goodness to goodness."

65

1. Cf. Matthew 6:33: "But seek ye first the Kingdom of God, and his righteousness; and
all these things shall be added unto you."
2. Luke 10:41–42.

66

1. Plato, *Phaedrus*, 247.
2. Plato, *Laws*, 5.728.
3. 1 John 5:19.
4. Isaiah 48:22 and 57:21.
5. The eagle is a symbol of Christ's resurrection and an emblem of St. John the Evangelist, owing to his "insight into the divine," his power to behold the divine light.
According to a medieval book of legends concerning animals, the *Physiologus*, the
eagle could look at the sun without being blinded and trained its young to do likewise, bearing them up on its wings. Thus it was seen as representing Christ, who
gazes on God the Father and raises men up to contemplate the divine brilliance.
The eagle also stands for rejuvenation, as in Psalm 103:5, "thy youth is renewed
like the eagle's," because, according to the *Physiologus*, when it becomes old and its
eyes are dimmed, it flies toward the sun, where in the burning rays its youth is
renewed and its sight is fully restored. See also Dionysius, *Celestial Hierarchies*,
15.8.337a.
6. 1 John 1:5; 4:8; 4:16.

67

1. This letter was translated into Italian by Ficino and included in his *Sermoni morali*
(second sermon) in MS Ricc. 2684.
2. Ficino in the preface to his commentary on the *Philebus* explains that these three kinds
of life exist because "men choose three paths to happiness: wisdom, power, and pleasure." See M. Allen, *Marsilio Ficino: The Philebus Commentary*, appendix 3, p. 480.
3. Ecclesiastes 1:18.
4. 1 Corinthians 1:20–21.
5. Isaiah 44:24–25.
6. This simile is taken from Plato, *Republic*, 6.508, which Ficino also uses in *De amore*,
1.3, and in a letter in praise of medicine (*Letters*, 3.14, *Opera*, p. 759): "Just as the
brilliance in the eyes discerns the brilliance of color within the sun's very light, creator
of both color and eye, so the truthful mind comprehends the truth of anything within
the highest truth, the begetter of every truth and of every mind."
7. The Sophists represented a profession rather than a school of thought, though some
taught definite philosophic views. They were itinerant teachers in ancient Greece who
from around 500 B.C. went from city to city giving instruction for a fee on a variety
of techniques related to advancement in society. Oratory and the art of disputation

were perhaps the most important of such skills. Plato attacks the Sophists in several dialogues for their pseudoreasoning, which he likens to a form of "flattery" in the *Gorgias*. In the *Sophist* he calls the Sophist a "magician and imitator of true being."

Ficino, in his *Commentary on the Sophist of Plato* (*Opera*, p. 1284), says that God alone is wise; the philosopher is a true imitator of God, but the Sophist is a pretentious and false imitator of the philosopher.

8. Kristeller quotes the passage from "Come friends!" to the end to show how Ficino identifies an important doctrine of ancient ethics, that the highest good is always associated with happiness, with knowledge of God, and the return journey of the soul to God. See Kristeller, *The Philosophy of Marsilio Ficino*, p. 291.

68

1. Plato, *Phaedo*, 118A; the last words of Socrates before his death were, "I owe a cock to Aesculapius."

69

1. The *Oratio* was translated into Italian verse by Lorenzo in chapter 6 of the spiritual poem, *L'altercazione*, in *Opere volgari* 3. Compare this *Oratio* with the theological prayers at the beginning of Augustine's *Soliloquies*, 1, in *Augustine: Earlier Writings*, ed. J. Burleigh, Library of Christian Classics, vol. 6 (London).

70

1. Respectively, the rivers of sorrow, hate, lamentation, and fire in the underworld. Plato, *Phaedo*, 113.
2. Ficino refers to his book, *De Christiana religione*.

72

1. This letter and the two that follow are the subject of a study by R. Klibansky, E. Panofsky, and F. Saxl in *Saturn and Melancholy*, pp. 257–58.
2. It is probable that this letter refers to a request by Ficino to be exempted from a tax levied on the clergy by the pope.
3. Diog. Laert. 1.34, 39. Quoted also in Plato, *Theaetetus*, 174A. His death is described in a verse by Diogenes Laertius:

    As Thales watched the games one festal day
    The fierce sun smote him, and he passed away;
    Zeus, thou didst well to raise him; his dim eyes
    Could not from earth behold the starry skies.

4. See Ptolemy, *Tetrabiblos*, 2.8, for the qualities of the maleficent and beneficent planets.
5. John, 19:19–22.

73

1. Floral city *(florentem urbem)* signifies Florence *(Florentia)*.

2. Ficino gives the supposed horoscope of Plato in his letter "on the life of Plato" (letter 47). In Plato's horoscope the house in the ascendant is also Aquarius.
3. The meaning is allegorical, since Ficino was not endowed with a robust physique—he suffered from poor health throughout his life. The vigor of his mind is really what Cavalcanti means, since it was through his translation and commentaries that Plato, Zoroaster, Hermes Trismegistus, and other great thinkers were rediscovered to the West.

74

1. Ficino attached great importance to the power of Saturn, following the Neoplatonists who attributed to it the greatest influence of all. It represented the highest faculties of the soul—reason and contemplation. Melancholy or "black bile" expressed its malign aspect. According to Ficino, the scholar and philosopher leading a life of study and contemplation had melancholy as their companion. Ficino also described Plato as being saturnine and melancholic. See Ficino, *De vita*, 3.2 (*Opera*, p. 533). In this letter, while Cavalcanti emphasizes the highest aspect of Saturn's influence, intellectual genius, Ficino stresses its malign aspect.
2. Aristotle, *Problematica*, 30.953A.

75

1. According to one account by Ficino, the tradition of wisdom led in an unbroken chain from Hermes Trismegistus in Egypt to Plato, through Orpheus, Aglaophemus, Pythagoras, and Philolaus.

    Ficino took his knowledge of Orphic philosophy mainly from the Orphic hymns, but also from the *Asclepius* of Hermes, Iamblichus, and Julian. See *Hymns of Orpheus*, 33, in *Thomas Taylor the Platonist*. Cf. letter 69.
2. *Hymns of Orpheus*, 7.
3. Cf. Newton, *Opticks*, 1.2, p. 160: "All the colours in the world must be such as constantly ought to arise from the original colorific qualities of the rays whereof the lights consist by which those colours are seen."
4. "Order" and "level" are translations of *genus* and *gradus*. Cf. *Platonic Theology*, 1.3 (ed. Marcel, vol. 1, p. 45); also Kristeller, *The Philosophy of Marsilio Ficino*, chap. 9.
5. See Plato, *Phaedo*, 110 seq.; *Timaeus*, 67–68; A. Chastel, *Marsile Ficin et l'Art*, pp. 103–104; Ficino, *De lumine*, especially chap. 12 (*Opera*, p. 981).
6. Aristotle makes the distinction between efficient, formal, and final causes. See *Platonic Theology*, 18.8 (ed. Marcel, vol. 3, p. 207).
7. *Platonic Theology*, 2.7 (ed. Marcel, vol. 1, p. 96).
8. Cf. *Kena Upanishad*: "That which makes the eye see, but needs no eye to see, that alone is Spirit." *The Ten Principal Upanishads*, trans. Purohit Swami and W. B. Yeats, p. 20.
9. Plotinus, *Enneads*, 3.8.
10. See letter 66, note 5.
11. Plato, *Republic*, 7.
12. Psalm 19:4.

76

1. See letter 58, note 1.
2. The substance of the argument from the beginning of this paragraph up to here is taken from Aulus Gellius, *Attic Nights*, 14.1.36.
3. Seneca, *Oedipus*, 980. The original reads *"fatis agimur, cedite fatis"* (We are moved by the Fates; yield to them).
4. Lucretius, *De rerum natura*, 1.79. Ficino has substituted *impietas* (wickedness) where the original reads *religio*.

77

1. On 26 September 1480 Saturn was conjunct with both Venus and the Sun in Libra, where its influence is magnified. Mars, 908 away in Capricorn, was exerting a strong adverse influence. This would be especially dangerous for Lorenzo, at whose birth the Sun was in Capricorn, which is ruled by Saturn and which also was his ascendant (i.e., the sign rising on the eastern horizon).
2. Apart from the abortive Pazzi conspiracy of 1478, in which Lorenzo came within a hair's breadth of being killed, a number or other plots against Lorenzo and the Medici were thwarted. On 6 April 1470 a plot hatched by certain exiles under Bernardo Naldi and Diotisalvi Neroni was foiled and the ringleaders and their accomplices, numbering twenty-seven in all, were executed. Earlier, in 1466, Lorenzo had been in danger from a plot directed mainly against his father, Piero de' Medici, by Diotisalvi Neroni, Angelo Acciaiuoli, and Niccolo Soderini.
3. Within a month of this letter, Landucci wrote in his diary that on 15 October 1480 a hermit, accused of an attempt on Lorenzo's life, died in the hospital of St. Maria Nuova from injuries received following his apprehension.

78

1. A translation of this letter by E. Gombrich is to be found, together with detailed notes, in "Botticelli's Mythologies," *Journal of Warburg and Courtauld Institutes* (1945). Recent research suggests that Botticelli's *Primavera* was originally commissioned for Giuliano de' Medici to celebrate his part in the jousts but, on his assassination, it was recommissioned for Lorenzo di Pierfrancesco on the occasion of his marriage to Semiramide Appiani, which was to have taken place in May 1482 (hence the symbolism associated with spring). The marriage was postponed to July 1482. See Mirella Levi d' Ancona, *Botticelli's Primavera: A Botanical Interpretation including Astrology, Alchemy and the Medici* (Florence, 1983). See also Umberto Baldini, *Primavera*, p. 94; and R. Foster and P. Tudor-Craig, *The Secret Life of Paintings*.
2. Virgil, *Aeneid*, 6.730: *igneus est ollis vigor et caelestis origo*. Ficino has *igneus vigor inest et caelestis origo*.
3. Ficino refers to seven gifts given by God to Man by the agency of the deities who rule the seven planets: contemplation through Saturn, government through Jupiter, magnanimity through Mars, intelligence and prophecy through the Sun, love through Venus, eloquence through Mercury, procreation through the Moon. See *De amore*, 6.4, *Opera*, pp. 1342–43.

4.   Cf. Plato, *Epistles*, 4.321B.
5.   A play on words: *Humanitatem, humi natum.*
6.   Virgil, *Aeneid*, 1.75. This description of human nature *(humanitas)* by Ficino may
     have inspired Botticelli to paint the central figure of Venus in his *Primavera*. It is clear
     from this letter that Ficino attached the greatest importance to the visual impression.
     Both the picture and the letter were for the instruction of Lorenzo di Pierfrancesco de'
     Medici.

79

1.   Both letters are from book 2 of the *Epistolae, Opera*, pp. 697, 717. An amended ver-
     sion of the text is given in Marcel, *Platonic Theology*, vol. 3, pp. 347, 370.
2.   *Imaginum* in the Latin.
3.   The light that blinded Paul, and his conversion, are described in Acts 9:1-9.
4.   A son of Phoebus who resolved to find his true origin. He requested of his father that
     he be allowed to drive the chariot of the sun for one day, but he was inexperienced at
     guiding the chariot. The horses were plunged into confusion, and heaven and earth
     were threatened with universal conflagration. Jupiter struck the rider with a thunder-
     bolt and hurled him down from heaven. Hyginus, *Fabulae*, 152, 154.
5.   The emperor Flavius Claudius Julianus, sometimes called Julian the Apostate, who
     was brought up as a Christian but was later converted to paganism. He was encour-
     aged to believe that he had been chosen to restore the pagan religion and he composed
     an oration for the pagan festival of the sun, *natalis solis invicti* (birthday of the invin-
     cible sun), held on 25 December.
6.   Claudian, who lived in the reign of Theodosius, was the last notable Latin poet of the
     classical tradition. He wrote an unfinished epic *De raptu Proserpinae* (The Rape of
     Persephone). Persephone was carried off by Pluto to the underworld. Phoebus and
     Persephone were both offspring of Zeus.
7.   St. Luke, physician and constant companion of St. Paul. See Colossians 4:14. Hierotheus
     is mentioned several times by Dionysius in *The Divine Names*, and is referred to as
     his teacher.
8.   Paul of Tarsus (St. Paul) is figuratively referred to as Aesculapius, the Latin form of
     the Greek Asklepios, physician and a god of healing.
9.   According to Plato, both Homer and Stesichorus were blinded because they sang pro-
     fanely about love and so offended the deity. See Plato, *Phaedrus*, 243AB.
10. Numenius of Apamea (second century A.D.) wrote extensively on the teachings of
     Plato and Pythagoras and the occult meaning of Greek mythology. For this anecdote
     see Macrobius, *Commentary*, 1.2.19 (ed. Stahl, p. 87). The Eleusinian goddesses ap-
     peared to Numenius in a dream dressed as courtesans to show him how, by his writ-
     ings, he had prostituted them to every passerby.
11. Pherecydes of Syros (*c.* 550 B.C.), a Pythagorean who wrote a work on comsogony.
     He was one of the first to write on the doctrine of the immortality of the soul. Diog.
     Laert. 1.116-122; Cicero, *Tusculanos*, 1.16.38.
12. "Hipparchus, being guilty of writing the tenets of Pythagoras in plain language, was
     expelled from the school and a pillar raised to him as if he were dead." See Clement of

Alexandria, *Stromata*, 5.9 (*Pat. Graec.*, 9); Iamblichus, *Life of Pythagoras*, 17.75. The "sacred seer" is Pythagoras.

13. The reference is to Dionysius II, tyrant of Sicily, who tried to use Plato's philosophy for his own ends. See Plato, *Epistles*, 3, 7.

14. Apollonian: the hidden meaning of Plato's philosophy; Apollo was the god of prophecy and oracles.

15. Ficino seems to be alluding to Matthew 7:6 (Vulgate). Cf. Matthew 15:26, Mark 7:27.

16. The Latin word is *davus*, a common name for slaves in classical times. Ficino may be thinking of a passage in Terence's *Andros*, 1.2.24: *"Davus sum, non Oedipus."*

17. The disciple who restored Saul's sight. Acts 9:10–18.

18. Lorenzo de' Medici was born on the first of January (1449).

80

1. Ficino, *De amore*, "Oratio Prima," 4, *De utilitate amoris* (ed. Marcel, pp. 141–42).

2. Plato, *Symposium*, 206. Also see *Republic*, 3.402D. Ficino says in *De amore*, "When we speak of love we mean the desire for beauty . . . There is a triple beauty: beauty of the soul, beauty of the body, and beauty of sound. That of the soul is perceived by the mind, that of the body by the eyes, and that of sound by the ears alone. Since therefore mind, sight, and hearing are the only means by which we can enjoy beauty, and since love is the desire to enjoy beauty, love is always satisfied with the mind, the eyes, and the ears. What need is there of the senses of smell, taste, and touch?" ("Oratio Prima," 4; ed. Marcel, p. 142.) And again, "Of those six faculties of the soul, three belong to body and matter, that is touch, taste, and smell; but the other three, reason, sight, and hearing, pertain to the soul. Therefore the first three, inclining more to the body, are more akin to it than to the soul . . . But the three higher senses, most removed from the material, are much more closely related to the soul." ("Oratio Quinta," 2; ed. Marcel, p. 179.)

81

1. See Plato, *Phaedrus*, 255.

2. See Plato, *Lysis*, 214; and Ficino, *De amore*, "Oratio Secunda," 8 (ed. Marcel, p. 158).

3. Astrology in the Middle Ages was closely linked with astronomy and medicine. See Kristeller, *Renaissance Concepts of Man*, p. 138.

4. Pythias (or Phintias), a Pythagoraean, condemned to death by Dionysius of Syracuse, begged a period of liberty to arrange his affairs. Damon pledged his life for the return of his friend and Pythias returned before the day appointed for his execution. Dionysius, impressed by their friendship, then released both. See Diodorus Siculus, 10.4; also Plutarch, *Pericles*; and Iamblichus, *Life of Pythagoras*, 31.189 seq., and 33.234 seq.

Pilades was the faithful friend of Orestes, son of Agamemnon. See especially Euripides, *Iphigeneia in Tauris*.

82

1. *Amantissime atque amatissime mi Amati*: rhetorical figures that do not translate into English.

2. Virgil, *Aeneid*, 4.532.
3. Ibid., 4.298.
4. Ibid., 4.100.
5. Horace, *Heroides*, 1.12. The word human *(humanus)* has been added by Ficino.
6. Ficino frequently uses this idea: see letter 81, which may be derived from Plotinus, *Enneads*, 4.4.41.

84

1. Plato, *Theaetetus*, 176B.
2. Plato, *Republic*, 7.519A.
3. Ibid., 6.508.
4. John 14:6.
5. This essay on friendship is repeated in the preface to Ficino's translation of Alcinous, *De doctrina Platonis* (*Opera*, 2.1945), also dedicated to Cavalcanti.

85

1. Iamblichus, *Life of Pythagoras*, 22.102 and 33.232.

86

1. Bembo was born on 19 October 1433, the same day and year as Ficino. He first came to Florence as Venetian ambassador in January 1475 and was introduced to Ficino's Academy in February of the same year. In a letter to Marescalchi (letter 68) Ficino says he was seriously ill in August 1474, and he vowed to declare the Christian teaching with greater zeal and devotion. The Italian version of his book on the Christian religion was completed in 1474, i.e., before 25 March 1475, which was when the Florentine year ended. See also letter 81; *De amore*, 6.4 and 7.9.
2. Cf. letter 68.

87

1. Matthew 7:24–29.
2. Cicero, *De officiis*, 2.20.71.
3. Plautus, *The Pot of Gold*, 239.

88

1. For this idea see Plato, *Laws*, 4.721C: "Now mankind is coeval with all time, and is ever following, and will ever follow the course of time; and so men are immortal, because they leave children's children behind them, and partake of immortality in the unity of generation."
2. Compare Plato, *Phaedo*, 97C–98C, where Socrates describes his disappointment on finding that Anaxagoras was not capable of teaching him the causes of existence. Socrates had two wives, Xanthippe and Myrto; Diog. Laert., 2.26 (Life of Socrates).
3. See Augustine, *De vera religione*, 3.5.
4. Plato, *Laws*, 4.721C; 6.774A.
5. Hermes Trismegistus, *Pimander*, 2.17a.

6. Cf. Aristotle, *Politics*, 1.1253A.
7. Virgil, *Aeneid*, 1.630.

89

1. Pace was secretary to the archbishop of Florence, Rinaldo Orsini.
2. *Pace* means "peace" in Italian.
3. Lorenzo de' Medici. Some metaphor is intended here: Phoebus represents song and music, and Jove is the "heavenly Father." Lorenzo was a poet and Orsini was archbishop of Florence.
4. E.g. Aristotle, *De generatione et corruptione*, 2.1; *Physics* 1.5-6.
5. Written in 1478, according to Kristeller (*Sup. Fic.*, vol. 1, p. xcix), since it is mentioned in a subsequent letter in book 5 (*Opera*, p. 806, 3) as having been written a few days before the wars of the Pazzi conspiracy. If the date is correct, this letter was written less than a fortnight before the Pazzi conspiracy, which was immediately followed by war.

90

1. Plato, *Gorgias*, 527E.

91

1. See Iamblichus, *Life of Pythagoras*, 17.71-72.
2. Apollonius of Alabanda was a Greek orator who discouraged anyone from attending his school whom he considered unsuited to be an orator. See Cicero, *De oratore*, 1.28.126.

92

1. Panaetius was a Stoic philosopher who wrote a work on the duties of man discussed by Cicero in his *De officiis*, 3.2.7.
2. Aristotle left the Academy while Plato was there and only returned after his death when Xenocrates was head of the Academy. Diog. Laert. 5.2.
3. Psalm 51:15, etc.; Hermes Trismegistus, *Pimander*, 13.17-19.
4. Plato, *Epistles*, 7.331D; Diog. Laert. 2.98 (Life of Aristippus): "It was reasonable . . . for the good man not to risk his life in the defense of his country, for he would never throw wisdom away to benefit the unwise. He said the world was his country."

93

1. Plato, *Republic*, 5.462. See also for this and following paragraph, Plato, *Laws*, 10.903B, and *Laws* 4.716C-718. Shortly before Lorenzo's death he gave this advice to his son Piero: "Consult the interests of the whole community rather than the gratification of a part." From a letter of Poliziano to Jacopo Antiquario, quoted in Roscoe's *Life of Lorenzo de' Medici*, p. 328.

94

1. See Plato, *Laws*, 4.716A.
2. See Plato, *Laws*, 10.903B, for the idea that man is created for the sake of the whole.
3. See Plato, *Republic*, 5.462, for the idea of the state as a single being.
4. See Plato, *Laws*, 4.715.
5. Ibid.
6. Seneca, *Thyestes*, 607–12.
7. Goddess of justice, who lived on earth during the Golden Age but, disgusted by the wickedness of men, fled to heaven during the Bronze Age and was placed among the constellations as Virgo. She is represented as a virgin holding a scale in one hand, a sword in the other. Ovid, *Metamorphoses*, 1.150; Seneca, *Octavia*, 424.

95

1. Luke 24:36; John 20:19, 21, 26.
2. This is one of three letters to the pope. All three are masterpieces of irony. This letter was probably written in the autumn of 1478, soon after the outbreak of the hostilities between Rome and Florence that followed the Pazzi conspiracy. The armies of the papal alliance, led by Alfonso, duke of Calabria, son of King Ferdinand (Ferrante) of Naples, came within seven miles of the city of Florence. Florence was also ravaged by famine and plague. Ficino may not have sent this letter.
3. According to Herodotus (*Histories*, 2.73) the phoenix was a legendary bird of great longevity, and only one could be alive at any time. It built its nest in the topmost branches of a tree and every five hundred years it came to Heliopolis in Egypt, constructed an altar, set fire to itself and rose again, young and beautiful, from the ashes of the pyre. It was, therefore, a symbol of resurrection and immortality. Ficino may be ironically indicating that through Sixtus philosophy may be reborn and the Church revived.
4. Minerva was the Roman goddess of arts and crafts, and later of war. She was identified with the Greek Athena, and thus with wisdom.
5. Plato, *Laws*, 4.711–13.
6. The idea of repeated cycles, composed of four great ages of gold, silver, bronze, and iron, is present in both Vedic literature and such classical writers as Hesiod, Plato, and Virgil. It may be understood as a sequence, with the Iron Age passing into the Golden Age of a new cycle, or as the simultaneity of the four ages offering the possibility for men of one age to pass into the higher consciousness of another. Renaissance Florence probably owed to Ficino the concept of its own epoch as a Golden Age. In a letter to Paul of Middelburg in 1492 Ficino writes: "For this century, like a Golden Age, has restored to light the liberal arts, which were almost extinct: grammar, poetry, rhetoric, painting, sculpture, architecture, music, the ancient singing of songs to the Orphic lyre, and all this in Florence." *The Portable Renaissance Reader*, ed. J. B. Ross and M. M. McLaughlin. See *Opera*, p. 944.
7. The hunger and disease experienced by the speaker—the Christian flock itself—refer to spiritual hunger and disease as well as to their literal counterparts.

8. The ravenous wolf refers to hunger and starvation; the roaring lion, to pillage, plunder, and rapine; the huge elephant, to desolation and waste; and the noxious dragon, to plague and disease. "The Turk" includes all these evils. In 1480 the Turks landed at Otranto in southern Italy. They slaughtered the inhabitants, sacked the town and held it for a year. Sixtus was shaken by this unexpected disaster and he was encouraged to reach an early peace settlement with Florence in the face of the Turkish threat.

9. Cicero, *Academica* 1.5.18.

10. 1 Corinthians 13:7-8.

11. The Latin *vicarius* means "substitute." In the Roman Empire under Diocletian, the *vicarius* was an important official, while in the early Church the title was used for a representative of the pope at Eastern councils. In the eighth century, the popes were designated Vicar of Christ, which eventually replaced the older title, Vicar of St. Peter.

12. Colossians 3:8, 14.

13. The god Pluto (Dis), the son of Saturn and Ops, inherited the underworld from his father, while his brother Neptune received the sea and Jupiter heaven and earth. He was god of death and the infernal regions. He held the keys to his kingdom, so that the soul who entered might not leave again. Ficino indicates that Sixtus has the power to stop Pluto from opening the gates to the underworld, thus preventing souls from entering hell, and, like St. Peter, he has the power to unlock the gates of the kingdom of heaven, allowing souls to enter therein. The number two was sacred to Pluto; hence he was in opposition to the unity of the kingdom of heaven. The doors of the temple of Janus in Rome were closed only in times of peace when the god was considered resident, whereas in times of war he was with the troops. See Matthew 16:18-19 for reference to the keys of the kingdom of heaven.

14. John 21:15-17.

15. Matthew 18:21-22.

16. Matthew 18:12-13.

17. John 10:11-14.

18. A reference to Lorenzo de' Medici.

19. Cf. Virgil, *Aeneid,* 9.60 and Dante, *La divina commedia, Paradiso,* 25.1-12. Florence is likened to a goodly sheepfold, behind the walls of which Dante can sleep safe and sound in the knowledge that the wolf, i.e., the enemies of Florence, cannot harm him.

20. Virgil, *Aeneid,* 4.173-90.

21. This may refer to pamphlets published at the same time as Gentile de' Becchi's attack on the pope, or it may refer to this very letter!

22. Psalm 33:9.

23. Constantine was the first Christian Roman emperor, having been converted by a visionary experience while campaigning with his troops. In A.D. 313 he issued the Edict of Milan, granting toleration to Christians and subsequently he believed himself responsible to God for the good government of the Church. Ficino is pointing out that the Roman armies after Constantine's conversion were fighting for Christ against barbarians and not merely to serve the Roman state. "The barbarian wolves" confronting Sixtus are the Moslem Turks on the threshold of Italy.

24. Psalm 91:7.
25. John 12:47.
26. 2 Corinthians 10:4.
27. Ficino is telling Sixtus to free himself from the bad influence of his lower nature. At the time of Sixtus' birth, 3 July 1414, Saturn, Venus, Mercury, and the Sun were all in Cancer (producing a strong sense of family); the Moon was in the opposite sign of Capricorn and Mars was in Libra square to them all (i.e., at 908), indicating conflict. The benign influence of Jupiter, which gives authority to rulers, is strengthened by being in its own sign of Sagittarius. Thus, according to the contemporary system of astrology, this chart helps to explain Sixtus' position of authority as pope, his nepotism, and his aggressive policy of extending the papal states. Ficino reminds Sixtus to call forth the love of Venus to overcome his aggressive Martian tendencies and the magnanimity of Jupiter to overcome the rigidity of Saturn. If he follows Ficino's advice Sixtus will use his ability to establish love, peace, and law, and will extend his idea of family to include the whole Christian flock. Ficino, referring to Sixtus' divine nature, is suggesting that the surest way to overcome evil is to allow divine providence to prevail, so that he may be free of the influence of the stars, and may even rule over them. See also letters 72 and 77 in this volume; *De amore* 5.8 and 6.4.
28. John 18:36.
29. Luke 2:14.

96

1. Plato, *Protagoras*, 321-22.
2. According to Ficino, the powers of government are given to men by Jupiter, using Mercury's gifts of ingenuity and skillful speech. See *De amore*, 6.4.
3. Proverbs 21:1.
4. John 19:11.
5. Romans 13:1.
6. "Michael is called Lord of the people of Judah and other angels are assigned to other peoples. For the Most High established the boundaries of the nations according to the number of the angels of God." Dionysius, *Celestial Hierarchies*, 9.2.4. See also Psalm 91:11; Matthew 4:6.
7. Psalm 127:1.
8. Proverbs 8:15-16.
9. The introduction of practices of sacrifice and augury, prior to important state actions, was attributed to the second king of Rome, Numa Pompilius (715-672 B.C.), whom Livy and Plutarch both regarded as the founder of Roman religion.
10. "Scipio Africanus, the younger, often used to go to the Capitolium in the second half of the night before the break of day, instructing that the shrine of Jupiter be opened and would remain there a long time alone, as if consulting Jupiter about matters of State . . . the dogs that guarded the temple never barked at him or molested." Aulus Gellius, *Attic Nights*, 6.1.6.
11. See Plato, *Republic*, 6.488-89 and *Laws*, 4.709.

97

1. In the archetype MS M9, this letter was addressed to Lorenzo de' Medici. In most subsequent MSS and the printed editions the name of Lorenzo Iuniori has been substituted.
2. Cf. Dante, *La divina commedia, Inferno*, canto 1, lines 2 and 32–53; also Proverbs 24:30–31, "I went by the vineyard of the man void of understanding and, lo, it was all grown over with thorns, and nettles had covered the face thereof." See Plato, *Republic*, 10.611–12.
3. Cf. Plotinus, *Enneads*, 1.6.5, for a similar comparison.
4. Cf. Daniel 12:3, "They that be wise shall shine as the brightness of the firmament; and they that turn many to righteousness as the stars for ever and ever."

98

1. Homer, *Iliad*, 11.514.
2. Greek god of medicine, son of Apollo and the nymph Coronis. Homer mentions him as a skillful physician whose sons, Machaon and Podalirius, are the physicians in the Greek camp before Troy. Aesculapius was said to have learnt the art of healing as well as hunting from the Centaur Chiron. See *Iliad*, 4.193.
3. Hippocrates, *Works*, vol. 9, ed. Littré (Paris, 1839), p. 325.
4. Ibid., vol. 9, p. 339.
5. See Iamblichus, *Life of Pythagoras*, 15.64, and Porphyry, *Life of Pythagoras*, sec. 30.
6. This refers to Mithridates VII, king of Pontus, surnamed "the Great," whose skill in medicine is attested by ancient authors: Appian, Strabo, Justin, etc.
7. An Arabian medical writer, also known as John of Damascus, who lived in the first half of the ninth century. His collected works were printed in Venice in 1497. (See Jöchers, *Lexicon*, vol. 4, p. 1547.)
8. Saints who were brothers and physicians in Cilicia. Martyred in A.D. 303.
9. Hippocrates, *Works*, vol. 9, p. 325.
10. *Galeni Opera*, vol. 11, *Ad Glauconem*, 2.4.f.97 (ed. Kuhn, 1826).
11. Hippocrates, *Works*, vol. 9, p. 387.
12. Plato, *Timaeus*, 89.

99

1. This letter appears in the appendix to the first volume of letters.

Notes on Ficino's Correspondents
and other contemporaries mentioned in this volume

Details are given below of correspondents and contemporaries about whom significant details are known to the translators. The following abbreviations are used in the notes:

Cosenza	M. E. Cosenza. *Biographical Dictionary of Humanism and Classical Scholarship*. 5 vols. Boston, 1962.
Della Torre	A. Della Torre. *Storia dell' Accademia Platonica di Firenze*, 1902.
Diz. biog. Ital.	*Dizionario biografico degli Italiani*, Rome, 1960-.
Iter Ital.	P. O. Kristeller. *Iter Italicum: A Finding List of Uncatalogued or Incompletely Catalogued Humanistic Manuscripts of the Renaissance in Italian and Other Libraries*. 3 vols. London and Leiden, 1963, 1967, 1983.
Kristeller, *Studies*	P. O. Kristeller. *Studies in Renaissance Thought and Letters*, 1956, 1969.
Marcel	R. Marcel, *Marsile Ficin*, 1958.
Sup. Fic.	P. O. Kristeller, *Supplementum Ficinianum*.
Vespasiano	Vespasiano da Bisticci, *Lives of Illustrious Men of the XVth Century*. Trans. W. George & E. Waters, with an introduction by Myron P. Gillmore.

Peregrino Agli (1440-1469): poet and humanist. At the age of fifteen he was already writing poetry that was admired by men of learning. A member of Ficino's Academy; his teacher was Francesco da Castiglione.

> F. Flamini, *Peregrino allio umanista poeta e confilosofo del Ficino* (Pisa, 1893); Della Torre, pp. 552-53; *Sup. Fic.*, vol. 2, p. 322; *Diz. biog. Ital.*, vol. 1, pp. 401-402.

Girolamo Amazzi: physician, musician, and member of the Academy. He apparently helped Ficino to resolve the difficult question of whether a cause can produce contrary effects in one and the same subject.

> Della Torre, p. 779; Cosenza, p. 158.

Riccardo Angiolieri of Anghiari (1414-1486): priest and theologian, and member of the Florentine College of Theologians.

> Della Torre, p. 770 seq.; Cosenza, pp. 184-85.

Oliviero di Taddeo Arduini (died 1498): distinguished Aristotelian philosopher who taught natural philosophy and theology at Pisa University (1474-1487). He took part in the Camaldolese dialogues described by Landino, and once had a discussion with Ficino on the soul. His writings have not survived.

> Della Torre, pp. 743-45; Cosenza, pp. 265-66.

Marco Aurelio of Venice: scholar who held public office. He was secretary to the Venetian senate *(secretario ducale)*, and succeeded Giovanni Pietro Stella as grand chancellor of Venice. He went on an embassy to the Turks. Ficino sent him a letter in praise of philosophy and one in praise of medicine (*Opera*, pp. 757, 759; see also letter 42). Many letters from Filelfo are addressed to him. He also corresponded with Giuliano de' Medici, Bernardo Bembo, Guarino and Nicolo Sagundino.

> *Sup. Fic.*, vol. 1, p. 119; Cosenza, p. 336; *Iter Ital.*, vol. 2.

Francesco Bandini (*c.* 1440-1489): priest and diplomat who came from a wealthy family; was sent on many diplomatic missions by the Medici. His relationship with Ficino was very close and he belonged to Ficino's Academy. He was appointed master of the wine cup *(architryclinus)* at the Platonic Symposium, described by Ficino in *De amore* (see also letter 23). Ficino dedicated his *Life of Plato* (*Opera*, vol. 1, p. 763) to Bandini. In 1476 he was sent by Lorenzo to the court of King Matthias of Hungary and possibly stayed there till his death. Ficino continued to correspond with him and through him informed the king and the humanists of the work of the Academy.

Della Torre, p. 768 seq.; *Sup. Fic.*, vol. 1, p. 121; P. O. Kristeller, *Studies, pp. 395-435 and passim.* Cosenza, pp. 388-89; *Diz. biog. Ital.*, vol. 5, pp. 709-10.

Bernardo Bembo (1433-1519): Venetian statesman and orator, father of Pietro Bembo. He was appointed Venetian ambassador to Florence in 1474; the friend of Lorenzo, Poliziano, and Ficino, who dedicated the fifth book of letters to him. In Florence, Bembo's platonic love for Ginevra de' Benci was celebrated in numerous poems of Braccesi. In Venice Bembo frequented the literary circle of Aldo Manuzio.

Della Torre, *La prima ambasceria di Bernardo Bembo a Firenze*, in *Giornale Storico*, 35 (1900), p. 258 seq.; *Sup. Fic.*, vol. 2, p. 346; Cosenza, pp. 489-90; *Diz. biog. Ital.*, vol. 8, p. 103 seq.

Antonio Di Paolo Benivieni (1443-1502): greatest Florentine physician of the second half of the fifteenth century and important for his studies in pathological anatomy. He was a member of Ficino's Academy and a friend of Lorenzo and Giuliano de' Medici. He possessed an excellent library of philosophical and medical works, and was interested in astronomy and astrology. Both he and Ficino were consulted by Filipo Strozzi as to the right time and place for laying the foundation stone of the Strozzi Palace in 1481.

Della Torre, pp. 780-83; Cosenza, pp. 512-13; *Diz. biog. Ital.*, vol. 8, pp. 543-45.

Francesco Berlinghieri (1440-1500): Florentine patrician, poet, and geographer. He was a friend of Lorenzo de' Medici and a member of the Compagnia dei Magi. His teachers were Cristoforo Landino and Giovanni Argyropoulos, who taught him Greek. He held various public offices connected with the magistracy. His most famous work is a translation into Italian *terza rima* of Ptolemy's "Geography," entitled *Sette Giornate della geografia di Francesco Berlinghieri* (1480), dedicated to Federico, duke of Urbino. Begun when Francesco was twenty-five, this work occupied him for fifteen years. The preface to the book contains an *apologia* from Ficino to the duke (published as a letter in book 7 of the *Letters*, which is itself also dedicated to Berlinghieri). Francesco was a close friend of Ficino and a member of the Platonic Academy. Ficino once advised Berlinghieri concerning the choice of a husband for his daughter. (See letter 87). Together with Filippo Valori, Francesco helped to bring out a sumptuous edition of Ficino's Latin translation of Plato (1484). Ficino praises Berlinghieri in his commentary on Plato's *Timaeus*

(*Opera*, p. 1464 seq.). Berlinghieri's letters to the Medici are preserved in the Florentine state archives. Apparently, he preferred to express himself in Italian (Tuscan) rather than in Latin.

There are three letters to Berlinghieri in the *Letters*, two of them in the present volume (letters 87 and 96); and mentions of Berlinghieri (letters 46 and 70) indicate his close connections with Ficino.

Ioannos Bessarion (1403–1472): cardinal of Sabina, he studied under Gemistos Plethon. He came to Italy in 1437 for the Council of Florence, where he championed the cause of union between the Greek and Latin churches. He was made a cardinal by Pope Eugene IV and settled in Rome. One of the leading scholars of the time, many humanists including Platina and Valla gathered round him, and his house became known as the Academy of Bessarion. His collection of Greek manuscripts was the richest in Europe. Bessarion's work *In calumniatorem Platonis* published in 1469, made Plato known to a wide public and emphasized the harmony between Platonism and Christianity.

> Della Torre, pp. 584–85; L. Mohler, *Kardinal Bessarion als Theologe; Humanist und Staatsman*, 3 vols. (Paderborn, 1923); Marcel, p. 355 seq.; *Diz. biog. Ital.*, vol. 9, pp. 686–96.

Jacopo Bracciolini (1441–1478): son of Poggio, the famous humanist and chancellor of Florence. A member of Ficino's Academy and secretary of Cardinal Raffaele Riario. He took part in the Pazzi conspiracy and was hanged.

> Della Torre, p. 804; *Sup. Fic.*, vol. 1, pp. 121–22; Cosenza, pp. 693–94; *Diz. biog. Ital.*, vol. 13, pp. 638–39.

Antonio Calderini (1446–1494): lawyer and member of Ficino's Academy; an intimate friend of the Medici and Ficino. He was secretary to Cardinal Barbo in Rome (1485–1491) and interceded on Ficino's behalf when the latter was accused of heresy after the publication of his *De vita libri tres*.

> Della Torre, pp. 713–14; *Sup. Fic.*, vol. 1, p. 116; Cosenza, p. 768 seq.; *Diz. biog. Ital.*, vol. 16, pp. 592–93.

Andrea Cambini: historian and translator; friend of Ficino and Lorenzo di Bernardo de' Medici; he was a devoted student of Cicero.

> Cosenza, p. 800.

Giovanni Antonio Campano (1427–1477): poet and scholar. He began life as a shepherd boy. He studied law at Perugia and became professor of Rhetoric there (1455). Pope Pius II made him bishop of Cotrone (1460), and afterward bishop of Teramo. In Rome Campano belonged to the Greek Academy of Bessarion, and for many years was corrector and reviewer of classical texts; Pius II submitted to him the manuscripts of his commentaries. His many works include poetry, letters, and fables. His teachers included Demetrius Chalcondylas and Lorenzo Valla.

In 1471, Campano passing through Florence heard Ficino playing on his lyre, which he describes in a letter to Gentile Becchi.

Della Torre, p. 415 seq.; *Sup. Fic.*, vol. 1, pp. 132–33; Cosenza, pp. 808–13.

Giovanni Cavalcanti (1444–1509): son of a Florentine nobleman, he studied rhetoric under Landino and became a statesman and diplomat, going on an important mission to King Charles VIII of France in 1494. Ficino knew and loved Giovanni from the time when Giovanni was only seven years old. Ficino dedicated his translation of Alcinous and Speusippus to him in 1463 (see letter 84). In Cavalcanti's company Ficino wrote many of his works, such as the *Platonic Theology*. Cavalcanti remained devoted to Ficino all his life. When Ficino was afflicted with a "bitterness of spirit" (Corsi, 8), Cavalcanti advised him to write a book on love as a remedy for his illness and to "convert the lovers of transitory beauty to the enjoyment of eternal beauty." This work became the first version of *De amore*, the commentary on Plato's *Symposium*, which is dedicated to Cavalcanti.

Della Torre, p. 647 seq. & index; *Sup. Fic.*, vol. 1, p. 118; Marcel, pp. 340–46 & index; Cosenza, pp. 951–53.

Antonio di Donato Cocchi: professor of canon law at Pisa University from 1473 to 1490. He became vicar of Pisa Chapterhouse after the death of its titular holder, the archbishop Francesco Salviati.

Fabroni, *Historia Academiae Pisanae*, vol. 1, p. 133; Della Torre, p. 719; Cosenza, p. 1029.

Amerigo Corsini (1452–1501): poet and statesman who held important offices in the Republic. He was a member of Ficino's Academy. He wrote a life of Cosimo de' Medici in verse and a poem on Ficino's *De vita libri tres*.

L. Passerini, *Genealogia e storia della famiglia Corsini* (Florence, 1858), p. 128 seq.; Della Torre, pp. 662–64; *Sup. Fic.*, vol. 1, p. 113.

Luca Fabiano of Florence: For many years Ficino's secretary, Ficino left him a bequest in his will. He completed a handwritten copy of Ficino's translation and commentary on Plotinus for Lorenzo de' Medici within two months.

Sup. Fic., vol. 2, p. 333; Cosenza, p. 2018.

Bartolomeo della Fonte (1445–1513): Florentine priest, poet, and orator. He succeeded Francesco Filelfo (died 1481) as professor of rhetoric and philosophy at Florence University, but was forced to resign because of the hostility of Poliziano. After teaching in Rome, he regained his position in 1485 with the help of Lorenzo de' Medici. For a time he taught at the court of King Matthias of Hungary, whose library he helped to enrich. He returned to Florence in 1490 on the death of the king.

Della Torre, p. 420 seq.; C. Marchesi, *Bartolomeo della Fonte* (Catania, 1900); *Epistolae*, ed. J. Fogel and L. Juhasz (Leipzig, 1932). Cosenza, pp. 1448–53; *Epistolae*, ed. L. Juhasz (Budapest, 1931).

Sebastiano Foresi (born 1424): Florentine poet and musician, much admired by Ficino for his playing on the lyre. He addressed two poems in Italian to Lorenzo de' Medici, one a paraphrase of Virgil's *Georgics*; the other, *Il trionfo delle virtú*, in praise of Cosimo de' Medici. As a notary he served in the magistrature between 1446 and 1497. Ficino praised Sebastiano's skill on the lyre, and cherished their friendship on account of their mutual love of music and the lyre.

Della Torre, pp. 792–93; *Sup. Fic.*, vol. 1, p. 117.

Bartolomeo Fortini (died 1466): Florentine lawyer who held important offices in the Republic, a scholar in Greek and Latin and member of Ficino's Academy; a man of exemplary virtue, according to the *Lives* of Vespasiano da Bisticci.

Vespasiano, pp. 462–64; Della Torre, pp. 548, 550.

Lorenzo Franceschi: scholar who made an Italian translation of six dialogues of Plato from Ficino's Latin translation, and an Italian translation of Ficino's *Life of Plato*.

Iter Ital., vol. 1, p. 114.

Domenico Galletti of Monte San Savino (near Arezzo): member of Ficino's Academy and canon of Arezzo cathedral. In 1466 he went to Rome as an apostolic secretary and abbreviator (providing summaries of documents). He was a friend both of Cavalcanti and Ficino.

Della Torre, pp. 767-68; Cosenza, p. 1532; P. O. Kristeller, *Iter Ital.*, vol. 2.

Bernardo Giugni: Florentine statesman, diplomat and member of Ficino's Academy; also a man of exemplary civic virtue, according to the *Lives* of Vespasiano da Bisticci.

Vespasiano, pp. 326-32; Della Torre, p. 545 seq.

Giovanni Francesco Ippoliti, count of Gazzoldo: humanist, and friend of Ficino. In 1480 Francesco caused the first six books of Ficino's *Epistolae* to be transcribed. Ficino addressed a long letter (letter 46) to Francesco on the Platonic nature and function of a philosopher. Letters by him are preserved in the Archivio Mediceo avanti il Principato.

Antonio Ivani of Sarzana (*c*. 1430–1482): scholar who held public offices. He was chancellor of Volterra (1466–71) and Pistoia. He wrote a book on the sack of Volterra as well as a book in Italian on the family, *Del governo della famiglia* (ed. Bertoloni [Genoa, 1872]). His correspondents included Ficino and Donato Acciaiuoli. His unpublished letters are preserved in Sarzana (cod. Sarzan., 26).

Sup. Fic.,vol. 2, p. 324; *Iter Ital.*, pp. 144–45.

Cristoforo Landino (1424–1504): Florentine poet, scholar, and humanist, and member of Ficino's Academy. He shared with Ficino the duties of instructing the young Lorenzo. From 1458 he was professor of poetry and rhetoric at Florence University, and secretary to the Signoria until 1492. All his life Landino encouraged the study of the three great poets of Florence—Dante, Petrarch, and Boccaccio. His friends included Alberti and Bembo, and his pupils the Englishmen William Grocyn and Thomas Linacre.

Della Torre, pp. 380 seq., 579; *Sup. Fic.*, vol. 2, pp. 327–28; Marcel, p. 190 seq. & index; Cosenza, pp. 1909–16; *Carmina omnia*, ed. A. Perosa, 1939.

Lorenzo Lippi (1440–1485): poet and scholar, and professor of poetry and rhetoric at the University of Pisa (1473–1485). Lippi was a close friend of the Medici and their circle of poets, and his *Book of Proverbs*, dedicated to Lorenzo de' Medici, contains nearly 100 Greek and Latin proverbs.

Della Torre, pp. 702–706; Cosenza, pp. 1994–95.

Angelo Manetti: son of the famous historian and scholar of Hebrew, Gianozzo. Even as a boy he could speak and write Latin, Greek, and Hebrew. He possessed many manuscripts, some of which are now kept in the *Fondo Palatino* of the Vatican library (Vat. Pal. Lat. 958). He lived in Naples from 1460–68. He was a friend of Lorenzo de' Medici and of Vespasiano da Bisticci.

Vespasiano, pp. 305–310; Cosenza, p. 2109.

Francesco Marescalchi of Ferrara: Canon and member of Ficino's Academy.

Della Torre, p. 600; Cosenza, pp. 1484–85.

Carlo Marsuppini, the younger: son of the famous chancellor and orator of Arezzo. He was a member of Ficino's Academy and one of the speakers (Agathon) in the Platonic banquet described in Ficino's commentary on Plato's *Symposium*. He translated the first two books of Homer's *Iliad*. His poetry has not survived.

Della Torre, p. 658; Cosenza, p. 271.

Cosimo de' Medici (1389–1464): statesman, banker, scholar, and patron of the arts. Cosimo as a man towers above the many functions that he so ably performed. Steadfast in good fortune and bad, quickly and wisely decisive, freely extending help to all who sought knowledge and understanding. He was blessed with the widest vision and with a spirit of philanthropy that effectively deployed his immense resources without any sign of diminution.

From 1429 Cosimo was head of a great banking house with interests all over Europe and the Orient; from 1433 an active and devoted collector of ancient manuscripts; and from 1434, the first citizen of Florence. Inspired by Gemistos Plethon with renewed enthusiasm for the study of Plato, Cosimo determined to establish a new Platonic Academy in Florence. To lead the Academy he chose Marsilio Ficino, entrusting him in 1462 with the translation and interpretation of the Platonic dialogues. Two years later, as he lay dying, Cosimo heard Ficino read to him the words of Xenocrates, a disciple of Plato, on the consolation of death. Thus, at the age of seventy-five, he died a man exemplary in private and public affairs, the equal of the sovereigns of Europe, honored as "Pater Patriae."

A. Fabroni, *Magni Cosmi Medicei vita* (Pisa, 1789); Della Torre, p. 559 seq. & index; C. S. Gutkind, *Cosimo de Medici: Pater patriae* (Oxford, 1940); Marcel, pp. 255–62 & index.

Giuliano de' Medici (1454-1478): younger brother of Lorenzo and member of Ficino's Academy. Botticelli painted his portrait and Poliziano celebrated his love for Simonetta Cattaneo in the *Giostra*. He was assassinated in the Pazzi conspiracy. He left an illegitimate son, Giulio, who became Pope Clement VII.

Della Torre, p. 737.

Lorenzo de' Medici (1449-1492): grandson of Cosimo and son of Piero. Lorenzo was one of the most versatile and talented men of his time: perhaps the finest Italian poet of the century, he was equally accomplished in philosophic and religious poetry, love poetry, and comic poetry. An eminent statesman, his principles, particularly his respect for justice, arose from his love of religion and philosophy. Ficino, his boyhood tutor, he always regarded as a close friend.

He was only twenty-one when he found himself the effective ruler of Florence. He was faced with enemies both in Florence and outside. The most critical period of his rule was that of the Pazzi conspiracy (1478) in which his brother Giuliano was assassinated in Florence cathedral and he only narrowly escaped. After the conspiracy he was opposed in war by a powerful alliance of Italian states under the leadership of the pope, a war which his courage and statesmanship brought to a satisfactory conclusion. After this, through his statesmanship and the respect in which he was held, Italy enjoyed a period of comparative peace until his death.

From his love of knowledge and the arts Lorenzo revitalized the University of Pisa, discerned the latent talent in Michelangelo, and supported that group of artists, sculptors, poets, scholars, and philosophers who were close to the heart of the Renaissance.

A. Fabroni, *Laurentii Medicis magnifici vita* (Pisa, 1784); A. von Reumont, *Lorenzo de' Medici* (Leipzig, 1883, and London, 1876); Della Torre, pp. 737-42 & index; Marcel, p. 372 seq. & index; Cosenza, pp. 2272-75.

Lorenzo di Pierfrancesco de' Medici (1458-1503): the second cousin of Lorenzo de' Medici, referred to as Lorenzo the Younger. His fame has been assured for posterity by a letter to him from Ficino (letter 78) linking him with Botticelli's *Primavera*, as the letter describes the figure of Venus which is thought to have inspired Botticelli's Venus in the *Primavera* (see letter 78, note 6). Ficino sent Lorenzo a copy of *De vita libri tres* in 1489 as soon as it was published; and in his will Ficino bequeathed him a manuscript copy of the dialogues of Plato in Greek originally presented to him by Cosimo. Giorgio Antonio Vespucci was one of Lorenzo's tutors, and his friends included Poliziano and Bartolomeo Scala. His letters are preserved in the Florentine Archives. Lorenzo was sent on a diplomatic mission to France in 1493. He deplored the tyranny of Lorenzo's successor, Piero, and subsequently gave his support to King Charles VIII of France, who finally deposed Piero.

> G. Pieraccini, *La Stirpe de' Medici di Cafaggiolo* (Florence, 1924), vol. 1, pp. 353 seq.; Della Torre, p. 542. Sup. *Fic.*, vol. 2, pp. 331–32.

Michele Mercati: together with Antonio Serafico, one of the earliest and closest friends of Ficino. He was a monk and teacher. Ficino sent him an early essay, *Summa philosophiae*, summarizing different schools of philosophy, to help him in his studies. Ficino also confided his ideas on Epicurean philosophy and his youthful commentary on Lucretius' *De rerum natura* to Mercati (*Sup. Fic.*, vol. 2, p. 81). A story is told, based upon the testimony of Mercati's grandson, that Ficino appeared after his death to Mercati in order to prove the immortality of the soul.

> Della Torre, pp. 575–76; Sup. *Fic.*, vol. 2, p. 216; Marcel, p. 184 seq. & index; Cosenza, p. 2291.

Naldo Naldi (*c.* 1435–1513): professor of poetry and rhetoric at Florence University from 1484, and a member of Ficino's Academy. He was one of the most prolific poets of the Medici circle, and an intimate friend of Ficino who sent him the *De Christiana religione*. Naldi praised Ficino in his poetry and once for a Platonic symposium he rendered Ficino's *Life of Plato* into verse. He wrote religious and pastoral poetry, and love poems addressed to friends; three books of his Latin elegies were dedicated to Lorenzo de' Medici.

> Della Torre, pp. 503–505, 668 seq.; *Sup. Fic.*, vol. 2, p. 328; Marcel, pp. 170–72; Cosenza, pp. 2408–11; *Elegiae*, ed. L. Juhasz (Leipzig, 1934).

Piero del Nero (died 1512): held various offices in the magistrature. He financed the publication of Ficino's *De sole et lumine*.

> Della Torre, pp. 727–28; *Sup. Fic.*, vol. 1, p. 110; Cosenza, pp. 2431–32.

Lotterio Neroni: Florentine humanist of noble family, exiled in 1466 after being involved in a conspiracy against Piero de' Medici. He returned to Florence but held no public office. Friend of Ficino, Platina, and the poet Ugolino Verino. He compiled excerpts from Cicero's letters. Ficino wrote an important letter on the soul to him, *Anima in corpore dormit, somniat, delirat, aegrotat (Opera, p. 926)*.

Sup. Fic., vol. 1, p. 120; Cosenza, p. 2430.

Giovanni Nesi (1456–1520): poet, philosopher, and faithful disciple of Ficino. He held public office, was three times *priore* and *officialis* of the *studio* (university). His writings comprise poems, letters, and devotional orations, many of which were recited before the Compagnia dei Magi, a lay confraternity. He wrote a long visionary poem about Paradise, Neoplatonic in style. Nesi also frequented the convent of San Marco and followed the teaching of Savonarola, whom he praises in his *Oraculum de novo seculo* (1496). He had a deep admiration for Pico della Mirandola and corresponded with other poets: Poliziano, Naldi, and della Fonte.

Della Torre, pp. 692–701; Cosenza, pp. 2432–33; C. Vasoli, "Giovanni Nesi tra Donato Acciaiuoli e Girolamo Savonarola" in *Umanesimo e teologia tra 400 e 500, Memorie Domenicane*, 4 (1973).

Ottone Niccolini: lawyer and member of the Chorus Academiae Florentinae (an Aristotelian school). Niccolini once took part in a discussion with Argyropoulos and his pupils at Careggi in the presence of Cosimo de' Medici, the question being whether law was a branch of moral philosophy. Niccolini maintained that it was.

Vespasiano, p. 230; Passerini, *Genealogia e storia della famiglia*, p. 37; Della Torre, pp. 398, 545 seq.

Rinaldo Orsini: archbishop of Florence and brother-in-law of Lorenzo, who was married to his sister Clarice Orsini. When Francesco Salviati tried to obtain the archbishopric of Florence on the death of Cardinal Pietro Riario in 1474, Lorenzo bestowed it on Rinaldo instead. In June 1490 Ficino appealed to Rinaldo for help against a charge of heresy directed against him at Rome in connection with his book on medicine and astrology, the *De vita libri tres*. Rinaldo interceded in person on his behalf before Pope Innocent VIII and the charge was dropped.

Della Torre, p. 625; Cosenza, p. 3530.

Antonio Pelotti: poet and friend of the Medici. Ficino called him "Apollineus Academiae nostrae lepos."

Della Torre, pp. 659–62.

Leonardo Perugino (Leonardo Mansueti of Perugia) (died 1480): a Dominican who became general of his order in 1474.

Della Torre, p. 767; *Sup. Fic.*, vol. 1, p. 125; Marcel, pp. 416–17.

Angelo Poliziano of Montepulciano (1454–1494): eminent in the Medicean circle of poets and one of the greatest of classical scholars. He was in contact with all the leading humanists and statesmen of his day and his many writings cover a very wide range of subjects. He was a friend of Landino. Supported by Lorenzo, to whom he dedicated his Latin version of Homer's *Iliad* in 1472, he was proclaimed the finest poet in Greek and Latin that Italy had produced; but he also wrote important work in Italian.

Poliziano became tutor to Lorenzo's children but relinquished the post after disagreements with Lorenzo's wife. He became professor of Greek and Latin in 1480. He wrote odes, elegies, and epigrams, the *Orfeo* and *Stanze per la Giostra del Magnifico Giuliano de' Medici*. His pupils included the Englishmen William Latimer and Thomas Linacre.

Poliziano, *Opera* (Venice, 1498); *Prose volgari inedite e poesie latine e greche di A. Poliziano*, ed. Del Lungo (Florence, 1867); *Le stanze, l'orfeo e le rime*, ed. Carducci (Florence, 1863); Della Torre, pp. 657–58; Cosenza, pp. 2878–96.

Cherubino Quarquagli of San Gimignano: grammarian, musician, and poet. He was an early member of Ficino's Academy. Later he was in Rome in the service of Cosimo Orsini, the apostolic secretary, but continued to correspond with Ficino.

Della Torre, pp. 795–96; *Sup. Fic.*, vol. 1, p. 118; Cosenza, pp. 2978–79.

Raffaele Riario (Sansoni-Riario) (1461–1521): cardinal of San Giorgio and young nephew of Girolamo Riario; he was made a cardinal by Sixtus IV in 1477 at the age of sixteen while still a student at Pisa University. In the following year he was summoned to Florence. Jacopo Bracciolini, one of the Pazzi conspirators, became his secretary, and Raffaele was used as a tool in the plot against the Medici. He was consequently imprisoned by the Signoria after the abortive attempt to assassinate Lorenzo in the cathedral, and kept in confinement for six weeks for his own safety from an angry mob, and as a surety for Florentine citizens in Rome. When finally permitted to return to Rome on 12 June 1478, he was said to be more dead than alive from the terror he had endured and still feeling as if the rope were about his neck, as he had repeatedly been threatened with hanging by the mob.

Riario became the *camerarius* (chamberlain) of Sixtus IV, and Leo X made him chancellor of Rome University. In 1498 he was appointed bishop of Viterbo. In the conspiracy of Cardinal Petrucci against Pope Leo in 1521, Riario was accused of complicity, arrested and stripped of his office, but on paying a large sum of money he was pardoned and reinstated as a member of the College of Cardinals. He died shortly afterward (July 1521) in Naples, where he had taken up residence.

The patron and friend of humanists and one of the most long-standing members of the College of Cardinals (a member for over forty years), he was a man of considerable wealth. The Chancery at Rome was built on his orders to the designs of Bramante, as well as a splendid hunting lodge at Bagnaia near Viterbo. The plays of Terence and Plautus were performed at his villa in Rome and he was responsible for a revival of classical drama. Ficino corresponded with Riario for many years. His friends included Pomponio Leto and Lorenzo Buonincontri, who dedicated his commentary on Manilius' *Astronomicon* to Riario.

> Della Torre, pp. 93, 805; *Sup. Fic.*, vol. 1, p. 125; Reumont, *Lorenzo de' Medici*, trans. R. Harrison, pp. 324, 340-42.

Bindaccio Ricasoli (*c.* 1444-1524): member of Ficino's Academy. He held various public offices in Florence, and compiled a catalogue of the works of Ficino in 1493. He was a friend of Giovanni Corsi, who wrote the earliest life of Ficino.

> Passerini, *Genealogia e storia della famiglia Ricasoli* (Florence 1861), p. 155; Della Torre, pp. 59-60; Marcel, pp. 18-20; Cosenza, pp. 604-605.

Bernardo Rucellai (1448-1514): statesman, humanist, and historian. After the death of Lorenzo and Ficino, the Platonic Academy was invited to meet in his garden (Orti) which came to be known as "Orti Oricellarii." Bernardo married a sister of Lorenzo, and was a great friend of the Medici family and also of Luigi Pulci.

> Passerini, *Genealogia e storia della famiglia Rucellai* (Florence, 1861), p. 122 seq.; Della Torre, p. 824; Marcel, pp. 427-28; Cosenza, pp. 2513-14.

Francesco Salviati: made Archbishop of Pisa by Pope Sixtus IV in October 1474. Because Lorenzo de' Medici opposed the appointment, Salviati took office only in 1477. He was executed in 1478 for the leading part he played in the Pazzi conspiracy against the Medici.

> *Sup. Fic.*, vol. 1, p. 121; Cosenza, p. 3158.

Sebastiano Salvini of Castel San Niccoli: Ficino's cousin, priest and member of the Florentine college of theologians. He acted as Ficino's secretary.

When Ficino was invited in 1482 to go to Hungary by King Matthias to teach Plato's philosophy, he declined the invitation and tried unsuccessfully to induce Salvini to go instead. Salvini's letters are preserved in a Vatican library manuscript (Vat. Lat. 5140).

P. O. Kristeller, "Sebastiano Salvini, A Florentine Humanist and Theologian, and a Member of Marsilio Ficino's Platonic Academy" in *Didascalie*, ed. Sesto Prete (New York, 1961), pp. 205-43; Della Torre, pp. 94-104; Cosenza, p. 3164-65.

Francesco di Tommaso Sassetti (1421-1490): a wealthy Florentine merchant and patron of the arts. As an agent of the Medici he spent many years in France, where he made a collection of manuscripts that made his library one of the finest of his day. He corresponded with Ficino, who wrote his *Ricepte contro alla peste* (Remedy against the Plague) with the aid of Francesco's library. He was also a friend of Bartolomeo della Fonte with whom he shared an interest in classical inscriptions.

Francesco became general manager of the Medici bank soon after Cosimo's death. His interest in culture and patronage of artists and writers led him to neglect his business duties, and he has been held partly responsible for the general decline of the bank.

The Sassetti chapel in the church of Santa Trinita, in Florence, is decorated with frescoes painted by Dominico Ghirlandaio in 1485. Members of the Sassetti family appear in the painting together with Lorenzo and Giuliano de' Medici and Poliziano.

Della Torre, p. 781; *Sup. Fic.*, vol. 2, pp. 175-82; Sabbadini, *Scoperte*, vol. 1, p. 139; Cosenza, p. 3204; A. De La Mare, "The Library of Francesco Sassetti (1421-1490)" in *Cultural Aspects of the Italian Renaissance, Essays in Honour of P. O. Kristeller*, ed. C. H. Clough (Manchester and New York, 1976); De Roover, "Francesco Sassetti and the Downfall of the Medici Banking House" in *Bulletin of the Business Historical Society* 17 (1943), pp. 65-80; Aby Warburg, "Francesco Sassettis Letztwillige Verfügung" in *Gesammelte Schriften* (Leipzig and Berlin, 1932), 1.145 seq.

Antonio Serafico (Morali) of San Miniato (born c. 1433): one of the earliest and closest friends of Ficino; poet, musician and one of the first members of Ficino's Academy. He was an expert lyre player. Ficino dedicated an early essay on vision to him.

Della Torre, pp. 793-94; P. O. Kristeller, *Studies in Renaissance Thought and Letters*, p. 139 seq.; Marcel, pp. 224-29.

Pope Sixtus IV (Francesco della Rovere) (1414–1484): born into a humble Ligurian family and educated by the Franciscans, he entered the order at the age of nine, was chosen as the new vicar general of the order in 1464, and raised to cardinal in 1465. Della Rovere's early career was promoted by Bessarion, who was cardinal protector of the order from 1458 to 1472. Prior to his election as pope, Francesco appeared as a zealous reformer intent on keeping the peace in Italy and uniting the nations of Christian Europe against the Turks. On his election in August 1471, Sixtus appealed to the princes of Europe to prepare for a Crusade, and a fleet under the joint command of Venice and Naples succeeded in retaking Smyrna in 1472, but the allies fell out among themselves and enthusiasm for the war evaporated. Sixtus now turned his energy to furthering the fortunes of his own family; his nephews in particular. Pietro Riario (his sister's son) he made a cardinal and archbishop of Florence at the age of twenty-six. Giuliano della Rovere (his brother's son) was made a cardinal by his uncle at the age of twenty-eight and was later to become Pope Julius II. Another nephew, Raffaele Riario, was only sixteen when he was made cardinal. Yet another nephew, Giovanni della Rovere, was appointed prefect of Rome and made a captain general of the Church. When the dissolute Pietro Riario died at an early age, Sixtus now devoted his greatest care to promoting Riario's brother, the ruthless and ambitious Count Girolamo Riario, who was the pope's main instrument in enlarging the territorial possessions of the papacy. It was on his account that Sixtus became embroiled in the Pazzi conspiracy against Lorenzo de' Medici, and the costly war that followed that abortive plot. This was ended in 1480, following Lorenzo's impromptu peace mission to Naples, and the sack of Otranto by the Turks; Sixtus, in the face of this threat to Italy, was obliged to make peace with Florence and pardon Lorenzo. In 1481 Otranto was retaken and Sixtus resumed his intrigues and quarrels with the Italian states, seeking to win back control of lands in the Romagna and Umbria that had once belonged to the papacy. In one notable incident when the Pope had been in alliance with Venice against Naples and Ferrara (a small independent state), Sixtus made peace with Naples and requested Venice to surrender the gains she had won over Ferrara; when she refused, he laid Venice under an ecclesiastical interdict. At length a peace accord was signed between Venice, Naples and Ferrara, which ignored the Papal interests. On hearing the news of this settlement, the Pope was beside himself with rage; he died a few days afterwards.

Sixtus was accused of subordinating his dignity as head of the Christian Church to that of a mere Italian prince, and he was repeatedly threatened with a General Council. Powerful as he was as a secular prince, Sixtus was arguably even greater and more influential as a patron of the arts; his zeal left a permanent mark on the outward appearance of the city of Rome. In 1475 the Sistine Chapel was built, based on the proportions of the Temple of Solomon. In October 1481, some of the most celebrated names among Florentine artists, Botticelli, Ghirlandaio, and Lippi, were called to Rome to begin decorating the chapel with frescoes. It seems that Lorenzo de' Medici was instrumental in this project, perhaps as a gesture of reconciliation with the pope after the recent hostilities of the Pazzi; a contract drawn up in October 1481 names Botticelli, Ghirlandaio, Perugino, and Cosimo Roselli. Sixtus is acknowledged to have been the author of the program of decoration that culminated in the great cycle of frescoes painted by Michelangelo in the reign of Pope Julius II.

Sixtus gave the people of Rome some famous statues of antiquity, such as the She-wolf of Rome, complete with the legendary twins Romulus and Remus and he also had restored the colossal bronze statue of Marcus Aurelius which now stands in the center of the piazza on the Capitoline Hill (Campidoglio). He built the Sistine bridge from the blocks of the Colosseum, and he rearranged the irregular street plan of the City of Rome, widening many of its thoroughfares. In 1481 Sixtus gave the feast of St. Anne, the mother of Mary, a special place in the liturgical calendar, increasing the significance of the family of Christ. Effigies and paintings of the Holy Family increased, and Leonardo da Vinci painted his famous trinity of Anne, Mary, and the child Jesus. Sixtus promoted a new devotion to the cult of the Immaculate Conception, which was promulgated in a series of papal bulls (1477–83). These devotions were seen as a means of combating one of the most serious evils of the time: the widespread decline in social institutions, and especially that of the family.

Francesco Tedaldi: father of Lattanzio, he was an Aristotelian philosopher who dedicated his *Disputationes occidentalium philosophorum de anima* to Lorenzo de' Medici.

Sup. Fic., vol. 2, p. 339.

Baccio di Luca Ugolini (died 1494): poet and musician, skilled on the lyre ("improvisatore"). The friend of Poliziano and Lorenzo; he attended the first lessons of Ficino, who held Baccio in warm regard on account of their common love for poetry and music. Ugolini played the role of Orpheus, when the play of that name written by Poliziano was given its first performance in Mantua. He was made bishop of Gaeta in 1494.

Della Torre, p. 796 seq.; *Sup. Fic.*, vol. 1, pp. 119–20; Cosenza, pp. 3506–7.

Tommaso Valeri of Viterbo: physician.

Della Torre, p. 779 & index.

Carlo Valguli of Brescia: scholar and tutor to the sons of Tommaso Minerbetti; secretary of Cardinal Cesare Borgia and friend of Poliziano and of Cardinal Piccolomini of Siena.

Sup. Fic., vol. 1, pp. 114–15.

Giorgio Antonio Vespucci (1435–1514): priest and canon of Florence cathedral, he was an early member of Ficino's Academy, and became an eminent tutor of the classics. He built up a rich library of Greek and Latin manuscripts. Ficino gave Vespucci his Latin translation of Plato to revise. He was an uncle of the navigator and explorer, Amerigo Vespucci (after whom America is named).

Bandini, *Vita e lettere di Amerigo Vespucci* (Florence, 1745); Della Torre, pp. 772–74; *Sup. Fic.*, vol. 1, pp. 111–12; Cosenza, pp. 3654–65.

BIBLIOGRAPHY

Text of Works by Ficino

Ficinus, M. *Opera omnia*. 2 vols. Basel, 1561; 2nd ed., 1576; Paris, 1641 (following 1st ed.). 1576 ed. reprint, Turin, 1959.

——. *Epistolae libri XII*. Venice, 1495.

Ficino, Marsilio. *Lettere I: Epistolarum familiarum liber 1*. Ed. S. Gentile. Florence, 1990. First volume of a full critical edition of the text of the *Epistolae libri XII*. Further volumes in progress.

——. *El libro dell'amore*. Ed. S. Niccoli. Florence, 1987. Full critical edition of the Italian text of Ficino's *Commentarium in convivium Platonis de amore*.

——. *Consilio contro la pestilenzia*. Ed. E. Musacchio. Bologna, 1983. The Italian text based on the *Editio princeps* of 1481.

——. *Mercurii Trismegistis liber de potestate et sapientia dei*. Florence, 1989. Facsimile reprint of the *Editio princeps* of 1471.

Kristeller, P. O., ed. *Supplementum Ficinianum: Marsilii Ficini Florentini opuscula inedita et dispersa*. Florence, 1937. Reprint, 1973.

——. *Studies in Renaissance Thought and Letters*. Rome, 1956, 1969. Contains unpublished writings of Ficino, including *Summa philosophiae* and *Divisio philosophiae* with additional notes on the manuscripts and printed editions of his works.

——. *Marsilio Ficino and His Work after Five Hundred Years*. Florence, 1987. A reissue of Kristeller's contribution to the proceedings of the Ficino Conference of 1984, with full indices of manuscripts, documents, and literature concerning Ficino, including the text of unpublished letters—with addenda and corrigenda.

Shaw, P. "La Versione Ficiniana della 'Monarchia.'" *Studi Danteschi* 51, (1978), pp. 289–408. The Italian text of Ficino's translation of Dante's *De monarchia*.

Translations

Allen, M. *Marsilio Ficino: The Philebus Commentary*. Los Angeles, 1975. Text and translation of Ficino's *Commentarium in Philebum Platonis de summo bono*.

——. *Marsilio Ficino and the Phaedran Charioteer*. Los Angeles, 1981. Text and translation of Ficino's *Commentarium in Phedrum Platonis*.

——. *Icastes: Marsilio Ficino's Interpretation of Plato's Sophist*. Los Angeles, 1989. Text and translation of Ficino's *Commentaria et argumenta in Platonis sophistam*, including five studies on Ficino's philosophy.

──. *Nuptial Arithmetic: Marsilio Ficino's Commentary on the Fatal Number in Book VIII of Plato's Republic.* Los Angeles, 1994. Text and translation of *Commentarium in locum Platonis ex octavo libro de Republica de mutatione Reipublicae per numerum fatalem.*

Biondi, A. and G. Pisani. *Marsilio Ficino: De vita.* Pordenone, 1991. Text and Italian translation of *De vita libri tres,* with notes.

Boer, C. *Marsilio Ficino: The Book of Life.* Irving, Texas, 1980. A translation of *De vita libri tres,* with notes.

Burroughs, J. *Five Questions Concerning Mind.* An English translation of *Quinque quaestiones de mente* from Ficino's second book of letters, in *The Renaissance Philosophy of Man.* Ed. E. Cassirer & P. O. Kristeller. Chicago, 1945.

Ficino, M. *Epistole philosophice di Marsilio Ficino Platonico Fiorentino.* Rome. An early translation of the first book of letters.

Figliucci, F. *Le divine lettere del gran Marsilio Ficino.* Venice, 1546, 1563. An Italian translation of the twelve books of letters.

Jayne, S. R. "Marsilio Ficino's Commentary on Plato's Symposium." *University of Missouri Studies* 19, no. 1. (1944). Text and translation of Ficino's *De Amore.*

──. *Marsilio Ficino: Commentary on Plato's Symposium on Love.* Dallas, Texas, 1985. A new translation of *De Amore,* with notes.

Kaske, C. and J. Clark, *Marsilio Ficino: Three Books on Life.* New York, 1989. Text and translation of *De vita libri tres,* with introduction and notes.

Marcel, R. *Commentaire sur le banquet de Platon.* Paris, 1955. Text and French translation of Ficino's *De Amore.*

──. *Théologie Platonicienne de l'immortalité des âmes.* 3 vols. Paris, 1964-1970. Text and French translation of Ficino's *Theologia Platonica sive de immortalitate animorum,* the third volume containing the text of *Opuscula theologica* from the second book of letters.

Montoriola, K. von. *Briefe des Mediceerkreises aus Marsilio Ficino's Epistolarium.* Berlin, 1926. First book of letters translated into German with notes.

Selected Studies on Ficino and the Academy, His Correspondents, and Source Material

Acton, H. *The Pazzi Conspiracy: The Plot against the Medici.* London, 1979.

Allen, D. C. *The Star-Crossed Renaissance.* Durham, N. C., 1941. Reprint, London, 1966. The first chapter discusses Ficino's attitude toward astrology.

Allen, M. *The Platonism of Marsilio Ficino: A Study of his Phaedrus Commentary.* Los Angeles, 1984.

Anon. *Vita di Marsilio Ficino.* Biblioteca Nazionale Palatinus 488. (Italian text published in R. Marcel, *Marsile Ficin,* pp. 694-734).

Boccaccio, G. *The Life of Dante (Trattatello in laude di Dante).* Trans. V. Z. Bollettino. New York and London, 1990.

Branca, V. *Poliziano e l'Umanesimo della Parola.* Turin, 1983.

Burroughs, J. *Platonic Theology* (including translation of books 3.2, 13.3, 14.3, 4) in *Journal of the History of Ideas* 5 (1944), pp. 227-39.

Caponsachi, P. *Sommario della vita di Marsilio Ficino.* Archivio di Stato di Firenze. Ms 191-v.

Chastel, A. *Marsile Ficin et l'art.* Geneva, 1954. Reprint, 1976.

———. *Marsile Ficin. Lettres sur la Connaissance de soi et sur l'astrologie,* in *La Table Ronde* 2 (1945). A French translation of selected letters.

Copenhaver, B. P. *Hermetica: The Greek Corpus Hermeticum and the Latin Asclepius in English Translation.* Cambridge, 1992. With notes and introduction.

Copenhaver, B. P. and C. B. Schmitt. *Renaissance Philosophy.* Oxford, 1992.

Corsi, G. *Marsilii Ficini vita in Philippi Villani liber de civitatis Florentinae famosis civibus.* Ed. G. C. Galetti. Florence, 1847. Reprint in R. Marcel, *Marsile Ficin,* pp. 680–89. English translation in volume 3 of *Letters,* pp. 135–48.

Cosenza, M. E. *Biographical Dictionary of Humanism and Classical Scholarship.* 5 vols. Boston, 1962.

Creighton, M. *A History of the Papacy from the Great Schism to the Sack of Rome.* 6 vols. London, 1903. Vol. 4 is on Sixtus IV.

Cristiani, E. *Una inedita invettiva giovanile di Marsilio Ficino in Rinascimento.* Dec. 1966. Contains an early letter of Ficino.

Dante. *The Divine Comedy.* Trans. C. S. Singleton. 3 vols. Princeton, New Jersey, 1975.

Della Torre, A. *Storia dell' Academia Platonica di Firenze.* Florence, 1902.

Ficino, M. *Marsilio Ficino e il ritorno di Platone, studi e documenti.* 2 vols. Ed. G. C. Garfagnini (Istituto Nazionale di Studi Sul Rinascimento). Florence, 1986. Papers read at the Ficino Conference of 1984.

———. *Marsilio Ficino e il ritorno di Platone, manoscritti, stampe e documenti.* Ed. S. Gentile, S. Niccoli, P. Viti. Florence, 1984. Catalogue of an exhibition of manuscripts, prints, and documents held in the Laurentian Library to commemorate the 500th anniversary of Ficino's Latin translation of Plato.

Field, A. *The Origins of the Platonic Academy of Florence.* Princeton, New Jersey, 1988.

Festugière, J. *La philosophie de l'amour de Marsile Ficin, et son influence sur la littérature française au XVI siècle.* Paris, 1941.

Fubini, R. "Ficino e i Medici all' Avvento di Lorenzo il Magnifico." *Rinascimento* 24 (1984).

———. "Ancora Su Ficino e i Medici." *Rinascimento* 27 (1987).

Garin, E. *Prosatori Latini del Quattrocento.* Milan and Naples, 1952. Includes text and Italian translation of Ficino's *De sole.*

———. *Lo Zodiaco della vita.* Bari, 1976. English trans. C. Jackson and J. Allen. *Astrology in the Renaissance: The Zodiac of Life.* London, 1982.

Giannetto, N. *Bernardo Bembo umanista e politico Veneziano.* Florence, 1985.

Gombrich, E. H. "Botticelli's Mythologies: A Study in the Neoplatonic Symbolism of His Circle" in *Journal of Warburg & Courtauld Institute* 8 (1945), pp. 7–60. Reprint in *Symbolic Images.* London, 1972.

Hak, H. J. *Marsilio Ficino.* Amsterdam, 1934.

Hankins, J. *Plato in the Italian Renaissance.* 2 vols. Leiden and New York, 1990. Includes a full study of Ficino's translations of the dialogues.

———. "Cosimo de' Medici and the 'Platonic Academy.'" *Journal of the Warburg and Courtauld Institutes* 53 (1990).

———. "The Myth of the Platonic Academy of Florence." *Renaissance Quarterly* 44 (1991).

"The Hymns of Orpheus." Trans. T. Taylor, in *Thomas Taylor the Platonist: Selected Writings.* Ed. K. Raine and G. M. Harper. London, 1969.

Jayne, S. R. *"Ficino and The Platonism of the English Renaissance." Comparative Literature* 4 (1952), pp. 214–38.

——. *John Colet & Marsilio Ficino.* Oxford, 1963. Contains unpublished correspondence between Ficino and Colet.

John of Salisbury. *The Statesman's Book.* Trans. J. Dickinson. New York, 1927. Books 4, 5, and 6 of the *Policraticus* and selections from books 7 and 8 comprising the political sections.

——. *John of Salisbury's Frivolities of Courtiers and Footprints of Philosophers.* Trans. J. B. Pike. 1938. Reprint, New York, 1972. A translation of the remainder of *Policraticus.*

——. *Policraticus.* Trans. C. J. Nederman. Cambridge, 1990.

Klustein, I. *Marsilio Ficino et la théologie ancienne—Oracles Chaldaïques—Hymnes Orphiques—Hymnes de Proclus.* Florence, 1987. A study of the Chaldaic oracles and Orphic hymns quoted by Ficino, with Greek text and anonymous Latin translations.

Kristeller, P. O. *The Philosophy of Marsilio Ficino.* 1943. Reprint, 1964. German trans., Frankfurt, 1972.

——. "Sebastiano Salvini, a Florentine Humanist and Theologian, and a Member of Marsilio Ficino's Platonic Academy." *Didascalie.* Ed. Sesto Prete. New York, 1961.

Lee, M. *Sixtus IV and Men of Letters.* Rome, 1978.

Lowe, K. *Francesco Soderini (1453-1524), Florentine Patrician and Cardinal.* Ph.D. diss. University of London, 1985.

Il lume del sole, Marsilio Ficino medico dell' anima. Florence, 1984. Catalogue of an exhibition including essays on Ficino's medicine and astrology to commemorate the 550th anniversary of his birth. Contributors: P. Castelli, P. Ceccarelli, A. Mazzanti, C. Paolini.

Macrobius. *Commentary on the Dream of Scipio.* Trans. W. H. Stahl. New York, 1952, 1990.

Marcel, R. *Marsile Ficin.* Paris, 1958.

Medici, Lorenzo. *Lettere di Lorenzo de' Medici.* Ed. R. Fubini, N. Rubinstein, M. Mallet. Florence, 1977-1990. The letters of Lorenzo the Magnificent. 6 volumes printed to date; further volumes in progress.

Newton, Sir Isaac. *Opticks.* With a foreword by Albert Einstein. 1931. Reprint, New York, 1952 and 1979. Based on the 4th ed., London, 1730.

Novotny, F. *The Posthumous Life of Plato.* Prague, 1977. Chap. 20, "Marsilio Ficino: The Florentine Academy."

Pastor, L. *History of the Popes.* Vol 4. 5th ed. London, 1950. See section on Sixtus IV and the Pazzi conspiracy.

Plato. *The Dialogues of Plato.* Trans. Benjamin Jowett. 3rd ed. 1892.

Plotinus. *The Enneads.* Trans. S. MacKenna. 4th ed. London, 1969. Loeb ed. trans. A. H. Armstrong. 7 vols. Harvard and London, 1966-88.

Poliziano, A. *Della congiura dei Pazzi (Coniurationis commentarium).* Ed. A. Perosa. Padua, 1958. Poliziano's account of the Pazzi conspiracy.

Renaissance Philosophy: The Italian Philosophers. Ed. A. Fallico and H. Shapiro. New York, 1967. Includes an English translation of Ficino's *De sole.* pp. 118–41.

Reumont, A. von. *Lorenzo de' Medici.* London, 1876.

Robb, N. *Neoplatonism of the Italian Renaissance.* London, 1935.

Rochon, A. *La Jeunesse de Laurent de Medicis (1449-1478).* Paris, 1963.

Roscoe, W. *Life of Lorenzo de' Medici.* London, 1884.

Ryder, A. *Alfonso the Magnanimous.* Oxford, 1990.

Saitta, G. *La filosofia di Marsilio Ficino.* Messina, 1923. 3rd ed. Bologna, 1954.

Shumaker, W. *The Occult Sciences in the Renaissance.* California, 1972.

Sieveking, K. *Die Geschichte der Platonischen Akademie zu Florenz.* Göttingen, 1812.

Thompson, D. and A. Nagel. *The Three Crowns of Florence: Humanist Assessments of Dante, Petrarch and Boccaccio.* New York, 1972.

Vasoli, C. *Filosofia e religione nella cultura del Rinascimento.* Naples, 1988.

Vian, F., ed. *Argonautiques Orphiques.* Text and French translation. Paris, 1987.

Walker, D. P. *Spiritual and Demonic Magic from Ficino to Campanella.* London, 1958.

Warden, J., ed. "Orpheus and Ficino." *Orpheus: The Metamorphosis of a Myth.* Ed. J. Warden. Toronto, 1982.

Zanier, G. *La medicina astrologica e la sua teoria.* Rome, 1977.

General Bibliography

Chastel, A. *Art et Humanisme à Florence au temps de Laurent le Magnifique.* Paris, 1959.

Cosenza, M. E. *Biographical Dictionary of Humanism and Classical Scholarship.* 5 vols. Boston, 1962.

Cronin, V. *The Florentine Renaissance.* London, 1967.

da Bisticci, Vespasiano: *Lives of Illustrious Men of the XVth Century.* Trans. W. George & E. Waters. New York, 1963.

Dizionario Biografico degli Italiani. Rome, 1960–.

Klibansky, R. *The Continuity of the Platonic Tradition during the Middle Ages.* London, 1939.

Kristeller, P. O. *Renaissance Concepts of Man.* New York, 1972.

——. *Eight Philosophers of the Italian Renaissance.* London, 1965, and California, 1966.

Lewis, C. S. *The Discarded Image: An Introduction to Medieval and Renaissance Literature.* Cambridge, 1964.

Panofsky, E. *Studies in Iconology.* New York, 1939.

Pevsner, N. *Academies of Art Past and Present.* Cambridge, 1940.

Sandys, J. E. *A History of Classical Scholarship.* 3 vols. Cambridge, 1908–1921.

Schevill, F. *Medieval and Renaissance Florence.* 2 vols. New York, 1963.

Thorndike, L. *A History of Magic and Experimental Science.* 6 vols., New York, 1923–1941.

Walker, D. P. "Orpheus, The Theologian, and Renaissance Platonists" in *Journal of Warburg and Courtauld Institute* 16 (1953). Reprint in *The Ancient Theology.* London, 1972.

Yates, F. A. *Giordano Bruno and the Hermetic Tradition.* London, 1964.

INDEX

Also from Inner Traditions

THE PROPHET OF COMPOSTELA

A Novel of Apprenticeship and Initiation

Henri Vincenot • ISBN 0-89281-524-8 • $19.95 pb

In *The Prophet of Compostela,* award-winning French author Henri Vincenot addresses the themes of journey, initiation, and spiritual growth in 12th-century Burgundy. Seen through the eyes of a young builder's apprentice, it is a tale of youthful adventure, an exploration of Gothic architecture and Freemasonry, a meditation on the relationship between Celtic wisdom and Christianity, and a spiritual allegory of self-knowledge.

THE MYTHIC IMAGINATION

The Quest for Meaning Through Personal Mythology

Stephen Larsen, Ph.D. • 0-89281-574-4 • 432 pages • $16.95 paperback

"An extraordinarily rich and wide-ranging compendium of the psychological uses of mythology. Stephen Larsen has given us stimulation for the mind, a feast for the imagination, and a multidimensional road map for the soul in quest of its truth."

Roger J. Woolger and Jennifer B. Woolger
Authors of *The Goddess Within* and *Other Lives, Other Selves*

"Stephen Larsen has achieved a synthesis of mythic story, psychological theory, and clinical experience that extends the work of his teacher, Joseph Campbell, toward a more practical understanding of the relevance of myth for each of us."   **David Feinstein, Ph.D.**
Co-author of *Personal Mythology* and *Rituals for Living and Dying*

REVOLT AGAINST THE MODERN WORLD

Julius Evola • 0-89281-506-X • $29.95 cloth

In what many consider to be his masterwork, Evola analyzes the spiritual and cultural causes for the decline of modern Western civilization. Agreeing with the Hindu philosophers that history moves in huge cycles and that we are now in the Kali Yuga, an age of decadence and dissolution, he compares the characteristics of the modern world with those of traditional societies and boldly challenges the materialism and meaninglessness of life in the twentieth century.

"Evola uses the bow, hitting his target with consummate accuracy and illuminating in a few words a whole area of thought hitherto unrecognized by most of us."   **Gnosis**

HARMONIES OF HEAVEN AND EARTH

Mysticism in Music from
Antiquity to the Avant-Garde

Joscelyn Godwin • 0-89281-500-0 • $12.95 paperback

Exploring music's perceived effects on matter, living things, and human behavior, Godwin shows how the spiritual power of music can be found throughout folklore, myth, and mystical experience, and includes theories of celestial harmony from Pythagoras to Marius Schneider.

"Through a rich, eclectic mix of mythological, philosophical, literary, and scientific references, the deeper meanings of sound and music are revealed."   **Gnosis**

THE DIVINE LIBRARY

A Comprehensive Reference Guide to the Sacred Texts and Spritual Literature of the World

Rufus Camphausen • 0-89281-351-2 • $12.95 paperback

From the Angas to the Zend Avesta, from Apocryphal writings to the Yogini Tantra, and from the Bible to the Zohar, this quick-reference guide is the first to offer a concise directory to the primary religious literature of past and present cultures. The author traces many sacred texts back to their source in the oral tradition of pre-literate civilizations. He offers bibliographical references to available editions, translations, and commentaries, with a glossary and indexes.

"More than 120 entries delineate important works of religious literature of yesterday and today. A comprehensive, accessible guidebook."

Library Journal

ARCHING BACKWARD

The Mystical Initation of a Contemporary Woman

Janet Adler • 0-89281-577-9 • $19.95 cloth

"Rarely are we given the gift of reading a story of a direct *embodied* experience of the numinous. Adler's account of her initiation rings with authenticity as she is taken through the mystical spirals of hell and heaven. A splendid book!"

Marion Woodman, author of *Leaving My Father's House*

"*Arching Backward* is an eloquent and lyrical prose poem, riveting testimony from a modern mystic. Janet Adler offers this narrative of her extraordinary journey, traversing territory both intensely intimate and primordial, luminous and transcendent. This is a heroine's mythic journey, as fascinating as it is mysterious."

Daniel Goleman, author of *The Meditative Mind*

TAMING THE TIGER
Tibetan Teachings on Right Conduct, Mindfulness, and Universal Compassion

Akong Tulku Rinpoche • 0-89281-569-8 • $12.95 paperback

With wit and wisdom, Akong Tulku Rinpoche teaches how to tame the tiger of the mind—the ceaseless mental chatter within. True peace, he explains, may be achieved through a practical program for cultivating awareness and bringing the spiritual into everyday life. He provides a series of exercises by which to change our patterns of living and achieve the kind of happiness that also brings happiness to others.

TEMPLE OF THE COSMOS
The Ancient Egyptian Experience of the Sacred

Jeremy Naydler • 0-89281-555-8 • $19.95

"A valuable and original work." **John Anthony West**, author of *Serpent in the Sky*

"An ambitious and lucid interpretation of ancient Egyptian consciousness, especially with respect to the experience of the sacred. As such the book also sheds light on the wild and mysterious psychospiritual currents of our present time, including the Goddess re-emergence."
Robert Masters, Ph.D.
Author of *The Goddess Sekhmet*

These and other Inner Traditions titles are available at many fine bookstores or, to order directly from the publisher, send a check or money order for the total amount, payable to Inner Traditions, plus $3.00 shipping for the first book and $1.00 for each additional book to:

Inner Traditions, P.O. Box 388, Rochester, VT 05767
Be sure to request a free catalog